FALL
OF THE
DAWN

BY NICOLE C. BOYD

Contents

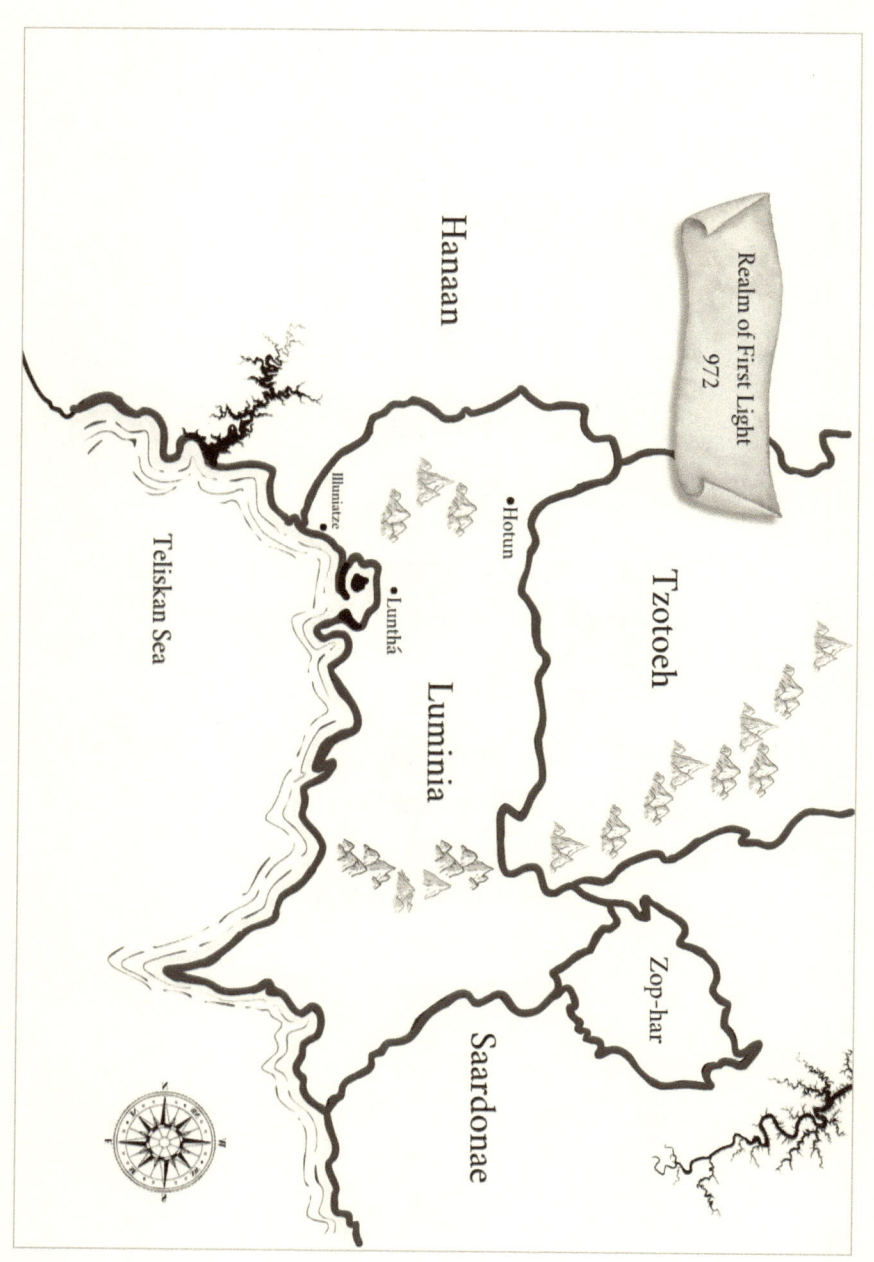

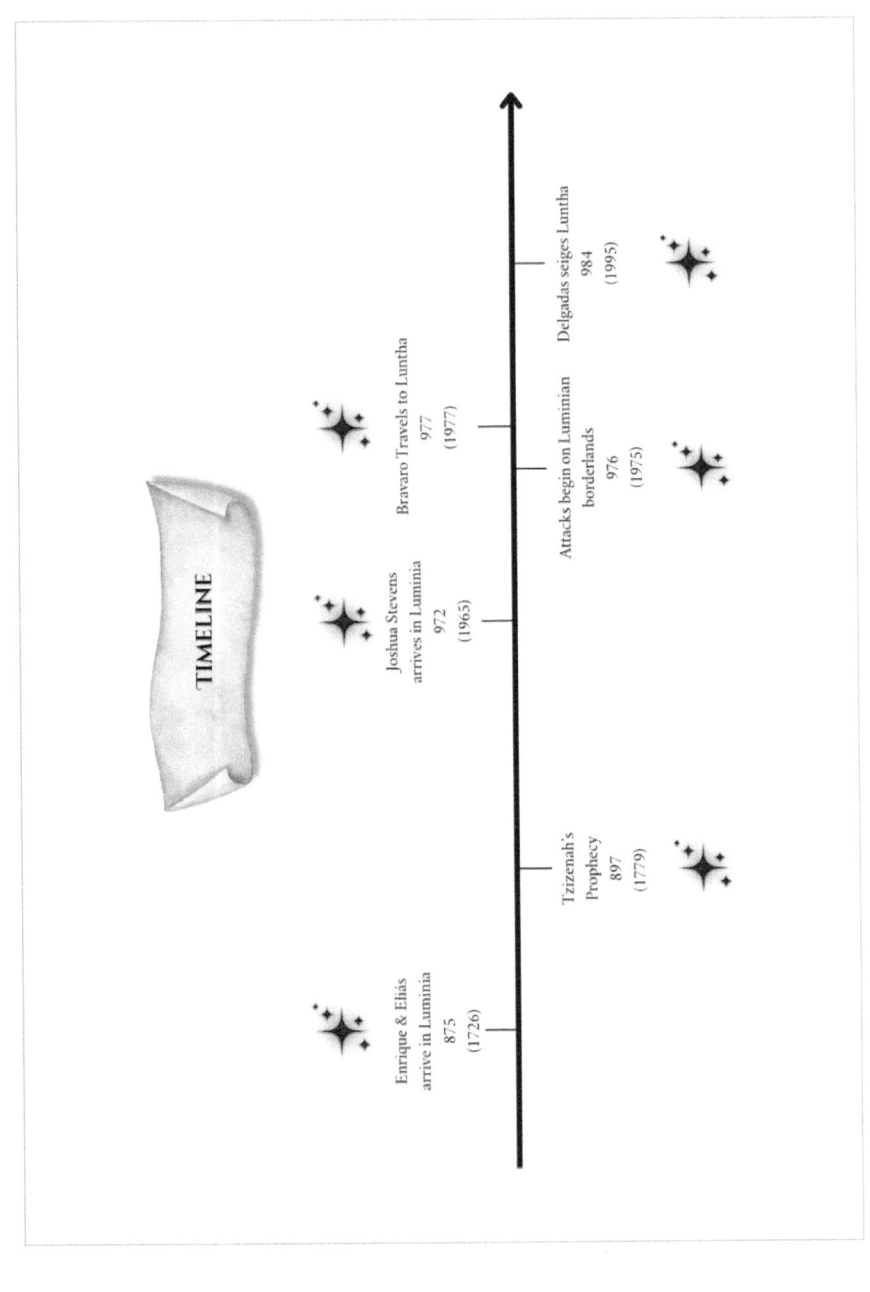

TIMELINE

Enrique & Elias arrive in Luminia
875
(1726)

Tzizenah's Prophecy
897
(1779)

Joshua Stevens arrives in Luminia
972
(1965)

Attacks begin on Luminian borderlands
976
(1975)

Bravaro Travels to Luntha
977
(1977)

Delgadas seiges Luntha
984
(1995)

DEDICATION

For Colton, the love of my life.
Without you, this book would still be just a
dream. Thank you for always encouraging and
challenging me. I love you, Sug.

And for my little loves, Kaleb (my drummer boy)
and Kallie (my singer and dancer). You both are
the light of my life. I am so proud and honored to
be your mama.

PART ONE
ADVANCING SHADOWS

"A day without music is to stumble in darkness."
-Ancient Luminian Proverb

CHAPTER I
PROLOGUE

Clatsop Territory, Pacific Northwest Coast
August 1726

They were dead.

At least, they would be in a matter of minutes if they did not find cover. Enrique Justiano stumbled through the sand and jagged rocks, his chest heaving as he ran for his life.

"Wait!" his partner, Eliás de Soto, yelled as he crashed through the darkness behind him.

Enrique spun behind a colossal rock just in time to dodge another arrow. Eliás joined him behind the massive formation, placing his hands on his knees as he sucked air into his lungs.

"What are we going to do?" Eliás asked through gulps of air. "They're going to kill us!"

Enrique could barely hear their pursuers now, creeping through the grey light and sea mist toward their pathetic hiding place. It would be dawn soon, but would they live to see it?

He peered around for somewhere better to hide. The braves would be on them in minutes and then it would all be over. "I suppose that is what we get for trying to escape."

Enrique wiped his brow with the back of his arm, his cotton shirt soaked in perspiration. He looked down as a sharp pain throbbed in his right thigh. Blood oozed out of a long slash, soaking his shredded trousers. They had been on this God-forsaken coast for months, with no hope of making it home to their beloved Spain. And now he might not even live to see another sunrise.

"We must do something, *mi compadre*," Eliás whispered, eyes wild with fear. As far as the eye could see, there was only this stretch of beach—with rocky cliffs to their left and the unending sea to the right. Waves crashed on the shore, a deafening reminder that they were hemmed in.

Enrique peeked around the rock. Warriors cloaked in shadow sneaking closer, ready to end their miserable lives. The finality of their plight made Enrique's heart slow to a dull thud. Tingles traveled up his spine as Death's warm, stinking breath wheezed down his back while the hairs on his arms and neck stood on end.

They were going to die–

He pressed his back into the rock once more. Out of the corner of his eye, Enrique saw a small depression in the jagged coastal cliffs. Caves were numerous in these parts, or so he was told by the locals. "There!" he whispered, pointing it out to Eliás.

His partner followed his gaze, and he nodded in assent. At least it was something. They ducked low to the ground as they moved toward the entrance of the cave. Enrique gritted his teeth against the pain searing his leg, willing himself to keep going. Just a few more feet, and they would be safe.

Eliás entered the cave first, crawling deep into the dark recess. Enrique stumbled along behind him, trying to keep his loud panting under control so as not to give away their location. Minutes passed as they pressed their backs against the cave walls, slick with sea water–watching, waiting. By now the sun had risen over the eastern hills, but the beach was still covered in thick darkness thanks to the cliffs casting long shadows. The natives came into view before the hideout, speaking in their strange tongue. Enrique had learned a little of their language while they had been captives. But he did not want to know what they were planning to do to them if they were found. He closed his eyes, offering up a silent prayer to God. *¡Dios, protégenos!* God, protect us!

Enrique waited as the warriors seemed to be in some sort of debate. He turned his face away, wishing, for once, that the blackness would envelope him. Usually, he held onto the light for as long as possible, dreading the onset of darkness, when the nightmares stalked him in his fractured sleep.

They had stumbled on this land after their ship had sunk off the Pacific Coast. Of the 211 men on board the Spanish galleon, only four of them had survived. That terror-filled night spent at sea, clinging to the boards that had come loose during the wreck, had been one of the longest of his life. It was not the chill sea water or the near-death experience that haunted him so, but the desperate pleas of his fellow sailors that could not swim. Eventually they were all dragged beneath the merciless waves, never to be seen again.

Enrique and the other three survivors had collapsed on the beach in the early hours of the morning. They been roasting corn on the beach, stolen from one of the nearby fields, when a lone native girl had found them. Enrique had tried to warn them that building a fire out on that open stretch of beach was foolish. But they had all been so hungry.

They had tried to hide, but the natives soon found them and had taken them prisoner, keeping them as slaves over the following months. They had worked hard, but the natives had also treated them with mercy. He had heard that many native tribes in New Spain had the custom of enveloping captives into the tribe, after an allotment of time. And there were also tales of men who had been taken prisoner and decided not to leave, even when they had been given their freedom. Of course, it was all hearsay in this wild land. Until they had become a statistic in the legends.

Being enveloped by the tribe, taking a native wife, and settling down to his fate was not for him. Enrique had a family to get home to and had known he could not just sit around and wait for help to come. If they wanted their freedom, they would have to take it. After months of waiting for their opportunity, he had finally seen one. He and Eliás had jumped at the chance. Enrique had thought they would have a better chance of survival on their own in the woods, heading East first and then South to try to seek sanctuary from one of their outposts. However, the natives had been much too quick to realize they were missing, and he and Eliás had been forced to retreat to this beach.

One of the leaders made a loud grunt, and motioned for the braves under his command to move along down the beach. They moved away from the opening and Enrique let out a short breath. If they could wait out the natives, take the daylight hours to rest and make a plan, then they could sneak out when night fell and make their escape. One thing was sure: no one knew where they were. No one was coming to help them. Indeed, no one had been this far North in years, and never without their galleons or supplies. The storm that had driven them so far off course had forced the rest of the armada to turn back. Likely, their commander thought them all lost to the sea.

"That was close, *mi amigo*." Eliás whispered.

"We are not out of trouble yet," Enrique snapped. He winced as he put his hands around the slash in his thigh. He could see to the bone, the flesh flayed open to reveal the layer of fat and muscle underneath. "Give me a part of your hem."

Eliás did as he asked, tearing off a long, thin strip of his shirt and handing it to him. Enrique closed the wound as best he could, then wrapped the strip of cloth around his leg, tying it tightly. It would only be a temporary fix. If he was going to survive, he would need to find a way to sew up the wound. And soon. "How far back does the cave go?" he asked through clenched teeth.

Elías left his side and walked further into the cave. "I cannot see the end of it. I think it may recede into the cliffs quite far. Do you want to move away from the entrance?"

"Yes, I do," Enrique winced. "But I will need your help."

His friend came back and supported him as they walked deeper into the cave. Enrique sat down on the damp ground with a grunt, the smell of salt air and rancid, dead fish wafting up to his nostrils. "We will have to find a way to get some food. I wasn't able to stow much away before we fled."

He pulled out the bit of leather he had made into a pouch from under his shirt and laid out the contents on a nearby boulder. They had stowed away some dried salmon jerky and corn cakes from their daily rations, but it would not last long if they had to travel South to their Spanish outposts, where they could find a ship back home. The journey would likely claim both of their lives before they even had a chance to make it a quarter of the way.

Beside their secreted foodstuffs, the only other supplies they had with them were a small whittling knife and a leather-bound Bible—Enrique's prized possession. Elías started poking around the cave, going in deeper than Enrique thought wise. "Do not go too far! I am in no shape to come after you," Enrique snapped. He leaned his head against the craggy wall, slick with moisture from the fine sea spray that floated on the air. He licked his lips then sat up, hating how dry his tongue was, like he'd swallowed a handful of sand. What they needed to find before they moved too much further down the coast was a water source.

He leaned his head against the wall again, closing his eyes. Poor Comete and Huerta. They had not been able to escape with them and would likely never see their families again. Of course, the natives kept a close watch on them all. Comete had been especially valuable to them. They had called him "Konapee". He was a blacksmith, and thus invaluable to the tribe. After they had been captured, the natives who called themselves the Clatsop, had salvaged parts of their ship and gathered the metal, forcing Comete to refashion it into weapons, tools, and even jewelry for their wives and daughters. The tribe had grown wealthy in native standards, thanks to Comete's skill.

"We only have enough food for the next few days. We will need to hunt, or fish, after we get far enough from the village," Enrique said, keeping his eyes closed. He was exhausted from the midnight escape. When Eliás did not answer, Enrique lifted his head, looking around the cave. "Eliás?"

His voice echoed and came back to him. But Eliás was nowhere to be seen. His heart again started to race. "Eliás?" he called again, more sharply this time. He got up on his hands and knees, wincing in pain as he crawled in the direction Eliás had gone.

Now that his eyes had adjusted to the dreariness of the cave, he could see a small tunnel leading further into the cliffs. Enrique sighed. Eliás had always been the more reckless of them.

"Eliás, answer me," he commanded. He stuffed their belongings back into the makeshift pouch and started crawling further into the darkness. However, as he continued, a pinpoint of light shimmered in the distance. Curious, Enrique forced himself to keep going. "What on God's green earth–?"

The tunnel widened and lengthened until Enrique was able to stand. The light grew, and he could hear birdsong, unlike any species he had ever heard before. He raised his arm to shield his eyes from the brilliant light surrounding him when he exited the cave. *"Dios mío–"* he breathed.

He was unsure what he was seeing, but he could only assume the cave let out into the forest outside the village where they had spent the last six months of their lives. But the trees in this part of the forest were ten times the size of the forest near the village. A bright purple and blue bird landed in front of him, cocking its head to the side. It trilled a little song, as if to greet him, then promptly flitted away. He had never seen anything like it. "Eliás?" he called slowly, not knowing if he was hallucinating from the loss of blood or if what he saw was real.

His partner appeared from under one of the giant ferns to his right, and Enrique uttered a sigh of relief and frustration. "What are you doing? I told you not to go too deep into the cave." He limped toward him. "We should go back—" he grunted, his leg burning from the strain. But as Enrique turned, he could no longer see the cave opening. He limped back the way they had come, running his hands over the rocky cliff. "*Imposible*. It was just here–!" The cave was gone, as if the mountain had swallowed it back up. Enrique took a shaky step back, looking up at the mountain soaring above his head. His mind swirled with thoughts of doom. *Trapped.*

"That is the least of our worries," Eliás said, his tone filled with dread. Enrique's blood ran cold. He turned around slowly to find a band of strangely dressed men standing just before the tree line. They held long bows and one of the men had an arrow nocked and ready to fly. These were not the natives who had been chasing them minutes before. They carried themselves with quiet dignity, and looked as shocked to see him and Eliás as they were to see them.

One of the men stepped forward, towering a few inches over Enrique. It was impressive, for Enrique was not a small man—at least he was not back home.

"*Sepsit nitz sikome?*" The man's language was like music to the ears.

"I don't understand—" Enrique replied in Spanish, then gulped. He tried again in English, which he had learned while he had been in one of the American Colonies before coming around Cape Horn to the Pacific. "I am sorry, I do not understand," he said a little louder, hoping they were able to understand. They only stared at him blankly. He limped backward, overwhelmed by what he was experiencing. Suddenly, he thought of his wife and babe waiting for him in Spain. She had been pregnant when he'd left, fool as he was. He would never see his wife again, never get to meet his son or daughter. And he had promised Esperanza he would return. Fear gripped his heart, wondering what would become of her.

The savages lowered their weapons, talking excitedly to one

another in a tongue he had never heard before. One of them came close and waved Enrique's hand away from the wound on his thigh, peeling away the makeshift bandage. While the man poked around his injury, he listened to the language. It did not even resemble the sounds of the Clatsop he had encountered, nor the surrounding tribes that had come to trade for the iron workings that Comete had created.

He glanced at his friend, dread settling over his head like the upper arm of the pillory, making it impossible for him to move. "Eliás, where have you led us?"

CHAPTER 1

JOSHUA

Butte Falls, Oregon
August 1965

"Curse this wretched heat!"

Joshua cringed at his father's angry tone. The birds went silent, and he scooted closer to his mother on the trail, gripping her hand tighter as they trudged through the woods. Joshua had never been camping before, and Mama was taking the whole family to her favorite spot.

"Don't curse in front of the children," Mama whispered. Father cursed a lot, mostly when he drank his special drink.

Father turned around and glared at Mama. His muscled arms strained under the straps of the heavy pack on his back. Joshua met his father's eyes and was surprised that he was looking straight at him. Ducking behind Mama's leg, he tried to hide. He was afraid of that look.

"Don't patronize me, Diana. If I want to cuss, I'm darn well going to cuss." Father turned and kept walking. Joshua squeezed Mama's hand again, feeling the tension crackle like the sky during a thunderstorm, with the promise of a lightning strike.

Joshua didn't like lightning storms. It reminded him of Father and Mama yelling when they thought he was asleep. He always burrowed under the blankets and covered his head with his pillow when they fought. He hated to hear Mama cry, feeling helpless to do anything for her.

"Daddy? Are we almost there?" his cousin whined behind them.

Joshua glanced over his shoulder at his cousin. Carson was nine and as wild as a rabid raccoon. At least, that's what Mama said.

Uncle Jeff was loaded down with the tents and camping chairs but still managed to turn to look at Carson on the narrow trail. "Almost, son. Keep moving, and we'll be there before you know it."

Uncle Jeff let his kids call him 'Daddy' instead of 'Father.' Joshua's stomach lurched, making him feel sick remembering the one time he had dared to call his father 'Daddy.' Father had just returned from fighting in the war, and Joshua had let the word slip out as he and Mama had greeted him at the base. Father had slapped him across the face when they had arrived home and told Joshua never to disrespect him like that again. Joshua swore he would never would.

"Are you alright, Sweetheart?" Mama leaned down and helped him over a fallen log. "Come on." Joshua grabbed her hand and continued down the trail. Mama was so pretty, with her long, blonde hair trailing over her back. She turned and flashed a smile at him, with her big blue eyes sparkling with life. She seemed so much more at peace in the woods, as if nothing could harm her out here. But he also knew she was a master of masking her true feelings. They had both had to do so since Father's return almost a year before. He'd been wounded in the line of duty, but Mama had never told him where he'd been injured.

Joshua was glad when they crested the hill, the land sloping down to a beautiful meadow. "Wow!" he exclaimed. To his six-year-old mind, he had never seen anything so beautiful.

Mama sighed. "I know." They stopped at the top of the incline while the rest of the family went down to a large wooden picnic table in the meadow's center, right near the fire pit. Mama knelt and wrapped her arms around Joshua's middle from behind, hugging him close. "My daddy built that table over thirty years ago," she whispered. "This has been our special camping spot since I was a baby. I hope to bring you here every summer. And someday, maybe you'll want to bring your family here, too, hmm?" She kissed his cheek and stood, grabbing his hand.

Joshua screwed up his nose. "Will I have to kiss a girl to get a family?"

Mama chuckled softly under her breath. "Well, someday, you'll want to kiss a girl." She tousled his hair. "Come on, I'll race you."

She started to move away, but Joshua pulled her back. "Can't we come up here alone, sometimes, Mama? Just me and you?"

Mama's eyes flickered with untold pain but she quickly covered it up. She chucked him under the chin. "Of course we can, Sweetheart. But for this week, let's have as much fun as we can."

They ran down the hill together, hand in hand. Joshua squealed with delight, enjoying the warm sunshine on his face. When they arrived, Father let the packs slide off his back with a loud thud, uttering a foul word. He and Uncle Jeff got right to work setting up the tents.

Carson lost no time making a nuisance of himself, chasing his sisters around with a spider he had killed. Their shrieks seemed to echo around the whole forest. The girls raced past the men as they wrestled the tents. His cousin Lisa slammed into Father, knocking him into the pile of tent poles and canvas.

Father scrambled to his feet, uttering a low growl that sent Lisa and Charlotte scampering back to their mother. "Send the boys off on a hike or something, Diana!" He stomped over to Mama, and she placed a protective hand on Joshua's shoulders. "How are we supposed to work with the kids getting under our feet?" Father's accusation rang out across the forest as if the whole incident were Mama's fault. "I don't wanna see them again until this camp is set up!"

Mama stepped back, getting as far away from Father as she hurried to do his bidding. She waved Carson over and took Joshua's hand, helping him off the picnic table. Mama put her hands on Carson and Joshua's shoulders. "You boys go up that trail there a ways and explore. Carson, look out for Joshua, okay? I want you boys to stick together no matter what. Do you understand?" Her voice was firm but kind, and he could hear the fear behind her words.

Joshua eyed the woods warily. "Do I have to go, Mama?" Carson was always mean to him when she wasn't looking.

Carson huffed and rolled his eyes. "Come on. Don't you want to go explore?" He started to walk away. "Only babies stay in camp. And girls." Never mind the men who were setting up where they would sleep for the next week, Joshua thought. But he held his tongue.

Mama knelt before him, brushing the hair away from his eyes. "It'll be alright, Joshy. You like to explore, don't you? You don't have to go too far away, just stay on the outskirts of camp where you can see me. It won't be long before your father and Uncle Jeff have everything set up." She tried to give him an encouraging smile. Father stopped what he was doing, pinning them both with a dangerous glare. Joshua knew he should hurry out of camp before Mama got the brunt of his anger.

"Okay. And then can we go down to the river?" he asked.

"Of course, we can." She touched his cheek, pausing for a moment. Mama grasped a leather string hanging around her neck, pulling it up from under her t-shirt to reveal a pouch embroidered with tiny seed beads. "My mother gave this pouch to me when I was a little girl," she explained. "Your great-grandma was a full-blooded Clatsop. She sewed the beads into this pouch when she was young." Mama slipped the leather straps over his head, letting it rest against his chest. He ran his fingers over the beads of a brightly-colored native design with gentle awe. "It's yours now," she said softly. "It will keep you safe."

"All mine?" Joshua's eyes grew wide, amazed that Mama would give him such a precious gift.

"All yours." She laughed and turned him around by his shoulders. "Now, go find me some pretty rocks. They are all over the place up here. You can put them in the pouch."

His cousin stood with his hands on his hips, tapping his foot impatiently as Joshua heaved his little legs up the hill to join him. "It's about time!" Carson growled, trying to sound like one of the adults. Joshua sighed. Carson barely allowed him to catch his breath before he hurried off into the woods. Carson was always eager to be out of his parent's earshot, spoiled rotten. His parents never disciplined him for anything, while Joshua's father got him in trouble for the slightest mistake. Mama said that his time in the service had turned him mean, twisted something inside him until all the good had been wrung out. Joshua wasn't sure, but Father's sour-smelling drink could also be to blame.

When they had gone about a hundred yards, clambering over fallen lodgepoles and ferns up the incline, Carson stopped and put his lips close to Joshua's ear. "I hear these woods are haunted by Indian spirits." He leaned back to get a look at Joshua's face, probably to see if he was afraid.

Joshua's heart began to race. "M-Mama says there isn't any such thing as ghosts."

"Oh, pooh," Carson dismissed his fears, screwing up his nose at the ridiculous suggestion. "She just doesn't want you to be a-scared." Carson looked over his shoulder at camp. Joshua looked, too, waving at his mother.

Carson gripped his arm, drawing him out of his thoughts, and hurried him further into the woods. "Come on," he said impatiently.

Joshua tried to pull his arm free, but Carson was too strong for him. "Wait! Mama said to stay close to camp." He stumbled as he looked over his shoulder, trying to keep camp in view.

"Don't be such a baby! I'm nine, and you're only six." Carson said in a very bossy tone. "That means you have to listen to me." They were both out of breath when they reached the top of the hill. He shoved Joshua to keep him moving. They started down the other side of the hill, Carson goading him on against his will.

Joshua swung around, trying to get away from Carson. "I want to go back to camp," he begged.

"No way," Carson said.

They seemed to walk for hours after that. The air cooled, and Joshua wrapped his arms around his middle, trying to keep warm. A thin mist rolled in, covering the tops of the mountains in the distance, the wind howling angrily through the trees. His teeth began to chatter.

"I think it's this way," Carson said, leading him over a narrow deer trail that side-hilled gradually up the mountain. They followed the trail until they came to the north face. But instead of flattening out, they were stuck in a draw, with a steep cliff face rising to their right and falling a hundred feet to their left—the bottom nothing but sharp rocks. The ledge going forward was only a couple of feet wide. If they fell, it would be the end of them.

Joshua hesitated as Carson moved forward. "Hey, maybe we should head back. Do you even know where we are?"

"Don't worry," Carson called, waving him off. "If we climb up to the top, we'll be able to see which way camp is." He got to a place where it was not quite so steep and started clawing his way up the dusty incline. There was little else he could do but follow. At least if they were together, they might be able to help each other if they got in trouble.

When they reached the top of the mountain, there was nothing but forest in all directions. Carson looked this way and that, shielding his eyes from the late afternoon sun. He pointed. "I think it's this way." He started walking, but Joshua stayed planted on the spot, tired from the long, steep climb.

"You don't know for sure, do you? You're just guessing." Joshua crossed his arms and squatted. "I'm staying right here until Mama comes for us. She always says to stay put if you get lost."

"No way. I'm in charge and I say we go down. Camp is probably just over that hill." Carson tried to grab his arm again, but Joshua side-stepped, moving well out of the way.

"I'm not going anywhere with you. You're just going to get us even more lost!" Joshua yelled. Carson reached again, and this time, he managed to grab his forearm. Joshua yanked his arm away, and to his surprise, Carson let go. But then he was falling backward, sliding down the side of the mountain amidst rocks and loose dirt.

Joshua screamed, clutching at manzanita bushes and ferns, anything to stop his fall. He slid close to the cliff's edge, with a sheer drop yawning below him. At the last second, Joshua was able to grab onto a manzanita branch and hang on for dear life.

Carson appeared about fifty yards above him, looking more frightened than he had ever seen him.

"Help me!" Joshua screamed. He looked back over his shoulder, tears streaming down his face. Carson stood frozen for a moment, then seemed to come to his senses and scurried down the hill, scooting on his backside. Joshua's fingers were slipping. He gritted his teeth, trying to hold on.

Finally, Carson made it down to him, and he grabbed him by the wrist. He then reached for a slim pine tree sapling and hung on. "On three, try to pull yourself up while I push with my legs," Carson instructed. Joshua nodded, and Carson pulled with all his might. Slowly, Carson was able to pull him up and out of harm's way. They lay on their backs, panting and hanging on to the sapling just in case.

After a few minutes, Joshua sat up and wiped furiously at his tears. "Now, let's climb down this mountain and wait at the bottom for someone to come and find us! I bet Mama and the rest of them are looking for us by now."

"Wait. Look," Carson said. He pointed a few yards to the left, and Joshua followed his gaze. A small cave was nestled against the side of the mountain, partially hidden by trees. From below, it would have been easy to miss it.

"Come on. Let's go check it out," Carson said.

"No," Joshua argued. "We've already gotten into enough trouble."

"Well, I'm going. Look," he pointed upward at the sky. Ominous clouds were forming overhead, heavy with rain. "You can stay here if you want, but don't blame me if the wolves get you, or you get sick from the cold." Carson headed off, leaving him before he had had a chance to think. Joshua hurried after him, careful to stay as far from the edge of the rocky cliff as possible. He did not want to be any wolf's dinner.

"Let's make it quick," Joshua conceded. He stood beside Carson before the mouth of the cave, his heart tripping with fear. The sooner they could look around the cave, the sooner Carson might allow him to return to camp.

Carson stepped inside cautiously. "Doesn't it look like a Native American temple? I bet it's just littered with bones from sacrifices." His cousin rubbed his hands together in anticipation.

Joshua stayed where he was. "Alright. We've seen it. Now, let's go back," he pleaded.

"No way! We're going in there to explore." Carson stepped through the opening and motioned for him to follow. When Joshua would not go in, Carson grabbed his arm. "Don't be such a chicken. What if there's Indian treasure in there? We could be rich!"

"I don't wanna be rich!" Joshua wailed. "I wanna go back to Mama!"

"Nothin' doin'! Get in here!" Carson heaved, dragging Joshua further into the darkness. He pulled a lighter out of his pocket and grinned. "I took this from my dad's glove box." He ran his thumb over the top until it lit and handed it to Joshua. "There. Now you don't have to be scared."

Joshua held it far from his body, knowing Mama would be upset he was playing with fire. It did help him not to feel so frightened as Carson pushed him further into the cavern.

He tried to be brave, not to let the tears pooling in his eyes drip onto his dusty cheeks. Joshua had only ever been to the Lava Beds in Tulelake, California, for a school field trip. And those caves had been wired for light. This one was scary and dark, with water dripping from the ceiling. Joshua jumped every time a droplet hit his head.

When they had gone about thirty feet into the cave, Joshua stopped. He could no longer see the entrance. He'd lost track of which way to get back since following Carson through the curving tunnel. "This is far enough," he said, jerking to escape Carson's hand pushing against his back. This time, Carson let him go. He walked around Joshua, looking like he had discovered a new, exciting world. There was no treasure, and there were no bones. Only rocks and boulders littered the floor of the cave. Huge spikes hung from the ceiling, making Joshua nervous. What would happen if they talked too loudly? Would the cone-shaped formations fall and stab them?

"We should go. This is not safe. Do you want to get killed dead?" Joshua whispered.

Carson rolled his eyes again. "Fine, we can go." Without warning, Carson snatched the lighter from Joshua before he could react. The tiny flame fluttered and danced on his cousin's face, reminding Joshua of a Jack-O-Lantern. At that moment, he thought his cousin looked about as evil as one of the carved pumpkin faces with teeth bared in silent screams.

Joshua gulped. "Alright, you lead the way then." He would say anything to Carson to give up his schemes so they could return to camp.

Carson held a hand out, pushing against Joshua's chest. "Stay here by yourself for one minute. Prove that you're not afraid of the dark, then you can be an Indian brave like me."

Carson started backing away, but Joshua refused to stay put. He didn't like the sound of being left alone in the dark. But before he could say yes to the plan, Carson turned and ran back the way they had come. Joshua scrambled after him but tripped and fell into the cavern wall.

"Hey! Wait!" Joshua panicked, his heart racing as he tried to follow Carson before the light was gone. He stumbled in the oppressive blackness. Fear gripped his heart, threatening to stop it entirely. "Carson!" he screamed, his voice echoing throughout the cave.

No answer came from the darkness. Joshua sank to the cold floor and brought his knees to his chest. Wrapping his arms around his legs, he lay his head on his knees and shut his eyes tightly. He counted down from ten since he didn't know how long a minute was.

"It'll be over soon," he whispered, trying to summon what little courage he had. "Mama, come quick—"

CHAPTER 2

JOSHUA

After what seemed like an eternity, Joshua looked up. It took a while for his eyes to adjust, but he could soon make out the shapes of the rock walls. "Carson?" he called. He listened for his cousin's voice, wishing the minute would be up. It seemed like an awfully long one. "Carson!" he shouted again. His reverberating voice was the only thing that greeted him.

Standing, he looked around the cave, wondering if he could find his way out alone. He started walking back the way they had come, the rocks invisible in the oppressive blackness. Joshua tripped as the toe of his shoe caught on a jagged rock, and he fell to his knees. He yelped with pain as the splintered rocks dug into his skin. "Carson, please!" he screamed, his voice raising in terror.

No answer.

Joshua forced himself to stand, gingerly touching his knees. His fingers came away sticky. His heart tripped inside his chest to an unsteady rhythm, his palms wet with sweat. He began walking again and felt something dripping down his shins. Joshua had heard stories of people wandering in the dark, lost and walking in circles as they tried to find their way out of caves. For that very reason, his mother had warned him not to wander away when they had visited some of the caves in the Lava Beds. Now, he was going to die, and Mama would never find him.

Maybe he shouldn't move. But he was desperate to get out. Joshua fumbled around in the dark, tears streaming down his cheeks. It was apparent Carson had either planned to leave him there as a part of his cruel joke or had grown bored of waiting for him and wandered off.

Joshua dried his tears and found that he could see much better, the dimness in the cavern decreasing as he let his eyes adjust. He ran his fingers along the cave walls, then felt in front of him for any obstacles. Finally, he stumbled into a tunnel with a faint light shining at the end. Relief washed over him as he scrambled over boulders and loose rocks to reach the opening. "My mama's gonna spank you so hard when she finds out what you did to me, Carson!"

However, when Joshua finally did return to the daylight, Carson was nowhere to be found. Nothing looked the same as he searched for his cousin. The rock ledge that had dropped off in front of the cave was gone. Instead, the land spread out flat before the entrance. The air was thick with heat and the sounds of insects buzzing. This unfamiliar forest looked nothing like the one he had just left. Everything was green—much greener than his forest.

Panic again assailed him. "Mama? Mama!" The trees were different, like the ones he and Mama had seen in the books about the jungle they had gotten from the library. The ferns could have hidden him completely under their mammoth fronds. Even the light looked different as it cascaded into the small clearing before the mouth of the cave.

"I must have taken a wrong turn—" Joshua whispered and started back toward the mouth of the cave. But when he turned around, the cave's opening had vanished. His mouth hung wide open, shocked and dismayed.

"Mama! No!" he screamed, limping toward the sheer cliff rising far above his head. The cave had been there a moment before. Now, it was gone forever. Joshua ran his hands over the rocks. "It was here!"

Suddenly, Joshua heard rustling in the trees behind him. He swung around, seeing a shadow dart past him to the right. Then another to the left, closing in. He pressed against the cliff wall, swallowing the scream bubbling into his throat. He gulped, looking for a place to hide. But there was nothing around him, only the open space of moist black earth sprinkled with tree roots and vines.

A shower of small rocks and earth cascaded onto his head, and he looked up in time to see a rope net being thrust at him from above. Joshua ducked, covering his head as the net wrapped around him. Men exploded from the trees and ferns around him, whooping and hollering until Joshua thought he would die of fright. Without thinking, he closed his eyes and screamed. He yelled for Mama, hoping against hope that she would miraculously appear and rescue him.

The men only laughed at him, and one of them nudged him with his bare foot. "*Atonk peata!*" he said and then laughed. The others joined in. Joshua had no idea what they were saying but was too scared to look at them.

One man lifted the net off of him and grabbed him by the arm, hauling him to his feet. Joshua was shocked by the sight of him. He was covered from head to foot in black and red tattoos. His teeth were yellow and black, and his breath smelled like he had swished a mouthful of Father's special drink. Joshua gagged.

The man said another phrase he couldn't understand and shoved him roughly away from the cliff. Another grabbed him and tied his wrists behind his back. Joshua did not care if Carson thought he was a baby or not. He could not stop the tears from rolling down his cheeks. As they headed off into the forest, Joshua looked back over his shoulder, trying to catch a glimpse of the cave. But his eyes had not lied to him. It had disappeared without a trace.

His savage-looking captors wore little more than loin cloths made of vibrantly-colored animal skins. They carried slingshots and bows with quivers full of arrows made with bright blue and purple feathers. Joshua bit his lower lip and tried to calm down. He did not want the bad men to shoot him before he had a chance to get back to Mama.

Suddenly, something whizzed past Joshua's ear. He instinctively ducked as the man on his right yelled orders in his language, motioning with his hands. The kidnappers formed a circle around Joshua, their weapons at the ready. Another whizzing sound caught Joshua's attention. A second later, a man dropped to his knees a few feet away, clutching at his chest. In the confusion, Joshua was shoved to the moist earth. Joshua turned his face to the ground, praying that the invisible attacker would not hurt him, too. With cries of agony, the men fell to the ground around him one after the other.

Joshua again closed his eyes, wishing he could wake up from this crazy dream. It had to be a dream. "Mama will be here soon. Mama will be here soon—" he repeated as the battle went on around him.

One of the men tripped over him, grunting as he fell to the ground with a loud thump. The man scrambled away and found cover in the ferns. Joshua's head smarted, pain prickling through his scalp after the man had fallen on him. He lay very still, hoping if he pretended to be dead, the unseen attacker would leave him be.

After several minutes, the forest went quiet, and Joshua risked opening his eyes. When he saw no movement, he sat up. It wasn't easy to do with his hands tied behind his back. He grunted and struggled, trying to sit up and bring his legs out in front of him.

Suddenly, strong hands gripped him from behind and hauled him to his feet. He opened his mouth to scream, but the person covered his mouth before he could utter a sound.

"*Kyeth, pedonae,*" a man's voice sounded. His voice was soothing and calm, even though Joshua could not understand what he was trying to tell him. The man turned him around so his back was to him, and he felt the ropes being cut off his wrists. Joshua sighed in relief, and the man took him by the shoulder, hauling him into the cover of the forest.

He only had a moment to look at the carnage around him. The six men who had captured him lay dead in the dirt, their bodies and limbs contorted in strange ways. Joshua looked away from them, not liking their wide, staring eyes.

"Who are you?" Joshua asked. He felt like he should trust this man. After all, he had just saved his life. Mama would be thankful that the man had been so brave, taking on six men all on his own to save him.

The man stopped dead in his tracks, frowning in awe. He knelt and said something else in his strange language. But, of course, Joshua could not understand. All he knew was this man was different than the others. He had lighter skin and no frightening tattoos. He also did not look much like a warrior, dressed only in baggy pants that puffed out around his legs, his bare chest heaving with the exertion of battle.

The man stood suddenly as a twig snapped in the distance. The man lifted a finger to his lips, signaling him to be quiet. He then motioned for Joshua to follow him deeper into the woods. Joshua quickly obeyed, not wanting to be left out in the open with whatever was coming for them.

CHAPTER 3

JOSHUA

J oshua snapped out of fitful slumber, his ears prickling with the sound of fern leaves rustling over head. Someone, or something, was watching him. He could feel their eyes boring into him, even though he could not see anyone. Joshua rubbed his eyes, looking around his lush surroundings. He could not remember when they had stopped or how long he had been asleep. But his eyes felt like he had accidentally flicked sand into them with his toy shovel, like he had done when he and Mama went to the river.

A shadow moved in the foliage nearby. He sat up, backing further into the cover of a giant fern at the base of a Redwood tree. Joshua's chest felt like there was a little man trapped inside beating a drum. He wished he had had time to run.

There was no time. A man appeared in the distance, coming down a small winding path from deep within the forest. Joshua peeked out from behind the frond. It was the same man who had rescued him from the tattooed warriors. He had been bare-chested before, with his ballooned pants spreading around his legs and gathering at the ankles. He wore a long cloak now and carried a gnarled walking stick. The man stopped as if listening. Could he sense Joshua's gaze?

After a few seconds, the man turned his head, his eyes piercing the fern leaves and resting on Joshua's face. Joshua gasped, burrowing deeper into the fern. But the trunk of the monolithic tree at his back blocked any further escape.

"*Hetot ni'it.*" The man's voice sounded deep and musical. He took a cautious step toward Joshua, offering his hand in friendship. When Joshua did not come out, the man dug in his satchel and held out what looked like a piece of dried fruit. The man nodded, urging him to take it.

Joshua rubbed his eyes, wondering if he was awake or dreaming. He took the fruit carefully and backed under the cover of the fern again. The man straightened, turning his back on him. He went and squatted a few feet away and tore at his own piece of dried fruit.

Joshua studied him for a moment, trying to decide if he did trust him after all. The man looked a little older than his parents, with white salting his black beard. His kind brown eyes searched the shadows of the fern. He held out his hands, palms open as he approached Joshua.

"*Ti'inta sik filou tziksoe?*"

Joshua shook his head. The strange language sounded like a song, with the man's melodic voice calming his fears. He had a kind face. Mama would probably not mind if he spoke to him, even though he had always been told not to talk to strangers.

"*Donde esta tu madre?*" the man tried again.

Joshua inched out of the fern's cover. "I'm lost," he whimpered. He looked up at the man, wondering if he had just made a mistake.

The man knelt a few feet from the fern and raised his hand in a show of friendship. "En-leesh?" His words carried the accent of his language. Still, Joshua relaxed, thinking that the man might be able to understand him. "You speak Enlish?" The man asked again, a little louder this time.

"Yes." Joshua stood, inching out of his hiding place in front of the fern. The man straightened, watching him closely. Joshua closed the distance between himself and the man. He might be the only one able to return him to Mama. Joshua extended his hand, just as he had seen Father do when he greeted other men. "My name is Joshua."

The man looked at his hand and then back at Joshua's face. He bowed slightly at the waist. "I am Manemna." He placed his hand over his heart and smiled. "Where you come from?"

Joshua cast a worried glance around. He had fallen asleep after their long walk through the woods. He no longer knew where the cave was or even the direction of the cliffs. "I got lost in a cave. Carson left me all alone and played a dirty trick on me. I wandered around until I came out in this jungle, but when I tried to go back into the cave, the opening was gone." Joshua sniffed, a shiver running up his spine. "And then those men caught me in their net."

Manemna nodded and jutted his chin in the direction that lay behind Joshua. Would the man believe him? "I see," was all he said. He extended his hand, and Joshua took it. "Storm is coming. I take you home tonight, and we see what to do in morning." It was difficult to understand with the halting way Manemna talked.

Manemna's hand enveloped Joshua's, its warmth spreading into his. Manemna looked down at him, then took off his mantle, doubled it over, and wrapped it around Joshua's shoulders. His body instantly radiated with the heat, warmth spreading through his chilled bones.

"Come," Manemna instructed, leading him to the path winding through the trees. As they walked, Joshua took in their surroundings. Looking up, he noticed again how much bigger the trees were than the ones back home. It would take twenty men, hands clasped and arms extended around the base, to reach all the way around it. He remembered Mama talking about the Redwood trees in California and thought that maybe these were the same kind. But even those were dwarfed by the ones here. Maybe this forest was older. The treetops seemed to reach the sky. Their branches blocked the sunshine from reaching the ground, save for tiny spaces where it allowed the cool evening light to filter to the ground.

Joshua relaxed, feeling safe with Manemna. He wondered what it would have been like if his father was more like this man. He had only known him for a short while but already felt more at ease with Manemna than his own father. "What is this place?" he asked as he got more comfortable.

Manemna waved his hand slowly before him as they came to another clearing amid the trees and ferns. "This my village. *Hotun.*"

"I've never heard of this place. Is it very far from Butte Falls? That is where I live with Mama."

Manemna frowned slightly but still wore a congenial smile. "I never hear of this *Bee-yoote Falls.* I never hear of any place like that in Luminia."

It was Joshua's turn to frown. "Luminia?" The word sounded strange. "Is that your state?"

"No. Luminia is name of my country." He halted as they came to the tree line. Joshua could see small houses dotting the clearing and wondered if he had fallen through the center of the world and come out in China. Mama had told him it was impossible, but now he was unsure.

Manemna knelt in front of him so they could be eye to eye. "Shos-hua." Joshua thought the way Manemna pronounced his name sounded funny and exciting all at the same time. "I believe you come from Other World."

It took a moment for Joshua to understand what he meant. Manemna took a stone necklace from around his neck and held it in front of Joshua. "Here. Take." Manemna motioned for him to put it around his neck.

Joshua gave the man a halting glance before he took the smooth, blue stone in hand. He turned it over. "What is it?"

"It will give you tongue of Luminia—so we understand each other better. My Enlish not good." He smiled and nodded, encour-

32

aging him to put the necklace on. Joshua did as he was told and waited for something extraordinary to happen. But nothing did.

"There. Now you have the *Luminsilkis*," Manemna said. At first, his words came out in the strange gibberish he had used before, then slowly morphed into English. Joshua raised his brows in shock. Manemna stood, looking down at Joshua with pride. "Come. I will introduce you to my wife and daughter." He understood him perfectly now, in unbroken English.

Joshua looked down at the necklace, marveling that something so simple could allow him to understand Manemna. He shook his head, feeling overwhelmed by everything that had happened. Joshua followed Manemna into the village and tried not to show how frightened he felt as the other villagers stared at him.

He slipped his hand in Manemna's, finding comfort as his fingers closed around his. Manemna bent slightly and lowered his voice. "Do not be afraid. They are only curious, my son."

The dome-shaped mud and wattle houses were laid out in a circle around a communal fire pit. Joshua counted eight houses in total, each with a well-worn path leading from the front door to the fire pit. Over to the left was a long path leading to another circle of eight houses. And beyond that, another and another, more homes than Joshua could count. Young children ran about the fire pit, playing a game involving a ball woven out of reeds and short sticks. Joshua thought it looked a bit like hockey, only there was no ice.

The air seemed heavy and wet, making it difficult for Joshua to catch his breath. He had never been in a place as warm as this. His skin felt sticky, and his clothes restrictive. He noticed that some of the younger boys wore only loincloths, like the men who had kidnapped him. Their clothing was made of tanned animal skins, not fur. The girls wore simple dresses with no sleeves. The children playing the game stopped as he and Manemna passed, looking at them with large brown eyes. They all had beautiful brown skin tanned by the sun. His skin was pasty white in comparison, making him feel even more out of place.

They passed a field where some younger men were working, their bare chests glistening with sweat. They wore long, baggy pants just like Manemna. It looked like they had taken skirts and tucked the back hem through the legs and up into the front waist-band, the material gathering tightly around the ankles. Some of the older men wore the same strange ballooned pants and sleeveless mantles that were open in the front. Women sat outside their houses, grinding grain in large rocks with depressions in their centers. They wore the same sleeveless dresses as the girls, except with long sashes to accentuate their waists. All the villagers wore various earthy colors: browns, reds, muted oranges, greens, and mustard yellows.

Joshua followed Manemna around the fire pit, people stopping their tasks to eye their new arrival with curiosity. Joshua stuck close to Manemna's side, nervous at the wide-open stares.

When they arrived at the last hut on the other side of the last fire pit, Manemna halted. "My home," he said and motioned toward the front door. He moved a plain canvas covering aside from the doorway and led Joshua inside. "Souni! I have brought a visitor!" he called.

They stepped down into the house, which was larger than it appeared from the outside. The floor had been dug a few feet down into the earth, hard-packed and covered with clay around the perimeter walls and floor. There were three doorways off the back of the main room leading to bedrooms. It was unlike anything he had ever seen before, even in cartoons.

It took a moment for Joshua's eyes to adjust to the dimly lit space. The light was minimal, even with the foot-wide holes that dotted the top of the dome-shaped roof. Joshua supposed on a sunny day, there would have been floods of natural light. However, dark clouds covered the sky, obscuring the sunshine. Manemna had said a storm was brewing, and Joshua wondered how they kept the inside of the house dry with so many holes in the roof.

As his eyes adjusted, Joshua spotted a woman sitting at the

hearth, stirring a pot. Whatever was in it smelled heavenly. Joshua's stomach grumbled as she turned around.

"Who is this?" she asked her husband, rising from her task and joining them at the door. Her face was round and kind. She looked to be quite a bit younger than Manemna. Her dark brown hair was done up in an elaborate braid.

"This is Shos-hua." Manemna introduced him. "I found him on the outer reaches of the forest, near the border." Lowering his voice, he leaned in to whisper in his wife's ear. "I believe he came from the Other World. I had to rescue him from a band of Tzotoen soldiers." Manemna turned and smiled at him, but Joshua could sense the tension in the air. He was used to picking up on things like that.

Souni's eyes snapped from her husband's to Joshua's. "The Other World? That has not happened in nearly one-hundred *kis-llzuto*." She looked at Joshua in alarm, studying him as if he were a part of a circus act. She looked like she wanted to reach out and touch him to make sure he was not a ghost.

"I know." Manemna replied softly. "And that raiding party may also be a cause for worry."

"Are you a warrior?" Joshua interrupted, his nervousness overcome by curiosity.

Souni laughed and put an arm around Joshua's shoulders, ushering him further inside. "We are farmers. But Manemna works the hardest. He is the *pitpak* of Hotun, our leader, and must set the example."

For a man who was not a warrior, Manemna had undoubtedly held his own in the fight against Joshua's captors. He was not sure it would be a good idea to mention that they all lay dead on the forest floor now, brought down by Manemna's bow.

Souni looked up as a small shadow darkened the front doorway. "Ahh, and here is our daughter, Intza."

Joshua turned to see a young girl peeking around the curtain at him. She looked to be about four years old, with shoulder-length brown hair touched with streaks of gold from the sun. She had strikingly bright green-brown eyes, unlike the other children whose eyes had been various shades of brown. "Kyasen?" Her big eyes grew even wider when she saw Joshua.

Joshua looked up at Manemna and noticed a cloud of sadness pass between his and Souni's eyes. Souni shook her head, going to the front door to draw Intza into the house. "No, my flower. This is Shos-hua." She had Intza stand in front of her and laced her fingers over the girl's chest. "He has come to us for help. He was lost in the woods outside our village."

Intza came forward slowly, studying Joshua. "You look like my brother," she said simply. She touched his short, dark hair as if he were not real. Joshua noticed Manemna and Souni's pained expressions once more. "Kyasin died in the river," Intza went on.

Joshua felt somewhat uncomfortable under the girls' bold stare. "I'm sorry."

The girl shrugged and sat down at the low table. "Mama says he went to be with *Ilyo Na'ada*."

"And so he has, my flower," her mother interrupted, placing a hand on the girl's back and steering her toward the door, her voice quaking with emotion. "Now, run along and play while Shos-hua rests." Souni shooed Intza back out of the hut and ushered Joshua in front of the fire. "I have some clothes that might fit you. Let us get you out of those filthy ones and see about some food. You must be hungry."

Souni searched for the clothes while Manemna had him sit at a low wooden table in the middle of the room. Joshua sat cross-legged on a woven mat before the table, instead of in a chair. There were no chairs in the whole house that Joshua could see. Manemna served him some stew, steaming from a clay bowl, and set it before him. Joshua took a tentative bite but dug in when the savory flavor of meat and vegetables spread through his mouth. His stomach growled in response, urging him onward. Joshua could not remember when he had last eaten—unsure how much time had elapsed since breakfast and when he had suddenly found himself stuck in this strange land.

Soon, his belly was full. Manemna had even allowed him to have a second helping of the delicious stew. Joshua's eyelids grew heavy and his body relaxed. Manemna had seated himself beside Joshua and had been carving on a small piece of wood. Mesmerized by the slow, steady strokes of Manemna's knife, Joshua soon began to nod off.

When Souni returned, she helped him change into some long, baggy pants he had seen the older men wearing. They felt much better than his tight shorts and shirt, bathed in sweat after the long walk through the humid woods. Souni did not give him a shirt to replace his other. Joshua did not need it, thanks to the heat.

It was only then that Joshua realized something was missing. His hands flew to his neck, and he looked around the floor. "My pouch! Mama's pouch! It's gone," he said. The language stone still hung about his neck, but Mama's leather beaded pouch was gone.

Souni looked up at Manemna. "Well, maybe you dropped it on your way here. Manemna, will you look around for it?" she asked.

"Of course," he replied. "But for now, I think he should sleep."

Souni placed her hands on his hips and readjusted the waist of the ballooned trousers. She bit her lower lip. "They are a little bit big for you, but that will have to do for now," Souni said. She ran her hand over Joshua's head and cupped his cheek tenderly, just as Mama would have done. His heart clenched at the thought of Mama. She would be worried sick.

Souni took a breath, standing all of a sudden. Her eyes were clouded with tears. "I suppose you are tired. Would you like to sleep for a while?" she asked. Joshua nodded, his eyelids growing heavy from the long day. She smiled and showed him to a small pallet in an adjoining room. A single hole, maybe a foot in diameter, was drilled through the top of the smaller dome covering the sleeping chamber. He lay down, and his eyes slipped closed all on their own.

He was asleep before Souni tucked a thin blanket over him, patting his chest as she stood. "Sleep well, Shos-hua."

CHAPTER 4

SOUNI

Souni backed out of the room, the smile seeping away from her face like water soaking into the cracks of a barren riverbed. When she turned, Manemna stilled. "The Other World—" she breathed. "Not since Tzizenah's day has anyone seen someone from there." She came to the table, sitting down cross-legged in one fluid motion.

Manemna nodded solemnly, resting his forearms on his thighs. "I know. Of course, neither of us were born when the first two arrived." Souni glanced at the room that had belonged to their son, where the strange boy now slept.

"He was exhausted. I wonder how far he came." Souni shook her head, amazed by the implications. What did this boy's arrival mean? Why here in the sleepy village of Hotun? Why now?

Manemna reached over and took her hand. She scooted closer to him, and he wrapped an arm around her shoulders. It was uncanny how Intza had noticed a resemblance between Shos-hua and their departed son. Of course, it was not in outward appearance but in spirit. Shos-hua possessed a noble soul and a courage that was rare in one so young, just as Kyasen had. Might the boy's arrival mean a

monumental change was coming, just as the Spanyaard's arrival had
so many years before?

Souni studied her husband's troubled face. She smoothed her
hand down his jawline. "Whatever his purpose for being here, we
will care for him." She looked back at the doorway, smiling at the
sound of soft snores issuing from it. "He seems a sweet child."

Manemna nodded once, his face hardening. He released her and
stood, heading toward the front door. Souni was not so much
worried for the boy but what his appearance meant. As the *pitpak* of
the village, it was his duty to protect them. No doubt, that was chief
on his mind as he watched the men coming in from the fields. The
women would be finishing their preparations for the evening meal,
while the children scampered around the fire pit.

He glanced over his shoulder at her. "Do not grow too attached,
my love."

Souni scrambled to her feet and joined him in the doorway.
"What do you mean? We cannot just turn him out to fend for
himself."

Manemna finally met her gaze. Her turquoise eyes, which had
been dull and full of sadness since the passing of their son, now
sparked with renewed fire. "We must do all in my power to see him
reunited with his family. I must take him to Lunthá and inquire of
the King what should be done for him."

"And if there is nothing to be done, though—"

He kissed the top of her head. "We cannot keep him here. He
belongs with his family in the Other World."

She pushed away from him, wrapping her arms around her
middle. Over the last year, they had passed the mourning period
with difficulty. She knew the ache would lessen with time but never
entirely disappear. Kyasen had been a joy to their family, protective
and strong, exhibiting the signs of becoming a good leader one day.
It was unjust that he had no heir to pass along the *pitpaksin* when
Manemna died. His absence had left a hole that Souni was unsure
would ever be filled again.

She pushed her grief away, tired of the toll it had taken. She had thought to move past it until this terrified boy with frightened eyes had appeared on the edge of their domain. Not only that, she feared what purpose the Tzotoen bandits had in roaming along their borderlands. Manemna came up behind her and squeezed her shoulders. "I will do what I can for him." He left the house and she watched him walk to the communal fire. She could not help but wonder, what did this solitary, frightened boy mean for the fate of Luminia?

CHAPTER 5

ADAGIO

The Royal City of Lunthá, Luminia
Year of the Jaguar, 972

R*un.*

That was all his mind had time to register. Adagio's heart beat wildly, like the thundering hooves of a hundred horses. His eyes darted back and forth like a fear-crazed animal, searching over his shoulder for what hunted him. Before he could make his escape, a hand grabbed his ankle and sent him hurtling to the ground.

Landing hard on his forearms, he sucked in a breath as sharp rocks sliced his skin. He flipped over onto his back, scooting away in a desperate attempt to escape. A shadow appeared before him, the cloaked figure advancing slowly and menacingly. The icy grip of fear wrapped around his heart when, all of a sudden, he heard a shrill cry in the distance. "Mama! Where are you?" The shadow jerked its head toward the sound and disappeared into the woods. Adagio scrambled to his feet, his fatherly instincts kicking in as he searched for the child.

What was a child doing out in these woods? He knew instinctively that the shadow-man was after the boy now. Perhaps it was easier prey.

43

"Mama!" he heard the cry again. Adagio snapped out of his thoughts, knowing he had to find the child before the shadowed-hunter did. As he moved through the dark foliage, he stumbled over a small boy who looked up at Adagio with sheer terror pasted on his dirty face.

Adagio knelt and took the child by his shoulders. "Are you lost, my boy?"

The boy spoke in garbled sobs, crying for his mother.

"Where did you last see her?"

The boy named a place Adagio had never heard of. He looked around, straining to hear if anyone was calling for the boy. The usual bird squawks and rustling of the leaves grew chillingly silent as he listened. Gooseflesh rose on his arms as he searched the surrounding woods for signs of the shadow-man. Adagio knelt before the frightened child again. "What is your name?"

"Joshua," he sniffed. Adagio raised an eyebrow. It was a very unusual name.

"I will help you find your mother. Do not worry." He reached out his hand for the boy to take, but as he did, the boy grew before his eyes, changing into a full-grown man. Adagio stumbled backward and rubbed his eyes in shock.

Out of the darkness, a voice called to Adagio. "This is the one I have sent, Adagio. When you see him, the destruction of Luminia is at hand..."

Adagio gazed at the young man, his muscled arms holding a bow and quiver. A sword was strapped to his side. "I don't understand," he said to himself. "Luminia has not had war for over six-hundred years."

"Do not fear," the voice sounded again. "I will send a deliverer to free you from the bonds of silence."

From the corner of his eye, he saw the shadow-man step around the trunk of an enormous Redwood tree, glaring at the young man. The specter removed his hood, making his face clearly visible. Adagio could hardly believe his eyes. "Lord Delgadas?" he whispered. The man's gaze pierced his heart like so many daggers, his eyes glowing with an other-worldly green hue. Adagio's hands began to shake. Delgadas was one of the king's advisors...

A twig snapped in the distance, and Delgadas disappeared before Adagio's eyes. When Adagio looked for the young man, he was also gone, leaving only the sword and bow lying on the ground in his wake. He knelt and touched the blade's hilt but was thrust backward with the force of a bolt of lightning coursing through his body. Paralyzed, Adagio watched the world disintegrate into darkness.

ADAGIO ROUSED from the dream with a start, sweat dripping down his forehead and coating his bare chest. He sat up and ran his shaking hands through his jet-black hair. The vision hung around him still. Even the strange voice echoed with a warning around the room and slowly fade. He swung his legs over the edge of the feather-stuffed mattress, rubbing his calloused hands over his face. The peculiar dreams had become nightly occurrences during the last few months. But none had shaken him as this one had. He could not help but wonder if trouble was on the horizon. The fact that Lord Delgadas had made an appearance in his dreams was even more unsettling.

He stood, padding across the marble floor of the spacious bed chamber. He parted the silk curtains hanging over the archway, allowing the moonslight to flood the room. He took a deep breath, a cool breeze greeting him and helping to chase away his disturbing thoughts. He felt that the voice in the darkness had been *Ilyo Na'ada*, warning him that there was danger afoot.

"Adagio?" His wife, Ritenueta, rolled over and called to him from the bed. Smiling, he left the window and came back to her side. He sank down with a sigh and felt her shift onto her knees and come to him. Running her slender fingers down his spine, she lay her head between his shoulder blades and held him close. "Is everything alright, *itim tziapia?*"

Adagio smiled at the use of the familiar endearment and lay back down, propping his arm under her neck. *Itim Tziapia*—My Love.

"Everything is fine. Go back to sleep. You have a while yet before we need to leave for the palace."

"Everything is not fine." Ritenueta sat up, leaning up on her elbow. She pouted, looking up at him, pleading with him not to go.

"It is nothing to trouble you with," Adagio said. He ran a finger down her jaw, kissed the tip of her nose, then coaxed her back to a prone position. "I wish I could stay, but you know I cannot start the day right if I skip my morning walk. I shall not take a long one this morning, do not worry."

She groaned and rolled over. "Whenever you say *it will not take long*, I can know for certain we are going to be late."

He chuckled, then stood and dressed quickly, padding down the cold marble staircase. Halting momentarily to don a pair of leather shoes that tapered at the toes, he exited by the front door. Adagio sucked in a breath, his lungs refreshed from the early morning chill. The shock helped chase away the last remnants of the dream from his mind. He bounded down the steps and descended the steep hill toward the marketplace. Fog hung in low clouds over the island city, rolling in from the lagoon almost every night. *This is what it must feel like to walk among the clouds*, he thought.

The moons were still high in the sky, illuminating the mist as it moved around him in feathery wisps. *Ni'inta*, the largest of the moons, led the two smaller moons in their race across the summer sky. At this time of year, *Dyros* stayed right on *Ni'inta's* heels, drawing ever closer while *Ruvot* lagged behind. But *Ruvot* would bypass the other two in the winter as if by magic, finishing the race in the lead as the New Year was celebrated. The 'Three Sisters' were like old friends to Adagio, guiding him as he walked. Indeed, they were like the guardians of Luminia, ever steady as the world changed below them.

The land of Luminia, or Dawn Land as some called it, had always been Adagio's home. His father had held a position of trust and fond regard in the palace, and Adagio had followed in his footsteps. Nothing could have prepared him for the weight of responsibility that had fallen on his shoulders when his father had passed away. Not only was he responsible for leading hundreds of Musicians in the art of bringing Luminia to life, but he was also an esteemed advisor to the king.

Adagio halted as he came to the bottom of the hill, which flattened out on a terrace. The island had been shaped over the centuries, with terraces to help with water run-off and provide places for the houses and gardens to be built. He looked up at the horizon, noting the barely visible gray light. It was as if the sun was held back. It was like a great horse pawing at the ground, impatient to begin a race. And indeed it was. For the sun would not rise until Adagio and his family deemed it so. Since the beginning of Luminia, *Ilyo Na'ada* had given The Musicians the weighty responsibility of bringing their world to life through song.

Turning toward the *chilput,* or laborer's quarter, his footsteps echoed off the mud-brick homes. Wispy clouds of fog swirled around him, giving him the appearance of a specter. Adagio had taken a walk before every sunrise since the time he was a child. This tradition started with his father carrying Adagio on his back as a small boy. Adagio had perpetuated the tradition with his own son. However, as of late, his son, Molto, had become increasingly interested in his readings of the ancient prophecies. And thus, much too tired to go on their walk together.

Adagio did not really mind but instead encouraged his son's increasing appetite for learning. He remembered a time when his own thirst for knowledge had been insatiable, just as it was now for his eldest child.

He looped around the *chilput* and then walked back up the steep steps towards the town's wealthier section. The *tilput* was where the politicians, merchants, and Musicians lived. Stone and mud-brick homes gave way to clay stucco houses, then to gleaming white marble mansions as he climbed higher and higher. The fog dissipated from the lower sections of the city until it hung like a halo around the mountaintop palace grounds. Adagio entered the clouds once more, making his way home.

As he neared the summit, he turned and looked out over the capital. From this vantage, he could see for miles across the lagoon and into the lush forests beyond. It was so still now, as if he were the only person on earth. He relished the feeling of peace and contentment that came before his busy day as he looked out over the slumbering city. *If only this peace would last...*

CHAPTER 6
ADAGIO

Adagio ducked inside the servant's entrance of his home and was immediately greeted by the tired smiles of his family. "Oh, good, you are all awake," he breathed a sigh of relief.

Ritenueta gave him a knowing look. "What did I tell you?" She planted her hands planted on her hips, a mischievous smile touching her lips.

"Yes, yes, I know." He leaned in for a kiss. "And still you love me?"

"Always." She rested a hand against his chest and searched his gaze. Her eyes grew troubled, and he again tried to hide his unease before turning from her. "Come along everyone. You know that the sun will not rise without us," Adagio beckoned.

Melodia, his middle child, yawned and came over to wrap her little arms around both his legs. "Is that really true, Papa? What would happen if we slept in one day and didn't play for the sunrise?"

Adagio wrapped an arm around her and patted her head. "Well, we say it would not rise but that is not entirely true. It would rise eventually, but much later in the day. And there would be rains such as you have never seen before."

49

"Like a flood?" she asked, looking up at him with her sweet innocent face.

"Somewhat. Now, we really do need to be off."

Molto helped gather the instruments, and they were soon out the door. Ritenueta laced her fingers through his as they climbed the steep hill toward the palace. The simple gesture helped to calm his nerves.

He glanced over his shoulder to be sure his twin daughters were keeping up. At only five years old, their little legs had difficulty climbing the arduous steps as quickly as the rest of them. Adagio halted, waiting for them to catch up. Melodia skipped happily to her mother's side and took her hand. "Mama! Has the queen had her baby yet?"

Ritenueta eyed her husband, shooing the children up the incline. "Not yet my dear, she has a few months yet."

His heart went out to their beloved queen. After so much heartache and loss, he hoped this birth went smoothly.

"Mama!" Melodia whined, her shoulders slumping forward. "I am tired of waiting. Why do baby's take so long to make?"

Ritenueta chucked her gently under the chin and laughed. "That is the way of things. Now, do not worry anymore. We will be some of the first to know when the baby does come. I promise." Ritenueta rolled her eyes heavenward as Adagio picked Haarmonae up and continued walking. His youngest was usually the more excitable of the two, but she did not like early mornings. Melodia and Haarmonae seemed to have switched personalities over the last few weeks. Melodia asked them when the royal baby would be born at least twenty times a day. Because of her excitement, she had been having trouble listening to her lessons and sitting still.

"It could be any day, my little songbird. But you must promise to study hard during your lessons," he told Melodia. "We will be responsible for announcing the royal birth, you know. And it must be spectacular."

They soon arrived at the palace gates and were admitted by the guards. They made their way across the spacious courtyard to the Musicians Steps, leading to the palace roof. The rooftop afforded a view over the island city's terraced hillsides and the mountainous landscape beyond. Surrounding the capital was a vast crystalline lagoon, reflecting the few stars still visible in the gray light. The lagoon was fed by a small inlet leading from the sea, allowing for a port on the leeward side of the island. On the island's western side were chalky white cliffs with a naturally arched entry. It was the only inlet from the sea. The rest of the cliffs acted as a natural buffer from storms and invaders alike.

Adagio turned from the view to gaze at his young family with pride. They sat together on a long, half-moon-shaped bench under a spacious pergola. Wisteria and roses climbed the pergola columns and hung from the trellis above. Their blooms were ready to open at the first rays of light.

They readied their instruments and looked up at Adagio, awaiting his signal to begin. Adagio nodded, and the first low note from the guitar caressed the air, life emanating from the gentle vibrations. As each instrument joined in, it brought a different part of their world to life.

Dim light colored the eastern horizon, accompanied by Adagio's gentle strum of the guitar. His fingers danced expertly over the eight-stringed instrument. The horizon brightened as he continued, clouds parting for the sun to crest over the majestic mountains. He looked at Melodia and nodded, signaling her to join in.

Melodia brought her little flute to her lips and began to blow. At first, she was reticent, closing her eyes as she found her place among the guitar's rich vibrations. Far away, in the forest beyond the royal city, a bird woke from its slumber and whistled its tune along with Melodia. Soon, birds of all kinds joined in, starting with the far bank's outer reaches and moving inward until there was a symphony of birdsong all around them. A brightly colored *chi-zitke*, or dew bird, landed on the trellis above Melodia and ruffled its purple, blue, and turquoise feathers. It seemed to wink at her as it joined in with the song, drawing a look of delighted wonder from Melodia.

Adagio raised his eyebrows, smiled at her, then leaned over to Haarmonae and signaled her to join. When her bow touched the strings of her violin, a gentle breeze picked up and carried the sound out to the forest. The notes awakened the trees, the wind making it look like they were stretching their branches over their heads as a child would after a good sleep. The flowers began to open their delicate petals at the dancing melody, turning their heads east in unison to the growing light of dawn.

Molto met Adagio's gaze, knowing his time to join had come. Molto caressed the top of his animal skin drum, running his hand over its top in a circular motion to draw out a low rumble from its belly. He then tapped the drum's edges three times with its sharp, high tones and once in the center to bring out the low tones. He repeated the beat over and over, growing louder each time. His drumming awakened the rest of the animals in the forest. On the outer bank of the lake, a mother bear and two cubs came out of the trees for a drink, the mother's lumbering movements in contrast with the gleeful wrestling of her cubs. A doe and her fawn came to the shore to drink as well, with no fear of attack from the sow. Adagio flicked his head toward the scene, relishing the joy on his children's faces. Predator and prey were in perfect harmony whenever the Musicians played, instinctively holding to an ancient truce not to attack each other during these sacred moments.

Ritenueta was the last to blend into the song, her rich alto voice awakening the sea. The waves could be heard crashing on the rocks just over the cliffs, bringing in the tide. A playful breeze brought the refreshing scent of saltwater up from the lagoon. Fishermen could be seen heading out in their boats, ready to gather the bounty that *Ilyo Na'ada* provided. As Ritenueta's voice rose, so did the swells. Adagio could see one of the waves take the shape of a maiden, twirling her skirts in a happy dance as she lifted her face and hands to the sky. As the wave neared the shore, the water-maiden leapt into the air and disappeared as the salt spray crashed against the rocks.

The sun peeked its head over the horizon as the song grew louder. Ray's of delicious sunlight illuminated the city, touching the Musician's Terrace first and then cascading down like a waterfall. People stirred and began preparations for the day. Soon, the capital was alive with voices and bustling crowds headed toward the market. Grays gave way to a light blues as the sky brightened, the sun bursting from behind fluffy white clouds tinged in pink.

Adagio nodded once again, and the song faded away in the breeze as each of them ended their portion in turn. Ritenueta was the last to finish, her clear voice carrying over the terrace. They sat in wonder for a moment, basking in the beauty of the sunrise they had helped create. "Well, I do believe that was one of the best sunrises we have ever played." Adagio's heart swelled with pride as he looked around at his family. It seemed they grew more confident in their arts each day in their arts, blessed by *Ilyo-Na'ada* himself.

"I agree," Ritenueta said. She placed her hand on Molto's head and pulled him close for a hug. "Well done, all of you. Now, store your instruments, children. We have a long day ahead."

The children did as their mother instructed, storing their instruments in protective leather cases. Ritenueta came to Adagio's side and placed her hands on his shoulders as he bent to put his guitar in its case. Leaning down, she whispered in his ear, "Are you alright? Your muscles seem tight enough to break bone." She began to massage his shoulders gently and some of the tension left. Usually, his wife would have let the matter rest, knowing he did his best to protect her from taking on burdens that were not hers to bear.

He turned and placed a hand over hers. "I am better now. After that sunrise, who could be nervous? Did you see the water-maiden?" he asked.

"I did. I have not seen one in months. Today must be a very special day," Ritenueta smiled, no doubt searching his face for clues as to what could be bothering him. "And do not try to distract with me talk of the water maiden." She ran her fingers down his cheek, and he closed his eyes momentarily, leaning into her caress. "I wish I could help ease your burden."

Adagio glanced at the children. "We are ready, Mama!" Melodia called from the stairs that lead them down into the palace kitchens. He nodded and started toward them, wrapping an arm around his wife's slender waist.

Ritenueta let her hand fall to her side and gave Adagio a bolstering smile. "Shall we?"

"I think we had better," he said, nodding toward the children. They were ready for the customary cup of warm *chatla*, a special tea made from the fire flower's petals. It would give them the energy they needed before beginning their studies and various tasks about the palace.

"Go ahead, my loves," Ritenueta instructed. The children raced down the steps to the Musician's Courtyard, just outside the kitchens, where a plentiful breakfast would be laid. Ritenueta and Adagio took their time descending the steep staircase, knowing they would have little time to spend together until they returned to their villa that night.

"You are still worried, Adagio. Won't you tell me what is troubling you?" Ritenueta whispered. "Surely it would be better to unburden yourself before you attend the court sessions with His Majesty."

Adagio let out a sigh. He should have known that his wife would ask him about his strange mood sooner or later. And it would do him well to have a clear mind. "It is not something I can put into words. It is only a vague disquiet I feel." He went first down the narrow, winding stairwell to steady her.

"Your nightmares grow worse," she said. "I can feel you thrashing in the night."

He halted at the bottom step, holding her as if it were a lifeline meant to haul him to a ship after being thrown overboard. Ritenueta joined him on the bottom step, looking deep into his eyes. However, he could not keep his gaze locked on hers, afraid she would guess at his thoughts. She had a habit of doing just that.

"I do not want to burden you, it is true. Let us simply say that I am warned of things to come." Lord Delgadas' appearance in his nightmare had put him on edge. As one of King Nissim's advisors, it would not bode well if he were found to be a snake in dove's clothing. He did not want to burden Ritenueta with his thoughts, especially if it turned out that he was wrong in his suspicions. Adagio would watch Delgadas closely to see if there were any signs of disloyalty in him.

Adagio cupped Ritenueta's cheek, offering an encouraging smile. "Everything will be well." He wished he could wipe away the furrows worrying her brow. She relaxed a little as he drew her in for a quick peck on the lips. "I will spend some time at the temple in prayer this afternoon."

"Perhaps we all should, if it is as serious as that?" she offered.

"Thank you, but I would have some time alone to entreat *Ilyo Na'ada*." They came to the arched doorway leading into the courtyard. The voices and laughter grew louder as they approached. Adagio took a deep breath, wiping the worry off his face. He would have to pretend that nothing was amiss for the sake of his children, not to mention the rest of his students. Ritenueta nodded solemnly before entering the Musicians Courtyard, set aside especially for the Musician families to rest and take meals together at the palace during their various duties. Adagio watched his wife join a group of mothers, starting a lively conversation that he could only begin to guess at.

Adagio watched for a moment, the Musician's Courtyard filling with families. He was responsible for all of their welfare. He only hoped he was up for the task should something change. He could not know what his dreams foretold, only that change was coming. When it did arrive, would they even be able to recognize their beloved homeland?

CHAPTER 7

JOSHUA

J oshua started, feeling warm breath on his cheek. His eyes flew open, and he came face to face with a little girl. She studied him curiously, her nose just inches from his own. He tried to back away, his senses still clouded from a deep sleep. But there was nowhere he could go. Where was he?

The events from a few days ago slowly filtered into his mind. He had lost Mama. Carson had abandoned him. He had ended up in this strange land, where this girl and her family had taken him in. Sadness overwhelmed his heart and tears pricked at his eyes. Would he ever see his mother again?

Suddenly, the little girl placed her hands on his cheeks and touched the tip of her nose to his. He dared not move, his eyes darting to the right and the left as if he might find someone to help him. She squeezed his cheeks together, making his lips pucker like a fish.

"Kyasen?" she questioned.

"No, Intza. Not Kyasen," the girl's mother poked her head into the small room, scooped her up in her arms and took her out to the table. Joshua sat up slowly, rubbing the sleep out of his eyes. His heart pounded in his chest.

"How do you feel today?" Souni called from the living area. "Your fever broke late in the night."

Joshua stretched his lower back, his mind in a fog. He felt like he had been asleep forever. He had only been awake for little snatches here and there. Shortly after arriving at Manemna's home, Joshua had fallen ill. Not too much to cause alarm, but he had not been well enough to travel to the royal city as Manemna had hoped. Joshua exited the sleeping chamber and joined Souni and Intza in the common area, rubbing his hand over his face.

"Where's Mama?" His back and neck were sore from sleeping on a reed mat on the floor. He missed his bed back home. He missed Mama.

"I do not know, child. We are going to try to get you home. Are you hungry?" She motioned toward a spot at the low table and placed a hand on his shoulder, gently nudging him to join the little girl. "Do you remember our names? Mine is Souni, and this little rascal is Intza."

Joshua relaxed a little as he was seated. "I remember. She is very curious, isn't she?"

Intza smiled at him, and he thought maybe she wasn't so bad after all. Intza didn't seem afraid of anything, even though she was younger than him. "Where is Manemna?" he asked, taking up a slice of fruit that looked similar to an orange, except the flesh was a deep pinkish-purple. He took a bite, and sweet juice filled his mouth, dripping down his chin and onto the table. Joshua laughed and wiped his chin with the back of his hand. "This is good."

When Souni turned, her eyes were filled with sadness. "Manemna is out in the field. He usually would not return until after sunset." She set a wooden cup in front of him, steam rising from the liquid's surface. She sighed, seating herself next to him. "He will return soon. He wants to try to get you back to your family today, if he can."

"And if he can't?" Joshua asked. "Will he have to take me to the king?"

"If you are well enough to travel." She brushed her fingers over his forehead, moving his hair out of the way. Mama would do that to check his temperature sometimes. "Yes, you seem much better." Souni did not seem to want to talk any more about him leaving, so he quietly ate his fruit.

She picked Intza up and situated her on her lap, resting a hand on the table even as the other wound around the girl's middle.

Joshua nodded to Intza. "Does she go to school?"

Souni frowned. "I do not know this word: *school.*"

Joshua couldn't believe she had never heard of school. His heart lifted: maybe he would not have to spend his days trapped inside, like he had been back home. "You know, it's the place where children go to learn things–like numbers and letters."

"Ahh, I see. You mean *hatchem?* Parents are responsible for teaching their children all they need know. Some of the brightest students are sent to Lunthá for training in special skills, but most of us follow in our parents' footsteps."

"Kyasen would have been a farmer, like Papa. But he fell in the river—" Intza chimed in, but her mother covered her little mouth gently before she could finish.

"That is enough, my flower." Souni whispered. Souni stood and was about to set Intza back on the cushion when the little girl squirmed her way out of her arms and bounded out of the house to play. Joshua touched Souni's hand, then slipped his hand into hers, giving it a light squeeze. Mama always seemed to like that when she was sad.

Souni's eyes filled with thankfulness and tears, although she did not let them fall to her cheeks. She sat down beside him once more, hanging her head.

"Intza still does not understand. I suppose it is difficult for small children to understand death. She thinks Kyasen will return one day." Souni looked to where Intza played outside in the dirt as if she feared the girl would be taken from her if she took her eyes off her for a moment. "Kyasen is with *Ilyo Na'ada* now."

Joshua took another bite of fruit. "What is *Ilyo Na'ada?*"

"He is God," Souni replied. She looked at him as if he should have known already.

"Oh, like Jesus? Mama takes me to church sometimes when Father is gone. He doesn't like church much."

Souni frowned slightly, but a small smile played at the corners of her mouth. "Perhaps they are similar," she replied. "Two men came a long time ago, much the same way you did. They told of this thing called *church and Shess-ooss.*" Joshua was confused but finally understood she meant to say *Jesus.*

"Why do you say my name like that? *Shos-hua?* Don't you have a sound for "J" in your language?"

"No, we do not," Souni explained. "It is a very strange sound to us. Too harsh."

Before Joshua could ask another question, Manemna came in from the fields. "Good morning, Shos-hua. How are you feeling?" He came over to the table and rested his hand on Joshua's head.

"I'm fine." He continued to eat the bountiful breakfast of sweet bread and fruit. Manemna motioned for Souni to follow him to the other side of the room near the hearth. Intza returned, trailing after her father no doubt, and sat beside Joshua. Manemna and Souni spoke in hushed tones while Joshua and Intza ate.

Intza snatched up a piece of fruit, then scurried off her chair and over to the corner where a few toys were piled up. She returned to his side, clutching a rag doll with a bright blue dress and black pebbles for eyes. She crawled onto his lap, and he watched as she tried to feed the doll the remainder of her fruit. He was unsure what to do with his hands as Intza played with her doll, as if sitting on his lap was the most natural thing in the world. Finally, he wrapped his arms around her waist as he had seen Souni do, and Intza smiled up at him. Of course, the doll could not eat the fruit, so the juice dripped down its fabric face and all over Joshua's lap. He glanced at Souni, who came to his rescue.

"That is enough, Intza. Go and fetch us some water," Souni instructed. Intza bounded off his lap and grabbed a small clay jar by the door.

Manemna waited until Intza was gone, sitting at the table across from him. "Shos-hua, I want to take you back to the place I found you a few days ago. Do you think you could show me the way you came? Perhaps we can deliver you back to the Other World."

Joshua nodded his head slowly. "I can try."

"Very well. Once you have finished eating, we will go."

"Go before Intza returns. It will be easier for her," Souni suggested. She looked as if she might cry again.

Joshua hurried to finish and wiped his hands on his pants, eager to be on his way home. "I'm ready!" Souni saw them off at the door, hugging Joshua tightly at the last second. She nodded, her lower lip quivering. Then she turned and disappeared inside the house.

Manemna rested his hand on Joshua's shoulder as they left the village. He told him about the different plants and animals they saw. Joshua noticed that the animals in this world were much more colorful than the animals back home.

About an hour later, they arrived at the spot where Joshua had entered a few days before. Nothing looked familiar.

"Where is this cave you spoke of?" Manemna asked.

Joshua searched for the mouth of the cave, but he had not been dreaming. It was as if the rocks had shifted and morphed, covering the cave entrance until it was nothing more than a part of the mountainside. He took a few steps closer to the base of the cliff, searching for signs of an opening. He placed his hand on the rough surface and looked at the cliff face. If there had been a cave there, it was gone now. None of this made any sense to his young mind.

He tried very hard to be brave, but the tears came anyway. Joshua sniffed hard and put the heels of his hands into his eyes. "It's gone! I don't know how, but it's gone." Despair overwhelmed him, and he sat down in the mud. Tingles traveled up his spine, the breeze skittering over his bare back. How was he ever going to get to Mama now?

"Do not worry, my son. Let us walk around a bit and see if you can remember." Manemna took Joshua up in his arms and began to walk around the cliff's base, stopping every few minutes to see if he recognized anything.

As they went, Joshua looked around for the pouch Mama had given him, too. However, it also was nowhere to be seen. Was there some unseen power that willed to separate him from everything he knew, from anything that might be from the Other World?

"No. I think it's gone forever," Joshua said. Tears spilled over his cheeks. He was getting tired and was unable to control his emotions. All he wanted was to curl up and go to sleep, to forget he was lost in this strange place.

Manemna set him down, placing his calloused hands on either side of his face and gently dried the tears with his thumbs. His hands were scratchy, calloused from long years working in the fields. He smiled comfortingly and hugged him. "It is alright. We will go to Lunthá. I am sure the king will be able to help us," Manemna said. He carried him on his back on their return to Hotun.

Joshua wondered if there were other fathers as kind as Manemna. His own father would never have been this understanding with Joshua. Father did not like it when Joshua cried, even when he got hurt and there was blood. If he could find his way back to his mother, Joshua could bring her back here, and they would live in Hotun with Manemna and Souni. Maybe then Mama wouldn't cry so much. And Father would never be able to hurt her again.

Intza was overjoyed to see Joshua again as they appeared at the village entrance. She bounded toward him, and he patted her on the head. She gave him a confused look. She made him bend down so she could pat his head as well. She then took his hand and led him over to the house. Intza pulled him into a squat position before the front door to examine a bug she had found. They were soon scrounging around the front of the house, looking under rocks and in the ferns for more specimens. Joshua busied himself building a small coral-type structure to hold their collection of insects. He was so busy, he barely noticed Souni and Manemna walk into the house.

CHAPTER 8

SOUNI

"Did you find anything?" Souni asked as Manemna approached the front door. Manemna motioned her inside so they could talk in private.

"I think I should take him to Lunthá to see the king. Perhaps he can help us," Manemna suggested. "I am only a simple farmer. There must be something the royal archives can tell us about the Other World."

Souni said nothing. She bit her lower lip, fighting against her selfish instinct to keep Shos-hua here with them. She was growing attached to the boy. Her husband raked his fingers through his hair. "The longer Shos-hua stays, the more difficult it will be for all of us to let him go," Manemna whispered.

"Are you even sure he comes from the Other World?" Souni asked. She watched the children playing in the front yard, thinking of Kyasen. It had been difficult on Intza to lose a brother. They had been so close. To see her opening up to Shos-hua... How could they take him away from her now? It broke his heart to think of that eventual reality.

"My dear, he does not know our language. He speaks the tongue of those from the Other Land. Even his skin is a different color, similar to the Spanyaards, if the legends are true."

She nodded, unable to dispute the fact. Souni's gaze fell on Joshua, her heart breaking. The boy had only been with them a few days, but Manemna had spoken true. She was growing to love the boy as if he were another son. "What if *Ilyo Na'ada* sent Shos-hua to us for a reason?"

Manemna pulled her into his arms, and she gained solace in his warm embrace. "I know you are fond of the boy, as are we all. But I made him a promise to do whatever I could to help him find his family." He wished he could take the burden of grief from her. Shos-hua was a good boy, but he could never replace their son. Tears rolled down her cheeks. He lifted her chin and gently wiped them away. "I want him to stay with us as much as you do, my love. If the King cannot help us, I will bring him home and we will raise him as our own."

She nodded, placing her hands on his chest. "Then do what you must."

"Papa! They are building the fires!" Intza announced as she scrambled into the house, towing Shos-hua along behind her. "Will you tell a story tonight?"

Manemna glanced at the boy, his eyes wide with expectant pleading. "Yes, of course I will."

Intza squealed and they ran back outside. "Papa tells the best stories."

Souni smiled and he enveloped her hand in his as they walked to the hearth fire being built outside their circle of houses. The other bonfires were being built. The *kynezpak*, or *leaders of eight*—in charge of leading the eight households surrounding each fire pit—would tell stories and lead the festivities for the evening. Each *kynezpak* answered directly to him as *pitpak*. It would be a treat to get to tell the stories this night.

Souni settled beside hr husband. Manemna waited until

everyone had come to seat themselves before the blazing fire, then halted when he came to Shos-hua.

"*Tapin hanaa,*" he began. *Many years past...* "In the years following our ancestors' arrival in Luminia, *Ilyo Na'ada* established the rule of music, binding all created things to the rhythms of melody and harmony, of cadence and vibration. He placed inside their hearts the mysteries of refrain, and we have been singing and playing ever since.

"But there was a time when darkness tried to overcome this ingrained melody. There was a ruler named Salaam Pe'sik, king of all Luminia at the time, and he entertained in his heart to overthrow the order of things. He had grown jealous of the Royal Musicians, and took it upon himself to steal away the sacred arts for his own greedy gain."

Her husband looked around the circle, every eye fixated on him with wide-eyed wonder, even though they had heard the old tales many times before. All, save for Shos-hua. The boy sat up straight, waiting with bated breath for Manemna to go on.

"For many days we fought against him, secreting the Royal Musicians ftom the armies of Salaam Pe'sik. Those who had defected to protect the Musicians faced certain death on the battlefield. But their leader, one Baetanu-Liz, told the rebels to stand firm and hold to *Ilyo Na'ada.*

"Salaam Pe'sik's army began the charge, and still those with Baetanu-Liz stood firm. When the assailing army reached the midpoint of the field, a mighty roar like thunder came from the sky—a cloudless sky. Down from the heavens poured fire, and a wind likened to a billows spread the judgement so quickly that none escaped. So it is said that on a cloudless day, His thunderous answer will arise."

"How long were the Musicians made to hide, *pitpak?*" A little girl who had come to sit at his feet asked.

He smiled down at her and knelt. "Eight days, little one. It was a miracle. The Musicians were allowed to resume their playing, and a short ways away from the battlefield, on an island encased by sea, they built what is now Lunthá."

"What does it mean, on a cloudless day?" another child asked. It was encouraged that the children ask questions, and thus were taught from a young age that their queries were valid.

"When all seems impossible," Manemna said, standing once more. "When all seems lost, we can count on *Ilyo Na'ada* to rescue us."

Souni touched her husband's arm, and he allowed her to speak. "Even when all hope is lost, you can know that *Ilyo Na'ada* will come through, as He cares for us so much."

The boy nodded, as if he understood. Whether they were able to find a way home for him, or he stayed, *Ilyo Na'ada's* will be won.

CHAPTER 9

JOSHUA

Joshua wished they had cars in this world. His little legs were tired after walking for most of the morning. Manemna seemed to sense his exhaustion and halted on the mountain path before they started down yet another steep incline. "Here, let me carry you." He knelt and motioned for Joshua to sit on his shoulders. "Are you warm enough?" He rose back onto his feet and started plodding down the stepped pathway.

"Yes, just a little tired," Joshua replied. He enjoyed his new perspective as they continued on. The wind whipped his brown hair around his face, and he wished he had a hat to keep his bangs out of his eyes. Maybe when they arrived back at Manemna's village, Souni would cut his hair close to the scalp like the other young boys.

Mama had insisted on keeping his hair longer. Father said it made him look like a sissy. That was the one thing Joshua agreed with his father about. He wanted to grow up so he could protect Mama. Maybe then Father wouldn't be able to hurt her so much.

"Are you alright up there, Shos-hua?" Manemna asked. Joshua nodded, wiping away a tear that had escaped and streamed down his cheek.

"Yes. I was only thinking about Mama. Do you think the king will be able to help me get home?" Joshua asked. He was eager to get back to her. Souni had told him it had been four days since he had arrived in Luminia. Would Mama spank him for being away so long? She hadn't often spanked him. Only when he needed it, she had said. But this time, he was sure Carson was the one who needed it.

Manemna sighed heavily. "We will just have to wait and see, son."

"Do you have any siblings, Shos-hua?"

"No, I don't have any brothers or sisters," he answered. "Mama is too old and rundown to have any more babies. That's what Father says." Joshua pouted. "But I think Mama is so pretty. She could have lots more babies."

Joshua pointed ahead of them on the path and asked about the animal that scurried across. "That is *aarnat'e*. I believe in your world they are called squirrels."

"But squirrels aren't blue!" he exclaimed. The creature looked like a squirrel but had a much larger body, and while its base layer of fur was gray, it seemed to change color in the sun, reflecting a deep navy blue tone as well.

"Perhaps not in your world. They come in all sorts of different colors. I think it is based on what they eat. The *aarnat'e* from our region are more of a yellowish-orange color. Up here in the mountains, they are the cooler hues: blues, purples, and deep greens," Manemna explained. "Are your animals not as colorful as they are here?"

"Nope. Mostly they're brown and black and white. Some of the birds are blue and red, but I have never seen animals with colors like you have here."

They stopped under an ancient oak tree to rest and eat at midday. Joshua was glad for the rest, since they had woken before the sun and headed out of the village.

Joshua lay down in the soft grass, looking up at the sky. "I like your sunrises here."

"Ahh, yes. They are my favorite part of the day. You should see them from the fields—like a painter is creating his masterpiece before your very eyes." Manemna got a far-off look in his eyes as he spoke. Joshua had to crane his neck to see his face. He was a tall man, taller than Father. Joshua could have listened to his calm, steady voice all day.

"You said before that the Musicians play for the sunrise. What does that mean?"

Manemna sat down, and spread a feast before them. "I will tell you," he said. However, he first handed Joshua a bit of bread, and motioned for him to choose whatever else his heart fancied. Joshua's mouth began to water. Souni had packed them a basket full of fruit, bread, cheese, and *chatla* for the journey, wishing them safe travel as she waved from the front door. Intza had still been asleep. He hoped if the king could get him back to his world, he would be able to say goodbye to the little girl before he left. He had liked having a sister, even if only for a few days. And he would miss Intza. Maybe Mama would reconsider having more babies once he told her how much fun it was to have someone to play with.

"Many *bu'athe* ago, *Ilyo Na'ada* created all that is seen and unseen. He sang each element into existence, and each note or pitch brought something new into our world. After He had created all things, he mandated that a special band of people would be the ones to keep the order of life going—the Keepers of Music."

"Like in the story from last night?" Joshua asked.

"Yes. The Keepers play their instruments every morning, greeting the sun as it returns from its journey through the Dark Lands. They play again each evening, to bid the sun a safe journey through the darkness once more. The sunrise differs each day, depending on what the Musicians decide to play."

"Can I become a Musician? I mean, if I cannot get back home?" Joshua asked.

"No, my son. Only children born into the Musician families are allowed to replace their parents. But we have our own special calling.

We work the land and raise our families in peace. It is not so glamorous, I suppose, but everyone has their place."

Joshua and Manemna ate in silence for a time. As his belly got full, his eyes began to droop. Manemna seemed to sense this, and patted his leg before he could fall asleep. "We had best press for the Royal City before nightfall. Perhaps if we hurry, we may make it in time to see the sunset."

Joshua helped him gather the untouched food into the knapsack. They started down the mountain, Joshua doing his best to keep up with Manemna's long strides. When they reached the forest below, he sighed with relief that they did not have much further to go. The land flattened out, and the air grew warmer. The Redwood trees loomed overhead, spreading their exposed roots out toward the road, as if they were reaching for them. Insects buzzed and hissed as they whizzed through the humid air. Flowers of all shapes and sizes, many larger than Joshua's head, dotted the vines that intertwined themselves with the tree branches, and around the base of the ferns. The air grew moist as they climbed down the mountainside and came to the outer city of Lunthá.

"It's so big," Joshua breathed. He was awestruck at the sight set before him.

"Yes, it is," Manemna said, a smile tinging his voice. "What do you think of her?"

"Her?" Joshua asked.

"Yes, our Lunthá—the Jewel of Luminia. That is what we call her." Manemna wrapped an arm around his shoulder, then knelt beside him. He pointed to the West, where the sun would set behind the white sea cliffs soon. "There is the archway leading out to the sea. At the summer solstice, the sun will pass directly through the center of it, and alight on the island city, coming into perfect alignment with a certain point at the top of the temple. It only does so once a year."

Joshua leaned into Manemna's chest, his legs tired from the long journey. Manemna did not even flinch, but held him up as he pointed out more about the city. Joshua liked watching the ships and boats coming to and from harbor most of all. Their sails seemed to glisten with golden magic as they whipped about in the breeze.

"Well, the sun will be setting soon. Let us get into the city, and we might just find a good spot to watch from," Manemna said, winking at him.

They walked through the crowded streets of the outer city. The din might have scared other young boys, but not him. He was fascinated by everything he saw, especially the marketplace. There were so many sights and scents and colors to experience. He hoped Manemna would take him there after they saw the king. When they came to a long bridge leading out to the center of the lagoon to the inner island city, Manemna pointed to the top of the land mass. "That is where the palace is."

Joshua craned his neck to see, but there were only a few rooftops that were visible behind the lush gardens of the surrounding mansions.

When they reached the inner city, Manemna picked Joshua up and carried him up the steep steps. He knocked at a house near the harbor and waited. Finally, a portly woman opened the door, recognition lighting her face instantly.

"Manemna? Is that really you?" She waved them in and wrapped Manemna in a hug. "Come in at once. What a lovely surprise!"

Joshua liked the woman immediately. She ushered them into the one-room home and had them sit down by the hearth, as if she were gathering her chicks.

"Well, to what do I owe this honor?" The woman asked. "And who is the handsome one?" She leaned down to smile at Joshua. "A new apprentice, perhaps?"

"This is Shos-hua," Manemna introduced. "That is, *Joshua.*" Manemna did his best to pronounce the hard "j" sound. However, it still came out funny. Joshua covered his mouth to hide a giggle.

"I am Joshua," he said, stepping in to help.

Manemna laid a hand on Joshua's shoulder. "And this is Posentut, one of Souni's and my dearest friends."

Joshua held out his hand as he had seen his father do when he met someone new. "Pleased to meet you."

Posentut gave a surprised laugh and laid her hand in his. "Well, my goodness. What a little gentleman you have brought me." She raised her eyes to Manemna's, question stirring in their depths. "Where is he from?"

"Shall we go up onto the roof and watch the sunset? Shos-hua has never seen one from the royal city," he replied.

The adults led the way up to the roof, and Joshua sat at the edge of the flat precipice, leaning against the short lip that went all around the stone and mud brick home.

Manemna and Posentut sat near the rear of the roof, and began talking in hushed tones. Joshua was engrossed with the changing colors of the sky, and the faint sound of the music floating down from the Musician's Terrace. However, he still kept his ears open for anything that might be said about him.

For a brief moment, everything stopped when the Musicians played: the market booths closed down, children stopped playing, and all household work ceased for these few moments as everyone listened.

Posentut lowered her voice, the cushion rustling as she leaned over to Manemna. "What is going on? You never leave that farm of yours if you can help it, and there are no festivals for months yet." Joshua perked up at this. "I have never heard a name such as *Joshua*. Where does he come from?" She tried to pronounce his name the way he had shown her, but was unsuccessful.

"He claims to be from the Other World."

"The Other World?" she breathed. "But—"

"I know," Manemna said before she could finish. "Do you know if Lady Tzizenah's daughter still lives?"

"No one has seen her, or the strange man she married, for over fifty years. Nor their offspring." Posentut heaved a sigh. "This is impossible."

"I know," Manemna said again. "But here we are." Joshua could almost feel their eyes boring into his back. He held his breath, hoping they had not guessed he was eavesdropping.

Manemna soon continued. "I fear it is all too real. Posentut, will you help us get into the palace tomorrow? It is imperative I speak to the king about him. Perhaps someone who works in the royal archives can find the prophecies handed down from Lady Tzizenah. That is why I asked about her daughter. Perhaps she can help us find a way to return the boy to his own."

Posentut paused for a moment. "I wish I could help you with Lady Tzizenah. She lived many years before either of us were born. The best I can do is try to get you an audience with the king. I have my contacts," Posentut replied. "If anyone can help him, it is King Nissim."

CHAPTER 10

JOSHUA

Manemna straightened Joshua's tunic as they made their way up the palace steps. A servant showed them into the royal court, where people brought forward cases for the king to hear. As soon as Manemna had told the official at the gate why they had come, they were rushed to the front of the line of supplicants.

"Now, remember how I showed you to bow? That is what we must do when we are presented to the king." Joshua nodded, remembering how Manemna had shown him to bow, first by placing his hand on his heart, then getting on his knees and leaning forward to touch his forehead to the floor.

"I remember." Joshua struggled to keep up with the men as they entered the palace. True to her word, Posentut had pulled strings to get them into the royal courtroom that day, instead of having to wait for days on end.

The hallways were open to the outside world, with spacious courtyards filled with flowers and plants. A cool breeze blew through the courtyards and corridors, bringing the scent of spices with it. Sunshine seemed to fill every corner of every space. Postenut smoothed down his hair as they walked. It must look a frightful mess after sleeping at a strange angle all night. He was still not used to sleeping on the hard floor, with only a reed mat under him.

Servants passed by them in the corridors, dressed in simple garb, but unlike the clothing back in Hotun. They mostly wore shades of white, ivory, or tan. Then there were others, men dressed in vibrantly colored fabrics that draped around them for what looked like miles of material. Most of them looked very important, but none of them seemed to notice him. Then there were the women, who wore lovely dresses embroidered with gold, in every color imaginable. Joshua thought they looked beautiful, like something from a storybook.

When they came to the court, two great wooden doors were flung open, and they stepped into the dim room. Their footsteps echoed off the high walls and ceiling. A man dressed in flowing ivory robes embroidered with gold leaned forward as they came near and bowed with their faces to the ground. Joshua's heart beat wildly, hoping he was doing his bow correctly.

"Rise, please."

Manemna nodded to Joshua, and they stood together. Joshua reached for Manemna's hand as the man stared at him with open curiosity. "Do not be afraid, Shos-hua," Manemna whispered. He turned to the man and began to explain why they had come.

"Your supreme Majesty, I have come with a matter of grave importance. Indeed, something like this has not happened for nearly a hundred years."

Joshua looked to the couple on the raised platform, seated gracefully on their thrones. The king was younger than he had imagined. He didn't even have a beard. He wore white ballooned pants, but of a fabric much more costly than the ones Manemna wore. Every move he made seemed to make the fabric shimmer, as if little specks of sunshine were trapped between the weave. He wore a loose-fitting shirt, with long sleeves and gold embroidery at the cuffs and open neckline. And his crown was unlike anything Joshua had ever seen—purest gold, but in a very odd shaped circle. It resembled thin tree branches that had been wound around and twisted together.

"Continue," King Nissim said. His voice was deep and resonant, but not unkind. Not like Father's.

"This boy claims to be from the Other World. I found him wandering alone in the woods—" Manemna hesitated. "Well, that is not exactly true. He had been captured by Tzotoen bandits."

King Nissim straightened on his throne, then looked to the woman at his side. "Tzotoen bandits? Whatever were they doing on our side of the border?" He raised a brow, but Manemna could not give an answer. "And you rescued him from them?"

"Yes, Majesty."

"This is grave indeed." King Nissim rubbed his chin, deep in thought.

Joshua shrunk back behind Manemna's leg as the conversation took a frightening turn. The woman at the king's side rose. "We are scaring our young guest. Could you not better discuss this in the gardens, my lord?"

King Nissim nodded and rose to take his wife's hand. "Of course. Manemna, Shos-hua, will you follow us this way?" He waved toward a side entrance, and the king asked for Manemna to walk beside him so they could discuss the situation.

The queen came down from the dais, her dress also glittering like the kings, although with more of the dancing light that had so fascinated Joshua. She knelt before him so she could be at his level. Joshua immediately fell to the ground, placing his hand on his heart and touching his forehead to the ground.

She laughed, such a musical sound. "Oh, my dear boy, please rise." She helped him up, clicking her tongue as she ran her finger gently over the goose egg that was starting to form in the center of his forehead. "Did you hurt yourself?"

Joshua blushed. "No, Your Majesty. I'm tough."

The Queen didn't seem to understand the word *tough*, but said nothing of it. "I am sure you are. Now, come along with me. We can follow the king and your friend while they talk, and we can have a little talk of our own."

"Thank you, Your Majesty."

She offered him her hand and they started off toward the side door of the courtroom to catch up with the men. "Please, call me Lutep-Tzia."

Joshua nodded, but didn't think Manemna would approve. "I like your dress."

"Oh, this? Thank you," she replied. Joshua could not take his eyes off the queen. She had beautiful olive skin, and silky, raven black hair that fell below her waist. Her shimmery veil made her look like an angel. They continued to hold hands even when they caught up with the king and Manemna. "Now, why don't you tell me your version of the story, hmm?"

Joshua could have talked to her for hours as they walked the halls. He told her all about Carson, and Mama, and how Carson had played that dirty trick on him and left him alone in the cave. The queen gasped when he got to the part about being left alone in the dark. "My goodness, you are a brave boy."

When the men went out into the garden and started winding around the curving pathways, the queen suggested they sit on a marble bench near a weeping willow tree. "This is one of my favorite spots," she said and smiled at him. She placed a hand over his. "I am sorry you were separated from your mama. But if my husband is able to do anything, he will not rest until you are reunited."

Joshua's heart surged with hope. "Do you really think so?"

"I know so," Queen Lutep-Tzia beamed down at him. Then she reached up and touched his hair, smoothing it away from his eyes. Just like Mama used to do. "I have a little sister about your age. How many years have you?"

"I am six." Joshua frowned. "You have a sister my age? You look too old to have sisters."

Queen Lutep-Tzia laughed, then nodded, pretending to be very serious. "I have eleven sisters. And four brothers."

"Do they live here with you? It must be nice to have so many people to play with."

"Indeed it was. But no, they do not live here with me. I am from Saardaonae. My father is the brother of the king of Saardonae. Most of my siblings are grown, but there are a few of us left in my parent's house."

"Do you have kids? You're very good with children," Joshua said.

Queen Lutep-Tzia shook her head, some of the joy going out of her eyes. "Not yet." She touched her belly, which Joshua just then realized was quite big. "But soon."

"That is good, Your Majesty. I am the only one back home."

She grabbed Joshua's hand again. "If you do not find your way home, I should very much like it if you would come here and live with me." She brushed his hair aside again. "Would you like that?"

Joshua hung his head. "I really want to get back to Mama." He squeezed her hand like he often did for his mother. "But if I do get through, can I bring Mama back here? I like it ever so much!"

Queen Lutep-Tzia gave one of those musical laughs again. "Of course, you can. Soon, I will have a son or daughter, and I should very much like if you would come and be their special companion."

"Me?" Joshua asked, even though he wasn't entirely sure what a companion was. But if he got to stay here with his new friends, and Mama could come, he was sure he would like it. "Yes, please."

Just then, the men rounded a bend and came into view. The queen stood, and Joshua followed suit. "Well, is there anything that can be done?" she asked the king.

"I have told Manemna that I will consult the chronicles and the royal diaries. There must be something from when the Spanyaards came."

"Indeed, there is," Lutep-Tzia started off in the opposite direction, but her husband called her back.

"My love, I will have Adagio consult the books. I believe Manemna and Shos-hua are eager to be on their way," King Nissim knelt before Joshua and placed a hand over his heart. "I will do whatever I can for you, Shos-hua. Be brave."

"I will, Your Majesty." Joshua looked up at Manemna, who wrapped a protective arm around his shoulder.

"Thank you both for your invaluable time." Manemna started backing away, and a palace guard met them at the archway leading back into the palace.

As they were making their to the front of the palace, a man dressed in splendidly dyed purple and blue robes approached. At first, he only gave him and Manemna a passing glance. Then he stopped, looking back over his shoulder at Joshua. "Wait! You there!"

Joshua froze.

"Yes, my lord?" Manemna asked. He put a protective hand over Joshua's chest and moved him behind his leg. "Is there something amiss?"

The man shook his head, as if he were trying to chase away the last vestiges of sleep. "No, forgive me. I am Adagio, Leader of the Musicians."

Manemna bowed at the waist and put his hand over his heart. Joshua followed his lead, but continued to look at the man curiously.

"Where are you from?" Adagio asked, pinning Joshua with a wild stare, his voice haunted.

"He is from Hotun," the king said as he came up behind Adagio. The queen and he looked perplexed as to why the head musician had stopped them.

Adagio did not take his eyes off Joshua. "He is the one, Your Majesty." He looked at the king. "The one from my dreams."

The adults all looked at each in bewilderment. But Joshua was only curious. "You had a dream about me?"

Adagio nodded. He tried to cover up his shock, but Joshua could still tell he was having a hard time staying upright. "I did."

"Was it about me and my mother?" He looked at the queen. "She said I could bring my mama back here with me, if I can get back."

King Nissim shot his wife a concerned look. "There is no guarantee we will be able to get you back to the Other World."

"The Other World—" Adagio breathed.

"Yes," King Nissim said, trying to keep the mood light. "I have said you would be happy to look through the sacred books and see if there was any way to return him there, to his mother."

"Of course, Your Majesty." Adagio continued to look at Joshua with awestruck wonder, but managed to regain some of his composure. He then offered to show Manemna and Joshua out to the front gates, and the king and queen went on their way.

"I must confess, I am stunned, Manemna," Adagio replied as they walked. "This is unprecedented."

"Except for the one other time we know of when people have come from the Other World." Manemna stopped when they reached the grand steps that led down to the front courtyard and beyond to the main gates. Joshua spotted Posentut waiting for them near the gates.

"Yes, except for that," Adagio shook his head. "I will consult my books. In the meantime, are you willing to look after the boy? If he would rather stay here with me and my family. I would be more than happy to oblige."

"No, thank you, my lord. I promised my wife and daughter that I would bring him back to my farm, if it were at all possible." Manemna smiled.

"Of course. Well," Adagio leaned down to address Joshua. "If you ever need anything, either of you, please do not hesitate to write or come and see me."

"Thank you," Manemna said. As they turned to leave, another man, dressed in even more finery approached from a darkened hallway.

As they turned to leave, Manemna nearly bumped into him. Adagio immediately tensed.

"Forgive me, my lord," Manemna said and hurried Joshua along beside him.

The man wiped off his shoulder, as if there was unseen filth transposed from Manemna's person. The man looked down his nose at them, but his brows shot up as he looked at Joshua. He frowned, studying the boy closer. For some reason, his heart leapt into his throat. What was it about this man's eyes that put him so on edge? He got the same feeling when he saw a hawk eyeing him from the treetops, as if he'd like to pick his bones clean for its next meal.

"Who are you?" Lord Delgadas demanded. He tried to reach for Joshua, but he stepped behind Manemna's leg for protection, clinging to his side. Manemna put a steadying hand on Joshua's back.

"Lord Delgadas. Attend me in the courtroom, please," Lord Adagio snapped, joining them in the archway. He looked at Manemna and nodded, encouraging them to go on their way. "Safe journey," he said in dismissal, then turned the other lord by the shoulders and they walked back to the courtroom.

Manemna hurried him out of the palace. Joshua snuck a glance over his shoulder, the older lord following him with his piercing green eyes. A shiver ran up his spine. If he met Lord Delgadas again in his lifetime, it would be too soon.

CHAPTER II

MANEMNA

Two Months Later...

Manemna stood proudly to one side of the communal fire pit, waiting for Shos-hua to appear alongside his wife and daughter. They exited their small home and walked forward to meet the rest of those gathered in the community. After weeks and months of searching, Manemna had received word from Lord Adagio. He could find no clues about how to return Shos-hua to his family in the Other World. Manemna and his fellow villagers had done all they could to find the elusive cave entrance, to no avail. Shos-hua was theirs now. In a public naming ceremony, he, Souni, and Intza would officially welcome the boy into their family.

Shos-hua had mixed feelings about the ceremony, Manemna knew. However, he was starting to come to terms with the idea that he lived here in Luminia now. And Manemna could not help but wonder if it was for some special purpose, as Lord Adagio had alluded to in his missive that had come a few days before.

The boy sniffed back tears, trying to hide his emotion from Souni. Shos-hua had grown to love them as they loved him. It was difficult for anyone to forget the family they had come from—good or bad. He still held onto hope that he would see his birth mother again. Manemna was not about to squash that hope.

"Step forward," Manemna instructed as Shos-hua, Souni, and Intza arrived at the circle's edge around the fire pit. The crowd of villagers split to allow the boy to pass through, coming to face Manemna. Shos-hua had grown since coming to Luminia. The muted orange ballooned trousers Souni had given him from Kyasen's old stores now fit him much better. Shos-hua's little bare chest heaved with every breath, displaying his nervousness.

Manemna looked around those gathered, over 200 in all. He was responsible for leading them, and it was customary to hold the naming ceremony seven days after any new babe was born into one of the village's families. "My esteemed family and friends. Today we welcome Shos-hua into our lives. However, before we continue, I must ask if we are of one accord." He met several gazes as he turned, looking around the circle. "Will you accept this boy into your homes and your hearts?"

"We will," came the resounding answer.

Manemna beamed with pride. The boy had worked hard to prove himself over the last few months. He had removed the language stone from around his neck, working hard to learn their tongue without its help. And he had worked with Manemna in the fields, eliminating rocks in new fields that were being plowed alongside the other boys his age, pulling weeds from choking the crops, and carrying water from the stream to provide sustenance for the tender shoots.

Souni's eyes misted with tears, and she held Intza's hand. His daughter beamed at him, looking forward to "keeping Shos-hua," as she had so often said.

"Kneel," Manemna said to Shos-hua. He did so, keeping his eyes downcast. The colors of sunset played brilliantly amongst the trees, sending shafts of light dancing around Shos-hua's head. "From this day forward, you will be known as Bravaro," Manemna pronounced.

It was a name that he and Souni had discussed at length. It fit the boy perfectly, meaning "one of extraordinary courage and nobility."

"Bravaro," the boy repeated, trying it out on his lips. "I like it."

The gathered company tried it out as well, and then, one by one, each member of the village came and placed a hand on Bravaro's right shoulder, and he on theirs, welcoming him into the clan. When all had passed, Souni came forward with the shears and cut his long hair close to his head as the other boys his age wore it in the community. Manemna then dug a shallow hole near the fire pit and deposited his hair inside. "You are now a part of this ground, Bravaro. Just as we all have vowed to protect and provide for this community, so you, too, must vow."

"I vow to provide for and protect Hotun with my life," Bravaro recited, as Manemna had taught him. For one so young and so short a time among them, his *Luminsilkis* was flawless.

With that, drums began to play and small pipes to resound in songs of celebration, thanks to a small band of apprentice musicians Lord Adagio had sent from Lunthá.

Bravaro looked around at his new family and friends, then went to Souni, who wrapped him in a hug. Tears streamed down his cheeks, remembering his mother. He would never forget her. But he had to turn his eyes to this world now, and thankfully, he had a loving family.

Manemna watched as the villagers paraded Bravaro around to their homes, offering him food and drink as a symbolic gesture of welcoming. He released a sigh, and wrapped Souni in a hug.

"He does look handsome," Souni said. "Our son."

Manemna nodded. "He certainly does. He is one with us now, never to be taken away."

CHAPTER 12

DIANA

Butte Falls, Oregon
January 1966

"Frank, please!" Diana shrieked as her husband hurled another piece of their best china at her from across the room. She ducked just in time as the plate shattered against the wall above her head. The dishes were a priceless family heirloom her mother had given her on their wedding day eight years ago. Now, her whole life was shattering like the porcelain lying in a crumbling mess at her feet.

"You killed my son!" Frank slurred in his drunken rage. Another plate came whizzing through the air, and Diana tried to scurry away under the cover of the dining table before porcelain rained down on her. She did not make it far before a cup smashed above her head. Ducking down, she covered her neck, tiny pieces of the delicate china slicing her arms and hands.

"No, Frank! We'll find him—" Diana pleaded for her life before an unjust judge. The desperation rose in her throat once more, just as it had every time she had to face her husband when he was in this drunken state. Guilt gnawed at her insides like an army of cancerous ulcers. She knew it was her fault that Joshua was gone—that if she had just searched a little longer, she might have been able to find him.

"Shut up!" he bellowed. He staggered around the corner of the dining table and lunged for her, but she was too quick. Diana scrambled out of the way, springing to her feet as she rushed into the living room. Diana held her hands out as Frank strode toward her with murder in his eyes. She headed into the living room, trying to put as much distance between him and her. He had been angry with her plenty of times, but this time, he might actually go through with his threats to kill her.

Frank tripped over the coffee table as he sprang for her, crashing into the armchair. Diana hurried past him, grabbed the phone off its receiver in the kitchen, dialed 911, and locked herself in the pantry. She held the door closed, hand shaking, praying she had enough time to get through before Frank broke the door down and strangled her.

"911, what is your emergency?"

"My name is Diana Stevens, my husband is trying to kill me."

"Ma'am where are you?" The woman on the other end was calm and to the point.

"I'm hiding in our pantry now. My husband is in the living room. Our address is 1517 North Obenchain Road." Diana replied, trying to keep the terror from overcoming her. Tears blurred her vision, but she quickly wiped them away.

"Okay ma'am, stay calm. Can you get out of the house and drive to safety?" There was no police station in Butte Falls. The nearest squad car would be sent out from Medford—over forty-five minutes away.

Diana listened for a moment. Frank had either gone outside or passed out in the living room, for a deathly silence had settled over the house.

"I'm not sure. I don't hear him anymore," she whispered.

Diana cracked the pantry door and peeked her head out. She could not see Frank anywhere. She decided to step out into the kitchen and investigate. Her purse was on the counter. If she hurried, she might be able to grab it on her way out and get into her car before Frank could catch up.

"Ma'am?" The dispatcher asked, calling her attention back.

"Yes, I'm still here." She came around the corner and saw that Frank had indeed passed out. He lay in a heap on the floor, snoring loudly. She let out a sigh of relief and closed her eyes. "He is in the living room. He passed out."

"Can you get to the Ranger Station there in Butte Falls? I am sending a squad car out now."

Diana hated that it had come to this, but Frank had left her no choice. "Yes, I'll head there now," her voice shook. "I don't want to be here when he wakes up."

"Are you okay to drive?" the dispatcher asked.

"Yes, thank you." She hung up the phone and let her arms hang at her sides. Frank's words rang in her ears. *You killed my son!* She was unsure why he cared so much now that Joshua was gone. He had never seemed to care when he had been around. Joshua had been more of an irritant to Frank than someone to love and protect. More often than not, she had been forced to protect Joshua from *him*.

Frank shifted on the floor, rolling onto his side with a loud moan. Diana did not stick around to see if he would wake up. She grabbed her purse from the counter as she rushed out the front door to the car. She started the Station Wagon and pulled out of the driveway to the sound of gravel flying, making her heart beat even faster. Now that the ordeal was over, she started to shake as she came down from her adrenalin high. Tears streamed down her face as she drove through the darkness. The ranger station was on the city limits of Butte Falls. If Frank did follow her, she would be able to find someone close by to help her.

Diana had seen plenty of red flags after her and Frank had gotten married. When she had gotten pregnant with Joshua shortly afterward, she had spent most of her time alone, since Frank had been shipped out to fight in Vietnam. However, he was sent home after an injury, and was able to get an honorable discharge.

That had only been the beginning of her and Joshua's problems. It hadn't taken long for Diana to realize that Frank was not even the fraction of the man she had married. Whatever had happened to him in the war had permanently scarred him. She wasn't sure why, but Frank had had it out for Joshua since he had arrived back home, when Joshua was only five.

So many regrets. So little answers.

Diana pulled into town and was soon at the ranger station. There was a light on inside, despite the lateness of the hour. She turned off the car and hurried inside and out of the drizzle of rain that greeted her as she had driven into town.

She opened the door and the man behind the desk swiveled in his chair. "Oh, God, Diana. Are you alright?"

Diana sank to the floor, covering her face with her hands. The ranger came out from behind his desk and wrapped his arms around her protectively. Officer Tom Pederson was an old friend of her father's and had been with the forest rangers for over twenty years. He helped her rise from the floor and pulled up a chair for her. "I came in as soon as your name came over the dispatch. Are you alright?" he asked again.

"No," she admitted, but not with any bitterness in her tone. It was just a fact. She stared off into the distance as Tom offered to get her a cup of coffee. Joshua had been missing for over six months. The police and rangers had given up hope of ever finding a body after only a few weeks. They had all told her to move on. How could she? Her little boy was out there all alone in the woods. Her resolve to continue the search had not been diluted. At the very least, her baby deserved a proper burial.

Tom came back with a mug of black coffee, then frowned. "You're bleeding."

Diana touched her forehead and her skin immediately began to sting from the small cut above her eye. "I'm fine, Tom. Frank banged me up a little, but I'll live." *Unfortunately.*

She wrapped her hands around the steaming mug. Tom urged her to take small sips and went to retrieve the medical kit. He sat beside her and dabbed at the cuts around her face. There was also a larger cut on her hand that she hadn't noticed until then.

"This has got to stop, Diana. Frank is going to do something unthinkable while he is in one of his rages."

"I know," Diana replied. Her life was in shambles. Thoughts of suicide had slowly begun to encroach on every waking hour. But no, she couldn't end her life. What if Joshua found his way home by some miracle, and she wasn't there to welcome him home?

"Do you think you could go and stay with your parents for a while?" Tom asked after he'd finished fixing her up. Diana sat back in the chair, resting her head in her hands.

"I don't think they'll have me, even if I could get the courage up to ask for their help," Diana replied.

Her parents hadn't been in her life for the better part of eight years. They had not approved of her marrying an older man, especially with her right out of high school. With eleven years between them, and Frank already divorced from his first wife, her parents had warned her that it was not a good idea. They had wanted her to go to college and continue her education. But Diana had refused to listen. Frank had been newly divorced and home on leave from the navy. In his younger years, he had been involved in the Korean Conflict and had seen things she could only guess at. But from the way he seemed to be transported back to the heat of battle, especially when he was drunk, she didn't want to know.

"What are you talking about? If they knew what was going on, they would take you in in a heartbeat," Tom argued. He came around the desk after stowing away the medical kit and perched on the front of the desk. "I can call, if you think that would help."

Diana wasn't sure anything would convince her father to take her in. She had barely talked to her father over the last year, since

Frank had come home. "I don't know, Tom. Everything is a mess," she choked. Tears threatened to strangle her, and thankfully, Tom said nothing more, just sat with her until the squad car from the neighboring town showed up.

Tom stayed with her while the officer gave his report. "We went to your home but no one was there when we arrived. We did go in and check the place out," he hesitated. "The house was all smashed up and the front door was wide open."

Diana nodded. "That sounds about right. I doubt if I'll ever see Frank again after tonight." She wouldn't miss him, but she wasn't looking forward to returning to an empty house either. "I have a friend I can stay with tonight. Frank won't find me there."

The officer promised to come back in the morning and help them check out the property again to make sure she was safe. If there was any sign of Frank, they would take him into custody.

Tom thanked the officer as he departed, then turned to Diana. "I can drive over there with you tomorrow, if you like. I can check the place out and change locks. Maybe a few of the people from the church wouldn't mind coming to help you clean up the house? I know Margie would like to help."

"Thank you. I'll let you know if I decide to go back tomorrow." Diana was bone tired, and didn't want to think about the next five minutes, let alone tomorrow. She headed to her friend's house, the one place she would not receive any judgement. All she wanted to do was clean herself up and go to bed, to forget for a few hours what a sham her life had become.

The following morning, after a fitful night's sleep, she met Tom at her home. And as she suspected, Frank had not returned. "I'll check the garage," Tom offered.

Diana only gave a silent nod. She walked up the steps and went inside, looking around at the utter destruction Frank had wrought. The home she had dreamed of and striven to build for the last few years was in shambles. And not only that, she had lost her family right along with it, dysfunctional as it was.

"His truck is missing from the garage." Tom came into the house and whistled. "My goodness—" Tom breathed, looking around the living room at the shards of glass and porcelain lying about. She was sure he had gone on a rampage after he'd awoken and found she was missing. One of the living room windows was broken, and all the furniture had been busted up. "You're lucky he didn't kill you last night, Di."

She gave a derisive laugh. "Yeah. Lucky." She walked over the bits of porcelain scattered on the floor, her shoes crunching as she unwittingly ground them deeper into the carpet. She sighed as she looked around at the destruction, thinking of the countless hours it would take to get the house back in order. It was the silence she couldn't stand more than the disarray. Joshua had been a lively boy when his father was not around. He was always full of questions, so curious about the outside world.

"Is there anything I can do?" Tom followed her through the house as she took a mental survey. She could clean the house, alright. What she couldn't do was bring her boy back.

"Can you find my son?" she asked dully, not bothering to look up at him.

Her question must have stunned him, for he was silent for several seconds. "We've looked all over these woods, Di. I know it's the last thing you want to hear right now, but Josh is gone."

Diana turned around and nodded, a lump forming in her throat. "Then, no, there's nothing more you can do for me."

Tom stayed for a while longer, no doubt, to make sure she wouldn't take her own life. She assured him over and over again that she would not do anything drastic as that, and he finally seemed to believe her. At least, for the time being.

When he left, she packed a duffel bag and camping gear, locked up the house as it stood, and headed toward the back of her property and up into the BLM in the mountains. The search for Joshua may have been over for everyone else, but it was not over for her.

It would never be over.

CHAPTER 13
QUEEN LUTEP-TZIA

Lunthá, Luminia

Queen Lutep-Tzia breathed deeply as the music floated down from the Musician's Terrace. She sat with her back resting against the marble wall, enjoying the fresh breeze blowing up from the lagoon. The balcony outside her lavish rooms was one of her favorite places to seek solace. This calm was likely the last she would experience before the chaos and excitement of the birthing chamber.

Lutep-Tzia loved watching the sunrise, the music bringing the colors back into her world after the long night. Every morning was different as the Creator, *Ilyo Na'ada,* and his Musicians painted the sky together. *This may be the last sunrise I see for a few days,* she thought, a smile of anticipation crossing her lips. She looked forward to sharing this spot with her husband and children in the years to come.

She sucked in a breath as a contraction tightened her abdomen. They had started early that morning, growing more intense as the darkness gave way to light. When she could no longer bear lying still, she had gotten out of bed and walked to the balcony to watch the sunrise.

The sound of footsteps padding across the marble floor alerted her to her husband's presence. She smiled to herself, waiting for him to join her.

"Tzia, should you not be resting?" She turned to see her husband, King Nissim, standing under the archway, watching her with his arms crossed over his bare chest. He joined her at the small marble bench and sat down, turning her so that she could rest against his chest. His hands spread over her burgeoning belly.

She covered his hands with hers. "I could not stay abed another moment. I had to see the sunrise from the best seat in Luminia," she whispered. Leaning her head to the side, Nissim kissed the soft curve of her throat. She turned slightly so she could look up into his kind, brown eyes and then closed hers as he leaned down and kissed her lips. The baby kicked inside of her, moving Nissim's hand. They laughed, and she straightened, stretching the sore muscles in her back.

"Little one, I do wish you would hurry up and come." Sighing softly, she rubbed her abdomen as another contraction tightened her belly. Nissim chuckled, unaware of the change in her expression. Lutep-Tzia wanted a few more private moments with him. When she told him of the pains she had been experiencing, their chamber would immediately be filled with midwives, nursing maids, and attendants. She grasped his hands and placed them on her belly, moving them so he could feel the next kicks that were sure to come. He splayed his fingers, nestling his cheek beside hers.

"I think he is just as anxious to see us as we are to see him." Nissim tucked her into his chest, wrapping his arms around her protectively. Even though their marriage had been arranged, their relationship had blossomed quickly in the nine years since their wedding. She could not have thanked her father enough for choosing such an outstanding partner for her.

Lutep-Tzia turned, mischief dancing in her eyes. "What do you mean *him?* It might very well be a girl." She snuggled in closer, resting her head on his shoulder. Nissim chuckled softly. He studied her, only able to see her profile. She seemed nervous. And well, she may be. There was much expected of a royal wife and queen.

"And she will be just as gorgeous as her mother," he whispered.

His breath tickled her ear as he said the words. She looked out over the water and tried to relax as another pain came. They were growing more intense now, and she knew she could not camouflage her discomfort from Nissim for much longer.

The sun had fully risen by then. Nissim pointed to the bank on the opposite shore. A doe and her fawn could be seen drinking from a happy little stream flowing into the lagoon. Birds sang as they hopped from branch to branch in the citrus trees lining the terraces below their balcony. The palace was built on the pinnacle of the island, with the whole of the western slopes being reserved for their private gardens and terraces. She was glad of the privacy it afforded Nissim, for he carried a heavy burden as king. However, he carried it all with such wisdom and strength. She longed to be able to afford him the one thing he so desperately needed if he were to continue the *Tzoruenian* line, which had ruled for the last sixteen generations.

She could see his frown out of the corner of her eye as she drew in a sharp breath. He turned her, no doubt seeing her face was lined with sudden pain. Her abdomen contracted and the worry lining his face only grew. That had been a hard one. She let out a breath slowly, frowning at the intensity of the contraction.

"Why did you not tell me you were beginning your labor?" Nissim stood up and knelt before her. "Someone! Please, someone, help!" he called. A frown of annoyance crossed his face. "Where is your maid? She should be here to hearken to your every need." He looked around and no doubt saw that the small adjoining servant's room was empty.

"Nissim, it is not so urgent. I sent Hatel to get me some *chatla.*" Lutep-Tzia laughed, but her strained smile quickly died away. She must try to be brave. "I have been having little pains since early this morning," she said through gritted teeth. The pain started to ease, and she forced her facial muscles to relax. "That was a bad one."

"What? Why did you not wake me as soon as your pains started?" Nissim jumped up and would have left had she not grabbed his hand and pulled him back down to her.

"Nissim, I am well," she soothed. "The baby will come when he is ready. It may be hours yet. Please, let's sit here just a little longer."

Nissim settled back down beside her but was tense, his muscles ready for action. She understood his concern. They had lost too many in years past. A little more of her spirit drained away as they were forced to bury a piece of her heart with each stillborn babe. "Should we not send for the midwife?" he asked.

Lutep-Tzia shifted to face him, fear filling his eyes like ink spreading through water. Another pain gripped her, and she could not speak for several moments. She grabbed his hand until it was over. When it passed, she let out a breath, "Perhaps you should. I think it is coming faster than I thought." Try as she might, she could not keep the fear at bay either.

Nissim stood, lifting her into his arms to carry her to the bed. Her maid returned at that moment. He lowered his voice, but Lutep-Tzia still heard that anger in his tone. "Stay here with your mistress. If I learn you left her side for a moment, you will have me to deal with,"

Hatel cast a frightened glance at the bed, nearly toppling the small tray with the silver cup and pot of hot *chatla*. She bowed her head and hurried to her side. Nissim watched to ensure she was settled before he disappeared into the hall, leaving the door wide open.

Lutep-Tzia watched her husband hurry out the door, shaking her head as she looked up at Hatel. She laughed weakly, "Expecting fathers..."

She tried not to panic as yet another wave of pain overtook her body. It was all happening so fast. The midwife had warned her that her first delivery would likely take hours if not days. This was the only pregnancy she had been able to carry to full term, and for that, she could at least be grateful. This blessed child would have been their fifth had not her body expelled her earliest pregnancies in the first few weeks. The other two had ended in stillbirth.

She spread her hands protectively over her abdomen as another pain came. *Just breathe,* she thought as she arched her back and let her head fall into the pillows, closing her eyes against the blinding pain. It was all she could do to focus on that one thought. *Breathe...*

When Nissim finally returned with the midwife, Lutep-Tzia could no longer control the guttural screams that exploded out of her. "Something is not right," she choked, leaning over the side of the bed just in time to vomit. Nissim came to her side and took her hand, wiping her mouth tenderly with a satin cloth. She had just enough time to give him a weak smile before another pain enveloped her.

"Breathe, my lady. There now." The midwife patted her leg as a mother would, her voice swimming to her through a sea of torment. It took every ounce of strength to decipher the woman's words.

Nissim brushed a few stray hairs away from her eyes. "You are doing splendidly, my love. I'm going to stay right here."

But before he could finish, the midwife stepped in. "No, my lord. I must insist that you leave the birthing chamber and allow us to do what is needed."

Lutep-Tzia gripped his hand, her eyes reflecting his fear for her. "No, do not leave me!"

Nissim looked up at the older woman and shook his head. "I will remain with my wife," he said in a tone that left no room for argument. The midwife's eyes darted from his hardened face back to hers. It was apparent the old midwife disapproved, but she could not do this without her husband.

"My lady, I need you to scoot to the end of the bed so I can examine you." The midwife went around the end of the bed and encouraged her with a wave of her gnarled, wrinkled hand. Nissim helped her get into position. Lutep-Tzia gripped his hand, holding back the groan of pain.

The midwife conducted her examination in silence, placing one hand on her abdomen to feel the baby's position. An alarmed expression spread over her face, and though she tried to cover it up, Lutep-Tzia's trepidation grew. Fear rippled through her chest. "What is it?" she demanded.

"You are doing wonderful, my lady. Drink some *chatla*, as it will ease the pain a bit. My apprentice will sit with you for a while. I need a word with His Majesty."

Nissim leaned in to kiss her on the forehead before he departed the room. "I will return in a moment. I will never leave you," he whispered.

She watched him go, leaning her head back against the pillow. She had thought this child was a miracle, a promise. But what if they both died this time? She would never forgive herself if she had come this close to giving Nissim a living baby, just to fail once more. Tears streamed down her cheeks. If they died, would *he* ever forgive her?

Nissim followed the midwife out into the corridor. He frowned at her when she hesitated. "What is this?" he asked, anxious to return to his wife's side.

"The baby is not in the correct position, Your Majesty. It is feet down, rather than head down." She cast a concerned look toward the bed where his wife sipped at a cup of *chatla*. It seemed to ease her pain a little, and she lay back. "I noticed her ankles are slightly swollen. Has she been complaining of headaches the last few days?"

Nissim frowned. "I do not believe so. If she has, she has not told me."

"You would do well to send a message to the queen's parents, Your Majesty. Perhaps the queen might feel more easy with her mother by her side." She looked past Nissim's shoulder and into the chamber. "And perhaps it would not hurt to send for your personal physician."

"Of course." Nissim followed her gaze to his wife's figure, settling a little with the help of the *chatla*.

"I believe the queen has a long labor ahead of her," the midwife said, lowering her voice.

Nissim's stomach dropped. He could not lose her. He rubbed his palms together and nodded. "I will send the message to her parents immediately." Anything to ease his wife's suffering as she labored to bring their child into the world.

The midwife nodded, likely glad to see him out of the birthing chamber for a little while. Nissim went on his way, striding toward the east end of the palace to write the missive and have it sent. "She will be well," he said aloud. "She has to be."

CHAPTER 14

QUEEN LUTEP-TZIA

"My lady. My lady?"

A voice swam to her through a blur of pain. Lutep-Tzia struggled to own her eyes, a face appearing before her. The midwife touched her shoulder and signaled for her apprentice to help Lutep-Tzia lean forward and bring her knees to her chest.

"It is time to push again, Your Majesty."

Lutep-Tzia closed her eyes and pushed with the contraction. When it passed, she fell back on the pillows and fell into fitful snatches of sleep. How long had she been here? She could no longer keep track of the passage of time. People milled around her, their furtive whispers growing more distant as the hours turned to days.

"Nissim—" she whispered as another pain gripped her. Where was her beloved? The midwife would want to keep him away until after the baby was born, but she needed him now more than ever.

"We can see the baby's head, my lady. Just a few more pushes, and you'll be able to hold your child." The midwife had her lean forward again as she bared down. She had sent Nissim from the room an hour before to send him on another little errand, while they had tried to turn the baby. It was well that he gone, for he would not have stood idly by while she screamed in agony. It had been excruciating, but she would undergo any amount of pain to see her baby come safely into the world. Even if she could no longer be a part of that world...

"I want Nissim," she said when the contraction ended. She only had a few seconds of respite and tried to stay awake between the pains. But it was becoming more and more difficult.

"You are almost delivered, my lady. We will bring the king in shortly." The midwife said, leaving her request unheeded. "He will return shortly."

She tried to catch her breath, but the pain was almost too much for her. Somehow she sensed that there would be no time once the baby was finally born. She sat up and pushed again, gathering what little strength she had left.

Panting, she fell back again. "No. I want him *now*," she said with as much force as she could muster. "Bring him to me at once."

The midwife pursed her lips but did not argue. "Do it," she heard her say. The midwife turned back to her charge and asked for one more big push.

Lutep-Tzia grabbed the apprentice's hand and leaned forward again, pushing with all her might. She let out a labored grunt, feeling like she was being torn in half from the inside out. Sweat dripped into her eyes, and she screamed as the baby was delivered.

She fell back, too tired to look at her newborn. Fear gripped her as the room remained silent. Should the babe not be crying? Finally, after what seemed like ages, a piercing cry echoed through the room. The attendants cheered, and Lutep-Tzia uttered a relieved sigh. "You have a son, Your Majesty," the midwife smiled. She quickly handed the baby over to the attendant, who placed the baby on Lutep-Tzia's chest.

A wave of gratitude and love washed over her. His mouth worked, searching for nourishment. He was perfect. However, Lutep-Tzia's face contorted in more pain as the afterbirth was delivered. Her limbs grew heavy. She could not seem to lift her arms, the life draining from her. "Where is Nissim?" she asked weakly. She was barely able to keep her eyes open.

The midwife was busy at the end of the bed, her face white as death itself. Lutep-Tzia could feel the woman's unease even though she was trying to hide her rising panic. "The bleeding will not stop —" The midwife gritted her teeth, reaching for more cloths. The strain was evident in the midwife's tone, causing a ripple of fear to course through her. Suddenly, the baby was taken from her chest, but there was nothing she could do to get him back.

"It is alright, my Lady. The doctor will only take him for a moment to clean, salt, and swaddle him," Hatel said.

Lutep-Tzia had little time left in this world.

The door crashed open, making her heart skip a beat. "My love, I am here." Nissim's face appeared above her, and she tried to give him a smile. Tears dripping down her cheeks as Nissim settled beside her. He cradled her in his arm over her head and leaned back against the pillow where she lay. "You did beautifully, my dear." He brushed the tendrils of sweat-drenched hair from her forehead, misunderstanding the cause of her tears. She reached for his hand, wanting to hang on for as long as possible. It took every ounce of strength to lift it. Brushing her fingers over his cheek, her heart broke. He was so handsome and had always treated her like a treasure. They had both been so young when he had come to the throne. He had leaned on her, just as she did with him. How would he fare without her, especially with their son to care for?

"Where is he?" She tried to lean up and spotted their son being cleaned by Bosenia, her husband's personal physician. The older man glanced at her, and sadness filled his eyes. Hurrying over to the bedside, he deposited the tiny bundle in her arms and went to help the midwife.

Nissim was spellbound. He gazed at their son, and love filled his eyes. "He's perfect, my love. He has your chin and your eyes." He touched the soft skin of his son's cheek and beamed up at her. She studied the tiny face, his mouth working to find sustenance. The midwife's apprentice helped her position the baby to nurse, and he was soon suckling at her breast.

"Our son," Nissim said softly. "What shall we call him?" Her eyes drooped shut.

"Tzia?" When he spoke again, his voice sounded very far off. He touched her forehead and immediately jerked his fingers away. "Lutep-Tzia!" he called more forcefully when she did not open her eyes. Try as she might, she could not make her eyelids open. He shook her shoulder gently.

"What is wrong with her?"

"We cannot stop the bleeding, Your Majesty," Bosenia choked. He continued to work on her, frantically trying to keep her from Death's door. She hardly felt a thing now.

"No." Nissim grasped her hand again, willing her to open her eyes. "Please, do not leave me, my love. We need you."

She forced her eyes open, her vision blurred. She sucked in a breath and tried to sit up, her head swimming with pain. She had to try for the sake of her son, but she barely made it an inch before she fell back on the pillows, pressing a hand to her temple. "My head!" she said, clenching her teeth. Bosenia joined Nissim at the bedside and gently touched her shoulder.

"Do not try to move, Your Majesty. You need to rest."

"Well?" Her husband demanded of the physician.

"I am so sorry, Your Majesty. There is nothing more we can do. She is in the hands of *Ilyo Na'ada* now."

His words rocked her to her core, as if the executioner was raising the *slitsike* above her head to deal the death blow. The tapered stone hammer used to dispense of criminals had always given her nightmares. Now, her worst fear was coming true—to die before she had a chance to be a mother. "We must name him," she said hoarsely. Nissim helped her lift the gemstone necklace over her head and placed it atop the swaddled babe. The beautiful white stone glistened in the sunlight streaming through the windows. "Give this to him when he is older. Tell him how much I loved him. And that I am sorry I could not be here to watch him grow." Her voice cracked before she could finish, the pressure in her head building.

Nissim's face blurred again. Then suddenly, her mother's face appeared behind him. Relieved, she reached for her. "Mama! You're here!"

Nissim frowned, and a second later, her mother's face disappeared. She looked around frantically. "Mama?"

"Your mother is not here, Tzia," he whispered. Nissim brushed the damp hair away from her face, then looked over at the midwife. "What is wrong with her?"

"It is the head sickness, Your Majesty," the midwife explained. "We are not sure what causes it, but that is why I asked about the swelling in her ankles and the headaches. There is nothing to be done—"

"No, there has to be something you can do!" Nissim shook her shoulders again. "You will live, Lutep-Tzia. You will live, do you hear me?"

Lutep-Tzia opened her eyes once more. She was so tired. The pain in her head returned in full force. She knew he did not mean to deal harshly with her. His gaze softened, and he sat on the edge of the bed with her, wrapping his strong arms around her and the baby.

She touched the baby's cheek again and stared down tenderly at him. Lutep-Tzia studied his little face as if to memorize each contour to take with her into the next life. "Shoram. I want to name him Shoram."

"*Ilyo Na'ada is exalted.*" Nissim recited the familiar name's meaning. "It suits him." He bent down and kissed her forehead. She tried to lean into him, to savor what little time she had left with him and her son, before she closed her eyes for the last time.

CHAPTER 15

KING NISSIM

Nissim looked at his sweet wife's face and knew that time was short. He held her closer, not wanting to let go. "Please don't leave me, Tzia," he begged, his voice choked with emotion. How could he go on without her steady strength and bolstering smile? How would he raise their son to be the man he needed to be without his wife there to help him?

"I will always be with you, my love." Shoram had finished suckling and had fallen asleep, tiny drops of milk left behind at the corners of his mouth. He took the baby in one are arm turned his wife into his chest, the baby cradled tenderly between them. He kissed her lips gently, wanting to savor every last moment with her.

"I love you as my own life," he whispered, reciting the vow he had made to her on their wedding day.

"I am yours forever," she recited, barely above a whisper. Suddenly, her body went rigid. Nissim sat back, not wanting to crush Shoram between them. He handed the baby to the midwife and immediately went back to Lutep-Tzia's side. "She's not breathing," he said, searching her face, her eyes eyes staring as she tried to gasp for air. For several seconds, she could not control herself, and arched her head backward, her muscles tense enough to break bone.

"She cannot breathe!" He bellowed. "Help her!"

The midwife and attendants stood a few paces from the bed, but they had already told him there was nothing to be done. Still, he did not want to believe this was the end. He knelt at the bedside, frantic to keep her with him. "Please, Lutep-Tzia. Please, breathe."

Her body went slack a few seconds later. She took several gasping breaths, but did not open her eyes again. Tears wet his cheeks. She tried to say something, and he leaned in close to catch her words. "Don't be afraid to take another wife, Nissim. You will need help in your young reign."

Nissim wept all the more, wiping furiously at his tears. Even now, she was still thinking of him. He did not want to hear it—could not think about taking another wife now. Maybe not ever. His heart felt like it was shattering into a million pieces. "Never mind that, now." He kissed her forehead, still damp with the perspiration of childbirth. He nestled her body closer, tucking her into his chest. Her body convulsed again, her muscles going rigid. He kept hold of her this time, but she was slipping away like sand though his hands. He was powerless to save her. "*Ilyo Na'ada,* please!" he cried.

She seemed to stay locked in that position for an eternity, her back inflexible and convulsing. After more than a minute, Lutep-Tzia's body went limp, her eyelids open and staring with the coldness of death. Nissim gripped her shoulders, staring into her unseeing eyes for her to blink again. "Lutep-Tzia?" he called. But there was no answer this time. "Tzia–" he choked.

A second later, his son cried from across the room. Heart breaking, he looked up at Bosenia, his hands and arms covered in blood from the birth. Nissim could contain his grief no more, and roared with a pain that he had never experienced before. Afterward, all was quiet for the longest time as he looked at his wife's lifeless face. *Why?* Why had *Ilyo Na'ada* allowed this to happen? All she had wanted was to be a mother.

Bosenia came to the bedside and felt for a pulse as Nissim continued to hold her. He shook his head and took his fingertips away from her slender throat. "She is gone, Your Majesty."

Nissim could not speak, could not move. "Leave us." His voice held no inflection, just raw pain.

"We need to wash her, Your Majesty. And a wet nurse should be found for the baby."

The midwife came closer, cradling the baby in her arms. Nissim lay his wife flat, arranged her head on the pillows and took a step back. She looked peaceful now, all traces of pain swept away to leave a beautiful shell of the woman he loved. "Leave us," Nissim said again. Thankfully, Bosenia did not argue with him.

The people who had attended the birth slowly started to exit the room. Bosenia was the last to leave, offering his condolences once again. "Thank you, Bosenia. You will help the midwife attend to my son, won't you?" He did not take his eyes off his wife.

"Of course, Your Majesty. Do not worry about anything."

"Thank you." He waited until Bosenia closed the door, then sank to the floor. He took Lutep-Tzia's cold hand, bringing it to his forehead. His body shook as he finally gave in to gut-wrenching sobs.

CHAPTER 16

DELGADAS

"His Majesty awaits you in the courtyard, my lord."

Delgadas peered down his nose at the king's servant. "You may go." He waved a hand, sending the man away.

He walked through the archway, wondering if the king had gone mad. Clouds had begun rolling in the previous evening, after the queen's death. As was customary, music would not be played for three days as the whole country went into mourning. Soon, the torrential rains would commence. For himself, the absence of music was a relief, for practice of playing for the sunrise and sunset had always put his teeth on edge.

Lord Delgadas found the king sitting on a marble bench in the outer courtyard. He halted, watching, waiting. The king sat motionless on the bench, staring into nothingness. Delgadas's footsteps echoed against the high walls as he entered the small courtyard, thick with climbing vines and flowers. The place was deserted save for His Majesty, himself, and a bright yellow and green bird. The bird was busily hopping from branch to branch in the towering maple of the courtyard's westward corner. It shook its feathers and trilled a happy little tune. Delgadas snapped his head up and shot an annoyed look in the bird's direction. Afraid, the bird flew away to join its friends in the safety of the higher branches.

"Your Majesty. You called for me?" Lord Delgadas said, announcing his presence.

The king motioned for him to sit beside him on the bench. Delgadas sighed heavily as he sat. He adjusted his wide girth and turned to him. "I offer my condolences, Your Majesty. Queen Lutep-Tzia was a noble and gentle ruler. She will be dearly missed."

When the king did not respond, Delgadas went on. "I only wish there was some way I could help ease your duties," he offered, his tongue dripping honey.

"That is why I have summoned you here. I am sending you as the head of a delegation to Saardonae to alert our allies of what has happened."

Interesting.

Obviously, the king's missive to the queen's parents had not reached them in time.

A flicker of discontent crossed his features before he could think better of it. He quickly replaced his annoyance by a mask of feigned acquiesence.

"Me, Your Majesty?" Delgadas almost sneered. "Am I now a servant boy to be sent on errands?"

Nissim straightened. "You are one of my most seasoned officials, Lord Delgadas. I want to make sure all is done properly, and I would not trust such an errand, as you call it, to a servant boy." The king sighed, anger dancing behind his eyes. "Relaying the news of the queen's death will take considerable finesse. You leave at first light."

The phrase was an oxymoron now. The Musicians would be silent for the next three days. The sun would rise, but it would be much later in the day, bringing the rains along with it. "First Light" would not appear until the nooning meal. Which suited Delgadas just fine.

He bowed his head, becoming the embodiment of accommodation itself. "Of course, Your Majesty. I am deeply honored that you would bestow such a task on me." Delgadas stood, smoothing his hands over his long tunic and gave a slight bow to the King. He did not placed his hand over his heart, even though it was customary, and left the courtyard to complete his *errand*.

Delgadas stewed as he departed the patio. As he thought about it, this journey might prove far from an inconvenience. This new mission could afford him the opportunity he had been looking for. For years, he had bent to Nissim's will—the presumptuous little pup. He had served under his father for many years, enjoying a state of wealth, trust, and power that few others did. When the former King had passed away, Nissim had 'cleaned house,' leaving many of Delgadas' peers with minor titles or forcing them into retirement in the country. Nissim's radical reforms had not set well with the older generation of politicians.

I should be running the country. The thought had whirled around in Delgadas' mind since Nissim had taken the throne. He had been biding his time for years, and now it seemed that Fate would smile on him.

He wove through the maze of pristine marble corridors, feigning grief if anyone passed. It was true that Lutep-Tzia had been beautiful. He had seen it as fortuitous that she had been unable to do her duty and provide the king with an heir.

Until now. He thought of this with annoyance that she had finally been able to birth a living child, forcing him to change his plans. King Nissim would be weakened by his love of the babe and grief for his wife. Perhaps the prince's arrival could be used to his advantage.

Exiting the palace, Delgadas made his way to his lavish home through deserted streets. Already, word was spreading of the queen's passing, and all were preparing for the three days of mourning and darkness ahead. It was a short walk to his home, and when he arrived, he thrust his expensive mantle at the servant girl, positioned at the door at all hours to greet him and tend to his needs. "Send Dizedo to me," he ordered.

The girl draped the heavy cloak over her arm, stumbling under the weight. "Careful!" he snapped. "That mantel is worth more than you." The girl stood and hung his mantle reverently on its hook, treating it as more precious than a newborn babe. And well, she should.

The mantle had taken nearly two years to weave, using the fur of the *titzake*. The small rodent-like creature was revered for its soft fur undercoat that could only be harvested from the animals after first trapping them in their native snowy mountain peaks. The tufts of white fur were gently plucked as they shed their winter coats in preparation for Spring. One *titzake* gave a handful of fur no bigger than a sparrow's egg. Only a few artisan women knew the secrets of spinning the fur into thread, almost as thin as a spider's web. Thus, when finished, the material, called *titzake lumpay*, took years to make and even longer to fashion into clothing. Only the richest of Luminia's upper classes could afford the luxury.

Delgadas headed to the study to the right of the circular court-yard, where he entertained guests. When Dizedo arrived, he gave him a stern scowl. "You know I do not like to be kept waiting," he said, low and menacing. The boy could not be more than ten years old. He clasped trembling hands in front of him.

"Forgive me, my lord. I came as soon as I was summoned."

Delgadas waved him off impatiently. He did not have time for excuses. "Take down a missive for me." Delgadas picked his nails as the boy sat at a small writing desk in the corner, taking down his dictated message.

To my esteemed friend, King Nargod, mighty ruler of all Tzotoeh:

I write to inform you that our beloved Queen has died in childbirth. The time is ripe for Luminia to be plucked. I am leading a delegation to Saar-

donae and beg an audience with you in our usual place near the High Road. I am sending my servant along and will give him further instructions on the day and time to expect us.

In haste,

    Lord Delgadas

Delgadas smiled wickedly as he looked over the finished missive. Glaring at the boy, he leaned forward, making sure the boy knew he was serious. "You know that if you say a word of this, your life—and that of your entire family—is forfeit."

The boy visibly shook with fear of Delgadas. "I will say nothing, as you require, my lord." The boy placed a hand over his heart and bowed low to the ground, using his free arm to prop himself up. Delgadas made him wait for several beats before allowing him to rise. The boy had been in his household long enough to know that Delgadas did not give idle threats. The thought sent a surge of power through his veins, feasting on the fear of his household servants.

"Good," Delgadas said, satisfied that the boy would keep his word. "Now leave me."

The boy scurried out of the room with the rolled piece of parchment in hand and went to deliver the message. It would be a few days before it arrived in Tzotoeh, but Delgadas would slow their progress to Saardonae as much as he could to give the boy the time he needed.

Soon, all of Luminia would bow before him. Not to mention Tzotoeh. While King Nargod was a valuable ally for the time being, he was not a wise ruler. Once Luminia was under his control, Tzotoeh would fall easy prey.

Delgadas walked onto the terrace adjoining his study and looked out over Lunthá, the Jewel of Luminia. The city was starting to show signs of the death. The sun was trying to set, but with no music to see it safely below the horizon, there would be no glorious colors to accompany it. Gray clouds rolled in. By the morrow, the rains would come, and not the kind they looked forward to for crops. These rains could bring flash floods, mudslides, and all sorts of damage around Lunthá and the outlying communities.

However, when the three days were completed, Delgadas would be in a position to take power. Visions of a glorious empire rose before him. "Soon, you will be mine."

CHAPTER 17

DELGADAS

The following morning, Delgadas and his entourage left the royal city under cover of darkness. It would remain dark for several hours after the usual time. Delgadas did not mind. He was borne on a litter carried by six robust male servants and allowed himself to dose as they struggled down the steep inclines that were the streets of Lunthá.

Delgadas used the full day of travel to plan his next moves. With King Nissim distracted by the loss of his beloved queen, he could work in the shadows. Nissim would not even realize what was happening until it was too late, like a noose wrapping around the throat of a sleeping victim.

When they arrived at the border of Saardonae three days later, their progress stunted by the storms and mudslides, they were let through the border immediately. The guards were shocked when they heard of the queen's passing, but Delgadas charged them to tell no one. Of course, he was counting on them to do just the opposite, to stir up unrest on Saardonae. Would they blame Lutep-Tzia's untimely death on Nissim? All the better for his plans.

Once through the gates of the borderlands, Delgadas sent

runners ahead of him to the palace to be sure satisfactory accommodations were prepared for him. The country of Saardonae was not as lush as Luminia. The Redwood forests soon gave way to rocky bluffs covered in prairie grasses and sage scrub. And dust. Oh how he hated the dust.

Turning to the west, they traveled along the coast, the cliffs breaking away toward the sea hundreds of feet below them. The people of Saardonaenian capital, Raellu, had carved their homes from the cliffs, with only one road leading to the city's center. It was a brilliant way to cut off attacks from neighboring countries. But with no outlet, it also served as a trap, with cliffs at their back and the sea at their face. Delgadas studied the cliff city as he was borne toward the palace. Perhaps Saardonae would also prove useful in his plans for a powerful empire.

The road widened as they neared the palace grounds. Delgadas climbed down from the litter, stretching his sore muscles from the long journey. His litter bearers looked exhausted, but he did not give a care for them. A servant provided him with his *titzake lumpay* mantle, and he brought it tighter around his shoulders with bejeweled fingers. He had donned his most expensive jewelry in preparation for his audience with the king's younger brother.

He climbed down the steps heading toward the palace gates. He shielded his eyes from the glare of sunshine coming off the ivory limestone. It was a work of genius and absolute precision: the palace walls towering above their heads with intricate designs, the dome-shaped roofs that came to a fine point. There were open, airy courtyards below, with brightly colored cloths stretched overhead, shielding them from the warm sunshine. Lush green gardens broke up the white rock from which the palace had been carved.

A spineless little man greeted him as he entered the palace, descending a grand staircase leading to the castle's upper levels. The man bowed slightly at the waist but did not put his hand over his heart. Apparently, this steward thought he was more important than a lord of the Luminian realm. "My lord, what brings you to Saardonae?"

Delgadas brushed past him. "I have business with the King and his brother, Lord Chukze." The steward hurried to catch up with him before he could reach the grand staircase. Delgadas halted, looking down his nose at the infuriating man. "My mission is of the most urgent nature. I assume my runners arrived and told you of our visit? I would like to refresh myself before my audience with Their Majesty's."

The steward raised his brow. "Your message *did* arrive this afternoon, my lord. All has been made ready for you, but His Majesty and his esteemed brother are waiting for you in the courtroom now."

Delgadas waved him off. "Surely you can see that I am travel-worn. It seems that the only thing in more abundance from your country other than our imports from the sea is the fine dust that is all over my tunic." He paused and gave a wicked smirk. "It would not be unseemly for me to present myself to His Majesty without first making myself presentable." He pushed past the man again, who had no choice but to show Delgadas to his rooms.

The steward did not seem pleased as he showed him a set of modest chambers overlooking the sea. However, Delgadas could care less. He must take his time in delivering the king's message to Queen Lutep-Tzia's father.

Taking in his accommodations, he turned and dismissed the steward. "I suppose it will do," he said. "Please tell the King I will be ready in an hour."

A flicker of surprise lit the man's eyes. "The king is eager to hear what his ally has to say, Lord Delgadas. There are rumors that a death has occurred in the royal household."

Delgadas gave him an imperious scowl. "I am not at liberty to discuss these matters with a lowly steward. You are free to go."

The man glared. "As you wish, my lord." He closed the door, and Delgadas ordered his servant boy to draw a bath for him. He was not in any particular hurry to get on with his task. Delgadas needed to stall for as long as possible if he were to give King Nargod time to receive his message and be ready to meet with him on his way back to Luminia.

Two hours later, the steward came knocking at the great wooden doors, bringing a message from the King. "His Majesty requests your presence in the courtroom, my lord." Delgadas did not like his superior tone but went with him, satisfied that he had kept the royals waiting long enough.

When he arrived, he saw several of the Saardonaenian lords gathered in the courtroom, tension hanging in the air like a noxious mist. The ocean could be heard crashing against the rocks below the courtroom's arched windows. The large circular room held sixteen high-backed chairs where the lords sat for imperial sessions. Delgadas puffed out his chest, glad to see so many of the king's advisors would hear his news about the queen from his lips.

The King nodded as Delgadas came forward and gave a shallow bow. "What news have you brought from our esteemed ally, Lord Delgadas?" the King asked with obvious annoyance.

Lord Delgadas rose slowly from his bow. "Your Majesty, I come with grave news from Luminia. Our beloved Queen Lutep-Tzia has passed away in childbirth." Gasps filtered throughout the room at his announcement. He relished inwardly that his words could have such an effect. He loved to be the bearer of bad news, knowing full well that terms between Saardonae and Luminia would be weakened. There may even be enough unrest to spark a war between the historically peaceful nations.

King Botzena stood in shock, his queen dissolving into tears at his side. Lutep-Tzia had been a beloved niece to the sovereigns. Lord Chukze swayed beside the king. He gasped, but did his best to keep control of his emotions.

After several seconds, Lord Chukze stepped forward. "How could this happen?" he demanded, not so much of Delgadas, but of Fate, he supposed.

Delgadas bowed slightly. "One does not always know why these things happen, my lord."

"I must ride back to Luminia as soon as possible," Lord Chukze choked. "My daughter—" The gray old man did not even try to hide his tears now, causing Delgadas to scorn him. The queen rose from her throne and comforted her brother-in-law. But Delgadas had nothing but derision for the man. Showing weakness in front of one's peers and superiors was unacceptable.

"Of course, my lord. I had plans to return to the capital in a few days if you would like to accompany my entourage," Delgadas replied, secretly hoping he would decline the offer.

The king gave him a questioning frown. "Are you not anxious to return to King Nissim, Lord Delgadas? I am sure he has need of you in this trying time."

"I have been entrusted with one more mission from King Nissim before I can return to Lunthá. With your permission, Your Majesty, I beg your leave to stay overnight and be off in the morning."

The King gave him a curt nod of dismissal, granting him rest for the night. He then turned to Lord Chuck to comfort him. Delgadas left the courtroom, sighing in contentment that he had dispensed of his duties and could now look forward to his meeting with King Nargod.

DELGADAS WAITED in the shadows of a towering Redwood. He wrapped the plain, brown peasant's cloak tighter around his shoulders as a disguise and protection against the rain that seemed to pelt him from all sides. King Nargod had left him waiting for two days, and he grew anxious to rejoin his entourage. He feared they would come looking for him and discover his true purpose for being this far into the woods.

He inched nearer the small fire he had built to ward off the cold. However, with every gust of wind, his only source of warmth and comfort grew fainter, sputtering as the raindrops splashed onto the flames. "Wretched man!" he huffed. What if his servant, Dizedo, had not been able to get through the border? Or what if King Nargod had refused his summons? If the latter, the sovereign would have all the fury of hell to contend with.

Delgadas turned to retrieve a piece of damp wood from under the ferns he had used to try to protect them. He placed it on the fire, but it would not take. A crow squawked, and the sound of wings flapping made him snap his head up. King Nargod and four of his soldiers were in front of him sitting astride their powerful horses. Delgadas jumped, holding a hand over his heart. "You nearly gave me an episode, Nargod." He let out an annoyed breath and straightened.

King Nargod jumped off of his mount and strode toward Delgadas. Nargod was an impulsive young man of twenty-seven, powerfully built with a volatile temper. Red and black tattoos covered the right side of his face and trickled down his neck onto his chest. His arms and legs were also covered with garish tattoos. The Tzotoens were a backward people, warring amongst themselves and their neighbors. He could not expect refinement from these men, not even their king.

He was just the sort of man that Delgadas needed. He looked more beast than human, dressed in animal skins and wearing a bleached human skull atop his head, no doubt from a vanquished enemy. "What brings you to my domain, Lord Delgadas. More *plans*? Or are you finally ready to take your revenge on Nissim?" Nargod spat the king's name as if it were a curse.

King Nargod and Nissim had never seen eye to eye on anything. And in Delgadas's opinion, Nissim had not the backbone to do what was needed to run Luminia as it should be. With Luminia and Tzotoeh under his control, he could reunite the countries and finally have their rich resources at his fingertips. Nissim had refused to ally himself with the cruel king of Tzotoeh, going against Delgadas's advice.

"The time has come, Your Majesty." Delgadas feigned obeisance to the monarch, though there was little but distrust and carefully disguised malice between them. Delgadas knew that Nargod was likely using him, just as Delgadas was trying to use Nargod. "King Nissim has just lost his wife in childbirth. He will go into mourning, giving us the perfect opportunity to put our plans into action."

"Yes, I know. I believe King Nissim might be missing a messenger boy?" A wicked smile crossed Nargod's face.

Delgadas understood why the queen's parents had not been alerted of their daughter's impending labor, nor of her death. It had worked to his advantage of course. "And where is the messenger now?"

Nargod shrugged. "If he was good enough to gain entry, he would have made it to the Beyond by now." He crossed his arms over his chest. "You give the word, and I shall be at your disposal, my lord."

"I shall need to tread lightly in these first weeks. Nissim is grieving, but he is smart. I will send word when the time is right for your troops to storm the city."

Nargod nodded once, then motioned for one of his soldiers to approach. "I am sending along Futah to act as your bodyguard. If you find yourself in trouble, he will bring you across the border to Tzotoeh."

Futah looked even more menacing than Nargod, his face tattooed with black grizzly lines that covered nearly every inch of his skin.

"My thanks," Delgadas said sarcastically, keeping his eye on the towering soldier. He could not help but wonder if Futah was there to make sure Delgadas followed through with his end of the deal as much as for his protection.

Nargod gave a curt nod and remounted. Thanks to the forest's rain-soaked earth, he and the three other soldiers rode away without a sound. Delgadas waved at Futah, motioning him in the opposite direction and back toward the road. Shadows obscured his return, and as Delgadas weaved his way through the forest and back to the road, he glanced over his shoulder several times at his new protector, leading his towering horse behind him. When they were a few yards from the road, he pinned Futah with a superior stare. "Follow behind the caravan. And be sure that no one spots you."

Futah gave him a derisive smile. "No one ever sees Futah, unless Futah wishes it." Without a sound, the man turned and disappeared into the towering ferns, making his way to the back of their procession.

Delgadas huffed, a shiver traveling up his spine. He pulled his cloak tighter and made his presence known, crashing through the ferns as he came out onto the road. He refused to answer his servants' concerned questions on his late return.

"You have been gone for nearly two days, my lord. We thought a wild animal had killed you!"

"I lost my way, but thank *Ilyo Na'ada,* I am unharmed. Now, let us make haste." Delgadas changed quickly into his finery and settled into the litter. It began to rain with even more fury as they lifted him into the air and started inching down the incline. He reached up and moved the curtain aside slightly. "Pick up the pace!"

A servant appeared at his side, looking worried. "The men are tired, my lord. And these steep roads are dangerous. Would it not be better—"

"I do not care how hazardous they are. If my litter bearers are too clumsy to stay on their feet, they deserve to be left behind. Replace them with others who will!"

The servant hesitated.

"Are you deaf? Move!" Delgadas let go of the heavy curtain that protected him from the rain. He wrapped a thick blanket up over his waist and tucked it around his feet, relieved to be in the warmth of the cocoon-like litter. He did not care that his servants would have an arduous task carrying the litter in the dead of night in the pouring rain. His only thought was to get back to Luminia so he could put his plan in motion.

CHAPTER 18

KING NISSIM

K ing Nissim sat by the fountain leading up to the temple of *Ilyo Na'ada*. Water trickling over the rounded rocks, calming his frayed nerves. The crystal clear water ran down channels carved straight into the mountainside, feeding several pools and fountains at the base of the hill and the water-works throughout the rest of the palace. Steps had been cut on all four sides of the mountain until it was shaped like a rudimentary pyramid where the temple of *Ilyo Na'ada* stood at the pinnacle. Very often, it was nestled in the clouds and mist that rolled in from the sea, a world it's very own.

But Nissim had not gone to the temple since his wife's passing eleven days ago. Going to the holy sanctuary was forbidden when one wore mourning clothes. He fingered the red tassels on the fringe of his tunic, knowing that the time for grief was almost complete. At least, the official bereavement period allowed by the dictates of society. He would mourn Lutep-Tzia forever.

Nissim would allow music to commence at sunrise. His people were already feeling the brunt of having heavy rains for so many days. Their young crops would not take much more of this, rotting in the ground from too much moisture and not enough sunshine. While his country was ready to move on, he wondered if he ever would be.

Someone cleared their throat as they came up the steps, and he turned, seeing Bosenia shuffling up behind him. "Your Majesty," he greeted him solemnly.

"Bosenia," Nissim said by way of greeting, although his words were dull and lifeless. He could see something was the matter. "What is it?"

"Adagio begs an audience with you. He is waiting in the courtroom."

Nissim was reluctant to leave. But life would have to commence at some point. He let out a deep sigh and stood. "Let us go, then."

"Your Majesty, I would not have troubled you, but there seems to be a problem with Lord Delgadas." Bosenia clasped his hands behind his back as they descended the path toward the palace.

Nissim frowned. Adagio and Delgadas had always been at war, with Adagio's perspective leaning towards the religious teachings of *Ilyo Na'ada* and Delgadas taking a more practical and political approach. Exhaustion settled over this shoulders at the very thought of acting as their mediator yet again. "What is it now?"

"Adagio wished to speak with you in private, Your Majesty. He would not divulge what it was about, just that it was urgent he see you as soon as possible."

Nissim entered the courtroom, searching the dimly lit room for Adagio. His friend turned and bowed when he heard the king enter. Nissim joined him near the dais, greeting him with the tiny bit of enthusiasm he could muster. "How are you, my friend? Bosenia said you had something urgent to discuss with me?"

"I am afraid so, Your Majesty. It concerns one of your advisors. If we may, I would not discuss it here where we might be overheard." Adagio motioned toward the gardens outside the courtroom.

"Very well," Nissim raised a brow. It was not normal for Adagio to be so secretive. "This must be grave indeed."

"There is much at stake, Your Majesty." They walked out to the garden side by side, wrapping their *titzake lumpay* mantles about themselves to ward off the chill. Wispy clouds of fog were settling on the palace grounds, the mist carrying icy droplets that clung to their clothing. "I have just learned that Lord Delgadas took a detour on his way back from Saardonae."

Nissim shrugged. "I suppose he stopped at his country estate to check on things. There is nothing so suspicious about that."

"No, Your Majesty. He stopped on the High Road, leaving the entourage behind for two days and a night while he rode off into the forest. I believe that he may have met someone, perhaps a conspirator, and then came back with a story about being lost in the woods."

"And you do not believe his story?"

"Your Majesty, I have not told anyone of this, but I have been having strange dreams for the last few months. A few days before we had the visit from the boy who claimed to be from the Other World, I saw him in that dream. I believe it could have been a warning from *Ilyo Na'ada*."

Nissim frowned. "Do you claim to be a seer now?" If Adagio had seen a warning in a dream, why had he not relayed this to him sooner?

"No. But we all know that He reveals things to simple people at times."

"Very well. Tell on, my friend." Nissim motioned to a path leading away from the palace to ensure their conversation was kept private. A gentle rain fell, chilling rather than refreshing.

"I was in the woods and felt like I was being hunted, by what or whom—I did not know. Suddenly, I heard a boy crying, and I stopped. I saw his face very clearly and heard a voice say, *"When you see this boy, the destruction of Luminia is at hand."* Adagio paused for a moment. "Then I saw a cloaked figure emerge from the woods and stand before the boy. It was Lord Delgadas. His eyes held such hate, and I knew he would try to kill the boy if I did nothing. But then, I woke up."

131

"And you think Shos-hua has something to do with the destruction of our land?"

"No, Your Majesty. I believe he is only a sign that it is nigh. I think Lord Delgadas may have more to do with the forewarned destruction than anyone." Adagio paused, hesitating as he formed his next words. "I do not know to what extent, but the fate of Luminia may rest on our quick action. You yourself have voiced concerns about the amount of trust you should a lot to him."

Nissim halted on the path before a copse of weeping willows. "It is true that I have had my reservations about keeping Lord Delgadas in my court. But do you really think him capable of treason?" Nissim shook his head. "He was one of my father's most trusted advisors. What exactly do you think he plans to do, Adagio? And how does Shos-hua play into it?"

"I do not know, Your Majesty. I think it wise to check into his affairs, see if there is anything suspicious. What reason would he have to go off into a part of the woods so close to Tzotoeh? Unaccompanied. The man hates nature, and his servants reported that he was gone for two days. All I ask is that we find out if there is anything for us to be concerned about."

Nissim thought for a moment. "Yes, you are right. I will have my steward look into his financial affairs, and I will question those who went with him to Saardonae."

Adagio let out a sigh of relief. "Thank you, Your Majesty. I am willing to help in any way you see fit."

"You know that you will have to bring a formal annunciation of guilt against him, Adagio? He deserves to know why you are questioning his movements and financial affairs."

"Yes, Sire. I will write up the official documents this evening. I suggest we search his quarters here and at his country estate, for evidence of his betrayal."

Nissim nodded once and motioned for them to return up the hill to the palace. "I will send the palace guards to detain him under house arrest immediately."

He sighed and stood motionless, staring off into the void as his mind swirled with every possible explanation of what this new and frightening revelation could mean. He had never particularly liked Lord Delgadas, but he had never pegged him for a traitor.

Nissim found he could not sit still once he returned to his study and continue to mull over the many correspondence he had to get through. Since the queen's death, missives from their allies had been streaming in from all corners, and with the funeral procession due to take place on the eve of the coming day, there was much that was plaguing his mind. However, he could think of none of the preparations that needed to be seen to. His only thought was of his newborn son, only eleven days old, and his in-laws newly arrived from Saardonae.

He found his mother-in-law sitting with Shoram, cradling him tenderly as she would have done with Lutep-Tzia all those years ago. "Mother," he said, announcing his presence. The serving maid who had been found as a temporary wet nurse looked up and bowed low to the floor when she saw him.

Nissim bid her rise and asked to be given some privacy. She quickly left the nursery and closed the door behind her. "How is he?" Nissim asked, voice cracking with emotion.

Lady Sounprinetz rose gracefully with the infant and gave a weak smile. "He bears his mother's likeness, and he barely utters a sound, save to coo and gurgle happily in his sleep."

Nissim brushed a finger over Shoram's soft cheek. "He does not know the pain of losing her." He coveted Shoram's innocence. Then again, he did not. Shoram would never know his mother's smile or laugh, or the way she screwed up her nose when she was cross about something.

Lady Sounprinetz nodded, giving a heavy sigh. She transferred Shoram to his waiting arms. "No matter how many children I have lost, it never gets any easier." She sat down again and stared listlessly out the window. "Lutep-Tzia was special, indeed."

"Are not all children precious?" Nissim asked.

"Of course. However, I cannot say I had the same closeness with each of my children." She gave another weak smile. "I am a mother to thirteen, and I love them each equally. However, there was a kinship I shared with Lutep-Tzia—" Her voice broke. "Well, you knew how easy it was to love her."

"Yes, I do," he agreed. Shoram shifted in his arms, and Nissim bounced gently to help him settle. "Where is Lord Chukze?"

"My husband is at prayer," she replied.

Nissim was not surprised. The stone sarcophagus that now housed Lutep-Tzia's body was at the base of the mountain temple, and would be interred in the heart of the mountain tomorrow. Nissim had been spending much of his time there as well.

Thunder rolled overhead, reminding him of the near constant downpour they had endured since her passing. It was customary for the Musicians not to play for three days following a royal death. In his grief, he had ordered it be extended until the funeral procession.

"I will go to him," Nissim said. He handed Shoram back to his grandmother's waiting arms.

"I know that my husband has not spoken to you since our arrival," Lady Sounprinetz turned slightly so she could see him. "He is grieving, Nissim. But do not think he blames you for what happened."

Nissim bit back his reply. *He certainly made it feel as if he blamed me.* He simply nodded once, then left the room. His footsteps fell like stones to the bottom of a pond, he barely heard them echo through the corridors, deadened to the sound of anything else but the rain. It came down in sheets on either side of the covered corridors, the cool spray sending shivers up his spine.

When he reached the other end of the palace, he strode out into the deluge, not caring that he would be soaked in a matter of seconds. He made his way on the steep stone steps that had been carved into the pinnacle mountain, then stood at a distance, watching his father-in-law's still form.

Lord Chukze knelt in front of the stone sarcophagus that would be moved into the permanent resting place on tomorrow's eve. Nissim approached, angry tears mixing with the rain streaming down his face.

"Lord Chukze!" he called over the din of the rain hitting the stone roof where his wife's body lay. His father-in-law barely turned, refusing to say a word.

Nissim knelt beside him, past caring what Lord Chukze would do. "I know how you must hate me," he said. "I hate myself—" he broke. "I should have stopped trying to have a child. I should have insisted she not be put through that again."

His father-in-law's head snapped up, then his face softened. "There was naught you could have done," he said. "My daughter wanted nothing more than to be a good wife to you, and a mother to your children."

Nissim blinked, anger rising up again. "Then why do you refuse to speak to me? Why do you shut me out!" he bellowed over another clap of thunder. "You should blame me! It is my fault that she is dead."

Lord Chukze rose slowly, bracing himself on the stone coffin that encased his daughter. "*I* blame myself! I should have been here. Her mother and I both should have been here to say goodbye."

Nissim blinked. "No one could have known," he said. "I should have demanded they take the baby somehow," Nissim replied. "I have heard of cases where the mother and babe have survived if it is done that way."

"We cannot change what has been. We can only prepare for what will be," Lord Chukze said. "You must lead your country as Lutep-Tzia would have wanted, and prepare young Shoram for his reign."

Nissim hung his head, feeling like all the life had drained out of him, just as he had watched the life drain from his wife's eyes. "How can I? How can I when all I feel is anger that she is gone? That *Ilyo Na'ada* has taken her from me?" He raged more at the unseen power that he had devoted his life to, rather than his wife's father. He had not dared to voice that anger until now. "I gave Him everything, and he took the one person that was most precious to me."

He clenched his fists, fighting against the voices that told him to turn his back on *Ilyo Na'ada* for good.

"I know," Lord Chukze said. He offered nothing more, no words of fruitless comfort or needless explanations. "I know," he said again, and placed his hand on Nissim's shoulder. He then slowly drew him in and hugged him, weeping with him as the rain continued to pour down around them.

CHAPTER 19

DOSANYATA

"Kyin, wake up!"

Dosanyata shook her husband awake as a shadow passed their window. It had been impossible to hear anything with the onslaught of rain over the last eleven days, as the rain had beaten upon the rushes covering their roof. She only hoped the rain would not have rotted the entire roof. "Someone is without," she whispered.

Kyin stirred. "Have they come?" he breathed.

Dosanyata held her breath, as someone stopped before the door of the mud brick home. Heart pounding in her chest, she fumbled with the thin blanket and finally was able to disentangle herself. She went and picked up their one-year-old son, cradling him close to her bosom. A troubled frown crossed his little brow, before he fell back into peaceful slumber snuggled against her chest. "How could they have found us?" she whispered, voice quaking.

"I do not know," Kyin said solemnly. He got out of bed and went to stand before the archway that led from their tiny bedroom into the main living area.

"Kyin, no!"

"Stay here," he commanded. He met her gaze, hopefully for what would not be the last time. He then closed the threadbare curtain that separated their one room from the rest of the tiny abode.

A knock sounded at the door, but it was not as angry or persistent as she would have imagined the soldiers would be.

She could see through the many holes in the curtain that separated their one bedroom from the main living area as her husband made his way to the door.

There is no way they've discovered his disguise. Ilyo Na'ada, please...

Her husband opened the door and stood back, no doubt a little shocked at the small royal entourage that stood outside their humble abode. Kyin immediately took a knee, placing a hand over his heart. "My lord, what an honor."

A regal-looking man bowed his head and entered at Kyin's invitation. "Forgive our early morning intrusion, Kyin, is it?"

"Yes, Sire."

"Please, rise," the man beckoned. He looked about the room, as if to let his eyes adjust to the darkness. "Where is your wife?"

Kyin stood and looked over his shoulder at the curtain. "She has not yet risen, my lord. Is something amiss?"

"Not at all. I am sorry to have upset your home so early," the man went on. Dosanyata snuck over to the doorway, careful to stay hidden. She strained to listen.

"Not at all, Lord Adagio. I am at your disposal," Kyin said. No one would have been able to discern how nervous he was except for her. It was not for himself, but for her and their son.

"I have been placed on a special mission, Kyin. One of our palace contacts, Posentut, has suggested you and your wife might be willing to come and serve at the palace?" He cleared his throat. "As I am sure you are aware, the prince is only a few days old, and while we have been able to secure him a temporary nurse, the king has asked me to find a more suitable woman to act as a wet nurse, until the child may be weaned. I have come to inquire after you and your wife, at Posen-tut's urging, if you might be convinced to come and serve our young prince for the next few years?"

Kyin said nothing for a moment. "Well, that is a very great honor indeed. But I shall have to confer with my wife."

"Of course. Take all the time you need," Lord Adagio said graciously. "Shall we wait outside?"

"No, please be seated. I shall awaken her at once."

A moment later, Kyin burst through the curtain, and she reached out to touch his arm. He jumped. "Dosanyata! Did you hear?"

"It is difficult *not* to hear," she said. Her heart thundered in her ears. She drew him away from the curtained doorway and lowered her voice, their faces mere fractions apart. "Are you mad? You want to go to the very place they would be sure to discover your true identity?"

Kyin shook his head. "Do you not see? This is our perfect oppor-tunity, Dos. We would be hiding right under their noses, under the protection of the king himself. There is no reason they would ever find us, cloistered away in the private, royal nursery." He cast a wary glance over his shoulder. "If we make ourselves invaluable, the king may even be convinced to give us a permanent place there."

"As what? There is no chance of there being a need for a wet nurse after the prince is weaned. Unless the king marries again."

Kyin hung his head. "Perhaps I could put my extensive learning to some use at the palace?" he suggested. "Regardless, this is our chance to give Valian a better life, the life he would have inherited had our family not—" his voice dropped off, like the side of a moun-tain crumbling after years of erosion from the elements. Likewise, his family's esteemed position had eroded over the last decades, sending them into hunted obscurity. She looked down at their son cradled between them, sleeping peacefully. It would be a relief to not be on guard every moment of every day, wondering if today would be the day her beloved Kyin was caught and never returned.

She deftly nodded. "Very well then," she let out a shaky breath. "For Valian." She cuddled her son closer to her breast. Kyin helped her wrap a shawl around her shoulders, and they walked out to the main room together.

Lord Adagio rose when she entered, giving a slight bow. The other two in his company did the same. "Dosanyata?" he questioned.

She nodded. "I am at your disposal, my lord."

"You come very highly recommended. Well, what have you decided?"

"We accept, my lord," Kyin answered, wrapping a protective arm around her shoulders. There was no going back on their decision now.

"Excellent," Lord Adagio beamed. "Well, I will allow you two to pack your things. I will leave my two attendants behind to help you love your things to the royal nursery apartments. I must go now, so I can prepare my family to play for the sunrise."

They both let out a relieved sigh. "The king is going to allow it?" she blurted.

"Yes. Today ends our mourning," he answered, but unspeakable sadness filled his eyes.

"I think we will all grieve for the queen's passing for many years to come, my lord," Kyin offered. And it was true. However, he had been reckless to reveal his depth of feeling. Hopefully, Lord Adagio would not suspect that Kyin had any connection to the royal family by his remark.

Lord Adagio's face softened. "Indeed, we will." He exited the house, and the attendants stood aside to await their orders.

Dosanyata and Kyin stood frozen for a moment, looking at each other. Their lives had just taken a drastic turn, and it had not been for the worse as they had always assumed it would. "Well, I suppose we should make haste, my love. We do not want to keep these good people waiting any longer than is necessary."

"May we assist with any of your furniture while you start packing your clothing and the like?" one of them asked.

"We will leave the furniture," Kyin said. "Will you start closing the shutters and securing the rest of the house?"

He smothered the fire with water from a small clay pot, then hurried Dosanyata into the bedroom. They packed quickly. There really was nothing much of value or use. They had fled their mountain home with little more than the clothes on their backs.

Kyin dressed quickly and then took the baby so she could don her nicest dress, one of only two that she owned. "The chest," he ordered, and she went to retrieve it from the small hiding place Kyin had built into the walls of their home. One would not have been the least bit suspect that there was a small alcove cut into the wall, big enough for the ornately carved wooden chest that had belonged to his great-grandmother, handed down through the generations. Inside were treasures more priceless than any amount of rubies or gold that they could have acquired. He ran his fingers over the golden crest that held the key mechanism, tracing the symbol of a dove gripping a scroll with its feet. He looked up at her. "Not a word of this to anyone."

"I understand," she said. "We will have to secure a new hiding place, once we get to the palace."

"I will find one. Or I'll *make* one. At least that is one good thing about working as a builder for the last few years." Kyin stood and placed the chest in the bottom of a sackcloth bag. Dosanyata piled their clothes and other belongings on top of it and around it. No one would be any the wiser of their secret treasure.

Kyin picked up the cradle in the far corner of the room, and they were ready to depart.

The attendant motioned for Kyin to give him the cradle, and the other reached for the sackcloth bag. Kyin quickly stepped in. "I can carry it, thank you," he snapped. He cleared his throat and softened. "That is, my wife is very particular about who touches our son's things. You understand."

"Of course," the attendant said and backed away.

There was little else of value that they would need at the palace.

They followed their escorts to the top of the palace mount as the musicians began to play for the sunrise. Dosanyata's spirits lifted as the music chased the early morning shadows away, seemingly pulling back the dark grey storm clouds that had covered the land for the last twelve days. Finally, the gloom would be gone, and they could move forward with hope—in more ways than one. At last, they would be safe. She had to believe it would be so.

When they arrived, they were taken immediately through the winding corridors, open to the outside world through ornately carved archways that let in the sunshine that was starting to pour over the royal city. Finally, the rains would end, and the country would enjoy the light it had been denied for what seemed like an eternity.

One of the attendants slowed as they entered the inner part of the palace, the more cloistered and private part where the royal family was housed. Dosanyata had not seen such lavish surroundings in many years, since she and Kyin had been forced to flee for their lives...

She would not think of that now, not when their fortunes were suddenly changing for the better. Dosanyata caught her breath as they entered the nursery. The whole of their mud brick home could have fit inside it, and that was just the main gathering room. There was a low, carved table where they would take their meals. There was another low table near the shelves that lined the walls, all of them filled with accordioned books and rolled scrolls. Writing instruments with brightly colored inks sat on one of the higher shelves, along with empty bark pieces that could later be bound into books, or simply hung around the room. No doubt, the prince would enjoy drawing pictures as he grew older.

In one corner were several plush cushions, surrounded by carved wooden toys of animals, boats, miniature houses, and trees. Great care had been taken to prepare for the princes' arrival.

There were several rooms adjoining the main part of the nursery. Dosanyata's heart sank when a pitiful cry sounded from one of them.

Soon, a young girl, no older than Dosanyata had been on her wedding day, appeared. She carried a tiny bundle in her arms. She bowed her head and handed the tiny bundle into Dosanyata's arms. "I am told you have come to take over the prince's care?" she asked.

"I have," Dosanyata said. She suddenly caught the solemnity of the moment as she moved the warm swaddling away from the prince's face so she could look at him. He seemed utterly peaceful as he slept, his thumb stuck between his lips.

"He nursed about an hour ago. He has been waking every two hours to eat, so you should have a little time before he is ready to nurse again." The girl folded her hands in front of her and bowed low. "I will return to my duties in the kitchen now. Please let me know if you need anything as you settle into your life here."

Dosanyata reached out to the girl. It would be difficult to leave the baby, as she knew what a strong bond a mother made with a suckling babe, even a stand-in mother. "You will come and see him from time to time, won't you?" she offered.

Her face brightened. "If the king would allow it, I would gladly come and see the child." Her face clouded with sadness again. "Good day," she said quickly and hurried from the room, as if it were on fire.

One of the attendants shook his head and joined them. Kyin placed a protective arm around her, even as Valian started to wake from his slumber. "Who was she?"

"One of the kitchen maids. She was summoned soon after the queen gave birth and passed away."

"Why was the girl not promoted to royal nurse?" Dosanyata asked.

"She refused. She agreed she would fulfill the need until a more suitable nurse could be found." He sighed. "She lost her child about a month ago. Apparently, her husband wants to try for another child as soon as possible."

Dosanyata knew perfectly well what had happened. The girl would not be able to conceive if she were nursing someone else's child. Dosanyata's mood darkened, her heart going out to the young woman. Loosing a child was beyond imagination. She looked down at the prince. She could not imagine never knowing her mother, either. "I will care for him to the best of my ability."

The other attendant stepped forward and smiled at her. "You come very highly recommended to us, Dosanyata. As do you, Kyin. Posentut tells you have had some formal learning?"

Kyin's Adam's apple bobbed as he swallowed. "A little," he said. "Working in the laborers' quarters does not give one much free time for learning," he said. It was not a total lie. He had not been able to spend the time on his books and figures as he had in the past. Hopefully, that was about to change.

"Speaking of work, I should be off," Kyin said. "Is there a side entrance that I should come to to get in and out of the palace, instead of having to wait at the main gates every day?" he asked.

"Oh, you will not be working in the laborers quarters anymore. No, you will stay here with your wife," one of the attendants explained. "I am sure there is something more useful you can do here at the palace, especially if you are able to read and write?"

"Yes, I can read and write," he agreed.

Dosanyata's heart soared. It was a dream come true. And inside the walls of the palace, they would be truly safe. "He can also cypher and has some training in astronomy, sir. My husband is too modest to say such things."

Kyin's hand wrapped around her arm, tightening in a warning grip. She closed her mouth and stood back. "I am only a hobbyist when it comes to such things. see there are many books available here in the nursery. May I avail myself of them?"

"Of course," the attendant nodded. "When you are settled, I will show you the main library, below the palace. In the meantime, I will speak to Lord Adagio and His Majesty of your skills." He turned to his fellow attendant. "Perhaps he would do well as a tutor?"

Kyin tried to make his face a mask of indifference, but she knew he would jump at such a chance if it were offered. "I would be honored to help in any capacity I am needed."

"Very well. Please send your servant boy for us if you are in need of anything. He has been stationed right outside the door." The attendants bowed, then left them to settle into their new home.

Dosanyata turned to Kyin, still cradling the prince. "How did this happen?" she asked. In the space of a few hours, they had been living in squalor and then moved to one of the highest stations in the country. "Is it a dream?"

"It must be." Kyin set Valian down so he could toddle about the room, now fully awake and curious about his new surroundings. He wrapped her in a hug, the prince shielded between them. "One where we no longer have to feel as if we're being hunted."

"We *were* being hunted," Dosanyata recalled. She shuddered to think what would have happened if they had been found. It would have only been a matter of time. Now, they would be safe inside these walls. Kyin let go of her as the baby began to fuss. Dosanyata went to sit down on one of the cushions and begin the process of feeding the baby. Hopefully, it would not take too long for the prince to get used to her.

Kyin retrieved the sackcloth bag and removed the clothing and little toys they had brought along for Valian. He pulled out the chest and tucked it under his arm. "I think somewhere on the shelf will be the perfect place to construct a little hiding place." He took off some of the accordion books from one section of the shelf, set them aside, and slid the chest to the very back. "They must be kept safe at all costs," he said. He then replaced the bark books, covering the chest as best he could for the time being.

Her husband joined her on the cushion, then reached out to Valian as he crawled over to them. He took Valian up on his lap, who looked curiously over at her as the baby finally latched and began to nurse. "Baba," Valian said.

"Yes, baby," Dosanyata smiled. "It will be good for Valian to have someone close to his age to play with when they get older."

"Hopefully, we can make ourselves useful here and will never have to return to the *chilput*," Kyin said. "I will do whatever I must to make sure of it." He lifted a chain out from under his tunic, revealing the worn bronze key. Valian wrapped his chubby little hand around the key and tried to stuff it in his mouth. Kyin gently pried his fingers from the key and replaced it under his clothes. "One day, it will be your sacred duty to keep the chest safe, my boy."

CHAPTER 20

DELGADAS

Delgadas had just seated himself at the low table for his evening meal when the pounding sounded at his door. He looked up at the serving girls standing around the room as he reclined at the low table, annoyed by the intrusion. The funeral procession for the queen had taken up most of his day, with all of Luminia turning out to see her off to the great Beyond. He had been looking forward to getting off his feet and having a leisurely meal where he could lose himself in the undulations of the dancing girls who would soon appear.

"What is this?!" he bellowed, motioning for one of his servants to go and open the door. But before the serving girl could do his bidding, the doors were flung open, and the girl uttered a surprised cry. Lord Delgadas stood with some difficulty, thanks to his girth. Four sinister looking palace guards stepped into the arched doorway. Delgadas stammered out a string of incoherent curses. "What is the meaning of this?!"

"Lord Delgadas, you are being placed under house arrest." The captain of the guard replied, eyeing him warily.

"You must be out of your senses, Captain Shundol. I am one of the king's most trusted advisors—!" He shrieked, but the man cut him off.

"Not anymore, it would seem." With the flick of his wrist, Captain Shundol ordered his men to restrain him. "The king has commanded we confiscate your documents and personal records. You may want to cooperate. It will go better for you."

Delgadas was taken into the study. He tried to jerk free, but the young soldiers were no match for his rotund frame which was sorely unused to physical activity. They entered the study and the other two soldiers began ransacking the place, gathering his documents and personal belongings. Shundol followed Lord Delgadas' eyes as they darted to the desk. "There, in the desk. Be sure to inspect it thoroughly."

"This is an outrage! I demand to know what charges have been brought against me!" Delgadas screeched.

Adagio stepped out of the shadowy hallway and approached him. "Certainly, Lord Delgadas. Upon your return from Saardonae, I was told you stopped for two days at the road near the Tzotoen border. Would you care to tell me why?"

Delgadas sneered. "I do not answer to you, Adagio," he spat. One of the soldiers raised his hand to strike Delgadas, and he recoiled.

Adagio stayed the soldier's hand as he came closer, standing face-to-face with Delgadas. "You do now. Either you can cooperate, as Captain Shundol suggested, or you can go before the king and plead for your life."

Delgadas's mouth opened wide. He should have put his plan in motion sooner and gotten out of Lunthá while he had the chance. He had calculated on more time, with the king being absent for his mourning period. Now, he could see the foolishness of his decision. "Where are these charges?"

Adagio held up the official papers, unrolling the parchment. Delgadas noticed the documents bore the king's seal. His heart sank. He read the accusations against him, including suspicion of conspiracy to regicide, perjury, and mishandling of government funds. Delgadas gave a derisive laugh. "These will never hold up in our courts. Where is your proof?"

Adagio lowered the documents and rolled them up. "That is precisely what we are looking for."

Delgadas watched silently as the soldier broke his desk apart, looking for secret compartments. Soon, they had all his documents and personal records in piles and began taking them out. Thankfully, he had been smart enough to burn his correspondence with King Nargod, knowing it was too risky to keep such things on hand. They would find nothing but a tidy itemization of his government funds. What he had to worry about was being held at his country estate.

"Keep him here until I say otherwise," Adagio instructed. Adagio brushed past Delgadas, accompanied by Captain Shundol and the other soldier.

"Am I to be held up like this for the remainder of my house arrest?" Delgadas asked in a superior tone. The soldiers exchanged glances before they released his arms. He brushed the sleeves of his tunic off as if they had left a layer of filth behind from their hands. Delgadas walked back to the dining area in the open courtyard. The soldiers followed closely behind him, watching his every move.

Delgadas turned, eyeing them as if they were nothing but lowly beggars, more of an annoyance than anything to be genuinely concerned about. "May I sit down?" he asked, waving his hand toward his low table and the meal that had been set out before him before they had barged into his house. "I'm sure it is all cold now, thanks to you."

They nodded curtly and remained standing with their spears at the ready. Delgadas moved his robes with a flourish and sat down, digging into the meal despite his momentary loss of appetite. He did not want the soldiers to report to Adagio that he seemed too nervous to eat. Besides, he had to keep up his strength. He had to find a way to escape the royal city. It would only be a matter of time before they discovered his actual set of ledgers and pieced together his movements between Lunthá and Tzotoeh.

With dinner finished, he moved to the balcony. The soldiers were immediately on his heels. "Where do you think you are going?" one sneered.

"Am I now to be banished from taking some fresh air?" he asked with a superior tone.

They looked at each other and nodded. "I suppose not," one said and they backed away. His rooms were situated several stories above the ground, cutting off that means of escape. When Delgadas was sure he was alone, he pulled a note from his billowing sleeves and placed it in one of the potted plants along the railing. He then tore a length of his red mourning clothes at the hem and stuck it under the pot, letting it hang over the rail. He had in his employ a little street urchin skilled at scaling roofs. Delgadas had been due to meet him outside the city that evening to deliver a note the boy would take to Tzotoeh. When Delgadas did not appear at the rendezvous, hopefully, the wretch would know to come to his apartments.

"Alright, that is enough fresh air!" one of the guards called.

"Very well, I am coming." Delgadas turned, praying the boy found the note before it was too late.

CHAPTER 21

KING NISSIM

K ing Nissim dug the heels of his hands into his eyes and rubbed. He had been studying Delgadas' documents and financial ledgers for what seemed like days rather than a few hours. The candle flickered as a breeze blew in from the sea. Standing, he went to the balcony and took a deep breath. Lutep-Tzia would have drawn him away from his work, telling him to clear his mind and seek a different point of view.

The wind whipped his hair around in a sudden gust, and he smiled. Lutep-Tzia had often tousled his hair when she teased him. His arms ached to hold her, to hear her voice again. She had not been a member of the esteemed Musician families, but she had a sing-song way about her speech. At least, it had always calmed him and allayed his fears. Nothing seemed to keep him from the growing unease building in his chest now. Nissim had never been one to give in to anxiety. But he was finding it harder to keep his mind from distracting rumors of war and intrigue, coups and whispered secrets circulating the palace.

A knock sounded at the door, and he did his best not to shout at whoever it was to go away. Just once, he wanted to be left alone in his pain! He was the king and did not get the luxury of wallowing in his grief. He let out a sigh, reluctant to leave the balcony.

"Come!" he called sharply. Sitting down again at his desk, he tried to make a neat pile of all the documents he had gone through. "Ah, Adagio. I am glad it is you."

He rose, hopeful that Adagio would have some information for him so they could put this whole mess behind them. However, one look at his face told him that all was not well. "What is it, Adagio?"

"The soldiers you dispatched a few days ago have just returned from Delgadas' estate." He carried a small leather-bound ledger under his arm. "They found this hidden in a secret compartment in the wall of his study." Adagio handed over the volume, and Nissim opened it at the desk, flipping through its pages.

"He has been pilfering money from the royal treasury and paying bribes to his fellow nobles. He has also been accepting bribes—favoring other lords in court rather than seeking out the truth," Adagio explained.

Delgadas had kept meticulous records, noting the nobles' names and the amounts they had paid him or that he had paid them to cover up injustice, as well as secrets he had learned about each one. It was ghastly. There were also detailed notations of what the money had been for. Nissim could only guess he had kept these records for blackmailing purposes. "This goes back to my father and grandfather's reigns," Nissim murmured. He could hardly believe what he was seeing. Was his whole high council infected with Delgadas' treachery? The notations went on and on, making Nissim's head swim.

Nissim closed the ledger with a loud thud. "I have seen enough. Have Delgadas brought to the royal court." Nissim's face was set in a grim line, his heart thudding dully with the betrayal of his nobles. This was enough to send Delgadas to the *slitsike* to have his head bashed in. Before that kind of justice could be enacted he would first, have to root out the rest of the corruption in his court.

Nissim made his way to the courtroom carrying the damning

evidence with him. He had been a fool to keep Delgadas around for as long as he had. How long had he been undermining the government, looking the other way as his nobles lined their own pockets instead of fighting for justice?

Nissim sat down on the royal throne, wearing the crown of judgment on his head with its bright red ruby in the center. He had only ever worn it one other time, and he shivered to remember when he had been forced to dispatch a band of Tzotoen-born pirates raiding the shores of Saardonae and Luminia. Delgadas' treachery was even worse, for he had betrayed his own countrymen.

A half-hour later, the great doors opened with a loud creak. The soldiers pushed Delgadas roughly ahead of them as they entered. Delgadas looked as if he had not gotten a wink of sleep. It was just as well, for he should face much worse even if he did not admit his sins.

Delgadas huffed when he saw Nissim sitting on his throne, doing a poor job of disguising his disdain. "Your Majesty, will you allow them to treat me thus?" Delgadas asked, glaring at his guards.

"They are under my orders, Delgadas." Nissim did his best to keep his voice even, despite the rage building inside him. He held up the ledger.

All the color drained from Delgadas' face. "Where did you find that?!" he railed. "You have no right—"

Nissim stood from the throne, and Delgadas immediately went quiet. "I have every right! You have been stealing from the treasury, turning a blind eye as my nobles corrupt the law. You are a disgrace to the high council and to Luminia."

Delgadas balked. Nissim had never spoken to him that way, and for a moment, he was speechless. "I am being framed, Your Majesty. Anyone could have planted that at my estate—"

"How did you know it was found at your estate?" Nissim asked. He had divulged no such information. Delgadas realized his mistake too late. Nissim continued before he had a chance to make excuses. "I find you guilty of treason, Delgadas. You are this day stripped of your title and lands. Take him away." He waved his hand and turned his back on Delgadas, returning to sit on his throne.

As the soldiers took his arms and started to drag him out, Delgadas finally found his voice. He shook off their hands and hurried toward the dais. He offered a measly plea. "Your Majesty, think carefully. I have been nothing but loyal to you and your family for my entire life. It would be a difficult thing to replace me."

Nissim turned around slowly, not having had a chance to sit. "Loyal? I wonder, Delgadas, perhaps it was you all along who was sowing discord during my father's reign." He paused momentarily, seeing clearly for the first time. "Come to think of it, I am not entirely certain that you are not wholly to blame for my father's untimely death."

Delgadas stuttered, looking around the courtroom, first at Adagio, then at the other soldiers. "That is preposterous!" Delgadas' face turned even paler, if that was possible. Nissim frowned, coming down from the dais and striding towards Delgadas.

"Look me in the eye and tell me that you had nothing to do with it."

Fear flickered through Delgadas' gaze before he could mask it. Nissim seethed with fury. "Get him out of my sight!" he bellowed. Delgadas was dragged towards the doors. "On the morrow, you will face your just reward at the *slitsike*."

"You will regret this, Nissim!" Delgadas's voice rang out as he was taken from the courtroom to the dungeons below the palace where he would await his execution.

Something inside Nissim broke. The grief he had wrestled with after his father's death all came back to the surface, and now, Lutep-Tzia was not there to comfort him. After several seconds of standing still at the bottom step of the dais, Nissim called for his friend to approach. "Adagio." His friend was at his side in an instant. "Take as many soldiers as are needed and round up the lords and nobles whose names are written in this book. I want them all brought in for questioning."

Adagio nodded, bowing at the waist with his hand on his heart as he backed out of the courtroom. "Your wish is my command, Sire."

DELGADAS LOOKED over his shoulder as he was hauled away, watching Adagio leave the courtroom. Hatred boiled up inside him, overflowing into a snarl. He would show Adagio what it cost to go head-to-head with him. If he wanted to test his strength and position in the royal court, then so be it. He knew he still had nobles loyal to him, who would back his claim as king rather than siding with King Nissim. The foolish man! He would find out soon enough what his arrogance would mean for his beloved Luminia.

The soldier on his right shoved him without mercy as they walked down the steep stone steps, winding down and down toward the bowels of the island city. He was taken through the impenetrable iron doors, which offered no escape. Once he was encased in this awful place, there would be little hope of ever seeing the outside world again. Delgadas' heart began to beat irregularly with dread. When he did see the sky again, it would only be for a short time before he was forced to kneel in front of the *slitsike* stone. He would rest his head in the center of the hollowed stone for only a moment before the heavy tapered hammer came down and ended his life. Fear slithered through his limbs, making it difficult to remain upright.

He was shoved once more into a small cell encased by stones, carved to fit so perfectly with one another that not even a hair could be placed between them, no mortar needed. The soldier closed the iron doors with a loud clang of finality, sneered as the locks were bolted, and walked away. Delgadas wrapped his cloak more tightly around his shoulders to ward off the chill.

Delgadas lived in constant terror for the next few days. Contrary to the king's word, the soldiers had not come to collect him for his execution. With every day that passed, his hope grew that his errand boy had found his note, gone to King Nargod, and would return to break him free before Nissim was able to carry out his judgement.

Night passed much too quickly. The skies grew lighter to signal his end was upon him. The king had allowed the Musicians to play again to greet the sun. He could hear their cursed music floating down to him from the Musicians Terrace, mocking him. The cell to which Delgadas had been banished was rank with waste and mildew. Water constantly dripped from the ceiling above his head. Pools of stagnant water stood all over the cell, having gushed in through the one barred window set high in the wall.

He lay on the dirty pallet in the corner of the room, trying to get as far away from the window, and the music, as he could. "When King Nargod comes to lay siege to the city, Nissim will be sorry," Delgadas raved quietly. A water droplet interrupted his thoughts as it landed in the middle of his forehead. He jumped up from his pallet and was thrown into a rage. "Will this incessant dripping never stop?! Am I to be driven mad by this leaky cell?! I demand to be taken to the king!" Delgadas screamed. He began to bang and shake the iron door of his cell. But no one heard him. He was utterly alone. If only he could be given one more chance to speak his piece, he might convince the king to show him mercy.

When no one acknowledged his tantrum, he calmed down and returned to mulling over his misfortunes.

King Nissim had found records of all the money he had been stealing. However, the one blessing was that the alliance with King Nargod had not been found out. Fear again coiled in his stomach. It would only be a matter of time.

"He will not see me executed." Delgadas spoke aloud to himself, trying to rid his mind of the thought of dying before Nargod came to his aid. "What is taking him so long?" His voice echoed off the walls.

"Pst! My lord? Are you in there?" The familiar sound of his messenger boy's voice floated down to him from the alleyway.

"Finally! Tzedi, where have you been?" Delgadas scrambled to the window and stood on his tiptoes to reach the bars. He climbed up to the window on stones that jutted out of the wall and clung to the bars as if they were a lifeline.

"I returned as quickly as I could, my lord. I found your note in the flower pot."

"And? Did you deliver my note?" he snapped.

"Yes, but the king held me for the last day and a half."

"That stupid fool! Why?!"

"I do not know. They were celebrating some sort of festival to the Virgin Moons—"

"Never mind, never mind," Delgadas interrupted impatiently, "What news from the king?"

It was unfortunate his life hung on the decisions of one incompetent leader. King Nargod would rather lock himself away in his private chambers to drink wine and enjoy the company of his numerous concubines than attend to his nation.

"King Nargod says to be patient and sends this message," Tzedi handed a rolled piece of paper tied with a strip of leather through the thin slits between the bars. Delgadas quickly untied the knot and read,

Most Excellent Lord Delgadas,

My armies are not yet ready for a direct attack on Luminia. I will send a raiding party to escort you from the royal city. Futah will aid them. They will deliver you safely to me.

His Supreme Majesty,
*   King Nargod of Tzotoeh*

Delgadas crumpled the note in disgust and threw it in Tzedi's face. "Destroy this and tell me when the raiding party arrives. Time is short, and even if they arrive tonight, it may be too late." Delgadas did not take kindly to being delivered to King Nargod like a common slave. He did not belong to King Nargod any more than he belonged to King Nissim. However, it was better than having his head bashed in.

"I saw the square being made ready for executions on my way into the city—" Tzedi said. It was no secret to Delgadas that the boy disliked him, but he would remain loyal for fear of what Delgadas would do to him if he were ever betrayed.

"Yes, but you will not have the satisfaction of seeing me die. Of that you can be certain." Delgadas growled and hit the bars, making Tzedi jump back.

The boy came back but kept his distance lest Delgadas reach his hand through the bars and strangle him. "Be ready tonight at the turning of the second watch. They will come to break you free then."

"Why did you not tell me that in the first place, you little fool!!" Delgadas jumped up and tried to grab the boy by his shirt. It was a narrow miss, Delgadas's fingers brushing the boy's tunic. "Ahh!" Delgadas cried. "If I were not confined, I would ring your neck!"

"I am sorry, my lord." Tzedi feigned contrition, but Delgadas could see he was hiding a chuckle. He backed away a few inches more, and his smirk disappeared as Delgadas' face turned red with anger.

"Keep in mind that these bars will not always separate you from me. And I would remember your place if I were you. If I had not given you work, you would have been dead in some gutter by now after your parents abandoned you," Delgadas said ruthlessly. He knew Tzedi hated him all the more for reminding him of his past in Tzotoeh.

He was about to turn away when Delgadas yelled after him, "I am not finished with you! Go to the mansion and find the chest buried under the oak tree. Bring it with you when we meet outside the city gates at our usual place by the ancient tombs." Delgadas glared at him. "And do not even think about running out on me, because you know that I will find you no matter where you try to hide."

Tzedi's eyes filled with fear. The boy shook his head, as if to rid his mind of the image of the first and last man who had betrayed Delgadas. The traitor had been expertly dispatched in front of his servants, lest anyone get any more ideas of betrayal. No doubt the little wretch could still hear the traitor's agonized screams.

"I will not fail you, my lord," Tzedi said, his trembling voice.

"See that you do not." Delgadas let go of the bars of his cell and disappeared into the darkness.

That night, just minutes after the second watch's turn, the city was awakened by the shouts of alarm from the palace dungeon. Dozens of soldiers were sent out to search the streets. Every house was searched, but there was no trace to be found. Futah had made completely certain of that.

Delgadas watched the island city from the safety of the woods on the opposite shore, torches bobbing up and down as the soldiers searched for him in vain. "We must go," Futah whispered. The bear-like man towered over Delgadas, a satisfied grin on his face. He nodded. Nissim might have won this battle, but Delgadas would win the war.

CHAPTER 22

KING NISSIM

The Wildlands, on the border of Luminia and Tzotoeh
Year of the Serpent, 976

Nissim surveyed the village's skeletal remains, the hollowed-out house beams jutting like the rib cages of giant beasts. The ground smoldered with the after-effects of a raging fire that had destroyed the town. Smoke swirled around his steed's hooves, his bay coat smudged black with soot. This was the third village they had visited during their survey of the country, only to find it had already been laid waste. The raids had been scattered and random at first, but were growing steadily in frequency and cruelty. Still, they had been unable to pin down the attackers. They had suspected their savage neighbors to the north, Tzotoe– that lawless land of bandits. What he could not understand was why here, and why the intensified cruelty?

As in the rest of the towns, no survivors would be left to tell what happened. The remnants had been captured and taken to destinations unknown. Nissim was sure that Delgadas was behind these raids, as they had not started until after his escape from the royal city four years earlier. However, the more pressing question was, who was helping him?

"At this rate, there will be no one left on the borderlands." Nissim's general, Zalim, rode up beside him and looked out over the fuming ruins. "We must raise a counterattack, Your Majesty. Our food stores will not be able to take much more of this. With so many people fleeing to the safety of Lunthá, we will not have enough to feed everyone with the farms lying desolate."

Nissim knew all too well the state of the farms. At first, the attacks had come few and far between, allowing them to rally and continue with food production. Now, however, the attacks were growing more frequent, weeks—sometimes days—in between. "Perhaps we can persuade our farmers to clear some of the forest lands outside of Lunthá to start growing new crops." Until now, it had been difficult to persuade the people to spread out from the royal city. It would take a mountain of work to clear land, with the mammoth trees creating too much shade to allow enough sunlight to grow crops. Besides, the trees were regarded as sacred. How could he convince the farmers, let alone his nobles, to allow the trees to be taken down? Perhaps he could have the mammoth trees used for a good purpose? Just one of them would supply enough wood to fashion him an armada of new warships. And it would give his shipbuilders plenty of work.

Then there was the money to pay them all. Nissim's head began to pound with all the pressures of leading a country on the brink of ruin. What they needed was to find the raiders and bring them to heel.

"What is to stop the enemy from raiding the new farms, Sire?" General Zalim pointed out after a short pause. "We need to go on the offensive, Your Majesty, before all is lost."

Nissim nodded silently and glanced over at his old friend, Adagio. He had come along on this trip, insisting he needed to visit someone in one of the outlying communities. Adagio's shoulders hunched in defeat as he walked around the debris. Nissim could almost hear the terrified screams of the women and children as the wind whistled through the charred remains of a home.

"How are we to go on the offensive if we do not even know who the enemy is?"

General Zalim shifted in his saddle, worry lining his face. "I thought it was entirely obvious, Your Majesty. This is the work of Saardonae."

Nissim nearly fell off the horse. "*What?* No, it cannot be. They are our oldest ally. Do you forget so soon that my late wife was from Saardonae? Her father would never betray me."

"They are the closest country to this land, Sire. What reason would our other neighbors have to attack us? I admit that Tzotoeh is a barbaric land compared to ours, but I hardly think they would have the organization or the patience to carry out prolonged raids like this. King Nargod is not a patient man. Nor a wise one." Lord Lamik glared at him.

"Who else, then?" Nissim asked in frustration. "It is true we have not always been on friendly terms with the Asartians. They have always been jealous that *Ilyo Na'ada* gave us the gift and responsibility of music." Nissim pressed a finger to his temple, his head aching all the more.

"That leaves Ni'ich-slapak and Zuet'e, Your Majesty." Lord Lamik rode up beside the duo to interrupt. "Forgive me, Your Majesty, but I could not help but overhear. I will again state my disappointment that you did not follow my advice to build a wall around our borders. We are a prime target with so many neighbors, cut off as we are by the sea on our western shores."

"We have never had to fear invasion from these nations in the past. They all rely on us as the Keepers of Music. Without us, the rest of the world would collapse."

"Perhaps that is exactly what our enemies are after." Lord Lamik shook his head. "With Luminia weakened, it will invariably weaken our allies. Our enemies would be able to overrun us much easier."

Nissim let out an irritated sigh. "What do you suggest then, Lord Lamik?"

The aging lord cleared his throat. "I suggest we make an alliance with Detallma," he said.

Nissim had not been expecting that. Detallma was a powerful city with which they had long been on friendly terms, although they had never brokered an official alliance. The floating city-state was unequaled by any other in the world, the only one of its kind. Nissim had never had the pleasure of seeing Detallma in person. Still, his grandfather had told him stories of the warrior-king who had lashed ships together until they stretched as far as the eye could see. He had then built his gleaming city on top of it. His fleet was also second to none, making him a sought-after ally. The city could shapeshift at a moment's notice, splitting apart to allow their ships to float up rivers and inlets or even spread around a whole nation by sea and force surrender.

"What do I have to offer King Tzunam? Our fleet is not very impressive, not when compared to his. He is much richer than I and has the whole world at his fingertips." Nissim felt the weight of despair pressing down on his shoulders. Even in the early years of his reign, he had never felt so despondent or unprepared.

"King Tzunam has a daughter who has very recently come of age." Lord Lamik's words fell with the force of a mudslide, cutting off his air as if he were buried under rubble.

"Take another wife?" The very idea was preposterous to him. Nissim shifted in the saddle, shaking his head. "No."

"Yes, Your Majesty. It has been four years. Taking another wife would allow you to make a powerful alliance, and she could provide you with more sons in case—"

Nissim held up his hand, unwilling to listen to him anymore. "No! Shoram will be king."

Lord Lamik bit his tongue. "I am sorry, Your Majesty. I know that no woman could ever replace Queen Lutep-Tzia," he admitted grudgingly. "However, you cannot argue with the benefits of taking Princess Tamil as your new wife. A formal partnership through marriage would bring stability to Luminia."

Nissim nodded, doing his best to keep the unmanly tears at bay. "I will think on this. Now, I believe we should be heading to Hotun. Lord Adagio has someone he wants to see." He caught Adagio's eye and nodded toward the main road. They would not want to be caught in the open when night fell.

His friend mounted his horse and followed him, Lord Lamik, and General Zalim at a distance. Nissim worried for his friend. He had grown quiet over the last few years. Of course, Adagio had always been pensive, but this new silence unnerved him. Not to mention, Adagio had also lost a considerable amount of weight. He had been trim and muscled before, but his cheeks were now slightly sunken. Nissim pulled on the reins and allowed his general and Lord Lamik to advance.

"You need not wait for me, Your Majesty." Adagio said with an apologetic smile—a smile that did not reach his eyes.

"I am worried about you, my friend. You have not been yourself for a long time. What is troubling you?"

Adagio sighed. "There is much to trouble me these days. That is why I must go to Hotun to see the boy."

Nissim nodded. It would seem the decline of their nation and the boy's arrival went hand in hand. Luminia was falling apart around them, fraying slowly like the edges of a worn cloak. He felt powerless to stop it. Had *Ilyo Na'ada* abandoned them?

Adagio's brow furrowed as he spoke again. "I have spent many months in prayer, and still there seems to be no answer. I wonder if I have done something to elicit His silence."

Nissim shook his head. "It is unimaginable, Adagio. You are the most devout person I know."

"There is a difference between religiosity and genuine devotion, Your Majesty. I have been examining my heart, Sire, and I am disconcerted with what I see. We have enjoyed *Ilyo Na'ada's* blessing for many hundreds of years. Perhaps we have become complacent."

This gave Nissim pause. He had seen that complacency in the people at times. Some indulged in the good life they had been given, just as Delgadas had taken advantage of his wealth and position. There were others who struggled to provide the basest of necessities for their families.

However, there were many who still followed the old ways. "It is oney a difficult season, Adagio. I am confident we will find the attackers, and the people will soon focus their devotion wholly toward *Ilyo Na'ada* once more."

Adagio shook his head, and seemed angry with him. "Compromise is like a crack in a clay pot. It is unnoticeable at first. Eventually, when the freezing temperatures come, a little water in the gap will cause the entire vessel to shatter."

Nissim's heart began to race. "What do you suggest we do?"

Adagio took a steadying breath. "I cannot be sure, Sire. But I fear we will destroy ourselves from the inside out if things do not change."

"Are things really so bad? You always taught me that *Ilyo Na'ada* desires relationship with us, not just an empty ritual. I hope I have led the people well in that sentiment." Frustration boiled up inside his chest. "

"One cannot force a people to true devotion. It must come from the heart, or it was useless." Adagio rubbed his bearded jaw, as he often did when deep in thought. "The people grow restless. Callous, even. I have spent many months in prayer, wondering what can be done."

Nissim heaved a sigh, the weight of responsibility crushing him. "They want me to marry again," he said softly.

His friend did not seem the least surprised. "I know." Adagio hung his head. "It is not an easy decision to make, Your Majesty. Queen Lutep-Tzia was beloved by us all. No one could ever replace her in your heart. We know that well."

"And yet Lord Lamik is trying to do just that, it would seem."

"May I be so bold as to ask an impertinent question, Your Majesty?"

"Of course."

Adagio hesitated, his blue eyes brimming with compassion. "Do you believe Queen Lutep-Tzia would want you to be alone for the rest of your life? Or would she want you to have a partner?" Adagio let the words sink in before continuing. "The position you hold is a very lonely one. No one can understand that as well as you. A wife could help you bear the burden." Adagio sighed heavily. "I do not think Queen Lutep-Tzia would want you to be alone forever. She loved you, Sire. She would want you to be happy."

Tears sprang to Nissim's eyes. His friend was right, of course, no matter how much the thought hurt him. Lutep-Tzia had never been selfish. She would have told him to move on if she could have spoken from the Beyond. It would have broken her heart to see him like this.

"And marrying would bring us out of this complacency you speak of?" he asked coldly. Adagio's eyes sparked with hurt at his words. He knew his friend had not meant it that way, but it made his ire rise all the same. "I will think on it," he snapped as he spurred his horse forward to try to find some solitude.

ULTIMATELY, Nissim could think of no legitimate reason to refuse the alliance proposal. He had told them that when they returned from surveying the country, he agreed to send an envoy to Detallma. Their response had been swift. Later that day, the envoy had departed in one of their fasted ships.

"I do believe King Tzunam is eager to be rid of his last remaining daughter," Nissim said dryly as he read the missive. It had only been two weeks since he had sent the envoy. For some reason, he had thought he would have more time to come to terms with his decision.

Adagio opened his palms and spread them in front of him. "It is good that we have not had to wait long, Your Majesty. We may soon rely on Detallma if we are called to full-scale war."

Nissim simply nodded. Their meeting with the boy from Hotun had proved interesting, but he could not tell them anything about the raids or who was behind them, as Nissim had hoped. Adagio had spoken with the boy's adoptive mother and father as Nissim visited with the village children, who were all transfixed by his stories of Lunthá. However, he had watched Adagio and the boy as they conversed out of the corner of his eye.

Bravaro seemed like any other ten-year-old boy, full of energy and curiosity. He was bright for a boy his age and had mastered the Luminian tongue. Manemna had regaled them again on how he had found the boy wandering in the woods and given him the special language stone that blessed him with the *Luminsilkis* tongue. However, Bravaro did not need it anymore. They had learned nothing new from the boy that would give them intel on why these attacks were happening or who was behind them.

Adagio interrupted his reveries, approaching the desk as he summoned Nissim back to the present. "I know that things have not worked out as you would have hoped. I am also worried for Luminia's future, for the sake of my children. I hope that I might have the joy of seeing my grandchildren come into this world, *Ilyo Na'ada* willing. But if it is not, I want to leave this world better off than it is now. I believe you hold the same sentiments, Sire, or you would not have worked so hard during your young reign."

"I do," Nissim agreed. It was strange that people still considered his reign *young*. After thirteen years on the throne, he would have thought they would stop saying the phrase. He supposed, with his grandfather serving on the throne for twenty-seven years and his own father for forty-one, his time as king seemed short in comparison.

Nissim stood and began to pace. "I want to leave Luminia better off than when I received it—for Shoram and his descendants. My father seemed to be happy with the status quo, and I believe it was his undoing."

Adagio bit his lip. "Sire, about your father. We were never able to prove anything, as you well know. There are perhaps more of your nobles and even members of your high council who could be in on a conspiracy."

Nissim had had the same thoughts. At the time of Delgadas' escape, there had been more pressing matters. *Let the dead keep counsel with the dead* was a phrase that had often sprung to mind. "I thought you brought to heel all the members of the nobility that were arrested after Delgadas' capture. I do not believe we have anything to fear from them. They have received a life sentence in my dungeon."

"Delgadas escaped your dungeon, Your Majesty."

"What is it that you suggest I do, Adagio? Shall I execute everyone who ever had dealings with Delgadas?" Nissim struck out in frustration. He raked his fingers through his hair, trying to keep calm. "No. I will not be like my great-grandfather, who went mad and killed anyone he thought might be conspiring against him." After the famed prophecy from Lady Tzizenah, his grandfather had slowly slipped away from reality, suspecting even his shadow was conspiring to kill him.

Nissim did not believe he had anything to fear from regicidal nobles. Only three of Delgadas' cohorts were still alive, and they were locked away in his dungeon. They would soon be making their way to the Beyond, although their fate would not be much better in the next life than in their prison cells.

"That is not what I am suggesting, Sire. I only warn you so that we may be on the lookout. I would hate to see all your hard work go to waste. You are the keeper of your family's legacy and Luminia's future. We underestimated Delgadas. Let us not make the same mistake again."

Nissim gave a curt nod, hesitant to show emotion in front of his friend. His nerves felt too raw, too volatile these days. In a way,

Nissim envied Adagio. He still has his beautiful bride by his side and three wonderful children blossoming before their eyes. At least Nissim had Shoram to bring him comfort.

"Very well. I will heed your warning." Nissim sighed and headed out of the large private study. "Let us talk no more of this tonight. We should turn our attention to preparations for Detallma's arrival."

CHAPTER 23

PRINCESS TAMIL

Floating City of Detallma

"Tamil. You are a vision, my love."

Princess Tamil turned as her father entered the room, dismissing her attendants with a wave of his hand.

Tamil tried to smile but felt the tears pooling in her eyes instead. "Please do not make me do this, father." She went to him and knelt at his feet, bowing low to the floor.

"Stand up this instant. That is no way for a future queen to behave." Her father placed his hands on her shoulders, and she rose slightly. "Rise, my child."

Tamil sighed and allowed her father to help her stand. She felt so out of place in her lavish gown. Looking in the mirror now, she barely recognized herself under the heavy cosmetics and veils. At her mother's insistence, she had been turned into a 'proper young lady.'

She hung her head even as her father took her hands and squeezed them gently. "Look at me, my little sunbeam." She obeyed, not caring that her tears would smudge the carefully applied cosmetics. He wiped them gently with his thumbs and gave her a compassionate smile. "I suppose I cannot call you *little* anymore. You have blossomed into a radiant young woman."

Tamil turned abruptly and walked out onto her balcony. The sea breeze greeted her, its familiar playfulness a comfort. "You still have time to call off the betrothal." Her hands gripped the wooden railing of the ship, which comprised the royal household. Her knuckles grew white as she tightened her grip, trying to come to terms with her fate.

"I cannot." Her father's voice was firm but held a hint of sadness.

Her father followed her onto the balcony and joined her at the railing. Tamil's voice cracked with emotion. "*Why?*" Tamil pleaded. They looked out over the city together, marveling at the sea beyond. What her father had accomplished in building Detallma thirty years earlier was a feat to be envied. It had started as a small fleet of ships, growing into a thriving city—with lush gardens, bustling markets, and even an observatory. "I want to stay here and help you." She let out a choked sob.

He patted her hand gently, then placed it on his chest over his heart. He was having as hard of a time letting her go as she was with the thought of leaving him. "Tamil, all your other sisters have married. You are my last one, and your mother informs me at least twenty times a day that it was *'high time she was married as well.'*" He raised his voice to a higher pitch to denote her mother's grating tone. They shared a laugh, but it was short-lived. "When King Nissim's envoy came proposing this alliance through marriage, it seemed like a sign from *Ilyo Na'ada.*"

Tamil turned away once more, tearing her hand away from his chest. How could her father understand? "I have never been away from you and mother." What she really meant was that she had never been away from the sea. It was a part of her, almost as much as the blood running through her veins. The sea was freedom. How could she survive on land?

Her father placed his hands on her shoulders and gently turned her into his chest, holding her close. "Do not tell me that you are afraid?"

Tamil looked up into his tender gaze and felt ashamed. "I am, father. I have said nothing of this growing terror inside me for fear that I would disappoint you. But I am so unspeakably afraid of what my life will be if I leave you." She hung her head, unable to face whatever emotion she might find in his gaze. He lifted her chin and smiled down at her.

"I could never be disappointed in you. Why do you think I could not been persuaded to part with you until now?"

"I do not know. I always thought it was because I was the youngest. And I never have lived up to Mother's standards." She gave a wry smile. They shared a laugh at this, knowing the endless frustration she gave her mother. Tamil had always been a free spirit. She had never shown interest in her mother's lessons on how to please a man, the appropriate clothing to catch their attention, or in cosmetics to enhance one's beauty. Tamil would have much rather spent her time reading the skies or helping her father chart their course through the vast seas.

"One thing I know: you will make a marvelous queen. You may not feel like it now, but you will rise to the occasion. I am sure of it."

Tamil let out another sob and buried her face in his chest, savoring the feel of his strong arms protecting her. If only she could have stayed a little girl forever.

"I don't know anything about being a wife or mother. All the pretty clothes and veils in the world cannot cover that up. Sooner or later he will see that I am a fraud." Tamil's insides quivered at the thought of going to King Nissim as his wife. Her mother had told her little of what to expect *after* the wedding ceremonies were complete.

"Nonsense. There is more to running a country than pretty clothes." He stuck his finger on her forehead and gently nudged it. "You have your mind, Tamil. You are quick-witted and know how to give creative solutions to problems. Trust me, you will be glorious." He leaned in and kissed her forehead, taking her by the hand. "Now, enough of this emotional foolishness," he said, teasing her as he hauled her back into the chamber toward the door.

Tamil's heart flew into her throat, her blood pounding in her ears like the deafening gales of a cyclone. She would have preferred braving a cyclone to marrying a complete stranger. Her mother greeted her with a smile that was almost approving. She came to her side and linked her arm through hers. "Straighten her veils," she whispered to the attendants. Tamil gulped back the lump of fear growing in her throat.

Detallma was approaching the cliffs just outside of Lunthá. Her father had arranged for hundreds of the outer ships to build a bridge leading to the shore, temporarily connecting the two countries. It was a sign of the connection they would soon share when Tamil and Nissim were wed. There would be no escaping now, Tamil thought as she waited. Time passed much too quickly. From the palace rooftop she spotted the ships moving into position to create the bridge. Each of them took their signals from the various towers around the city using burnished bronze shields to reflect the sunshine. It was a mesmerizing dance over the water.

"Now, remember to bow when you are presented to King Nissim. It is customary for the Luminian people to cover their hearts with the right hand and kneel with their faces to the floor," her mother coached. Her mother had told her at least a thousand times, relaying several other customs she would have to learn. She only hoped she could keep all of the various court customs straight.

"You are not coming with me?" On any other occasion, Tamil would have been glad that her mother was not present. Now, she felt frantic at the thought of going through this ordeal without her guidance.

"Your father will accompany you to the presentation and alliance ceremony in Lunthá and then King Nissim and his court will come to Detallma for the betrothal ceremony."

Tamil nodded, unable to speak over her fear. Too soon, the ships were in place, temporarily making the nations one. "It is time, my sunbeam." Her father held out his arm for her, and she took it without thinking. It was as if she watched her movements from outside her body.

They made their way down from the rooftop to the litters that would carry them into Lunthá. Tamil wished they could have walked side by side instead of being trapped in the curtained litter alone. Her thoughts ran rampant, wondering what awaited her on the shores of Luminia.

When they reached land, Tamil felt as if she would be sick. She was only a girl of sixteen. Why was her father forcing her to do this?

Crowds of cheering people greeted them as they were hoisted through the steep streets of Lunthá. Never before had she seen a city like this, so different from the home she had grown up in. She felt terrible for the litter-bearers having to heave her up the dangerous inclines to the palace.

They came away from the port, mud brick homes lining the stone streets on either side of them. As they moved higher up the mountain, the homes became more lavish, built with more costly materials. The rooftop gardens were like nothing she had ever seen before, lush and inviting. She was utterly undone by everything around her.

A little girl ran up to her litter, holding out a flower. "Stop!" she ordered. The whole procession came to a stop, and Tamil parted the curtains. The little girl bowed low, then stood and handed the flower through the partitions. The girl's eyes grew wide. "My lady, you are very beautiful," she said.

The girls' mother came up beside her and pulled her back into the line of well-wishers. "Thank you!" Tamil called as the litter began to move up to the top of the palace mount.

Suddenly, the litter came to a halt as they again waited to pass through the palace gates. The litter-bearers set her down, but she did not make a move to exit. Not yet. She took several deep breaths to try to calm the wild beating of her heart and slow her breathing. Otherwise, she might faint from hyperventilation before she even made it up the palace steps. Tamil watched her father's shadow exit his litter and come to hers. He parted the curtains and offered her his hand. "Come, daughter. Your husband awaits."

Tamil took her father's hand and descended from the litter, gripping his hand for support. He helped her arrange her veils to cover her face, as was custom. She took a risk, glancing up the palace steps where the royal entourage waited to greet them. There in the center, dressed in gleaming white robes embroidered in gold, was the man she could only guess was her future husband.

CHAPTER 24

KING NISSIM

Nissim was sure Adagio could hear his heart beating as King Tzunam escorted his daughter up the palace steps. He could not tell since her face was covered in silken veils, but she seemed quite young. He wished he could see her face before they went through with this. Not that it would make a difference. He was not marrying her for her beauty, or lack thereof.

She was dressed in white, as he was. However, her clothing was much more of a loose fit than the women of Lunthá wore, something that would be fit for the sea. Her long flowing skirts billowed out around her. When they reached the top step, he could see her hand was shaking.

"Your Majesty," Adagio motioned him forward to greet their guests. Nissim bowed at the waist to King Tzunam and tried to give his most winning smile.

Nissim extended his hand and motioned them to follow him into the courtyard where the alliance ceremony would begin. "Your Majesty, it is an honor to welcome you to our humble shores. Please, come this way."

King Tzunam smiled, his sun-tanned skin making his deep blue eyes pop. Nissim wondered if his daughter had inherited his looks. King Tzunam was a roguishly handsome fellow, even though his short-cropped white hair belied his advancing years. Nissim did his best not to look at the princess, dreading the step he was about to take. There was no going back now.

When they arrived in the courtyard, Nissim made his way to the dais and sat on his throne. He felt awkward sitting above his royal guests, especially since Luminia was the one who needed their help. This did not seem to bother King Tzunam, however. He bowed at the waist, nodding to the lords and ladies around the court.

"Your esteemed Majesty, it is with great pleasure that I present my youngest daughter, Princess Tamil of Detallma." He waved his hand over to his daughter and took a step back. The princess stepped forward, placed a shaking hand over her heart and knelt, bowing her face to the ground.

Nissim was shocked that she would bow as a commoner, wishing he could step off the dais and help her rise. She stayed in this position for several seconds before rising gracefully, keeping her eyes downcast. He could barely see her face despite the sheerness of the veils.

"I am honored that you have agreed to become our allies through marriage. We have long been friends, with the bonds of faith and goodwill bringing us together." The speech seemed lackluster now that Nissim was saying it aloud. He had rehearsed it many times with Adagio, but now it felt false.

King Tzunam bowed his head. "It is fitting that we should be unified by bonds stronger than friendship, Your Majesty. Family shall be the thread that weaves us together from this day forward." He smiled and touched his daughter's back, gently nudging her forward. Nissim swallowed, standing to receive his bride. He walked down the steep steps, took her hand, and helped her climb to the dais. She turned to face the assembly, barely looking at him as a loud cheer rose from the crowd. He felt her jump slightly as the noise echoed throughout the chamber. He smiled tensely and was glad when the noise died down.

When the introductions were complete, he and the princess walked back down the dais and into a smaller courtyard where they could become acquainted. A contingent made up of his top three officials followed him into the patio, along with the visiting king. Three of King Tzunam's advisors followed suit. Soon, the noise was shut out by the heavy wooden doors of the courtroom, and Nissim allowed a sigh of relief escape his lips.

"Now we may begin the proceedings for the alliance agreement," Lord Lamik said. He seemed utterly pleased with himself, and for that, Nissim resented him all the more. He tried not to let it show, however, as the terms of the alliance were read. King Tzunam and Nissim then affixed their seals and signatures to the documents, and the deed was done.

"Your Majesty, now that the alliance is official, King Tzunam may reveal Princess Tamil—as is our custom." One of King Tzunam's officials stepped aside and allowed Princess Tamil to be brought forward. Nissim was surprised the woman had not fallen asleep as she had waited in the corner. It must have been very dull.

King Tzunam stepped to the young woman's side and lifted her veils, allowing them to cascade down her back. *Woman* had been an overstatement.

Nissim stood and took a few steps closer to the princess, silently taking in her features. She was beautiful, to be sure. However, she did not look like she could be over eighteen.

She kept her heavily lashed eyes dutifully trained on the floor. Her skin was tanned by the sun but not as dark as her father's. He saw dark red hair peeking out from the edge of her veils. She was, in every respect, the opposite of Lutep-Tzia. While his late queen had been dark, tall, and mysterious, Tamil was lighter of skin, bearing freckles from too much time in the sun and possessed a more petite build. Nissim willed the girl to look at him.

"It is a pleasure to meet you, Your Highness," he said, his voice cracking slightly.

Her eyes darted from side to side before she looked up at him, meeting his gaze with impossibly blue eyes. After a few seconds, he observed they were more blue-green. Fitting for a girl raised at sea. His heart skipped a beat, not from her beauty but rather from the terror he read in her gaze. The poor girl. She must be dreading this just as much as he was—perhaps more.

"I am your humble servant, Your Majesty." She bowed at the waist with her hand on her heart and again moved her eyes to the floor. A wave of frustration overtook him. He wished they had more time to get to know each other before the wedding ceremony.

"Very good," King Tzunam stepped forward and took his daughter's elbow. "Shall we make our way back to Detallma for the Betrothal Ceremony? The queen is very much looking forward to meeting you face-to-face, King Nissim."

"As am I," Nissim replied stiffly. He snuck one last glance at Princess Tamil before they were escorted off in a flurry of excitement. Their eyes met briefly, her face filled with inexplicable sadness. *Ilyo Na'ada!*, he cried out silently. *Have I just made the biggest mistake of my life?*

CHAPTER 25

PRINCESS TAMIL

Tamil could not have been happier returning to Detallma, even if only for a little while. She had been experiencing *tzuk-ho't*, or phantom sways, throughout the ceremonies in Lunthá. Her father had warned her of the malady common among Detallmanians when they spent any length of time on land, their bodies used to the rocking of the sea swells. To compensate for the waves' absence, the body mimicked the movement, making her dizzy and slightly nauseous.

"It will soon pass," her father whispered, handing her into the litter. She closed her eyes as they traveled back down the streets, finding comfort in the knowledge that she would be able to sleep in her own bed one last time.

Tears spilled down her cheeks. King Nissim was certainly handsome, almost too handsome for words. However, he was also quite a bit older than herself. When her father had lifted her veils, she had noticed the surprise flood his face. Was he sorry that he had gone through with the alliance?

When she had finally dared to look him in the eyes, she had seen tenderness there, along with grief and pain. She had wished to take

NICOLE C. BOYD

that from him for a moment, to see him smile. Her feelings confused her. She longed for the journey back to Detallma to stretch on, giving her time to sort through all her roiling emotions.

It was not to be. All too soon, she, her father, and King Nissim were back at the docks, and she had to climb down from the litter to be stared at by hundreds of curious Luminians. Tamil suppressed the urge to vomit as they prepared to walk over the bridge back to the royal flag ship. Hundreds of thousands of people had flooded the streets of her home, waving bits of brightly colored cloth in greeting. King Nissim came to her side and took her hand. They would walk over the bridge together this time, paraded and gawked at.

"You are trembling," King Nissim said softly. She glanced up at him but could utter no reply.

They said nothing more as they walked the length of the bridge. It swayed with the waves, which Tamil was used to. But King Nissim was less sure-footed, although he tried to mask it. She gripped his hand tighter as a large swell hit the side of one of the flat-bottomed boats. He flashed a small smile of thanks her way. They passed under the arched hole that led through the sea cliffs and out to sea, all the while feeling as if she were one of her father's exotic fish in a glass bowl.

Her father came to collect her when they reached the main body of ships that made up the city's center.

"Come, we must hurry," her father instructed. She let go of King Nissim's hand, almost reluctantly. His had been warm and reassuring as they had been forced to endure people's curious stares. "Your mother requires you to change into your betrothal gowns as quickly as possible." Her father went on, drawing her away. King Nissim and his entourage were also whisked away and soon disappeared from sight.

Tamil looked down at her gown and frowned. "I have barely worn this one. I don't see why—"

"Do not argue, Tamil. Come along," her mother stepped forward, herding her off to her rooms. Tamil stood silently as her attendants scurried around her, helping her change into the elaborate new gown. Her dress's silky, deep blue and shimmering turquoise fabric made her eyes sparkle. It was wholly different from the ones she was used to—of Luminian design, she was told. The gown was fashioned of one long piece of fabric. Starting in the center of her back, the attendant brought the ends forward and twisted them together in a knot at her sternum to cover her chest. Then, one side of the fabric was draped over her right shoulder and under the material at the middle of her back. It was then secured with a silver pin shaped like a sea star. The other length of material hanging down from her sternum was then spread loosely over her abdomen and around her hips several times to create the skirt. It was an alluring effect that she was sure would please the king. But it was more skin than she was used to showcasing. She much preferred the loose-fitting ballooned pants and shirt that was more practical for the sea-treading people.

The maids then attached a new set of long veils to her hair, which was left in loose curls around her shoulders. Several more silver sea star pins were used to secure the folds of cloth expertly draped around her slim form. Tamil turned in the mirror, the blue sheen of the fabric catching in the setting sun. She had to admit that she looked every bit a queen. She may have looked the part, but she still trembled like a frightened child. Her mother came up behind her and rested her hands on her shoulders, tears springing to her eyes.

"You look absolutely radiant, my dear, like the moons rising over a crystal blue sea."

Tamil frowned. "Do not cry now, Mother. Everyone knows you cannot wait to be rid of me." She turned away from the mirror and wrapped her arms around her middle, hating how she felt. Trapped. Exposed. Vulnerable. How could she be imprisoned on land for the rest of her life? It was unthinkable.

When her mother did not argue, she turned around. Tamil knew she had hurt her, and she softened. "I am sorry, Mother. I'm just so unhappy."

Her mother lifted her chin and placed her palms on either side of her face. "Look at me, Tamil. I hope you know I am not doing this to hurt you. I do this out of love. I want to see you settled with a family of your own. There is no greater joy than raising a family. Your husband is counting on you to help him produce an heir. As a woman, you get to be a part of his legacy. In fact, without you, his legacy dies. It is a great responsibility."

There was no use arguing with her. How could she make her mother see she was more than a pretty ornament to beautify a palace? Was she not worth more than just a brood mare to produce heirs? Besides, King Nissim already had his heir. Tamil hung her head and tried not to cry. The only purpose she served was as a pawn to secure the alliance between their two countries. Nothing more.

Suddenly, a sound more beautiful than words could describe filled her ears. She perked up and walked to the balcony, listening to the melody that sent shivers of delight up her spine. "What is that?"

Her mother smiled and opened her hand to her. "The Luminian Musicians are unmatched, are they not?" her mother asked. Tamil gulped, unmoving at the balcony railing, until her mother waved her over. "It is time."

Her mother gently prodded her toward her chamber doors. She then escorted her to the ship's helm, towering above the rest of the vessel. The music grew louder as they approached, floating down to Tamil's ears as they climbed the steps.

King Nissim was the first person she saw, flanked by his most trusted advisors and the famous Musicians of Luminia. The music seemed to course through her, giving her courage. She attempted a smile, and King Nissim returned it, even though she knew he could not see her face through the veils. When she had closed the distance between them, halting only a few feet from her soon-to-be husband, her mother lifted the veils and helped arrange them behind her back in a flowing train. He was dressed inn blue and turquoise, as she was. They must have been a striking couple for the many thousands of people who gathered on the ships around the royal vessel to watch the betrothal ceremony.

She took his offered hand, and they moved to the helm where her father waited. Her mother soon took her place by his side, and they looked on proudly as they waited for the new couple to join them. The music swelled, and as it did, it seemed to stir the sea into a frenzy of activity. Dolphins and whales came to the surface, as if drawn by the melody. Salt spray moved in unison with the notes, as if to showcase a dance all their own. Tamil stopped, looking over the side of the ship. A wave crashed against the side, and the sea spray suddenly took the shape of a little boy and girl, holding hands and skipping around each other.

Tamil halted, shaking her head. "Did you—?" She could not finished her thought, too overcome by surprise as she looked up at King Nissim.

He chuckled. "Yes, I saw. Have you never seen a water maiden before?"

"Never," she breathed, her nervousness forgotten momentarily in favor of awe. When they came to the bottom of the stairs just before the helm, they stopped and turned to one another.

King Nissim's gaze traveled the length of her person appreciatively. He seemed to catch himself and turned to the priest of *Ilyo Na'ada*. They walked up the steps to the helm and stood before her parents, the king's entourage, and the royal musician family.

"Esteemed guests, it is with great pleasure that we perform the Betrothal Ceremony in your beautiful city," the Head Musician said, his voice echoing over the terrace and down to the ships below. The crowds had silenced, straining to catch even a glimpse of the royal couple or hear a snippet of the speeches. "Do you promise to take this woman into your home as your wife, Your Majesty?"

"I will. And may *Ilyo Na'ada* strike me if I…" The words seemed stuck in his throat. Everyone held their breath until he swallowed and kept going. "If I fail to uphold my promise," he finished. He did not look at her as he said the words, the muscle at his temple clenching and unclenching as he ground his teeth.

Tami's stomach dropped. Was he thinking of his first wife's tragic death?

"Do you agree to go with this man into his house and become his wife?" Lord Adagio turned to her and waited for her answer. Tamil glanced at her parents. Her mother looked like she would faint, as if she had not breathed since the ceremony had begun. Tamil met Lord Adagio's steady gaze and swallowed.

"I will. And may *Ilyo Na'ada* strike me if I fail to uphold my promise." Tamil heard herself utter the rehearsed answer, as if she were watching from outside her body. The saying had always filled her with uneasiness. She closed her eyes as a rush of nobles came forward to congratulate them.

It was done. She was betrothed to King Nissim and would be the next queen of Luminia.

She barely heard the music strike up once more, a lively tune that seemed to set the crowd's feet to dancing. Tamil was whisked away from King Nissim's side, and they all made their way down to the banquet.

The celebration lasted long into the night and small hours of the morning. Tamil found it strange that she was seated at a separate table from her betrothed. A group of young nobles' daughters from Luminia and Detallma surrounded her. She did her best to follow the conversation but found it hard to focus.

"King Nissim is so handsome, do not you think? Your Highness, you are a most fortunate young woman!" one of her attendants gushed.

Tamil gave a stiff smile. "Yes, fortunate," she agreed half-heartedly. No one seemed to notice her foul mood. She glanced at King Nissim and watched him laughing with his friends and nobles. How could he be so calm? Of course, he had already been married once before. She was the one who was taking all the risk.

"Excuse me," she said and walked away from the low table. She made her way through the crush of bodies and up to one of the helms to try to find some peace. Finding a quiet corner, she leaned against a wall and pressed her back into the cool surface. She closed her eyes and let her head fall back.

What would become of her? The wind whipped the veils around her face. She tried to move them, but they kept getting in her way. Finally, she undid the silver clasps and ripped the heavy veils off in frustration, throwing them onto the deck beside her. She let the sea breeze brush against her cheeks and move her hair away from her face. "That is better," she breathed. The veils and gown were beautiful, but she had been uncomfortable all evening with the restrictive bodice cutting off her air supply, wrapped around her ribcage as tightly as it needed to be to keep it up. She much preferred her s seafaring garb to this finery.

"It seems we had the same idea," a deep male voice sounded beside her, and she jumped. King Nissim caught her by the elbow, helping to right her before she fell into one of the gigantic potted plants.

"Your Majesty. I do apologize," she said and made to leave the balcony. She spotted her attendants coming to look for her and rolled her eyes. Was she never to have a moment's peace again?

"No, please, do not go." His hand on her elbow was gentle yet firm. His touch sent shivers through her whole being. "Are you well?"

Tamil looked into his eyes and shooed her attendants away with a stern glance. They backed away, waiting for her at an acceptable distance. "I am quite well, thank you," she said more curtly than she had wished. She hung her head, going to the edge of the balcony. Tamil ran her fingers through her hair and realized her state of undress. Would he be offended she had taken off her veils? She was almost a married woman, after all.

He joined her, standing closer than any man who was not her father or brothers had ever dared. She unconsciously took a step away, keeping her eyes trained on the horizon. The first of the moons were rising out of the sea. Soon everything would be washed in The Sisters' silvery light. Tamil snuck a glance at him. Even with his hair starting to turn slightly grey at the temples, it made him look distinguished, wise even. What would he want with a mere child such as herself?

Tamil wrapped her arms around herself to ward off the chill. She wished she could don her usual attire. The breeze made gooseflesh rise on her skin.

"It's all very overwhelming, is it not?"

"Yes, it is," she said with difficulty. A familiar lump rose in her throat, and she did her best to swallow past it.

"Tamil—" he began, reaching for her hand. His fingers enveloped her hand, warm and assuring. "May I call you Tamil?"

"Of course, Your Majesty." Her voice shook despite her best efforts. She had never had to deal with these confusing emotions before. "You will have the right to call me whatever you wish after tomorrow."

He frowned, but quickly wiped it away. "Please, call me Nissim." He let go of her hand and rested his palms on the railing. He flashed her a sad smile and then looked out over the water.

A long silence stretched between them. Tamil racked her brain for something to say but came up blank. After a time, Nissim sighed and turned to her. "Would you like to meet my son?"

The question took her aback. "Yes. Please." She had been dreading this part all evening. She had seen little Shoram sitting on his nurse's hip at the ceremony. Would he like her? She had plenty of experience with children, thanks to her young nieces and nephews. Shoram would be different. Tamil would be his stepmother.

Nissim offered her his arm, and they returned to the banquet room. Thankfully, they only attracted the attention of a few people. They were able to sneak off to the corner of the room where Shoram was being kept occupied. His little face lit up when he saw his father, and Nissim bent to pick him up. "Hello, my son. How are you this evening? Enjoying much too many sweets, I can see."

His nurse bowed and stood aside to give them some privacy. Nissim sat down on the cushions. Tamil knelt in front of the pair, nervousness fluttering like hundreds of butterflies in her stomach.

"Shoram. This is Tamil—" Nissim met her gaze, hesitating for a split second, "—your...new mother."

His hesitation was like knife in her heart. Nissim did not want her to be Shoram's new mother. "He doesn't have to call me Mother. Tamil is just fine if you would rather."

Nissim simply nodded. Surprisingly, Shoram reached his pudgy hands towards her, and she grasped him under the arms to take him. He still had the full face of a toddler, but was showing sign of his transition from toddler to little boy. Tamil settled down on the cushion across from Nissim, and Shoram made himself comfortable on her lap.

"I'm pleased to meet you, my prince. How old are you?" she asked. She never once broke eye contact with Shoram, knowing how important it was for him to feel he had her uninterrupted attention.

"Four," he answered shyly. He fingered her hair, which she realized was still uncovered. She gasped and looked to where her mother stood on the other end of the room. She would be appalled when she saw. "Why your hair like fire?"

Nissim leaned forward and lowered his voice. "He has not seen many many people with red hair. Most Luminian's are of darker complexions."

"It is alright." She turned and smiled at Shoram. "Well, you see, I was very fond of candied fire flowers when I was little. My mother used to scold me for eating too many," she whispered.

Shoram's eyes grew wide. "You ate the flowers?"

"I did. Every chance I could get. I suppose that is why my hair is such a dark red now."

Shoram twirled a lock of her hair around his finger. "I want red hairs like yours. Can I eat some flowers? We not have those here."

Tamil laughed. "Oh, we have barrels simply full of candied fire flowers. I can have some brought to the feasting hall, if it is agreeable to you, Your Majesty."

Nissim chucked his son under his chin. "Yes, thank you."

The king sat down a few paces away, eyeing her and the young prince all the while, but it was impossible for her to decipher the look in his eyes.

After several minutes, he called the prince's nurse back over, and he led her to her table. Something had shifted between them, a mutual understanding,

Tamil rejoined her entourage, knowing her cheeks were flushed from the excitement. It took several minutes for her heart to slow its pounding and return to normal. She glanced over at King Nissim, who nodded to her. She flushed immediately and looked down at her plate.

Perhaps this will not be as bad an arrangement as I had imagined.

CHAPTER 26

PRINCESS TAMIL

"Your Highness? Your Highness!"

Tamil found it difficult to awaken. Her eyelids felt like she had been tossed about by the salty sea, with bits of grainy sand ground into her pupils. She had only been lost in a sea current once in her life, but it was once too many. She sat up groggily and rubbed her eyes. When her vision cleared, one of her attendants was kneeling at the bedside. "Good morning, Yupiltz. What time is it?"

"It is well past sunrise, my lady. Your mother has been waiting for over an hour in the antechamber, but you ordered us not to disturb you. You had such a late night and—"

Tamil sprang out of bed and gasped at her appearance. Deep, purple bags were under her eyes, the whites of her eyes marred by spidery, red lines. *"Ilyo Na'ada* help us! How will you ever make me look presentable for the wedding?"

The rest of her attendants came to her side and smiled at what they presumed was pre-wedding excitement. What they did not know was that she was dreading the coming day. Although, oddly, not as much as she had been the day before.

"Do not worry, my lady," said Yupiltz. "We will make you look breathtaking for your special day. But we must hurry. The procession will begin in a few hours."

Tamil sighed. This day was going to be grueling at best. "We have drawn a bath for you, my lady. May I suggest you get into it before we open the door to your mother?" One of the other three serving girls said, eyeing the door that led in from the antechamber warily.

She nodded. "Yes. Better she think I was soaking all this time instead of sleeping." She hurried into the adjoining room and peeled off her nightdress. She had tossed and turned during the few hours she had been allowed to sleep, unable to let her mind settle. Her skin was sticky with a layer of sweat, her anxiety over the wedding causing her to break out in feverish perspiration. She climbed into the warm water sprinkled with flower petals, a gift from Luminia's royal gardens. Tamil sighed as the steam surrounded her, relaxing her tense muscles. She allowed herself a few minutes before motioning one of the maids to help her wash.

Evidently, her attendants could not stall her mother any longer. Her thoughts of the upcoming nuptials were interrupted by her frantic mother, who came in to start ordering her maids about. "Really, Tamil. Have you not soaked long enough?"

"I suppose a bride should be clean on her wedding day, Mother?" Tamil quipped, not even opening her eyes.

"Well, you are not going to get any cleaner, my dear." Her mother patted Tamil's arm, and she sat up, opening her eyes wide. Her relaxation for the day was over. "Out, out! It will take ages for the girls to dress your hair. I wish you had not washed it this morning. It will be unruly." Her mother rolled her eyes, waving to the serving girl to help Tamil out of the tub.

"King Nissim might as well know I have curly, frizzy hair, Mother. It is just a fact." Tamil resisted the urge to roll her eyes as she stepped into a waiting dressing gown held aloft by one of her attendants. She wrapped the soft, thin linen fabric around herself and went to sit at the vanity, where her serving girls began to arrange her hair.

They tugged, cajoled, brushed, and pulled until she thought she would go bald. Finally, her hair was just as her mother had envisioned, piled high atop her head. The effect was quite breathtaking, with tiny seed pearls woven throughout the elaborate braids and curls. Several gold seastar combs also adorned her hair.

Tamil was allowed to dress in a thinner, dry dressing gown before the serving girls started applying cosmetics to her skin. First, they rubbed gold flake infused oils into her skin. The tiny specks of gold glistened every time the slightest ray of light touched her skin, making her look as if she shone with an inner light. White paint was applied to her hands and feet in intricate, swirling designs. They applied powdered gold on her eyelids and drew a dramatic black line on her top eyelid, just above her lashes. It gave her the appearance of a great cat, in her opinion. Then, they brushed a mixture of black soot, guano, and water onto her lashes to make them appear thicker and longer than they were. Finally, the juice of the fire flower was spread onto her lips. It made her lips swell ever so slightly and darkened them until they looked as red as a plump, ripe cherry.

Tamil sighed heavily when the girls stood back, allowing her to admire herself. She barely recognized the girl staring back at her. "It is perfect," her mother breathed. Tamil hung her head. Was this what her life was going to be like from now on? Was she merely a decorative piece of property?

"Stand up, my dear. We must hurry to get you dressed."

She stood up, feeling like she might tip over from the weight of the pearls and silver combs in her hair. She dreaded having to walk like this all day and knew her neck would probably have a giant crick in it by the end of the ceremonies. Tamil stood still, arms raised as the girls wrapped yard upon yard of shimmering white-gold fabric around her torso in the same fashion they had done the night before. The last thing to do was attach the sheer white veils to the sea star hair combs. However, this time, her face would remain uncovered.

She and Nissim would weave their way through Detallma and Lunthá, this time on foot, for all to see.

When all was finished, her mother opened a box, revealing a strand of exquisite raw-cut blue sapphires glinting in the sunlight. "These were your great-great-grandmother's, made especially for her wedding day. They have been passed down from mother to daughter for the last four generations. And today, you carry on that tradition."

She fastened the necklace around Tamil's slender throat and stood back to appreciate all her hard work. Tamil looked like a queen, ready to rule at her husband's side.

Weighed down by all the finery, she looked in the mirror. "I do not feel anything like myself."

"No one does, on their wedding day. The nerves will soon pass as you settle into your new life. There is nothing to worry about, Tamil." Her mother smiled at her, beaming with pride. Tamil wished she could be as happy as her mother on this momentous day. She turned away from the mirror and sighed.

"Well, I would say it was about time for the procession to begin, would you not? I do not want to keep King Nissim waiting." Tamil started toward the door slowly, allowing her attendants time to situate her impossibly long train. She was thankful she would be able to go barefoot through the streets. At least she would be steady on her feet instead of wearing the pointed shoes most Luminian women favored. She did not understand how they could wear them with their toes squished together.

King Nissim was indeed waiting when they exited her chambers and joined them on the deck of the enormous ship. Nissim stood with her father, his hands fidgety. He stilled when he looked up and saw her coming down the steps. He gave her an appreciative glance, his gaze sweeping her form quickly, then pointedly coming to rest on her eyes. For that, she was thankful. He held out his hand to her when she reached the bottom step. Her father joined them, his eyes sweeping over her with fatherly affection. "I have never seen you look so beautiful, my darling." Unshed tears filled his eyes, and Tamil took King Nissim's hand even though she wanted to collapse into her father's arms and cry.

Tamil kept her composure, however, and she risked a glance at her soon-to-be husband. He was dressed in an ivory white ensemble as well, with matching blue accents embroidered around the v-shaped plunging collar and sleeve hems, which gathered the otherwise loose-fitting sleeves at the wrist. He wore his royal crown, the gold glistening in the sunlight against his dark hair. He was indeed one of the most handsome men she had ever beheld. She tried not to let that thought distract her.

King Nissim drew her into the middle of the deck. Their family and friends surrounded them in preparation for the long day. Her father uttered a short prayer over them before they led the wedding procession over the ship bridge and through the steep streets of Lunthá.

He tightened his grip on her hand. "Are you afraid?" he asked as they started the slow walk to the palace.

"Nervous," Tamil admitted, although she was afraid, as well. What if she did or said something wrong during the ceremonies? She was more worried about what would come after the rituals and feasting.

He seemed to read her thoughts, giving her hand a gentle squeeze. "Do not worry, Tamil. Everything will be fine. You will see." He seemed to be telling himself as well as trying to reassure her.

Crowds had gathered on either side of the bridge leading into Lunthá. They threw flower petals and cheered as the couple passed by. Tamil did her best to paste a smile on her face, but the panic welled inside her as she left the only home she had ever known. It took hours to move through the compacted streets, moving at a slow pace so everyone would have a chance to see them. They finally arrived at the palace when the sun was high in the sky. King Nissim led her into the castle and up to the Musician's Terrace.

"This procession and walk up to the terrace signifies your

journey through life," one of the Musicians explained as they made their way up the stairs. "There will be difficult times and good times, but always you will have your partner by your side. You must help each other in the hard times, and rejoice together in the good."

Tamil's heart began to pound with the exertion of the steep climb and with the notion that she would soon be bound to this man for the rest of her life. There would be no escape once the vows were said. She licked her lips, feeling like her mouth was a desert.

When they arrived on the Musician's Terrace, she was greeted by a cool breeze. She was glad the pergola offered some shade from the sunshine, winding vines of wisteria hanging down to give off a refreshing scent.

The head Musician was waiting for them in the center of the terrace. He smiled at her and then bowed his head to the king. "Welcome, Your Majesties. It is my great honor to perform this first ceremony in front of all your loved ones and friends. Please, step forward."

They did so, and the Musician brought out a three-stranded cord made of purple, blue and golden threads. He took their wrists, placed her hand over Nissims', and began to tie them together. "This cord represents the unbreakable bond you will share from this day forward. The blue represents the man, and the purple the woman. The gold represents *Ilyo Na'ada*. Keep him at the center of your love and marriage always, and you will not be easily broken." The Musician then led them around the terrace eight times, their family offering prayers on their behalf. Tamil felt faint after all the walking, the heat and humidity growing more unbearable as the afternoon wore on.

Finally, after what seemed like an eternity, they were allowed to sit in the center of the terrace. A meal had been prepared for them and their guests. Tamil sank on the cushions gratefully, her feet throbbing. She gingerly moved her neck from side to side, wishing that her mother had allowed her a less elaborate hairstyle. She looked around at all the guests, seated a few yards away in a half-circle around them. She could not hear what anyone was saying. She felt like she was in a play, being stared at by an audience and was there only for their entertainment.

"Are you well?" Nissim leaned in close, whispering to her. His breath was warm against her ear, sending shivers down her spine. She backed away slightly, surprised by her reaction to him.

She blushed, looking away. "I am quite well, thank you."

"I know it is a lot to endure. But may I say, you look stunning." Nissim smiled down at her, his eyes alight with tender attraction. His comment made her blush all the more.

"Thank you, Your Majesty," was all she could manage.

"Nissim, please. We are married now, after all." He held up his hand, bringing hers along with it since their wrists were still tied together by the long cord.

"Yes," she replied, her voice shaking with emotion. She did not feel any different. Instead, she still felt like a frightened child being ripped from her home.

The feast lasted for several hours until the sun descended behind the hills.

Nissim looked up as Adagio approached. "Come. It is time to depart for the temple for the final ceremony, Your Majesty." Nissim stood, helping Tamil rise to her feet. She stumbled slightly, no doubt stiff after sitting for so long. Her gown looked like it weighed twice as much as she did.

"I am well," she said softly. Even so, she was grateful for his help. The guests followed them down into the palace and out into the gardens. They climbed up to the island's highest peak, water flowing in tiny streams on either side of the rough-hewn steps. The temple was a simple stone gazebo, its roof open in the middle. Adagio motioned for them to stand in the center, waiting in awed silence as the sun set and the moons rose. Adagio held up his hands in the soft glow of candles that the guests had brought. "In this, the last marriage ceremony, we join this couple in the light of the moons. Let your love be as the light of the moons, a reflection of the love *Ilyo*

Na'ada has for each of us. You cannot love one another without first experiencing the love of *Ilyo Na'ada*, the All-Father. Allow Him to shine his love on your heart, and let it overflow to your spouse."

Lord Adagio then took up a wine goblet, dipping the rim into the spring bubbling up from the heart of the mountain. The gurgling of the spring was the only sound that broke the silence of the holy moment. Adagio handed the cup to Nissim, and he took it with his free hand. He turned to Tamil and smiled at her, but it did not reach his eyes. Was he remembering the day he had promised himself to his first wife? "Tamil. As we partake of this cup, I pledge to love you as my own life. Forever." He lifted the rim to his lips and sipped the sweet waters. He then handed it to Tamil.

She took the goblet with shaking hands, refusing to look at anyone. If she was going to get through this without shaming herself and her family, she had to focus. She lifted the cup and recited, "Nissim. As we partake of this cup, I pledge my devotion and obedience to you. I am yours, forever." She managed to take a sip despite her quivering lips, handing the cup back to Adagio.

"Turn and face the assembly," Adagio instructed. Tamil gulped as they turned to face the gathered company. It might not have been so awkward if their wrists were not still bound.

"The married couple!" Adagio cried, the assembly erupting into applause. "May their bond remain strong in the power of *Ilyo Na'ada!*"

PART TWO
CRIMSON DAWN

"A nation cannot bear up under
a slave who becomes king.
Slavery is a state of mind
as much as a physical condition.
One cannot simply take the captive out of bondage,
but must take the bondage out of the captive."

- The writings of Tzizenah the Seer

CHAPTER 27
BRAVARO

Hotun, Luminia
Year of the Locust, 977

Bravaro stretched as a solitary bird chirped above him. It had landed perfectly, allowing him to see it through the round window at the pinnacle of the dome-shaped roof. He sat up on the reed mat and folded the thin blanket. In the heat of high summer, nothing more was needed during the mild nights.

He donned a clean pair of dark brown ballooned trousers, yawning as he went into the main room to find his mother squatting in front of the hearth, humming softly as she prepared the day's first meal. He smiled, joining her there. He wrapped his arms around her neck in a gentle hug, and she placed her hand on his arms. "Good morning, my son," she greeted.

"Mama," he said, releasing her. He sat down at the low table, eager to fill his belly with the sweet gruel she prepared from grain, fresh fruit and a sprinkling of sugared fire fruit. It was his favorite meal of the day—before the bustle of working in the fields took over or the intensity of stocking wild game had every muscle standing to attention. These moments of quiet with his mother were ones he looked forward to.

Especially after the strange dreams he had had the night before. Souni seemed to sense his mood and turned to cast a knowing glance his way. "You are troubled this morning?" she asked.

"More dreams," Bravaro admitted.

She served him a bowl of the hot gruel and sat beside him. He let the bowl sit untouched, allowing it to cool.

"Of your father?" she asked.

"No, not of my father," he spat bitterly. "Manemna was a kind and generous father to me, and I am glad whenever he appears in my dreams." He took a shaky breath. "No, the man that intrudes on my sleep was not someone I was ever proud to call father." He remembered little of his former life. The little he did remember was of a man who had once wished aloud that Bravaro had never been born.

Souni placed a hand on his shoulder. "It does no good to harbor unforgiveness in your heart, Bravaro. You know what I always say. Unforgiveness only hurts you, not them."

"I do not care," Bravaro snapped.

His mother blinked in surprise, then wrapped her arms around his shoulder and hugged him close. Even though he was nearly a man, he still craved her hugs. Especially now that Manemna was gone.

"You are better than that, my son." She kissed him on the cheek, urging him to eat as she rose slowly from the cushion.

Bravaro watched her carefully as his mother bustled around the kitchen. She had slowed in the year since Manemna's death. Sadness seemed to have seeped into her very bones, making even the slightest movements painful.

"I wish I could remember more," Bravaro said as he took his first bite.

Souni turned, casting him a curious glance. "Oh? And why is that?" she asked.

"There are many reasons," he said. It was not that Bravaro wanted to leave them. Hotun was the only home he had ever known. At least, it was the only one he still remembered. He knew that Souni lived in near-constant fear during those first months after his naming ceremony, afraid that he would suddenly find his way home just as one of the Spanyaards had many decades before. There had been no explanation. No goodbyes. The one called D'Tzoto had simply vanished back from where he had come, never to be seen in Luminia again.

And then there was the other one, Enrikae. Well, there was legend embroiled around his story as well. Who knew what the truth was?

Thankfully, Bravaro had done no such thing. Now that he had spent so many years in Luminia, he would not want to return home, unless he was able to bring his mother back with him.

"Perhaps if I remembered more of my birth parents and where I came from, I would not feel so lost at times. I know you and Manemna and Intza have always tried to make me feel like I am a part of Hotun. The villagers do as well. It is just that sometimes I wonder, how can I know who I am if I do not even know who my real father was?" *And why he wanted me dead.*

Souni's face softened, and she came to sit beside him again. She ran a hand over his short-cropped hair and rested her hand on his cheek. "My dear boy. From what you have told me of these dreams you have of him, I am glad you do not know more. I do not want you to grow up to be a bitter, drunk old man."

Bravaro shook her off. "You do not understand," he said.

"Knowing one's parentage does not make the man," Souni said. She rose again, turning her back on him as she stirred the gruel. "You must look to *Ilyo Na'ada* for that sense of identity and purpose, Bravaro. Or you will always be looking—trying to fill a hole in yourself that cannot be filled any other way."

When he did not respond, she sighed and went to wake Intza. "You are a good boy, Bravaro. Soon, you will be a man." She stopped before the curtained door of Intza's room. "You must decide what kind of man you want to be."

She leaned close to the curtain and called into his sister's room. "Intza, my little flower, time to wake up!" Intza groaned in complaint. Now nine, she was sometimes more of a handful than Bravaro ever dreamt of being. "Up!" she called.

Intza joined them several minutes later, rubbing her eyes and plopping down on the homespun cushion. "I swear the Musicians are making the sun rise earlier every day," she complained.

"We do not swear in this house, young lady," Souni reprimanded.

"Yes, Mama," Intza replied dully. Souni served her a dish of gruel, and her children ate in companionable silence for a while.

When they had finished, Souni sent them off to do their chores. Bravaro retrieved his longbow and quiver of arrows leaning against the wall by the door. Intza bent and picked up the clay water jar, balancing it carefully on her head once she cleared the doorway.

"*Ilyo Na'ada* bless you, my children," Souni said as they started out the door.

"*Ilyo Na'ada*, turn his light upon you," the children returned.

They walked together down the path leading out of town, Bravaro to the fields and Intza to fetch water for the household chores. He turned to see Souni watching them, her usual easy smile gone.

CHAPTER 28

BRAVARO

The air was thick with midday heat, making it difficult to draw breath. Thankfully, the shade of the forest's mammoth trees gave Bravaro a little relief as he crept toward the sound of the stamping of horses' hooves and muffled voices just sixty yards ahead. Flies buzzed about his mud-smudged head and face, but he made no move to shoo them away. Soundlessly, he crawled forward on his belly like a soldier sent to spy against the enemy. And well, he might have been, for the land he loved so much was again under attack, oppressed by raiders who struck in the night. After the king had married again, there had been a lull. Now, however, the attacks had begun with a force that threatened to bring the borderlands to their knees.

The dark, moist soil was cool against his skin as he inched forward. He had left his shoes behind, making it easier to go undetected, with his bow and quiver strapped to his back. Fern branches brushed across his face as he reached the edge of the clearing and peeked at the intruders. There in the shadows stood a band of half-naked Tzoetoen raiders, whispering in their guttural tongue that was harsh on the ears and the mind.

As of late, Bravaro had taken to spying rather than stocking game, keeping watch over his village. Souni would have died if she had known what he was up to, which is why he had not shared his daily tasks with her. Several weeks ago, raiders had rallied their attacks on the villages closest to the Tzotoen borders with renewed force. After several months of silence and peace, they had been lulled into false security. However, once again, they were at the mercy of their attackers. This time, they would know who their adversaries were.

Bravaro was determined to keep them from ravaging his village and their home, whatever it took. His mother's pleading words rang out in his mind unbidden, *"This is not your responsibility. An eleven-year-old boy with a stick-bow is no match for raiders with spears and swords!"* she had whispered harshly after a visit from the village elders.

A pang of loss clenched his heart, making it hard to breathe. His father, Manemna, had passed away the year prior. For that reason alone, his mother was wrong. It *was* his responsibility to protect her and Intza. Papa had made it clear that he was to step up as the man of the house when he was gone. As the one next in line to be *pitpak,* he had even more to prove.

Bravaro had made so many mistakes in the months following his father's death. Thankfully, the crops had done tolerably well, but fresh game was scarce. His father had taught him how to hunt since he was a small boy, taking him out more often as he grew. However, without his father's guiding hand and practiced eyes, he struggled to put food on the table for his mother and sister. The villagers shared everything they had with one another, so no one went hungry. Even so, he felt the pressure to do his part. He could only hope that, in time, he would make them proud.

Bravaro shifted to get a better view of the bandits' movements. All he could see were their legs, muscled and tanned by the sun. Shifting to a better line of sight, he marveled at the strange tattoos that laced their limbs. Strange symbols and ferocious beasts stood out in inks as black as Death and red as blood. It was rumored that their ill-bred brothers across the border put a toxin in the ink that caused their skin to stand in ridges when their shamans applied the tattoos. Mama called the Tzotoens *jutz-aka*. Heathens.

He held back a gasp with difficulty as one of the warriors came close, calling his fellow soldiers to accompany him. "I thought I heard something over here," he said in flawless Luminian, without so much as an accent. Bravaro raised a brow. Why would this warrior know Luminian? Indeed, he knew it so well that there was not even a hint of Tzotoen accent left on the Luminian words.

Bravaro's blood turned cold. There would be no way, unless one of their brothers had betrayed them. Nausea and fear mixing in the pit of his belly.

After several seconds of listening, the soldiers must have decided there was nothing to worry about and returned to their circle a few paces away.

What were they planning to do? There were several villages on the main road. The town of Eñgata was only a mile away to the east, while his village lay an almost equal distance to the west. Which village were they planning to attack first? He edged closer on his elbows, straining his ears to listen for anything that might give away the pinpoint of their next attack.

His heart twisted with fear. When the raids had commenced a few weeks ago, Bravaro tried to convince his mother to seek refuge in the royal city of Lunthá with his sister. BShe would not be convinced to leave him alone to protect their home. *"Ilyo Na'ada will protect us...."* she had said. She would not leave the land her husband had loved so much. He tried to reason with her that the attackers were coming closer every day.

"Tyiuput sik hechetsip," she would say. *Worry is futile.* However, her brow grew increasingly furrowed every time she said the phrase, and he knew she was agonizing over what to do for him and Intza.

A shudder ran down his spine and out through his toes. He had been to one of the villages after it had burned to the ground. Until the latest raid, there had been no casualties, only prisoners taken. But upon entering the still-smoldering town a few days before, Bravaro had found a young girl's charred remains hanging from a tree limb, her parents laying face down in pools of their own blood. The raiders had made blatant examples of the unlucky family to deter others from fighting back. He shook his head and tried to rid himself of the horrific images. After all, the young girl had been no older than his little sister. Somehow, he knew he would never be free of the nightmares that plagued him after what he had seen that day.

He inched a little closer and turned his ear up so that he might hear the band's leader more clearly. Even from this distance, he caught a whiff of unwashed bodies and the strong liquor the Tzotoens made from the fire flower. Their unholy use of the medicinal plant was another example of what set Luminia apart from their wayward brothers.

Bravaro scrunched up his nose at the stench and nearly cried out in alarm as one of the men stepped on his hand. He remained motionless as the dead, using the tricks his father had taught him to control his breathing as he stocked prey. Otherwise, he would become their next prey if he made a sound.

The man went deeper into the forest to relieve himself, and Bravaro sighed with relief. He drew his hand back, clenching and unclenching his sore fingers. Bravaro put his head down as the soldier rejoined the group, hoping his mud-caked hair would blend into the ground.

Bravaro peered out from behind the fern leaves, studying the group. There were about twenty men in all. Their leader came from around his horse and called all of them to attention.

"We will attack at twilight. Take all that you can alive. Lord Delgadas needs slaves to build up his fleet of ships. Futah!"

The name instantly brought a memory back of a man with cold eyes and a hard frown. Bravaro shook his head, unable to focus on the memory for now. A man at the far end of the group turned slightly, his foot tapping on the rich, black earth. He looked up slowly as if bored by the proceedings.

"Try not to lose your temper as easily this time," the leader said. "That little girl and her parents were capable of many months' work."

Futah sneered with disdain and gave a callous grunt in response. Bravaro pitched his head to the side to better look at Futah's features. A chill ran up his spine at the black and red tattoos weaving across his face. He was a bear of a man, made even more frightening as he sat sharpening an enormous blade with an ivory handle.

The commander continued, "Kill only as a last resort, do you understand?" The men nodded in affirmation, save for Futah. The men dispersed and began to cut portions of meat from a spit in the middle of their circle.

Bravaro had heard enough. He had to get back to his village to warn everyone. But which town should he warn? He could make it to Eñgata before twilight, but his home would be unprotected. Bravaro slowly backed out of his hiding place beneath the fern, looking behind him as he went. He slinked noiselessly behind a Redwood sapling, its diameter as big as a house.

He looked up at the sky, obscured by the towering Redwood trees and their full, dark green branches. Dusk was only an hour away. He stepped away from the tree as quietly as possible, but the top of his longbow caught on a fern leaf. The forest exploded with the echo as the leaf went crashing back into place, announcing his presence. Bravaro released an expletive under his breath and ran, throwing caution to the wind. His cover was blown now, and he was the last hope for his village.

"Get him!" he could hear someone shout behind him. A second later, an arrow whizzed by his head. Ducking to the right, he nearly careened with a tree but pushed himself off it to help propel him forward, zigzagging through the trees. He looked behind him and saw three men in hot pursuit. He gave a short laugh, taunting them while he ran, but when he turned his head face-front, a man stepped from behind a tree. His massive, muscled arms encircled Bravaro before he had time for another thought. *Futah!*

Bravaro thrashed and screeched, knowing there would be no escape for him. "Let me go!!" he yelled as the man brought him back into their camp. No matter how he tried, he could barely move since Futah held his arms to his sides in a sort of big bear hug. He flailed his legs, trying to kick at the soldier. Futah dropped him to his feet and slipped an arm around his neck, effectively cutting off his air supply. Stars danced at the edges of his vision. Bravaro stopped struggling as he tried to conserve what little oxygen was left in his lungs. *Ilyo Na'ada, save me!*

"Hold him down, over there," the commander snarled. Futah loosened his hold on his throat, and Bravaro filled his lungs with precious air.

He sputtered momentarily. "Let me go!" Bravaro shrieked again, only this time in English. All grew quiet, and the commander squatted to look at him closer. His ugly face was smeared with red paint instead of tattoos but somehow the effect was more terrifying, looking like he had rummaged face-first in a bloody carcass. Bravaro did not cringe or shy away. Instead, he glared right back at the man, seething with anger.

"Who are you?" the leader asked in wonder. Bravaro bit his lip. He hardly knew what to say. He had not spoken English for years, and he was unsure why he had done so now.

"I am Bravaro, son of Manemna," he said proudly in Luminian. "I am not afraid of you," he spat in the soil, narrowly missing the man's foot.

"Do you know what language you just spoke?" Bravaro made no reply to the man. He raised a brow, peering at Bravaro as if he were a freak of nature. "Lord Delgadas will be very interested in you."

The commander straightened, brushing his hands off. Staring down his nose at him, the commander inclined his head slightly and nodded to Futah. "Bind him. We shall take him to His Lordship tomorrow along with the prisoners we capture tonight."

The next instant, a filthy cloth was stuffed into Bravaro's mouth to gag him. Futah bound one wrist with a rope and wrapped it around a nearby tree trunk. He made Bravaro stand and face the tree, securing the other wrist with the loose end. He wished he had bound his wrists together. He might have worked at the knots to free himself if his hands were behind his back. Being bound like this would effectively keep him from loosening the bonds. Futah shoved his head to the side when he was finished. Bravaro stayed very still until all the men returned to the fire pit and continued eating, congratulating themselves on the prey they had caught.

When he was sure that no one was paying him any attention, he began to work at the ropes around his wrists one-handed. He only had a few more precious minutes until the sun sank below the distant hills. After that, it would be too late to warn his village and family. He struggled to loosen the ropes until his wrists were raw and bloody. The darker the sky grew, the more frantic he became. It was no use.

He stilled as the commander came to him again and gave him a cursory look. He nodded and then signaled for his men to climb onto their horses. Bravaro's heartbeat spiked, knowing his time had run out. "Do not worry. Your family will soon join you," the commander said with an evil laugh. Bravaro glared at him.

They rode out of the camp a few moments later, their horses' hooves kicking up the muddy ground. His village would never hear them coming in time, their approach muffled by the wet earth.

Bravaro pulled at the bonds, crushing his hands against the ropes until he thought his bones would shatter. Finally, one wrist burst free from the rope and he fell on his behind with a hard thud. His wrists were bleeding, but he had no time to take stock of how bad his injuries were. Loosening the rope on his other wrist, he raced out of the raiders' camp, weaving and bobbing between the trees as he headed toward his village.

Bravaro's heart sank as he neared Hotun and saw billowing clouds of dark smoke rising to the sky. Flames licked at the damp fuel, the fire creating twisted shadows on the surrounding trees as people ran for their lives. Smoke surged out of the houses nearest him, making it difficult to take stock of the rest of the town. Deadly orange gleams lighted his way as he rushed to where his home stood, still untouched by the inferno raging at the center of the village. He peeked into the doorway, but there was no sign of his mother or sister. He headed around the house and was about to turn from there and try to find his family when he saw his mother being dragged through the square by her lengthy, black hair. He gripped the side of the house and was about to run to her aid when their eyes met. The resignation he saw shining from her dark eyes made his heart stop. The soldier threw her to the ground, making her land hard on her hands and knees. Four men entered another house as the commander interrogated his mother. Crashing pottery and tumbling furniture soon filled his ears, and he clambered around the curve of the house to conceal himself.

"Where is the boy you call Bravaro? Where is he from?" the commander yelled.

His mother raised her chin with the grace befitting a queen. "He is gone," she said.

"That is not what I asked, woman. Where did he come from?"

"I sent my son to the royal city with his sister days ago." His mother said, her voice oddly calm.

"That is a lie. We have captured your son. He said his name was Bravaro, son of Manemna., who we know was your husband." His mother remained silent. The man kicked her hard in the stomach, sending her sprawling to the ground. She held her side, gasping as she tried to draw breath. Bravaro clenched his fists. He wished to break into the clearing and tear the man's throat out with his bare hands. However, there was little chance of him overcoming twenty seasoned warriors. The commander stood over her, ready to strike again. "We know he is from the Other World! How did he come to be here?!"

His mother shook her head, lying helpless on her side. "I do not know what you are talking about," she croaked. She turned her head ever so slightly, pinning Bravaro with her gaze. He reached for her, but she deftly shook her head, frowning.

The commander bent down and delivered a blow to her face with enough force to flatten a full-grown man. The commander took her by the shoulders and shook her, but she lay unconscious. "Useless woman," the commander spat, letting her fall with a sickening thump in the dirt.

Bravaro lunged forward, but the commander was quickly joined by five of his men. He did not have a chance against so many. He looked helplessly at his mother's still form as he backed into the safety of the shadows. Her chest moved up and down ever so slightly, and he breathed a sigh of relief. When the raiders took their leave, he would go to her and try to get her out.

He eased back into the forest's darkness, walking a few paces around the houses the flames had not yet touched. He searched the faces of the people being herded like sheep under the archway leading into the tiny town. Several raiders sat atop their steeds, keeping all the prisoners in a tight circle. The whimpering of children and babies' cries floated to him over the sound of the inferno.

He replayed the commander's disturbing words as he searched for his sister's face amongst the prisoners. Why would they want someone from the Other World? Why was Bravaro so vital to them?

"Get her out of my sight!" the commander screeched, kicking his mother's side again. She did not budge. "And search the woods beyond the village. I do not want anyone to escape and alert the king."

Bravaro watched in anguish as one of the soldiers dragged his mother through the dirt to the circle of other captives. One of the ladies bent down and cradled his mother's head in her lap as the man dumped her like a sack of flour on the ground. The woman gently dabbed his mother's bleeding nose with the hem of her skirt. After a few moments, his mother opened her eyes.

Bravaro made his way to the village entrance, ensuring those guarding the prisoners were not watching before he slipped into the crowd of captives. He knelt next to his mother, one hand on her arm and the other touching her face tenderly. She nodded toward the western hills and whispered his sister's name.

"Go, my son. Find Intza and keep her safe. It is up to you now." Bravaro's heart lifted with hope. If Intza had escaped, perhaps he could get his mother out as well.

"I will find her, Mother. But you must come with me. I can help you escape."

"No, I will only slow you down. And they are looking for you as it is. They know you are from the Other World, and that makes you of great value to them. Go," she prodded.

"But why, Mother? Why would they want me?"

She shook her head, her eyes closing for a moment. "No time to explain. Go, Bravaro. Intza needs you." The raiders started prodding the captives out of the village and onto the main road. One of the menfolk began making a scene at the head of the line, and the soldiers who were supposed to guard the back of the pack were called forward, giving Bravaro his chance to escape. His mother pushed him toward the forest, and he slipped away in the darkness. He turned once he was beyond the tree line, wanting to memorize every curve of her face. Would they ever see each other again?

Souni followed him with her gaze, her eyes filling with tears. The woman at her side helped her stand. She limped forward, leaning heavily on her fellow captive.

Intza was out there in the forest all alone. Souni searched the tree line as they were prodded out of the village. She met his gaze one more time. He placed his hand over his heart and nodded firmly, his eyes full of promise. He would find Intza and then come back for her. She shook her head as if willing him to stay away.

She mouthed the word "run," willing him not to lose another moment. Bravaro blew her a kiss, and seconds later, he disappeared into the forest, determined to find his sister before it was too late.

CHAPTER 29

BRAVARO

Bravaro stumbled as he came to the rocky shore of a stream, bending to slake his thirst in the crystal clear waters. After three days of searching for Intza, he had still not found a trace of her. He was hungry and exhausted, trying to fight the despair threatening to strangle him.

"Where are you, Intza?" Bravaro said as he collapsed onto his haunches and fell back on the rocky shoal. He did not care about the stones pressing into his back. He peered up at the sky as if the answers to his many questions were there.

He gazed at his surroundings, the peaceful scene in direct conflict with the dark emotions roiling in his chest. The leviathan Redwoods had given way to the much smaller aspen, pine, and madrone the higher up into the mountains he had climbed. Sighing, he closed his eyes but kept his ears alert for any approaching danger.

"You cannot stay here long," he chided himself. If he closed his eyes for too long, his body would give way to sleep, and he could not afford to do that again.

Sitting up with a grunt, he grimaced and looked down at his legs. He was filthy from head to toe after crawling through the mud to spy on the Tzotoen raiders. The grime of sweat, blood and dust was caked to his skin after days of searching for Intza in the wilds of the Luminian forests. Not his blood. His mother's blood.

He moved forward to soak his blistered feet in the icy waters. He grimaced as several more scrapes and cuts were made known to him. Without his doeskin shoes, he was slowed by the rocky ground of the mountains he had scoured. Bravaro scooted further down the bank and washed his feet. He was still several miles from Lunthá.

He needed a moment to rest if he were to keep pressing on later that afternoon and into the night. At least he was beginning to recognize his surroundings. He would soon be at the broad, winding highway that led to Lunthá. Perhaps Intza had also known enough to reach the road and seek refuge in the royal city.

An owl hooted in the distance, frightening him. What was an owl doing up at this hour? Bravaro searched the surrounding trees and spotted a gray owl, the ends of its feathers tinged in violet, soar through the air above the river and land on a fallen log not ten yards from Bravaro. He straightened, watching in awe as the bird moved its head to face him. Its piercing eyes stayed trained on his, an oddity since animals usually looked away in subservience after a few seconds.

Bravaro's heart pounded. Was this bird a messenger of some kind? He took his feet out of the water and squatted on the river bank, waiting. The owl cocked its learned head and blinked once.

"Hello, there," Bravaro whispered.

The bird straightened its head and winked before spreading its wings and flying back toward a stately tree on the opposite shore. Bravaro watched him go, awed by the encounter. He could not be sure if this creature was sent by *Ilyo Na'ada* or what the message was. However, he felt peace radiate in his heart. He was not alone, and that in itself was a comfort.

He finished washing his feet, glancing at the owl now and again. The bird stayed on the branch, watching over him as a mother would have watched over her children as they slept. He smiled up at his silent sentinel. "You are good company. Want to come along?" he asked, knowing it was doubtful the owl would leave its home wood to fly to Lunthá.

Bravaro lay back once more, propping his head in his hands. What would await him in Lunthá? He was perhaps the only person besides Intza who had escaped the raid on his village. Someone needed to alert the king to what was going on. And soon.

He dozed in the sunshine, lulled to sleep by the warmth and the sound of trickling water.

All too soon, he was jarred from sleep. Long shadows had crept up on him, and his owl friend had disappeared. He sat up. If he were to make it to Lunthá by nightfall, he had a lot of catching up to do.

He grabbed his longbow and slung the quiver strap over his shoulder. His stomach growled as he neared the road. Before stepping onto the white stones their ancestors had carefully laid, he looked up and down to ensure no one was there. He doubted any raiders would have come this far from the border, but he could not be too careful. After all, the raiders were bent on capturing him for reasons that still escaped him.

The road was deathly silent, and he cautiously stepped out of the tree's cover. He began walking, looking forward to the food that awaited him a short way down the road. He came around a curve and saw the unmistakable branches of the fire flower's tree. *Tahitzpil thotmin*, or the 'eternal tree,' was one of Luminia's many marvels, growing only in the soil around Lunthá. The bright red and pink blossoms were exported all over the country and beyond, used in medicines and for tea, which was a staple in Luminian homes. But what was unique about the tree was that it not only bloomed all year round but embodied every season of growth—bearing buds, blossoms, leaves, and ripened fruit all at once.

When he saw the trees that lined the king's highway, he quickened his pace, mouth watering for the delicious fruit. Indeed, the branches hung low with the bounty of this miraculous tree. He plucked one of the oblong fruits, its bright skin starting with a deep red at the top and fading to a brilliant orange in the middle and finally to bright yellow—like a candle's flame turned on its head. Juice dripped down his chin, staining his skin redder . He had forgotten how delicious the fruit was. Or perhaps he was so famished that anything would have tasted good. After he finished one, he picked two more and continued on his way.

Bravaro found himself on the outskirts of Lunthá just as the sun began its descent. He was taken aback for a moment. Life went on as usual. The city seemed unaffected by the raids, people still bustling to and fro about their business. How could the world go on as if nothing had happened? A thought struck him, and he froze at the gates leading into the city. No one would have heard about the raid on his village yet. How could they?

He wove his way through the compact streets of the outer city, stumbling now and again because of his torn and blistered feet. He caught the eye of a woman coming out of her house to dump a pan of dirty water. She froze, staring at him. Bravaro hurried on toward the gleaming white bridge that connected the outer banks to the inner island city. With the onset of dusk, the streets had cleared. He felt even more alone than he had in the woods for all those days by himself. Did no one care about their fellow man anymore? He hurried across the bridge and as he came to the other side, he caught a mother's eyes as she was bringing her children in from their game of ball and stick. She frowned deeply when she saw him and hurried her children inside, slamming the door behind her.

As he got closer to the city center, the markets were still bustling with activity. He wandered through the overcrowded streets, searching for the house where he and his family had often stayed when they came to Lunthá for festivals. After about an hour, he found the place and gave a furtive knock. His head swam as his vision blurred. No one seemed to notice how terrible he looked, the flow of humanity pushing around him like a stone amid a stream.

He knocked again and leaned against the door as his exhaustion took hold. Suddenly, the door opened, and he fell backward. Their old friend, Posentut, caught him by the arm and steadied him, uttering a low gasp. He righted himself, taking a step back.

Posentut's kind face appeared, concern making lines on her brow. "Bravaro! What in the name of *Ilyo Na'ada* are you doing here? What's happened to you?" She took his hand and pulled him into the house, clutching him to her breast. She then put her hands on his face and made him look at her. "Where are your mother and Intza?"

He splayed his hands, his fingers still caked in his mother's blood from when he had tried to stop the bleeding at her forehead. "I—I did not know where else to go," he mumbled, never once taking his eyes off his hands.

Posentut sat him at the table and bustled around the kitchen for a moment to get him some food. She then filled a basin with water and slung a rag over her arm. She knelt before him and examined his feet. He winced as she put his feet into the water and gently wiped around the scrapes and blisters. " Where are Souni and Intza?" she asked again, her voice full of dread.

Bravaro sucked in a breath, feeling slumber tugging at his eyelids. But no. He must not give in to sleep yet. "The village was raided four days ago. I am the only one who escaped. And Intza—" A sob stuck in his throat, and he hurriedly swallowed it. "Mama made it sound as if Intza escaped. I have been looking for her for days and found no trace. I thought maybe she would have come here?"

"No, I have not seen her," Posentut said. "Poor child. What horror you must have endured." She wet the rag again and wiped the blood from his hands and arms. She then removed his feet from the basin and dried them with a clean cloth. Tears sprang to his eyes as she bandaged his feet, remembering the tender touch of his mother tending him whenever he had injured himself. Would he ever feel that touch again? Bravaro's heart sank with the weight of his failure. What if Intza had been captured after all? It was all his fault.

He stood hurriedly on his freshly bandaged feet, wincing as he swayed dangerously to the side. He gripped Postenut's arm and fell back slightly as he tried to stand. "Thank you for everything, but I have to go. Intza is still out there." He tried to walk to the door but nearly fell to the floor. Posentut steadied him and helped him back to the cushion.

"But the sun is set and it is too late to go out now. Lunthá is not as safe as it once was." Posentut clicked her tongue. "Besides, you are in no shape to do anything but sleep."

Bravaro shook his head, "You do not understand, I have to find Intza. I promised I would take care of her!" He tried to stand, but she kept her hands firmly on his shoulders.

He let out a growl of frustration. He was just a child in her eyes. How could he make her understand? "If you will not allow me to go out and look for Intza, then I must go to the king. Someone has to tell him what happened. Who knows how many more villages they have raided since I escaped?"

Posentut thought for a moment, coming around his chair and kneeling before him. She searched his eyes. "My dear boy, I cannot imagine what you have been through. You should rest before you do anything else," she coaxed.

"I will not sleep until I have spoken to the king and told him everything I saw."

Another long pause ensued, deep lines furrowing her pensive brow. "Very well. I will take you to the palace. I cannot guarantee that he will see you, but the situation is urgent enough, I may be able to convince someone to let you in." She stood quickly, retrieving a shawl from a wooden peg at the door.

Posentut gave him a pair of her late husband's shoes, still resting in their usual place near the door. They were big but would be perfect with the bandages around his feet. She helped him stand and wrapped her arm around his middle to steady him. They made their way slowly up the steep streets leading to the palace, weaving in and out of passersby. "It will be a miracle if they allow us an audience at this time of night," Posentut said through gritted teeth, working hard to keep him upright as he stumbled around in the dark. "What use do these bandits have for raiding villages like this? None of this makes any sense."

Bravaro froze when he remembered what he had overheard the raiders talking about. "Posentut. I happened upon the raiders before they attacked and heard them talking about a man named Delgo, or something like that. They said he needed slaves to build his fleet."

Posentut froze. "Delgadas? *Lord Delgadas?*"

Bravaro halted next to her, trying to search her face in the faint light of the crescent moons. People filtered around them, some giving them nasty looks as they went. "Yes. That was his name, I think. Who is he and why would he want a fleet?"

Posentut shook her head. "I did not know he was still alive. He escaped from the king's dungeon years ago after trying to overthrow him. I assumed he perished in the woods, for they are wild, as you well know. Either that, or he had escaped to some far-off land, never to return." She started walking again, and he tried to keep up on his swollen feet. "It would seem the latter is the case," she said, speaking more to herself than to him.

When they reached the gates, the night guardsman poked at them with a spear through the bars. "It is late, woman. Can you not see that the gates have been closed for the night? Should have come when the king was holding court."

He turned to leave, but Posentut called out for him. "This boy has information about the raids! He says that Lord Delgadas may be behind them!" Her frantic voice rose over the palace courtyard, echoing off the great marble walls.

The watchman froze and turned slowly. "Delgadas, you say?" He returned to the gate, his piercing stare roving over Bravaro.

"Yes, sir. His men are behind the attack on my village, and I suspect on the other border towns." Bravaro held his breath as the man looked him over again, his brow raised as he decided whether or not to let them enter. Finally, the guard nodded.

"Stay here. We shall see if the king thinks this news urgent

221

enough to see you tonight." The guard walked away, leaving them outside the gates.

Bravaro let out a breath, leaning his back against the gates. "Well, now what?" he asked, sliding down until he was seated on the cobblestones. He was too tired to stand.

Posentut watched the guard walk away. "We pray they believe us."

CHAPTER 30

BRAVARO

"What is your name again, boy?" The guard came back, looking quite a bit more curious that he had before, studying him again. The man shifted his weight to his left foot, peering at him closely through the bars.

"Bravaro, son of Manemna." Bravaro tried to draw himself to his full height, ignoring the agonizing stabs of pain pulsating through his feet with every beat of his heart. Could the man see the lie in the face? In truth, he was an orphan, his real name but a fading memory amongst several painful flashes of his life before Luminia. He had been thrust into this strange place from a world he barely remembered. However, the pain of his birth father's words still haunted his dreams. Why could he remember that his birth father had wished he was never born but not one good memory? Perhaps bitter words were the ones that made the most impact. When the guard did not answer, only looking at them with a mixture of suspicion and caution, Bravaro let out a breath. "The king may remember me as Shos-hua. That was my name when I first came here to see him, five years ago."

Posentut put a protective arm around his shoulders. "He tells the truth, sir. Please, it is important that we see the king as soon as possible. The lives of the people on the borderlands are at stake!"

The guard grunted in response, nodding to the other guardsmen to open the gates. "Come on then." He led them through a maze of corridors, but instead of taking them to the courtroom where the king tried cases, he showed them to a private study. Bravaro held his breath as the soldier whispered to the king's aide, who turned and immediately opened the door for them.

The study walls were lined with myriad scrolls and books. Bravaro had never seen a room like it before. On any other day, he would have loved to explore the wealth of knowledge stored there. The village's few precious bark books had not been enough to quench his thirst for learning.

The king turned around, alarm marring his face as the aide whispered to him. Bravaro bowed as Manemna had shown him all those years ago. His memory jolted, remembering when he had come before the king before, and of Queen Lutep-Tzia who had been so kind to him. Images flashed through his mind: holding Manemna's hand as they walked into the courtroom, bowing before the king, walking with the queen as Manemna had spoken to the king of the *Other World*.

"Rise, my boy." King Nissim beckoned and came around to sit on the edge of the desk. Very casually, he folded his big arms against his chest, ready to listen. Bravaro did as he was told, giving a furtive glance back at Posentut. She gave him an encouraging nod.

Bravaro licked his chapped lips before starting in on his tale. "Your Majesty, I have come from the village of Hotun. We were attacked four days ago by a band of Tzotoen raiders. I was in the woods before the attack and overheard their plans—"

"You were spying?" The king leaned forward, peering at him. It was as if he was trying to remember something, like a song on the edge of memory—just out of reach.

"Yes, Your Majesty," Bravaro looked at him without wavering. "I could not stand aside while these bandits lay waste to our farms. But my spying proved useless. All the people in my village were captured, including my mother. I believe my sister may have escaped, but I could not find her. That is why I have come, Your Majesty. I have to find her," he pleaded, desperate to rally them to help his sister.

Posentut approached, stopping beside Bravaro before she bowed low to the floor. "He says he overheard them talking about Lord Delgadas, Your Majesty."

"Delgadas?" the king asked between clenched teeth. He stood up and began to pace, his anger billowing off of him like heat from a blacksmith's furnace. Bravaro hoped he would believe him, worrying that the news he shared might not be acted upon because he was so young.

The king halted, thinking for a moment. "You are sure the raiders are from Tzotoeh?"

"Most of them spoke the Tzotoen dialect, except one, and they all bore variations of their frightening tattoos. I am certain, Sire," Bravaro replied.

The King rubbed the back of his neck, "You speak Tzotoen?" he asked.

"My father taught me many of the Luminsilkis dialects, as well as *Tzoltlikis*" Bravaro replied. His heart skipped a beat, remembering why the raiders had wanted to capture him. "They seemed very intent on catpuring me, Sire. They knew I was from the Other World."

The king nodded solemnly. "It would seem that way, would it not? I am impressed with your grasp of our languages." He eyed him with open admiration. "Were you able to find out where they were taking the prisoners?"

Bravaro hung his head. "No, Your Majesty. I was captured by them before I was able to find out. I escaped after they left their camp and reached my village as they set it on fire. I was able to talk with my mother briefly before they took her, and she told me of my sister's escape."

His Majesty glanced at Posentut, and she nodded in confirmation of the story. He was undoubtedly a boy of abnormal bravery. "It is alright, my boy. You have done your utmost duty in coming to me with this information. I thank you." He looked to his steward and nodded. "Please give him any accommodation he may need. Bravaro shall be my special guest."

"Please, Your Majesty," Bravaro said, desperate enough to break custom and approach the king. "My sister?"

Nissim frowned, shaking his head. "I am not sure what I can do for you, Bravaro. I may be able to spare a small contingent of my men to search the area around your village. But I need most of my men to search for the raiders and put a stop to their attacks ."

"I respectfully request to join them, Your Majesty. I know the area well." Bravaro stood to attention, trying to appear taller than he was.

The king studied him for a moment longer. Finally, recognition dawned. "I have seen you before," he said after a short pause. "You are the boy Lord Adagio went to speak with while we were on survey of the country last year."

Bravaro was not one to lie. He gulped, hoping the king would be reasonable and let him leave. "Yes, Sire," Bravaro replied. "Manemna found me in the woods surrounding Hotun over five years ago." He hung his head, raking his teeth over his chapped lower lip. "I will never forget Queen Lutep-Tzia and how she tried to make me feel at ease that day."

The king stared at him with wide eyes. "I remember now. You *are* the boy from the Other World. *Bee-yoote Falls,*" he repeated the words. He approached Bravaro to get a better look. Bravaro shifted uncomfortably.

"I hardly remember that world. It was so long ago—" Bravaro faltered.

"You do not know anything, then, of where you came from?" the king asked. Bravaro only shook his head.

Sighing, the king went on. "It stands to reason, I suppose. You were only five or six years old when it happened—" The king's voice trailed off, leaving his thought unfinished.

Bravaro's heart began to pound.

"I would like you to stay here tonight. It is too late now, but in the morning you will ride with us to the borders and show us where they came from so we can try to track them down. They may be able to lead us to Delgadas." The king looked to Posentut. "He will be well taken care of, I can assure you. You are more than welcome to stay here with him, if you like."

"Thank you, Your Majesty, but I have my own home to look after. Will you be alright here, Bravaro?" Posentut looked as if she wanted to hug him but was unsure.

Bravaro closed the distance between them and wrapped his arms around her ample middle. She hugged him tightly. "Yes, I will come to you as soon as we are back in Lunthá," Bravaro promised. "Will you keep a watch out for Intza? I cannot imagine she would think to go anywhere else."

"Of course," Posentut replied. He hugged her tightly once more before a soldier escorted her to the gates.

Bravaro was shown to the royal nursery where the prince himself slept. He could not help but feel inferior as they walked through the brightly lit corridors of the palace. He was dressed in his simple ballooned trousers and the oversized shoes that Posentut had lent him. In contrast, those around him were dressed in richly woven fabrics dyed in bright colors. Like a fool, he had left his long bow and arrows at Posentut's home. But there was nothing for it now.

"My son's nurse, Dosanyata, will see that you have everything you need," the king knocked on the big wooden door, and a kind-faced woman opened it. King Nissim explained the situation to her and her husband. Bravaro was bid to enter the room. The woman placed her hands on Bravaro's shoulders, turning him around to face the king.

"We will take good care of him, Your Majesty." She studied Bravaro from head to toe. "You have been through quite an ordeal, I can see. Come and get cleaned up and have some food to revive you," she instructed. Another young woman approached him and led him to a smaller room adjoining the nursery, setting out fresh clothing for him. He began to change, but kept his head cocked toward the curtained doorway. The woman called Dosanyata lowered her voice.

"Delgadas has come back after all these years?" Dosanyata whispered, fear tinging her voice. The king simply nodded, no doubt wanting to keep the matter from the younger children. Bravaro finished changing and peeked out from the edge of the curtain, hoping to learn more. At that moment, a boy of about five years of age rushed in from one of the sleeping chambers and wrapped his arms around Dosanyata's legs, peeking out from behind her thigh. Another boy came barreling through the door after him, laughing. The younger boy took the king's hand.

"Papa!" He reached up, and the king took him up in his arms. He was about four years old, with long brown curls and soft green eyes.

The King smiled at the boy and tousled his hair. "How are you, son? I have missed you today. But why are you not in bed?"

The boy raised his arms, and the king scooped him up with a smile. Bravaro watched with a pang of loss, missing Manemna more than words could say.

"I heard your voice and wanted to come see you." The boy placed his tiny hands on the king's face and pinned him with a stare. "You are worried?" Bravaro turned and watched the exchange between father and son. The boy seemed to change from a little child to a full-grown man before his eyes, with perception beyond his years. Bravaro walked out into the main room then, but remained on the edges of the little group that had formed in the midst of the school room.

The king softened, and he nodded once. "It is alright, my son. But you may keep me in your prayers."

"I always pray for you, Papa."

"Good boy," the king smiled and put the boy down. He saw that

Bravaro had halted only a few paces away and motioned him over. "Bravaro, this is my son. May I present Prince Shoram?"

Bravaro placed a hand on his heart and bowed at the waist. Shoram gave him a brilliant smile. "Is he to stay with us in the nursery, Papa?"

"He is. I am counting on you and Valian to make him feel welcome." King Nissim leaned down and chucked the other boy under the chin, who seemed to find his courage and come out from behind Dosanyata's skirt. She placed her hands on the boy's shoulders and beamed at him with pride.

"This is my son, Valian," she introduced. Bravaro nodded at the boy, who returned the gesture with nary a sound. Bravaro could feel the exhaustion creeping up on him, threatening to send him into a deep slumber in the middle of the floor. Dosanyata seemed to sense this and reached for him. "I think it is high time you went to bed, Master Bravaro. You look ready to fall asleep on your feet."

Bravaro gave a nervous laugh. "I am quite tired," he admitted. "Perhaps I shall bathe and go straight to bed? I had some of the fire fruit on my way into the royal city."

"Ahh, well, you will be full for a while yet. Yes, you may wash and then go straight to bed if you like. This way," she said, motioning to the bathing chamber.

"Thank you, Dosanyata, for looking after him." King Nissim touched Bravaro on the shoulder and gave him an encouraging nod. "I will see you tomorrow, Bravaro. Try to get some rest. We have a long journey ahead."

He washed quickly and then lay on a bed of plush *titzake lumpay* cushions and pillows. He had never slept in such lavish accommodations in all his life. At least, he did not remember if he had.

Thoughts of his former life and the Other World plagued him. Sometimes, he would have dreams of a strange, far-off place. But when he would awaken, he would quickly forget. The only image that stood out in his mind was a woman's face framed by blonde, soft curls. Her eyes were ever-searching, her brow furrowed. He did not know how, but he knew the woman was his birth mother. And then there was the angry man who was always yelling or throwing things in his dreams.

Pushing the thoughts away, he propped his arms behind his head. A gentle breeze blew in through a small window above his head, bringing the scent of spices, fruits, and flowers from the gardens. All was still, and in the darkness, he felt so alone. He was accustomed to the sound of his mother and sister's steady breathing as they slept on their mats in the adjoining rooms, only a whisper away.

Before he knew it, he drifted to sleep, his dreams fraught with frightful memories of the raid and his long journey to the capital, all intermixed with the face of an angry man he had once known as Father.

CHAPTER 31
BRAVARO

Bravaro tried to settle the anxiety roiling in the pit of his stomach as they neared his village. The sight was far worse than he could have imagined. Before they even passed through the archway that had once stood proudly at the entrance of the town, Bravaro dismounted and ran to the center of the first ring of houses.

He looked to the right, staring at the remains of the home he had come to love over the last five years. It was completely consumed by flames, a charred skeleton of what had once been a beautiful sanctuary from the world.

However, the pile of rubble incited far less horror than the scene in the center of the square. A body was strapped to a wooden pole, smoke still rising from the remains. Whoever it had been, they were now unrecognizable.

Bravaro tried to push the bile back down, not wanting to embarrass himself in front of the king's entourage. When he looked around at their faces. They all seemed to struggling to hold down their midday meals, as well.

"*Ilyo Na'ada,* help us," the king breathed as he looked around the village. "It is just like the others."

A memory flashed in Bravaro's mind as the king said the words, remembering the unannounced visit from him and the Head Musician, Lord Adagio, over a year ago. He shook his head as his mind began to spin with memories. That visit had occurred only months before his father died. Had that visit somehow brought on the demise of his village or maybe even his father?

Bravaro's face heated instantly with a flash of anger. "You did this!" He pointed an angry finger at Lord Adagio. The man looked up at him in surprise, sitting pompously atop his steed. King Nissim had dismounted in preparation to survey the remains of the village, but he stalled now.

"I beg your pardon—?" Lord Adagio asked. He dismounted as Bravaro strode toward him.

"You came here when the raids started again over a year ago. You did nothing!" Bravaro lunged at Lord Adagio, but a soldier stepped before him, barring his advance. Bravaro threw himself at the man, who was twice his height and at least triple his weight. He did not care. He raged and threw his fists, trying to claw at Adagio. "The men who attacked this village were looking for me!" he screamed. "How else would they know I was here unless they heard from you?"

Lord Adagio raised a brow. "Let him go," he ordered the soldier after Bravaro had sufficiently calmed down. When he was released, Bravaro brushed himself off. "I did not tell anyone but the king of the circumstances surrounding your arrival in this land, Bravaro."

There was another explanation, he realized. There had been the run-in with one of the other lords as he and Manemna were leaving the court that day. Had the man recognized that he was not of their world? "Perhaps the palace is not as secure as we have been led to believe."

Bravaro wiped at his eyes, planting his hands on his hips as he shifted his weight. "Then why this?" he asked, his voice sounding more the pleadings of a frightened boy than the angry accusation he had flung at him a moment before. "Why now?" His bravado washed away under the weight of grief.

"I have no more answers for you than you have for me, Bravaro," he said gently. "But that is why we are here. To try and find out."

A falcon with orange and red-tipped wings squawked overhead and disappeared into the trees. Bravaro's chest tightened as his thoughts returned to the present. If Intza was still alive, she might have stayed close to the village to scavenge for what little food was left, just like the raptor that had flown overhead a moment before. Except the bird's fare was of another kind, making a shiver run down Bravaro's spine.

Bravaro knelt in front of Lord Adagio, humbling himself. "Is there anything that can be done to find my sister, my lord? She has been alone for over a week and I do not think she can last much longer."

Lord Adagio turned to the king. "Your Majesty?"

"Yes. Something must be done," King Nissim said. He left Bravaro and Adagio standing at the archway leading into the city and walked into the destruction.

Bravaro breathed a sigh of relief. "Thank you, my lord."

The King seemed overwrought as he moved through the remnants of the dome-shaped dugouts. Bravaro returned to his horse and retrieved the reins, leading her to a scraggly patch of dried grass.

He again turned to his village, his mind playing tricks on him. Heat and smoke still radiated from the houses' burned-out centers. The wind made a mournful tune as it whistled through the rubble, bringing to mind the flute songs they had played during their dances when they brought in the harvest. In his mind's eye, Bravaro could see silhouettes of his fellow countrymen and women dancing around the bonfires of the communal fire pits. Just as quickly as the images had appeared, they were gone—carried away with the smoke on the breeze.

King Nissim stood in front of him, shoulders hunched. His frame shook slightly, and Bravaro wondered if he wept for the village. Suddenly, the king turned, his face full of unveiled fury.

"I want all the border villages evacuated," he barked. "I want blockades on all the roads leading to Lunthá. We must find places for the refugees to lodge until these raiders can be brought to heel." He seemed to lose some of his vehemence, glancing over his shoulder at the smoldering city.

"How can you protect your people if we cannot catch up with these raiders? They attack at night, like specters from hell, and disappear without a trace." Lord Lamik asked.

"We have to try."

General Zalim nodded once and rode out of the town to relay the orders to fifty of Luminia's finest soldiers who had accompanied them. Adagio approached the king, whispering to him for a moment. The King turned and looked at Bravaro, motioning him over with a flick of his finger. "Take some men and go in search of your sister now," he instructed. He raised both hands with his fingers splayed, showing he needed ten men. "Do you know where she was last seen?"

"I do not, Your Majesty. She may have gone to a few of our old haunts. I thought I would start there." Bravaro was soon joined by the men who would accompany him in searching the forest.

"Very well. You go on ahead, and let me know if you require anything else. When you return, I will need you to show me where the raiders camped before they attacked Hotun."

"Of course, Your Majesty. Anything to help."

The King gave him a sideways glance, holding up his hand for him to wait. "Have you ever thought of becoming a soldier, Bravaro?"

Bravaro's heart fluttered. He had thought of it every waking moment since his mother had been captured. He could have saved her if he had known how to fight better. "Yes, Sire," he replied, trying to keep the shakiness from his voice.

The King nodded and turned to Lord Adagio. "When we return to

Lunthá, I would like to have Bravaro trained alongside Valian and my son."

Lord Adagio nodded his approval. "It will be done, Your Majesty."

The King instructed the soldiers to help Bravaro search the woods for his sister. But every place he went turned up void. His panic and sense of loss only increased as the day went on. And even though the soldiers did their best to bolster his spirits, deep down, he knew Intza had either been captured or perished alone in the woods.

He trudged into their temporary camp long after dark, the soldiers hungry from their long search. Bravaro sat down at one of the many fire pits dotting the jungle, but he had no stomach to take any nourishment. His family was gone. Once again, he was alone in this world. How had he been the only one to survive? Hanging his head, he wished to melt into the earth and perish, joining his family in the Beyond.

Adagio sat next to him, clapping a warm hand on his shoulder. Bravaro looked up at him, his heart clenching at the compassion in the older man's eyes. "Anything?" he asked.

"No, my lord. Not yet." Bravaro was cut to the quick. He had accused this man of bringing about this calamity, for which he was genuinely sorry. Lord Adagio had repaid his insults with kindness and compassion.

The older man let out a long sigh, raking a hand through his short dark hair speckled with quite a bit more white than when he had first seen him all those years ago. "I am sorry, son. Perhaps we can go out again tomorrow and try one last time."

Bravaro resisted the urge to cry. He was eleven, and the time for tears had long since passed. "No. We would have found something if she had escaped. It would seem she vanished into thin air. More likely than not, she was captured by the Tzotoens and taken to wherever Lord Delgadas is holding them."

Lord Adagio let his hand fall back to his sides. "I have two daughters, you know. They are about your age. Pray, how many *kis-llzuto* have you?"

Bravaro straightened slightly. "I have eleven years, sir."

"The King is right to start your training. Many of our royal guards are trained from infancy, but you seem to have the fighting spirit necessary to make something of yourself among our ranks."

Bravaro shifted his weight, turning in anticipation of Lord Adagio's offer. "I know how to shoot a bow, my lord. My father was training me to hunt before his passing." Bravaro was eager to begin training of another kind. It was all well and good to know how to hunt—but the skills he needed most were those of swordplay and military strategy. Whatever he could do to prepare himself to meet Delgadas, the better. Shame overwhelmed him. Manemna would have been horrified to know he would be a soldier. He had detested violence unless it was absolutely necessary, as had Souni. Manemna had never spoken of his rescue from the Tzotoen soldiers when Bravaro had first appeared in Luminia. However, they no longer lived in a world where he could lead a peaceful life as they had done, men tending crops and women caring for the hearth fires.

"Are you willing to make the sacrifices it will take to become a soldier?" Lord Adagio asked.

"He said I was to be trained with Valian and the prince. I am willing to make any sacrifice necessary, my lord." Bravaro's eyes barely moved away from the fire.

Lord Adagio nodded. "That is good. You will most likely be lodged with the prince and Valian in the palace then. No doubt, he means to make you one of their companions."

"That would be quite an honor, sir." Bravaro could not imagine such favor. He was a lowly boy from the outskirts of Luminia, and now he did not know if he was even that. What did the king know of his past and the Other World? He knew the woman who sometimes visited his dreams was his birth mother, and the angry man was his birth father. Bravaro hung his head, disturbed by memories he could not quite grasp. What could a boy such as himself have to offer a prince?

"I would be happy to train as a lowly foot-soldier, my lord. I only want to do my part to help protect Luminia," he said softly. In reality, he was unsure if the royal children would accept him. Why should they?

"Your humility is commendable, Bravaro. believe the king has bigger plans for you. Wait and see."

A second later, one of the soldiers came to retrieve Bravaro. "His Majesty is ready to see the raider's camp, Master Bravaro."

Lord Adagio rose with him and walked over to the king's tent. Nissim was dressed in dark clothing, ready to go.

"Can you find your way?" Nissim asked.

Bravaro nodded firmly. "I could find it with my eyes shut, Your Majesty."

The king smiled. "Good boy. Let us not waste another moment."

Bravaro led them through the forest, his new pointed soldier's boots crunching on the dried twigs and foliage. He would have rather made himself a new pair of doeskin shoes, but there had not been time. It was a short walk through the woods before they arrived at the Tzotoen's long-deserted campsite. Torches were lit as soon as they stepped out into the small clearing. Bravaro marveled at how they had destroyed the surrounding flora. They had chopped down every tender sapling in sight for their fire and not even bothered to bury their refuse or disguise their tracks.

Bravaro bent at the fire pit they had created. Beside the animal bones strewn about and the gut pile of a deer left to rot, there was little else to be found that might have clued them into where they were going next.

"I am sorry, Your Majesty. There is not much here that will be of use."

King Nissim surveyed the area for a moment before answering. "How many men did you say there were?"

"Twenty. Perhaps a bit more." A shiver ran up Bravaro's spine at the remembrance of Futah clamping a dirty hand over his mouth. Bravaro walked over to the tree he had been tied up with, and his heart stopped. Two Tzotoen symbols had been scratched in the bark, revealing the red-hued flesh underneath.

"*Beware, outsider,*" the king translated, running his fingers over the rudimentary hieroglyphs belonging to the Tzotoens. "Was this here before, Bravaro?"

Bravaro shook his head. "No, Your Majesty. I think they meant this as a warning for me. This is where they bound me," he replied.

King Nissim came to his side, placing a protective arm around his shoulder. "Do not worry, my boy. They cannot harm you now."

Bravaro said nothing, staring at the markings dug into the tree. He might be the king's ward, but he was not so sure he and his guards could protect him against a man such as Delgadas.

CHAPTER 32

BRAVARO

"Oh, how good it is to see you back safe and sound, Bravaro! Come in, come in. The boys were just sitting down to their lessons." Dosanyata opened the nursery door wide, flashing a smile as she ushered him in. She whispered with the king momentarily and then closed the door, leaving Bravaro feeling bereft. The king had allowed Bravaro to stay by his side throughout the return trip to Lunthá, asking about his past and his family. He had promised to do whatever he could to find his mother and Intza, and for that, Bravaro was grateful.

However, the king's questions had stirred something inside him, things he had preferred to leave buried. Memories of his birth parents pervaded his sleep, making the moments he closed his eyes something he had come to dread.

Despite their efforts to evacuate the remaining villages closest to the Tzotoen borders, there had been three more attacks. The assaults had grown more savage and violent with each town they happened upon. King Nissim grew increasingly pensive and withdrawn.

"They are starting to fight back," the king had whispered as they surveyed the last village. How could they fight against an enemy who abandoned common decency?

Bravaro felt sick every time he saw the death and carnage wrought by the bandits. He was helpless to save them.

Streams of refugees and pack animals had lined the road as they had ridden back to the royal city. People from all over the country, not just the borderlands, were starting to abandon their homes and fields to find refuge in Lunthá. Bravaro had seen the worry lining the king's face and heard him whisper to Lord Adagio as they rode past a group of road-weary travelers earlier that morning. "Where in the name of all that is good are we to put them all?"

"We shall have to deal with that when we get there." Lord Adagio had said.

Bravaro had been shocked to see how the crowds had swelled within the island city upon their return. It had only been a few weeks, and already the noise and stench of so many people packed together were unbearable. With relief, he rode through the palace gates with Lord Adagio and the king's entourage.

Now, faced with living with princes, he was overcome with anxiety. He was not of royal blood, and he was certainly not worthy of being a companion for the heir of Luminia. Bravaro looked up at Dosanyata, who touched his shoulder reassuringly. "Do not worry. They will not bite," she whispered. "At least, not very hard." Bravaro's face shot up, A twinkle of mischief shone in her eyes. She winked as she ushered him into the central room of the nursery.

With an encouraging nudge from Dosanyata, Bravaro stepped forward to join the two boys at the table where a tutor was starting to run through a history lesson. The man looked up and extended a hand as Bravaro neared. "Hello. Bravaro, is it? We have heard a lot about you over the last few weeks. Please join us."

Bravaro sat down, nodding to the other boys, who eyed him with open curiosity. "Hello," he said. The older boy, Valian, smiled shyly and hid his face.

Prince Shoram looked at him, cocking his head to the side. "You are a brave boy," he said and turned his attention back to the man standing at the head of the table.

Bravaro blinked, stunned by the prince's words. The hair on his arms stood on end as if the boy knew more than he should at four years old. He seemed wise beyond his years. Was he a seer of some kind, perhaps?

"I am Kyin," the man introduced himself, calling Bravaro's attention away from the prince. "I am Valian's father, but I also act as tutor for the boys." Kyin motioned to the older boy, and Bravaro was surprised he had been wrong about his parentage. He had thought the boys were brothers.

Kyin went on before Bravaro could respond. "The King has instructed me to educate you along with them. We will cover subjects on history, religion, *Luminsilkis,* governmental structure, arithmatic and literature. General Zalim will oversee your military training. The boys have already started theirs, but of course you will be far more advanced in your skills than they. Lord Adagio tells me you shoot?"

"I do, sir. I am honored that you are willing to tutor me." Bravaro shifted in his seat, unnerved at Valian's even gaze. He had decided to turn around and look at him since his father seemed eager to engage him in conversation. Hopefully, in time, Bravaro could prove that he was his friend.

"Not at all. It is a pleasure for me to help mold young minds, especially if they are willing to work hard. I hear that you have a proficiency in languages as well?" Kyin went to a shelf built into the wall, reaching from floor to ceiling. It was brimming with books and scrolls. They seemed to be beckoning him, inviting him to discover their secret wisdom. Kyin retrieved a rolled bark parchment, stylus and ink pot and returned to the table.

Bravaro swallowed hard, nervous at being the center of attention. "I do not know how proficient I am, Master Kyin. But I will do my best to learn everything I can from you, sir." He fingered the stone necklace Manemna had given him, hidden under his cotton shirt. He had not had to use the language stone, having practiced the language tirelessly since his arrival.

Kyin gave him an approving nod. "Well, then, let us get started by all means. We were just about to start reading from the Creation Chronicles, when *Ilyo Na'ada* fashioned the world, and handed us the responsibility of being the Music Keepers. You may follow along as I read, boys." Kyin slid the writing instruments to Bravaro.

Bravaro was unsure what to do with the instruments. He had learned to speak the Luminian language but had spent little time working with writing and reading. He glanced up at Kyin with an embarrassed smile. "I am not sure these will be of much use to me yet, sir. I do not know how to write very well."

"Oh, well, that is no matter. I am sure you will pick it up quickly. For now, you may listen as I read."

Prince Shoram scooted closer to him on the bench, lacing his chubby little fingers through Bravaro's. Bravaro looked down at the prince, his brown eyes shining with interest. "It is alright. Master Kyin is a great teacher," he whispered.

Bravaro was taken aback for a moment. How had he guessed at his thoughts? Shoram squeezed his hand, and the gesture reminded him of how Intza had held his hand when he first came to Luminia. Jumbled images flashed through his mind. Tears sprang to his eyes as he remembered wandering through the forest, crying for his mother. It seemed like an eternity had passed since he had come to Luminia, even though it had only been five years. Would he ever regain all his memories of the Other World? He had been so frightened and alone, only a little older than the prince was now. But Intza had welcomed him with open arms, making him feel like part of the family.

"She is safe," Shoram leaned over and whispered to him again.

Bravaro's heart nearly stopped. He looked down at Shoram, who regarded him with childlike faith. His eyes seemed to pierce Bravaro's very soul. "Who?" Bravaro asked with urgency. Had the prince the gift of second sight? Had he seen where his sister was?

"Boys," Kyin scolded gently. "Are we listening or having our own conversation?"

Shoram let go of Bravaro's hand and faced Kyin. "We apologize, Teacher. It will not happen again."

Bravaro nodded his agreement and quieted. But he could not focus on the lesson. He had thought only the Musicians had The Sight as a gift from *Ilyo Na'ada*. But perhaps He bestowed it on those of the royal line as well? Whatever the case may be, Bravaro's mind spun. Was Intza safe, as Shoram had said? Or had he meant someone else—Souni? Or perhaps his birth mother? Whoever he had meant, Shoram's words had given him hope.

Shoram seemed to sense that Bravaro was watching him, and he turned slightly, giving him a wide smile. Bravaro returned his smile, feeling at home for the first time since he had fled his village. *Ilyo Na'ada, hear my prayer. Keep Intza and Mama safe until I can rescue them.*

CHAPTER 33
BRAVARO

S everal weeks passed as Bravaro adjusted to palace life. He felt so out of place at times, but Prince Shoram and Valian soon welcomed him as an older brother. In Hotun, he knew what was expected of him. He had worked alongside Manemna in the fields and then on his own after his passing. Bravaro longed to be out of doors, training in the art of war, as King Nissim had suggested during the survey of the borderlands.

However, the training had not been forthcoming. When he asked Kyin about it, his tutor only told him to be patient. A quick mind was far more valuable in a soldier than a sharpened sword. He must learn to think for himself before he handled a weapon.

Bravaro tucked his knees up, sitting on the window's wide ledge overlooking the island city's west side. He much preferred to look over the gardens and down at the lagoon, separated from the sea by wave-smoothed cliffs. These days, the city was a jumble of human-ity, loud and pervasive. His heart ached. No word of Intza's where-abouts had come from the squadrons patrolling around the Luminian borders. The raids had quieted, only popping up now and again. It would seem that the bandits had slaked their lust for bloodshed. For the time being.

"What are you doing?"

Bravaro put his feet down and climbed back into the safety of the nursery. Prince Shoram looked up at him with innocent eyes, and Valian soon joined him. "I was just thinking," he said.

Prince Shoram grabbed his hand. "About what?" He reminded Bravaro of Intza when he had first arrived in Luminia. She seemed to ask many questions, especially *why*, until he thought he would scream. But he did not mind. Not really. Shoram's questions made him feel close to his little sister.

"Oh, I was just thinking about when I get to start training in the barracks with the other soldiers," Bravaro replied. He did not want to worry them with his thoughts about their borders' safety nor his personal troubles with finding Intza.

Shoram and Valian's eyes went wide. "Are you going to be a soldier?" Valian asked, his voice tinged with respect and awe.

"Someday. Soon, I hope," Bravaro replied. Shoram pulled on his hand, and they entered the main room.

"Come along, boys. It is time for our walk," Kyin said. Dosanyata said goodbye to the boys, and they followed Kyin down the wide, bright corridors. However, instead of heading to the gardens as usual, Kyin led them in the opposite direction.

"Where are we going, Master Kyin?" Bravaro asked.

"King Nissim holds a war council today. I have asked permission to allow you boys to listen in." They passed the main courtroom doors and headed up to the balconies where privileged men of the upper classes could listen.

"You must sit still and be very quiet," Kyin instructed.

The boys took their seats, and Bravaro wondered how long Shoram and Valian could do as their teacher said. Bravaro, however, was enthralled. He and Kyin sat on either end of the row, with the younger boys in between, boxing them in.

He leaned in to listen, the dome-shaped roof just feet above their

FALL OF THE DAWN

heads giving the room the perfect acoustics to hear what was going on below.

"We must fight back, Your Majesty," one of the lords was saying. "With Tzotoeh on the offensive, we can mobilize our forces and take back the borderlands. We can even take over Tzotoeh, make them pay for what they have done!"

King Nissim sat on the edge of his throne. "And how do you suggest we raise the funds for this war, Lord Lamik?" The king leaned forward, pinning the older man with a severe stare. "With the country just now settling after the raids, we have to turn our focus inward: crop production, stabilizing the farmers, and building this momentous wall that you have all pressured me to construct."

Bravaro could not see Lord Lamik's face since he looked straight down at the top of his head. However, he could tell from his mannerisms that he was unhappy with the king's response.

"We cannot sit inside Lunthá and do nothing, Your Majesty. With respect, Tzotoeh must be made to pay—to act as an example of what becomes of those who attack our fair country."

Bravaro did not like Lord Lamik's tone. He glanced at Kyin and saw that he wore the same look of unease.

"People are already suffering, Lord Lamik. Your suggestion would only make that suffering worse. Who do you think is going to work on the wall construction? Who will fight in the ranks? You? Or perhaps your sons and grandsons?"

"I would rather fight than wait! Sending people to the borders would solve one problem, Your Majesty. The royal city would not be so crowded if we relocated people to the borderlands for construction. You yourself know that we have had a rise in disease and sickness due to overcrowding. We could also relocate farmers to new fields nearer the walled sections to produce crops for the workers and for the royal city. It is beneficial for all."

Bravaro could think of no argument against this, and the king seemed to come around to the idea. King Nissim rose from the throne, clasping his hands behind his back as he paced on the dais.

"Very well, Lord Lamik. I see the wisdom in your plan. However, we will need financing to pay the workers. Will that be coming from your coffers?" he asked.

Lord Lamik grunted as if the idea was preposterous. One of the other lords stood and bowed at the waist before the king. "Your Majesty, I will put up three-thousand *atzantas* for the project."

Bravaro gasped. One *atzanta* was a poor man's yearly wage. Lord Lamik looked around the room for a moment, baffled. Bravaro could hear the amusement in King Nissim's voice as he bowed his head toward the generous man's offer.

"Thank you, Lord Danib. That is most kind. Lord Lamik? Surely you could match that?"

Lord Lamik hesitated for only a second more before he acquiesced. "Very well. I will also donate three-thousand *atzantas.*"

"As will the palace treasuries," King Nissim replied. "Now that that is settled, let us move on to the next order of business."

Kyin motioned for the boys to follow him, pressing his finger to his lips. They followed him out of the courtroom and down a narrow, winding staircase.

"Where are we going now, Papa?" Valian asked.

Kyin took his son's hand and continued down the dim staircase. "We are going to see the Musicians. Lord Adagio asked me to stop in and introduce Bravaro to some of the other children."

Bravaro felt like he was being paraded in front of the entire population of Lunthá. But his fascination soon overcame his hesitancy. Bravaro was enthralled by all the instruments when they arrived in the Musicians Courtyard. He had only heard a sunrise being played from a great distance the few times he and his family had traveled to the royal city for high festival days. To see how they were played up close was mesmerizing.

Lord Adagio stood at the head of the class, with children spread around him in a semi-circle, sitting on cushions as he took them through their lessons. "Ahh, Master Kyin. Welcome." He waved him to the corner, and Kyin directed them to follow. A boy about his age and two younger girls approached them.

"Bravaro, this is Molto, Lord Adagio's eldest. And these are his daughters, Melodia and Haarmonae. Twins," Kyin added.

"Pleased to meet you," Molto said. He had an animal skin drum at his side, attached to a strap that was slung over his shoulder, allowing it to rest next to his hip. He placed his hand over his heart and bowed at the waist.

"Hello," Bravaro replied.

Haarmonae stepped forward and began walking in a circle around Bravaro. "Are you really from the Other World?" she asked.

"Lady Haarmonae," Kyin scolded. "That is quite enough."

Bravaro glanced over at the group of children who were sitting at low square tables. Each had their assigned table, with a small clay pot, a writing brush, and pieces of thinly cut bark from the eternal tree. "What are you doing?" Bravaro asked. He had seen people write before but had not yet had the chance to learn how.

Melodia stepped up beside him shyly and motioned for him to follow her over to her little table. "We are practicing our characters." She sat down on the cushion, making room for him. She took up the brush and started to write a character. "This is *Aaya*. It also stands for the first musical note in the scale. You see?"

Bravaro was a little confused. He knew nothing of music. "I suppose," he said slowly.

Melodia gave him a patient smile. "Here. There are seven notes in the scale. *Aaya , Besha, Cadesh, Desha, Elash, Fetash, and Galet.*" She wrote the symbols for each note down one side of the bark paper. "Each character of our language has a musical note that goes with it. *Aa* is paired with the musical note *Elash*. Do you see?" she asked.

Bravaro nodded. "I think so."

"Essentially, you could sing someone's name to get their attention, if you did not want to call them," Melodia said excitedly. She seemed very knowledgeable for someone so young. Of course, being a Musician, he was sure they started their training from birth.

"Could you sing my name?" Bravaro asked.

Melodia thought momentarily, then wrote his name out, placing the corresponding notes below the characters. "Yes, here we are," Melodia said. She took a deep breath, opened her mouth and began to sing in a clear soprano voice. The sound sent chills up his spine, thrilled by the tune. He glanced at Valian and Shoram, who were just as captivated as he was.

"Do my name!" Shoram said, clapping his little hands as he jumped up and down. Melodia laughed and wrote the prince's name as she had done with his. Bravaro stood aside so Melodia could sing Prince Shoram and Valian's names next. Out of the corner of his eye, he saw Master Kyin and Lord Adagio stand aside, whispering. No doubt, they were discussing him—the strange boy from another world.

CHAPTER 34

KYIN

Lord Adagio gave the rest of the children a break, then motioned for Kyin to join him near the window that over-looked the gardens. "How is he today?" he asked, nodding toward Bravaro.

"He is about as well as we can expect. He is still anxious to find his sister and mother." Kyin eyed the boy. "I can understand his sense of urgency."

So many years had passed since Kyin had seen his own family. And still he kept his secret locked away, fearful of who might be lurking in the shadows. However, he now enjoyed a station of trust and security in the palace, thanks to his years of hard work. Kyin and Dosanyata had done everything they could to prove themselves valuable in the last five years, and it had paid off. He had thought that Lord Delgadas being taken to the dungeon would be the end of his problems. However, there were others still loyal to him, even on the king's counsel. The difficulty was trying to separate who was loyal to Nissim and who was loyal to Delgadas. Confronting them face-to-face was not an option for Kyin, not with his past. He could not risk being recognized by one of the lords who had been there during his grandmother's time...

"As can I," Lord Adagio agreed, bringing Kyin back from his dark thoughts. He put a hand on his shoulder and turned him away from the class, so none of the children could see their faces. "Perhaps you can speak with him? You are the closest thing he has to a father figure. He needs someone to lean on."

Kyin had tried. Sometimes he felt Bravaro was beyond reaching, especially with this obsession for training with the sword. "Yes, I can speak with him. I am not sure how much good it will do. But I can try."

Lord Adagio sighed. "He is here for a reason, Master Kyin. I do not know the purpose, but there must be a reason."

He lifted a brow. Perhaps Lord Adagio also had secrets, just as he did. "I will do my best to help him settle, Lord Adagio."

Lord Adagio's eyes filled with fear, something Kyin had never seen before. His heart instantly quickened it's pace. If Lord Adagio was worried, something must be seriously wrong. "What is it, my lord? You do not think Bravaro is a traitor–?"

"No, no. That is not it," Adagio said. However, his haunted eyes showed signs of growing terror. He shook his head, and his once-easy smile had trouble reaching his lips. "I am sure not."

Kyin raised a brow. Lord Adagio seemed to be trying to convince himself, rather than being sure of anything. He would have to keep an even closer watch of the boy. They turned around and watched the children gathering around Melodia and Haarmonae. They were regaling their friends with their name songs, laughing with innocent glee and wonder as they sang. Lord Adagio crossed his arms over his chest, worry hanging like a heavy cloud over his friend's head. He could not help but worry, too. If only their children's innocence could last.

CHAPTER 35

BRAVARO

A sharp crack rang out around the training facility as wood smacked against wood. Sweat poured down Bravaro's face, running into his eyes. Muscles cramping, he refused to give in to his teacher, General Zalim. He would not be bested again. Not if he wanted to move up in the ranks.

"Focus, boy. You are letting your emotions control you," General Zalim said, as if the physical exertion was nothing to him. He side-stepped Bravaro's subsequent attempt to strike with the headless spear. Bravaro stumbled as he lost his balance.

He let out a guttural cry as he turned and lunged for the seasoned soldier. His wrist exploded with pain, and General Zalim expertly hit the practice spear, sending it careening through the air. Bravaro sank to his knees, frozen in place as General Zalim's spear stopped only a finger's breadth from his temple. He looked up at his wizened teacher, his chest heaving. There was a flush on the older man's cheeks and beads of sweat now standing out on his forehead.

"Careful, Bravaro. Your recklessness will get you killed if you do not learn to control your anger," he whispered so only Bravaro could hear. Bravaro's blood still ran hot, but the General allowed the

253

wooden spear to touch his head ever so slightly, sending a shiver through him. It was a warning.

The general lowered the practice weapon and straightened. He placed a hand on Bravaro's shoulder as he rose, and they walked to the edge of the circular training paddock. "You have skill, Bravaro, especially for one who has only just begun their training. But wielding a blade or a spear takes more than physical strength. It takes quickness of mind." General Zalim dismissed the onlookers, sending them back to their exercises. "You care too much about advancing through the ranks than learning what you will need to know when you get there. It is a process, my boy."

Bravaro let out a frustrated sigh, propping the practice spear against the stone wall that enclosed the ring. "I don't have time to lose, General. I want to go out with the next squadron patrolling the borders. It might be that my sister is still out there somewhere," he said. He was eager to prove himself, not only to find his sister but also to feel as if he belonged. Ever since coming to the palace, he had felt more out of place than ever before. People gave him odd looks and whispered behind their hands when they thought he was not looking.

His skin was a lighter shade than almost everyone he met. And it was not because he spent less time in the sun. Natural-born Luminians had a darker tint to their skin—beautiful and rich. He was stuck with barely a tanned cast to his otherwise white skin.

Sometimes, he wished he had either been born a true Luminian of the blood or had never come at all. What was worse, his memories of arriving in this land were still fractured. It had been so long ago, and he had been so young.

"You are troubled, Bravaro. Let me say this: you will find no peace if you continue to run from your demons. You must face them. That is what being a soldier is all about. And you must harness your anger, not give in to it."

"How can you be a soldier and not give in to anger? I have never seen you lose your temper, General Zalim. But I cannot seem to handle it, no matter what I do." Bravaro tore off the calf-skin finger-less gloves and tossed them over the wall. After weeks of hard train-ing, his hands were starting to callous. His muscles were beginning to pop out on his arms and legs. His back and shoulders grew stronger every day. But the General was correct. He would never advance unless he got his rage under control.

"I did not say I was never angry. My blood still gets up still when I am in the ring, just as yours does. However, I have learned to harness and focus it. You will learn this, too, in time. But first, I think there are things that haunt you—in here," he said, poking him in the head. "—and here," he moved his finger to point in the middle of his chest. "You must first untangle these things that are holding you back."

General Zalim paused, studying the boy. "You have grown much in the last few months. You work harder than any of the other boys his age. There is a fire in you, a fierce protectiveness that boils to the surface whenever you are faced with a new challenge." The general faltered, showing emotion that he rarely allowed anyone else saw "If I had ever had a son, I imagine he would have been very much like you."

The general hung his head and cleared his throat. "Run through your interference paces, then go to Master Kyin for your lessons," he instructed.

Bravaro grimaced. He would much rather have kept training, then go straight to the special arena where the interference paces were held. Large boulders, walls of thorns, and many other obstacles were set in place, and the boys were timed to see how fast they could get through their paces. Bravaro was faster than most. Evidently, that did not matter to the general.

He raked a hand through his hair and went to do the General's bidding. It was almost too easy. Bravaro considered skipping his lessons with Master Kyin for the day and continuing his exercises. However, when he finished the course, Master Kyin was waiting on the sidelines.

"You get faster everyday," Master Kyin said. He wore a proud grin on his face. But it quickly faded as Bravaro came closer.

"A lot of good it is doing me," he muttered. He peeled the cotton shirt off and slung it over the low wall surrounding the course. "If it is just the same to you, I would rather stay here this afternoon."

Kyin glanced toward the watch tower, where General Zalim leaned against the turrets, watching his students. He gave a deft nod. Kyin nodded in return and put a hand on Bravaro's shoulder.

"Not today. I have a very special lesson for you. One for you alone," he replied. He turned and started toward the gate. Bravaro hesitated, curious as to what special activity Kyin could have planned for him. He followed, as if his feet had a mind of their own.

"You're to teach me on my own today?" Bravaro asked. "Why?"

"Because I can see that you are struggling with something. Why do you not tell me what it is?"

"I thought you knew everything," Bravaro said, only slightly teasing.

"I do," Kyin shot back with a small smile, teasing him in return. "But strong friendships are not built by one who is all-knowing and one who is not. It takes an exchange of ideas, one or both people checking their strengths at times in favor of relationship. It is what *Ilyo Na'ada* does for us." Kyin watched the boy expel a breath of resignation. "Why do you not tell me what is troubling you, Bravaro? You have been like this for days."

Bravaro shook his head. "I am sorry—"

"It was not a rebuke. I want to help, Bravaro, if I can." Kyin motioned for him to follow him out of the training facility and through the gardens.

Bravaro was grateful for the fresh air as they walked along the winding stone paths. He felt more at ease there than surrounded by the opulence of the palace. "I had a dream again last night. Well, for the last several nights, really." He plopped down on a marble bench, and Kyin sank beside him. "It was about my birth father."

Kyin raised a brow, curious. "And this upsets you?"

"Yes," Bravaro said simply. "He was screaming at my mother and me. But in the dream, everything is splintered. Dissonant. I cannot make out his face. My mother's is a little clearer, but still blurred." He sighed heavily, looking away from Kyin's perceptive gaze. "Sometimes I wonder if I will ever feel at home here. Living with Manemna and Souni, little Intza, I felt like I belonged, like I had a purpose. But here I feel—" He let his words trail off, not exactly sure how to put it into words.

"Lost?" Kyin finished.

"Yes, lost. I see how the others look at me. I hear what they say behind my back. I am a curiosity, someone to gawk at. Sometimes I wonder if I really belong anywhere."

Kyin placed a hand on his shoulder and hugged him. "You do belong. Bravaro, I am not sure what these dreams mean, but perhaps they are only memories, distractions meant to keep you from your goals."

"How can I belong? I do not even know where, or who, I come from!" Bravaro stood up, pacing away from the marble bench. He turned around, pleading with Kyin to understand.

"And you think that knowing who your parents are will make you whole?" Kyin asked.

It sounded silly when Kyin put it that way. He let out a breath of frustration. "I don't know!" He growled, glaring at the sky. "Maybe. All I keep thinking is if I don't know who my father and mother were, how can I know who I am? And how can I know where I fit in this world if I do not even know where I came from?"

"Come with me." Kyin rose from the bench, his eyes softening. Without another word, he started down the path, clasping his hands behind him. Bravaro followed hesitantly, knowing that there was likely a long lecture ahead. However, Kyin said nothing when he caught up. He only looked around at the lush terraced gardens and hanging vines, their tendrils reaching for the sun like children stretching their arms out to be picked up by their mother.

Kyin led him through a somewhat hidden wooden doorway off

the main path. Bravaro had to duck as he entered. The contrast between the warm sunlight and the cool, dimly lit space sent goose-flesh climbing up his arms. "The library? I never knew there was an entrance here."

"It is a special room off the library. This is where the most precious manuscripts in all of Luminia are kept. There are histories here that many have forgotten about. I have not brought you and the younger boys down here for lessons, as they are not ready. However, I believe you are."

Kyin walked deeper into the room. As Bravaro's eyes adjusted, he saw shelf upon shelf of bark books, all painstakingly detailed in *Luminsilkis*. He was still trying to master the written language. Still, it fascinated him to look upon the characters that seemed more like artwork to his untrained eyes.

He followed his master to a high table and waited as Kyin climbed a wooden ladder and retrieved a book from one of the uppermost shelves. When he came down, he unfolded the fluted bark book. It was no wider than two spans of his hand and three spans tall. "This is the history of Enrikae Hoostiano and Elee-ash D'Tzoto. They came from your world many years ago."

Bravaro's eyes widened, and he ran his fingers lightly over the rough-hewn surface, almost as if it were too holy to touch. The characters had been expertly carved into the woody flesh first. Then, white paint had then been applied to the crevices of the letters so they stood out against the dark brown wood. "There were others?" he asked.

"Yes. I know that you are struggling with where you belong, Bravaro. You have endured heavy loss in your young life. These men did as well. But as you will read, one of them came to love Luminia so much that, even when the chance to return to his homeland was presented, he chose to stay."

Bravaro frowned. He had wondered how Manemna had known he was speaking English when he first came to Luminia. Perhaps it would explain why Manemna had known enough to converse with him when Bravaro had stumbled into Luminia.

"Why are you showing me this?" Bravaro asked. Just because other people had come from his world, it did not help his cause. He was still an orphan boy, caught between two very different worlds.

"Perhaps you will find some answers within—when you become a little more proficient with your *Luminsilkis*." Kyin's eyes danced with mischief. "Let it stand as an incentive."

Bravaro met his gaze, and the compassion he saw shining from them was like a dagger in his heart. He had no right to act the way he had in the garden. Master Kyin had been nothing but kind and patient with him. He was ashamed of his outburst.

Kyin put his hands on his shoulders, waiting for him to look into his face. "Bravaro, knowing who your birth father is will not magically reveal your purpose—in this world or any other. If you anchor your identity in someone like that, in a fallible human, you are going to be disappointed. Now, I cannot say whether knowing where you came from might not give you some closure with your past. But trying to base your identity on who this man was is not the answer."

"Then what is?" Bravaro asked. He feared he already knew what Kyin's answer would be.

"*Ilyo Na'ada* is your Creator, Bravaro. He knows you better than any human ever could. He placed you here for a purpose. Perhaps that would be the best place to ask some of these questions." Kyin flashed him a wry smile. "He is an excellent listener, you know."

Bravaro did not want someone just to listen. He wanted answers. Kyin refolded the book and handed it to him. Bravaro took it, hanging his head. "I will try," he promised. However, the turmoil still swirled through his soul, like black sludge spreading through a crystal clear pond. Looking down at the history book, he wondered if he would ever find the answers he sought.

CHAPTER 36

BRAVARO

Year of the Dagger, 984

"Get him out of here!"

An angry voice echoed through the house, gaining in volume as it swelled like a great iron bell in Bravaro's mind.

"He's just a child, Frank. I will clean it up." Bravaro instantly recognized his mother's furtive pleas.

"I don't care if he's just a kid! I work my fingers to the bone to provide for this family, and to give you this house you begged me for. Coulda stayed in that dump on First Street if Joshua was going to ruin this place." He growled. "I wish he was never born."

Footsteps receded down the hallway. A door slammed in the distance, and Bravaro jumped. His eyes flew open as his mother touched his shoulder, drawing him out from behind the recliner where he had taken refuge. She pulled him into a hug, rubbing his back. "It's alright, son. Your father is just a little tired from work. You know better than to draw on the walls. What's gotten into you?" she asked softly, tousling his hair.

"I'm sorry, Mama," he said, sniffing back tears. "I just wanted to color a picture for Father."

261

"And that was very sweet of you to want to do for him. But the wall is not the place to do that, sweet boy. Come on, I'll give you some butcher paper and some crayons." His mother took him by the hand and led him toward the kitchen. However, he jerked his hand free, stalling in the center of the living room. Tears pricked his eyes. The more he tried to hold them back, the more upset he became. He did not want to be anywhere near his father now, much less draw a picture for him.

His mother turned around, kneeling in front of him. "It's alright, darlin'. Your father will go take a nap for a while and when he wakes up, you can give him your drawing."

He shook his head. "I don't want to draw anymore," he said dully. No matter what he did, he could not seem to make his father proud. Mama often made excuses for him. They could count on his father growing meaner by the minute whenever he drank that yellow-brown liquid from his glass bottle.

She placed her hand under his chin, giving him a sad smile. "He loves you, Joshua. It's just sometimes he doesn't know how to show it."

"I wish he would go back to the war. I liked it better when it was just me and you, Mama," he said. He touched her cheek, running his fingers down the poorly disguised bruise under her eye. She quickly turned her face away, standing. Mama covered her cheek with her hand, trying to shield him from her pain.

"Don't say such things, Joshua. We are lucky your father came home at all. We should be grateful," she said, her words echoing around him. However, he could tell she was having trouble believing what she had just said. Her face faded from his vision, clouded by a murky blackness.

No! He was not ready to leave her yet. Bravaro tried to hold on, to stay in the dream just a while longer. However, he felt his mind being pulled toward wakefulness. His mother reached for him, calling his name with such longing that it made his heart clench. "Joshua... Come back to me..."

~

BRAVARO AWOKE WITH A START. He sat up in bed, sweat pouring down his bare chest. He dug the heels of his hands into his eyes. When he looked up again, he saw gray light filtering through the curtains. The silky white fabric covering the windows was blown by a gentle breeze. He rolled off the cushions that made up his bed and stood, stretching as he padded over to the window.

The city was still fast asleep, with only a few people stirring in the marketplace as they readied their stalls to open once the Musicians played. The dream of his birth parents hung around him like flies buzzing around a carcass. No matter what he did, he could not be rid of them. What good was it to dream of his mother, knowing he was powerless to return to her? Of course, he had no desire to be reunited with his father. Only for her sake would he ever consider returning to the Other World.

He sighed heavily and retrieved his armor, sword, and training boots from the exquisitely carved wooden cabinet near his bed. The only thing that seemed to chase away the gloom that his nightmares brought was running drills in the training ring. For the last seven years, Bravaro had worked hard to show his worth as a soldier. He had excelled in his military training, becoming skilled with the sword and spear and improving his talent with the bow. Few trainees were as adept as him in hand-to-hand combat. Of course, he had not been tested in battle yet, but he felt that the time to prove his metal was on the horizon.

After donning his armor, he grabbed his sheathed sword and slipped silently from the room. He, Valian, and the prince had long since moved from their quarters in the nursery. He and Valian had moved into smaller palace quarters closer to the barracks. Prince Shoram had gone to larger quarters in the royal wing. Not only had they grown too old to be under Dosanyata's constant care, but they had had to make room for Shoram's half-sisters. Three daughters, all with the same flaming red hair as their mother, had been born to the royal couple since Bravaro's arrival at court. Bravaro had become fast friends with Prince Shoram and Valian, taking the role of an older brother. He helped them in their training, drilling them relentlessly.

Bravaro hurried through the spacious halls, stopping at the kitchens to swipe a freshly baked roll filled to the brim with seeds and dates. One of the cooks eyed him with a wry smile, swatting at his hand as he took the sweet roll off the baking paddle. "Behave yourself, Master Bravaro. I shall report you to Lord Adagio," she scolded with a good-natured smile.

He took a bite of the soft, warm roll and grinned. "You would not report me, Rysa. You would miss me too much," Bravaro shot back. His words drew a laugh, and she rolled her eyes, turning to knead the lump of dough before her on the wooden table. He hurried out the side door of the kitchens and across the cobbled path toward the training facilities at the palace's rear.

The hard-packed dirt floor of the training arena was silent as he entered. His compatriots, who slept in the barracks just outside the palace walls, would not be up until after sunrise. Bravaro liked to come here when all was still, giving rise to his thoughts before he was pulled this way and that by the needs of others. He was an aide to General Zalim, and his days were filled with errands or training exercises. Of course, he still had his lessons with Master Kyin and the boys. While he looked forward to his time locked away in the library, his restlessness only seemed to worsen with the threat of looming war. Delgadas and his horde had been quiet after the initial raids on the borderlands. Seven years after the alliance with Detallma had been concreted by the king's marriage to Queen Tamil, things had gone nerve-rackingly silent. The attackers had not come further inland after so many had sought refuge in Lunthá. Bravaro could feel that change was in the air. Delgadas would not remain silent forever.

To combat his growing unease, he spent more and more time in the arena, honing his skills for the moment he finally met blades with the Tzotoen raiders who had stolen away his family and friends. Perhaps *Ilyo Na'ada* would smile on him and give Lord Delgadas into his hands to exact revenge.

Bravaro began working through his daily exercises, swinging the blade this way and that. He dodged an invisible blow, twisting to the right and bringing the sword around as if to undercut an opponent's legs. He kept his momentum going, standing to his feet once more. Suddenly, a real blade flashed before him, and he deflected it at the last second, his heart thundering in his chest. A burst of energy surged through him, and he blocked another blow, catching sight of a hooded figure lunging at him from the shadows.

"You are getting old, Master Bravaro. Usually you would have heard me enter the ring." An unmistakable female voice sounded from the dark folds of the hood.

Bravaro gave a sardonic smile. "Perhaps you are finally getting better at stalking your prey, Lady Haarmonae," he shot back. "Heaven knows it has taken you long enough."

She lunged again at the insult, but he was prepared for her this time. He twisted to the left, evading the blow and came around with his sword, knocking her backward. The hood fell off her head, revealing her dark hair and olive complexion. He narrowly missed slicing her forehead, and she fell backward. "Careful!" she cried. "This is supposed to be a friendly fight," she laughed.

"May I remind you that you are the one who snuck up on me?" Bravaro shot back.

Green fire danced in her eyes. "True." She shrugged, and they were at it again, lunging and circling each other around the ring. They circled for several seconds until Bravaro spotted his opportunity. She stepped forward, raising the sword and bringing it down above his head. He knocked the sword from her hand, sending the heavy blade careening through the air. She gasped in pain, watching her blade whiz through the air and land with a ringing thud on the ground a few yards away. He stepped forward and sheathed his sword with a contented grin.

His features softened as she held her arm. "Forgive me. Are you injured?" he asked, taking her hand gently. "I have been known to be a bit rough."

She shook her head, wincing as he felt the bones in her slender wrist. "No, I am alright. I told you to treat me like the other students," she said. "Papa would be angry if he found me here, but I cannot sit aside and do nothing."

He continued to feel the bones, ensuring nothing was broken. Her heart rate spiked under his fingers. He took his hand away, helping her stand. "It doesn't seem to be broken," he said. "Your father is right to worry about you. If he is not careful, he will find your bed stuffed with pillows to disguise your disappearance when we march into battle," Bravaro teased.

"Yes, well, I prefer to leave the weaving and poetry-writing to my fair sister," she said with a mischievous grin.

"You are just as fair as your twin sister," Bravaro smirked. And indeed, she was beautiful. She and her sister had both bloomed over the last year or so. At sixteen, they were the envy of every lady they met and the muse of every red-blooded young man. They were alike in every way, pertaining to their facial structure and figures. The only difference in appearance between the sisters was that Melodia had inherited her father's light blue eyes and Haarmonae had her mother's green eyes. Melodia was the soft-spoken, imaginative twin with beautiful locks of flowing dark blonde hair.

Conversely, Haarmonae was spirited, stubborn, and passionate with darker waves of brunette hair. He knew she sometimes despaired of the family she was born into, longing for combat. Service in the army was forbidden to Musicians. Even so, she often met Bravaro in the training ring to practice swordplay or shoot her bow. While she was an accomplished Musician in her own right, it was not where her passion lay.

Haarmonae walked over to her sword, picking it up to replace it in the sheath at her side. They walked together toward the edge of the ring. "Perhaps we look alike. But she is much more graceful than I."

"You are a better shot," he argued. He had been teaching both of the girls about archery since coming to live at the palace. Although

266

he would not want to admit it, Haarmonae had long ago exceeded him in skill. He removed his belt and laid his sword atop the half wall surrounding the training ring. "Then again, you practice more. What are you doing up so early, anyway? Don't you have a sun to rise?" he teased.

She swatted his arm playfully. "I do. They are probably waiting for me now. Molto was already awake when I snuck out."

"And he didn't stop you?" Bravaro teased. "What kind of brother is he?"

"The pre-occupied kind," Haarmonae sighed. "He is obsessed with reading the prophecies, specifically those of Lady Tzizenah. He says that there is something coming that is worse than we could imagine." She sighed. "He has been trying to warn others. But no one seemed to want to listen."

"He would not tell father. Molto knows I need to get away from my lessons, to feel like I am doing something useful. Things have been so stressful lately, I could not sleep. It helps to get out some aggression. Thank you, by the way," she said with a sideways smirk.

Bravaro turned around and leaned against the wall, inclining his head toward the east. "Well, that is one way of taking out aggression, I suppose. You are lucky I did not take your head off, sneaking up on me like that."

Haarmonae joined him in leaning against the wall and crossed her arms over her chest. "What are *you* doing up so early? More bad dreams?" she asked, ignoring his halfhearted rebuke.

Bravaro stilled, sighing. "Yes, actually" he answered. "They are getting more frequent."

"They always seem to this time of year," Haarmonae replied. She had been a faithful friend, along with Melodia and their family. They knew of his true origins and had been there to offer comfort and friendship when his frustration threatened to drive him mad.

"Well, I should go. Perhaps the sunrise will chase your troubles away," she said, socking him playfully in the arm. She walked away, leaving her sword belt next to his. He pushed himself away from the wall, looking on in concern.

"Shall I walk you to the terrace?" he asked.

She turned around, walking backward through the training yard. "No. I must go home first. I forgot my violin," she said. She raised her shoulders in a self-deprecating shrug and rolled her eyes heavenward.

He chuckled. "What kind of Musician are you?"

Haarmonae's laughter echoed over the training ring. "The late kind!" She backed away, smiling all the while, then slipped through one of the side doors leading into the palace.

Sadness settled over him after she was gone. He sighed, heading to the weapons room to stow away his sword until he returned later that afternoon. A few moments later, a few of the other trainees entered.

"What are you doing here so early, Bravaro? You know you will never be as good as me." Sensha pushed into the room and took the sword Bravaro had just replaced. He unsheathed the blade and looked at it, then at Bravaro with a smirk. "He's so terrible he has to train with girls."

Sensha looked over his shoulder at the three boys standing behind him, all of them chuckling. Sensual was one of many of Lord Lamik's grandsons. He was cruel, just like his grandfather. Bravaro presumed Sensha's father, who had died last year, had sent him to the barracks to learn some respect. So far, it had not worked.

"What do you want, Sensha?" Bravaro asked. He did not have time to teach him a lesson. General Zalim was waiting for him.

"I want to know why you think you have to pretend to be better than the rest of us," he spat. "You are the first one here and the last one to leave, but you will never be one of us. You are just a pawn for the king. A nursemaid for his son." More laughter from Sensha's friends.

Bravaro clenched his fists. He knew Sensha was jealous. His father had wanted him to distinguish himself. He was a terrible swordsman, thanks to his temper. "Well, I will let you get out to the training ring. I am sure you have much to do." He turned to leave. General Zalim would not thank him for fighting with his own squadron. He heard the blade sing as Sensha pulled it the rest of the way from its scabbard. Bravaro kept walking.

"Come back, little Bravaro, if you are brave enough, and we will have a real fight," Sensha threw the challenge at his back. "I'll make you wish you were never born!"

CHAPTER 37

BRAVARO

He was angry enough to return and teach Sensha the lesson he so desperately needed. But it would have to wait until after he met with General Zalim. Sensha's words echoed in his mind, *"never been born..."*

It was what his birth father had wished. And he had gotten what he wanted, in a way. Had Frank been relieved when he had disappeared? Over the years, he had begun to remember more from his past, but none of the memories of his birth father were good. He sucked in a breath against the pain rising in his chest.

He stormed past the nursery, hating Sensha. He could not know the pain he inflicted by using those words. Bravaro was more than a *nursemaid* to Prince Shoram. They were like brothers. He would not let anyone hurt him no matter the cost.

The nursery door opened just as he passed, and he nearly ran Dosanyata over. He stumbled to the side, steadying her so she would not land on the floor.

"Forgive me," he said hurriedly. "Are you alright?"

Dosanyata righted herself, gripping his arm. She smiled, her eyes full of understanding. "I am quite alright. Forgive me, Bravaro. I did not hear you coming down the corridor."

Bravaro bowed slightly at the waist. "I should have been watching where I was going. Excuse me," he said more gruffly than he had intended.

"Wait. What has happened?" Dosanyata asked. She kept a firm grip on his arm. "Are you not feeling well?"

Bravaro did not want to burden her. "I am fine. Thank you," he said and tried to leave. However, before he knew what he was about, Dosanyata had pulled him into the nursery. She closed the door, pinning him with her knowing gaze.

"You are not," she argued. And she was right. "Sit down and tell me what is troubling you. Have you cut yourself again during training?" she asked.

"No. I am well, I assure you," Bravaro said. He tried to walk around her, but she placed a hand on his shoulder and pushed him down before the low table.

"You are *not* fine," she said again. "Now, tell me what it is. Or must I call Kyin?"

Bravaro shook his head, giving a short laugh. "No, please do not do that." Sighing, his mood turned serious. "Very well. I had another dream last night. About my real parents."

They had talked many times about his childhood back in the Other World. Dosanyata's eyes filled with concern. "And?"

"I wish I could be free of them, that is all." He picked at the calluses on his hands. He was seventeen—a full-grown man in the eyes of society. He did not have time to deal with his past. His father's words rang in his ears, like daggers stuck into his heart. He had grown and matured over the years, but sometimes, he still felt like that lost little boy cowering in fear of his father's rage.

"You cannot run from your past, Bravaro. No matter how far and fast you go, it will always catch up to you," Dosanyata said softly. She touched his arm, willing him to look at her. However, he could not meet her gaze. If he did, he knew the unmanly tears would start to flow.

Instead, he gave way to anger. "Why, Dosanyata? Why didn't he want me? I tried so hard to be the son he wanted. I tried to be good, to not get in his way. But it was never enough for him!" He jumped to his feet, pacing a ways away. Bravaro raked a hand through his hair. "Sometimes I wonder if it would have been better if I had died in those woods outside of Hotun."

Dosanyata rose, coming to his side. "Do not talk like that, Bravaro. You are here for a reason."

"Yes, but how can I know what that reason is when my own father wished me dead?" he pleaded. His anger abated, giving way to grief. "Why didn't he want me?"

Dosanyata wrapped her arms around him, and after a few seconds hesitation, he wrapped his arms around her shoulders. He stood a head above her, but he was comforted by her embrace. She was very much like his birth mother in many ways. Bitter tears pooled in his eyes, and he was ashamed.

"I do not know why he said those terrible things, Bravaro. I cannot imagine a father acting that way toward his only son. But I know that you were not placed in the world, or the Other, by accident." She pulled away, looking up into his face.

She fixed her eyes on his, searching their depths. "What else?" she asked.

Bravaro sniffed hard, looking up to try and keep the tears at bay. How could she know what he was thinking before he seemed to? "I am afraid I am becoming just like him. Sometimes, I feel this rage rising up inside me—enough to kill—and it frightens me."

"You are not him, Bravaro." She cupped his cheek when he would not look at her. "*You are not him,*" she said again with more force this time.

He hung his head, nodding. "I wish I could be sure."

"I am sure," she gave an encouraging smile. "I have seen the way you are with the children. You would lay down your life for Shoram.

You do not have to follow in your father's footsteps, Bravaro. You must let go of the past. Forgive your father."

Bravaro frowned. He was unsure he had the strength to do that. "How can I after the way he hurt my mother and me?"

Dosanyata drew him back to the table and made him sit. "Holding onto unforgiveness for your father does not hurt him, Bravaro. It hurts you." She poked a finger in his chest. "Forgiving him is the only way to be free of this pain, as you say you want to be. Let it go, Bravaro. Let go of the pain and give it to *Ilyo Na'ada*."

Bravaro nodded. He was not sure he was ready to give it up. Somehow, it felt as if the pain had become a part of him, giving him strength.

Dosanyata grabbed his hands, no doubt seeing the struggle. "My father was much like yours, Bravaro. When I was born, he was so sure I would be the boy he had been waiting for. But I was the last in a line of six girls. My mother died giving birth to me, and he blamed me for it."

He raised his brows. "What did you do?" he asked.

"I was angry for many years. And then I married Kyin, and tried to look to him for the healing I needed from the wounds my father inflicted. But he could not give it. Only *Ilyo Na'ada* can take that pain and turn it for good. If you allow Him, he will do that for you, Bravaro."

Bravaro thought for a moment. She rose and took his hands, gently tugging him to his feet. Dosanyata touched his cheek, then slid her hand to his chest, placing it right over his heart. "You are a noble man, Bravaro. I am proud of you. And I think, if your father could see you now, he would be, too. Most often the people who hurt us are acting out of their own private pain."

He exhaled, feeling like a part of the weight he had been carrying for so long was slowly starting to lift. "It is that simple, is it? I just forgive him?" he asked, still with a tinge of bitterness. It seemed like an impossible feat.

"Yes. Day after day—sometimes hour after hour—you choose to

forgive. One day, you will look back on this choice and realize that you no longer harbor hatred or bitterness. I know, because it is what I had to do." She let her hand fall to her side. "You do not have to let your past dictate your future, young Bravaro. The man I see in front of me is brave and loyal and kind. You were born to be a leader." A sad smile touched her lips. "I would hate to see him disappear under a cloak of bitterness."

Dosanyata could not know what her words meant to him. He felt the tears springing to his eyes again but quickly blinked them away. "Thank you, Dosanyata," he choked. She hugged him so fiercely that he feared she would crack a rib. He laughed as she released him.

They walked to the door, and she saw him off. "Hold your head up high, Bravaro." Her smile was radiant. "I am very much glad that you were born."

Bravaro gave a short laugh. "So am I." He thanked her again and started down the hall. As he headed toward his meeting with the general, he thought over what Dosanyata had said. Perhaps she right about his father acting out of his own pain.

But he was not ready to forgive him yet.

CHAPTER 38

ADAGIO

Adagio made his way up the steep hill toward his home at a much slower pace than had been his norm in years past. Indeed, it was not the physical ineptitude that held him back this morning but the weight of anxiety over their increasingly dire situation. Sometimes, he wished he had never taken up the vacant job that Lord Delgadas had left. The gray light of dawn was touching the eastern hills, and he quickened his pace as he rounded the sharp bend leading onto his street, knowing that he was on the verge of being late.

He nearly smacked into a young woman as he did so. He steadied her, offering apologies for almost running her down. "I beg your pardon, Miss." Trepidation settled in his chest. What was she doing on these dark streets so early in the morning? Lunthá was no longer safe for a lone woman, who might find themselves molested or worse by any number of vagabonds that roamed the streets. The men who had built the wall at their borders were now returned, save for the ones who had perished in the process.

"Papa!"

Adagio's anger swelled when he heard Melodia's voice. He pulled her toward their home, which lay only a few yards away, incensed. "What are you doing out at this hour? Without your brother or I?" His anger bubbled over, propelled by his fear for her. "I would expect something like this from Haarmonae, but not from you—" Haarmonae thought she was sneaky, but he knew of her early morning adventures in the training ring with Bravaro. He would have to have a long talk with the boy to make sure he was not encouraging her too much. Perhaps it was time he put a stop to it completely. Haarmonae's place was in the home, learning the secret arts of the Musicians, not swordplay.

"Papa, listen," she hissed, pulling him to a stop with a force that surprised him. "Delgadas is back!"

Adagio's heart nearly fell out of his chest. "Delgadas? That is impossible. How—" His mind reeled. He started toward the house but changed course mid-step. He had to get to the palace to ensure the queen's safety and that of the royal children. The king was away now, but that might be Delgadas's reason for coming. What could Delgadas manipulate the king into doing if he captured the prince? "We must get to the palace. Get Molto and tell him to alert General Zalim—"

Again, she interrupted him. "There is no time," came her furtive plea. "He is in the house right now. He has Mama."

Adagio sprang into action before he knew what he was doing. He hurried toward the house, remembering Melodia as an afterthought. He turned, grasped her hand, and they ran together to the front stoop. Halting at the cracked front door, he listened for signs of a struggle. All was silent.

"Stay here. You should be safe." He looked around, realizing her 'shadow' was missing. "Where is Haarmonae?"

"I spotted her sneaking out of our room over an hour ago." Melodia's voice shook, her eyes filled with inexplicable fear. "I was about to go after her when Lord Delgadas and his soldiers ambushed the house and took Mama. They are in there now, waiting for you in the inner courtyard." Her hands shook as she drew her mantle closer.

Adagio nodded once, placing his hands on her shoulders and pushing her toward the shadows behind the door. "Stay here, and if you hear things turn for the worst, run to the palace."

"Should I not run now, Papa?" Melodia was courageous in her gentle way. But he did not trust her to get to the palace unharmed.

"No. Let me see what Delgadas wants first. I would not want to risk your mother's life before I know the full extent of the situation." Adagio patted her cheek gently, trying to reassure her, even though he felt his fear might suffocate him. She gripped his arm briefly and disappeared into the shadows behind the front door.

Adagio entered his home, every muscle on alert. He fingered the handle of the small dagger he always carried on his person. It had become necessary since the Tzotoen soldiers started raiding their borderlands. People were prone to uncharacteristic violence when propelled by fear and hunger.

Adagio pushed these thoughts away, trying to silence his mind. He slipped off his shoes, inching through the foyer and down a short hallway toward the murmur of voices floating to him. The hallway opened into the central courtyard, where they took their meals and sat about the hearth, composing or reading as a family. He rounded the corner and saw his nemesis standing before the hearth. A fire was crackling in the hearth behind him, but even with that, he looked deathly chilled. He stood hunched over, peering over his hawk-like shoulder around the room.

"Adagio. At last. We thought you would never return."

The voice accompanying the words was gravelly, with a strange, high-pitched tone. Adagio remembered how Delgadas's voice would climb in pitch when he was upset. The hair on his arms stood on end. "Indeed? It is I who should be surprised at your return, Delgadas. It is a wonder you dare show your face here in Lunthá after everything you have done to bring destruction on us."

Delgadas turned slightly, and Adagio held back a gasp with difficulty. The whole right side of his face had turned an ugly, scaly black with three ridged red lines running diagonally over his eyelid and cheek. The cracks between the snake-like scales seemed to be radiating with a painful orange glow. His tight, evil smile made the skin on his right cheek go taught, and Adagio had to swallow hard to keep the bile from rising into his throat. Delgadas had lost a considerable amount of weight since Adagio had last seen him. However, the most unnerving part about Delgadas' changed appearance, was that his gray eyes had turned a bright, other-worldly green.

Adagio moved further into the room but halted when four armed Tzotoen guards stepped out of the shadows. Their chests and arms were naked, with nothing but simple calf-skin breeches covering their lower extremities. The customary blood-red paint had been splattered across their faces to instill fear in their enemies. And, of course, they all bore the black and red tattooed markings over their limbs. They leveled nasty-looking spears at him, the obsidian tips shaped like snake heads gleaming in the firelight. Adagio held up his hands, not wanting to further endanger his family by doing something rash.

"Always the fighting spirit, I see," Delgadas mocked him. "Sit down next to your lovely wife while I state my purpose in coming."

Adagio looked to his left, seeing his wife huddled on the floor with a spear aimed at her back. She turned her fear-lined face so she could meet his gaze. Adagio saw that a bruise was forming under her right eye. Anger welled up in his chest, and he clenched his fists.

"Adagio—" she choked. "I am so sorry—"

"Quiet, you she-dog!" Delgadas snapped, interrupting her. He was even more vile than Adagio remembered, and not just because his skin looked like it had been burned. Perhaps it was the fact his body now looked as grotesque as his heart had been all those years. His sickness was no visible on the outside for all to see.

The soldier at her side lowered his spear and promptly backhanded her across the face. She rocked back, no doubt trying to keep hold of consciousness. Never before had she been treated in such a way.

Adagio lunged for the man, and Ritenueta cried out in fear. "No,

Adagio! Do not, I beg you!" she warned. But he would not listen. Adagio punched the man squarely on the jaw before he could move a muscle, sending him reeling to the floor. Adagio knelt to gather her into his arms. He silently dared them to try and take her from him. He would kill every last one of them. Or die trying. However, another soldier was onto him in moments, yanking him back and pressing a steel blade to his throat.

Adagio released his wife, holding up his hands in surrender as he took slow, calculated breaths. Would that he could ring their necks with his bare hands. "Touch her again, and I swear on the holy books of *Ilyo Na'ada*, I will end each and every one of your miserable lives in the most painful way possible," he said through clenched teeth. His gaze met that of Ritenueta's, her silent pleadings that he use wisdom going unheeded. No one assaulted his wife in his own home. He would rather die fighting off a hundred foes than stand and watch.

"One more sound from either of you and I will be forced to lose my temper," Delgadas said, sinking into a chair. He drew his cloak tighter around his shoulders despite the room being overly warm to Adagio. His voice was oddly calm, like the solace before a storm.

The soldier behind Adagio snarled, taking the blade from his throat before he pushed him onto the floor next to Ritenueta. He glared at Delgadas. "I assume it was you who prodded these heathen Tzotoen half-breeds into attacking our borderlands?" Adagio asked.

He heard the soldier behind him raise his blade with an unmistakeable metallic ring. Before he could bring it down on his head, Delgadas held up a hand to stay the blow. An evil smile spread across his lips. "You think yourself so smart, and yet you are so slow. I wondered how long it would take you and that insolent pup, Nissim, to put it all together. It is too late now, of course." He folded his hands in his lap and turned his head to the side, reminding Adagio of a vulture eyeing his prey.

"What is it you want, Delgadas?" Adagio asked through clenched teeth. He wrapped a protective arm around Ritenueta's shoulders and felt her shivering with terror. She pressed into his side, and he felt a little better, knowing he could protect her from another blow if one were forthcoming.

Delgadas stood and threw his black cape over his left shoulder. Adagio was again surprised. Delgadas had lost more than a little weight over the years. He looked positively skeletal. He hobbled back over to the fire, standing as close as possible. It was as if his body could not absorb enough warmth no matter how close he got. Adagio almost pitied him, for he had brought it on himself. However, as far as he could tell, his disfigurement was not from the Tzotoen tattoos. No, his skin looked like lava after it had started to cool, the underside glowing red with heat while the top cracked and blackened. This was much more sinister than the toxic ink of the tattoos so popular with their estranged brethren.

"What I want is very simple, Adagio. I want you and your family to leave Luminia, and never return." Delgadas turned slowly, peering over his shoulder like a hawk.

Adagio was stunned, his heart sinking into his stomach. "We cannot do that. You know what will happen if Luminia—"

"Of course, I know!" Delgadas exploded, slicing the air with his right hand as he turned on him. "That is why I want you to do it!"

"But our world will be ruined," Adagio continued. "The sun will not rise without someone to play music, and if I leave, the other Musicians will disperse." He stood up slowly to face his enemy, his legs shaking with the surge of anger running through him. "Surely you do not want to conquer Luminia only to be left with a country— no, with a world—in desolation?"

"I tire of your diatribe, old man," Delgadas croaked. "Do as I say, or I will kill your son."

Adagio froze. Movement at the top of the grand staircase leading to the second-floor bedrooms caught his eye, and he snapped his head up. A soldier appeared at the railing, along with his son. The firelight glanced off the dagger held to Molto's throat.

Molto looked like he would come apart at the seams, his features contorted in shame. He had a keen protective instinct but lacked the skill to carry out a defensive attack on the men who had raided his home and abused his family. "Father, no! Do not listen—!"

Molto's words caught in his throat as the soldier pressed the blade closer to his Adam's apple. "Shut up, boy, if you value your life."

"I would rather die than see Luminia go to dogs like you!" Molto spat. He gave a muffled gasp as the soldier pressed the blade into his skin even harder, drawing a trickle of blood. It was a promise of what would come if Molto did not cooperate. Adagio lurched forward but knew he was no match for so many seasoned warriors. The Tzotoens were known for their brutality, thirsty for bloodshed. Adagio could not bear to watch his son die because of his youthful recklessness.

Adagio held up his hand for silence from his son. "Very well, Delgadas," he said, his voice pleading. "We will go. But first you must promise that my son will go free." Adagio hated how his voice shook. He clenched and unclenched his fists. Perhaps he should have taken greater precautions, stationing guards at his home instead of leaving them open for an attack such as this.

"Now, there is a wise man," Delgadas said with a condescending smile. He nodded to the soldier holding Molto captive, who shoved Molto ahead of him. He wrapped his muscled arm around Molto's neck, keeping the blade at the ready should he try to run. They ambled awkwardly down the stairs and finally joined them in the sitting area.

"There is more," Delgadas croaked. "I want Tzizenah's prophecies and the royal chronicles from the palace library."

"What for?" Adagio asked. "You never seemed to care about Tzizenah's writings before."

"You are not really in a position to refuse," Delgadas uttered a short, gasping laugh. "It is the price I demand for the safe return of your son."

Adagio clenched his fists. "Very well," he agreed.

"You have two days to bring me what I want, and then you will leave the city," Delgadas returned to Adagio. The grating sound of his voice was enough to drive a person mad, like listening to an out-of-tune violin that screeched with every note. "We will meet you outside the city gates after the second sunrise. There, we will release your son to you. And if you try to warn the king, we will know about it. We will watch your every move. If anything goes wrong, we will kill him."

Delgadas ordered his soldiers out of the house with Molto in tow at a single flick of his wrist. Their calf-skin shoes made nary a sound on the marble floors. Molto shot a furtive glance at his father, silently pleading with him not to go through with it.

Delgadas was the last to go, one soldier waiting to guard his retreat. He turned to Adagio and snarled. "Two days, Adagio. Do not disappoint me."

And then he was gone, like a phantom in the night. When the house was silent again, Ritenueta flung herself into his arms, weeping inconsolably for their son. All he could do was hold her, shame overwhelming him at how he had failed his family.

"What are we going to do?" Ritenueta wept. "Our son—" she croaked. "Our only son—"

Adagio held her tighter, kissing her hair as the tears streamed down his face. *Why Ilyo Na'ada?* he prayed silently. *Why have you abandoned us?*

He heard the front door close softly, and Melodia appeared. She rushed to them, clinging to them both. "Papa, they took Molto! I saw them leaving through the side gate—"

"I know, daughter. I know," he said, barely able to say the words.

"What are we going to do to get him back?" she asked, trembling.

"We will go along with Delgadas's plan. It is the only way." He spotted Haarmonae leave the shadows beneath the stairway, inching out into the open. She came to them, dragging her feet as if they were made of lead. He drew her into his arms, and the four clung together as if they were trapped on a wooden raft amidst an angry sea.

Delgadas had planned this perfectly, for the king and half the army were away surveying what was left of their country. Several outlying villages had been overrun with Tzotoen soldiers in recent years, shrinking their borders. The king had launched a defensive move, building a wall around the lands that were left to shield them from further attack. After seven long years, the wall was finally complete. However, he had not undertaken any offensive measures and gone after the raiders in full combat against many of his advisor's pleas. The king was surveying the wall, which had only been completed a few months prior. It was now useless if Delgadas' soldiers had found a way to get through the wall, as his presence in the royal city suggested.

Adagio tried to fend off the sinking feeling in his stomach. The bile again rose in his throat, and he was unsure he could hold himself back from being sick this time. He took slow, calculated breaths until the nausea eased. None seemed capable of speaking, trying to wrap their minds around what had just happened.

The fire was the only light in the house, the orange glow giving off a spectral aura. Adagio stilled. He could not let fear get the better of him. He had to be strong for his family. "Listen to me," he said after a while. "We all have to be on our guard the next few days. We must go to the palace, as usual, attend your lessons, and pretend as if nothing is amiss." Adagio's tone was stern, and he hoped the girls knew how dire their situation was.

"But they took Molto, Father! How are we to act normal when he could be killed?" Haarmonae asked in a tortured voice. She separated from the group, pacing a few feet away. He knew she would have rather gone after them, fighting and clawing to get her brother back. Adagio sighed heavily. What was he to do with her?

He let go of his wife and Melodia and touched Haarmonae's shoulder. "Molto is sick, do you understand? If anyone asks, say he is home with a fever. In two days, after we play for the sunrise, we will leave Lunthá to get Molto back."

"And then what?" Ritenueta asked, wringing her hands as she stepped forward. "We can never come back here." He knew exactly how she felt. Lunthá had been the only home they had ever known.

Even with all the changes wrought in recent years, he balked to think of what life would be like outside it. What would they do if they could no longer play for each sunrise and sunset?

"We will make preparations. Each of you must pack extra clothing and essentials for the journey. We will prepare enough food to last us a week or so, until I can find a place for us to hide in safety until Delgadas can be captured." Adagio's mind was reeling. Ritenueta was right, of course. They could not return to Lunthá until Luminia was removed from the Tzotoen threat.

"And how will you procure the books he's demanded? They are kept in the royal expository."

"Which I have access to."

"You mean to steal them? There are only a few copies of Tzizenah's writings. And the royal chronicles? What can Delgadas possibly want them for?" Ritenueta wrung her hands, on the edge of mental collapse. "What if he wants to destroy them?"

"I don't know what he wants them for. We can only hope to get Molto back safely, and deal with the loss of the books later." Adagio's head pounded. He pinched the bridge of his nose

"You really believe Delgadas is going to just release Molto without a fight?" Haarmonae asked, her voice dripping with disdain.

"We will get him what he wants from the library, and will not hand it over until we have Molto back."

Adagio had no way of knowing what Delgadas would do. The man seemed to be teetering on the edge of madness. But he had to try, for Molto's sake. "Do not worry about tomorrow. We must take each day as it comes." He gathered his wife and girls closer, kissing each of them on the forehead.

"Everything will be alright." Even as he said the words, Adagio tried desperately to believe them.

CHAPTER 39

ADAGIO

Adagio slipped into the library, holding his breath as he listened for the sound of books being unfolded, or tutors whispering to their students. It seemed all was quiet. He had hoped it would be, owing to the late hour.

Moonlight cascaded over the wooden floors, shadows nipping at his heels as he made his way to the royal depositories. The books that lay locked away in this innermost section of the library were only accessible to a chosen and trusted few. He swallowed hard as he unlocked the door and slipped inside, locking it behind him. Adagio's heart did a flip flop as he went to the shelves that held the most ancient and precious manuscripts. He looked on the dusty shelves for the writings that Delgadas had demanded. "Forgive me," he whispered as he found the musty volumes that held Lady Tzizenah's poetry and the famed prophecy that had been passed down for the last century. He then retrieved the five-volume scroll that held the royal chronicles. He gently tucked the scrolls into the large satchel draped over his shoulder. The weight pulled at his gaunt neck muscles, reminding him of the burden of guilt he carried. Was not his son's life not more important than books?

Haarmonae's words came rushing back to the forefront of his mind. "What if he means to change history, Papa? There is only one copy of the royal chronicles. Our history might be lost forever to that madman!"

Adagio's hand stilled as he reached for the last scroll. "*Ilyo Na'ada,* what do I do?" he pleaded into the musty silence surrounding the centuries of knowledge—knowledge he had taken for granted, he now realized. There was no time to make a copy of the chronicles, nor track down the few copies that had been made of Tzizenah's work.

No answer was forthcoming, so he stuffed the last scroll into the bag, moved the scrolls to disguise the missing volumes and slipped out once again.

Adagio locked the expository once more, then slunk out of the library. It would be safer to use the side entrance that let out into the gardens than the main doors that would take him right past the courtroom at the heart of the palace.

He paused to listen, then hurried on his way. The only sound he could hear was that of his own blood pounding in his ears, like the growing crescendo of a barrel drum. He had almost reached the secret gate that let out into the nobles quarters when a shadow caught the corner of his eye. Adagio pressed his back against the granite walls, eyes wide and searching. But there was nothing there.

"Lord Adagio?"

Adagio swung around, hitting his head against the bars of the hidden gates.

"Lord Adagio! Forgive me. I thought you'd seen us," Queen Tamil said. She and Prince Shoram emerged from the shadowed path on his left, a small lantern casting a yellow glow. Adagio looked to the place on his right where he had seen the shadow.

"I was lost in my own thoughts. Forgive me, Your Majesty," he said with a solemn bow. "My Prince." He nodded toward the young man with his hand over his heart.

"Is everything well at your home? It is very late for you to be working, my lord." Queen Tamil raised a concerned brow, lifting the lantern to see his face more clearly. He moved away, back toward the shadows. If she could see his face clearly, she might read the lie there.

"An advisor's work is never done, my queen. And now, if you will excuse me? I would not interrupt your walk." He tried to smile, if only to make his voice sound as if he were at ease. "It is much too pretty a moonslit night to waste talking to me."

"Nonsense—" the Queen went on. But she stopped mid sentence as Adagio bowed again and slipped through the gates.

"Good night then! We shall see you tomorrow after the sunrise!" Lord Adagio called, trying to disguise how shaken his voice was as he disappeared into the night.

CHAPTER 40

QUEEN TAMIL

Tamil glanced sidelong at her stepson. "That was very odd." They continued on their walk, rounding the corner to head back to the palace.

"Lord Adagio has been acting very strangely the last couple of days. I wonder if he is as well as he says he is."

"Well, I am sure he is worried for Molto. One is never quite right when one's children are sick," she said, shaking her head.

"I suppose."

Tamil placed an arm around Shoram's shoulders. "Let us go and see your father. Perhaps he is finished with his meeting with the high council."

They entered the quiet corridors and were soon standing outside the courtroom doors. However, one of the sentries bowed, then stood to attention with his obsidian spear tip glistening in the moonslight. "Forgive me, Your Majesty, but the King has moved the war council to his personal study."

"Are they still in session then?" she asked.

"Yes, my queen."

Tamil tried to push the worry aside, but it was difficult, knowing they had already been locked away in the courtroom for several hours. Tamil turned the prince away from the courtroom and they headed towards the royal wing. "It might be best if you retire for the evening, Shoram."

"No, I want to come," Shoram said. "If I am to be king someday, I should know of such things."

Tamil nodded once. "I suppose I cannot argue with that."

They arrived at her husbands personal study just as one of the elderly lords was coming out, muttering in frustration under his breath. He did not even acknowledge Tamil or the prince. She placed a protective hand on Shoram's shoulder. "Obviously it is not going very well. Are you certain you want to come? Your father may send you away as things stand."

"If he does, then so be it. But I would hear what goes." Shoram was already wise beyond his years. Poor lad. He was already having to step up into a man's role more and more everyday. It was the price of growing up in a palace as the heir, and having one's country torn apart from the inside out.

When they entered, there were only a handful of lords still present. General Zalim and his aide, Bravaro, were also in attendance.

"This would not be happening if you had taken my advice years ago and attacked those half-breeds! The attacks on our borders have dwindled our land holdings!"

"We have been through this already, Lord Lamik," Nissim said, rubbing his temple. He looked exhausted. "I cannot take back what has already been."

"That is why I urge you to take action now, Your Majesty!" Lord Lamik's face looked as red as the petals of the fire flower. Tamil was afraid he would pop a vessel if he did not calm down. "Ever since Queen Lutep-Tzia's death, you have refused to move in the offensive. Now is the time to strike, before they strike us!"

Nissim rose silently, the air thick with warning. "Do not ever say her name again," he said, low and menacing. She had rarely heard her husband speak that way, but she knew enough to not cross that line with him. Lord Lamik must have a death wish.

"I mean no disrespect, my king. But I agree with Lord Lamik in this one area. We have to at least look to our defenses. And we would do well to redistribute some of the refugees to other areas. As it is, we are too overcrowded here in the royal city. We need to send workers to the farms."

"I cannot force people to relocate, Bravaro," Nissim said. He turned, and it was only then that he seemed to notice them standing at the back of the room. Nissim sighed. "Many of our people are too afraid to go back to their homes near the border, even with the newly constructed wall. What of those who have homes on the other side of the wall, in areas that the Tzotoen bandits have taken for King Nargod? What more can I do?"

"Declare war," Lord Lamik said, slamming a fist into the wooden table in the center of the room, its face strewn with maps. "Tzotoen has gone unhindered for far too long, Your Majesty."

Tamil's heart went out to her husband. Even after all the years as his wife, and the warmth that had grown between them, she knew she would never see the hidden parts of himself that he kept only for Lutep-Tzia. in a way, Bravaro and Lord Lamik were right. It was as if he was afraid to declare war, that he would be letting down all the kings that had gone before him that had been able to rule in peace. More important, he was somehow letting Lutep-Tzia down if he did what had not been done in over five hundred years.

Tamil took a tentative step forward, her eyes pleading. Nissim nodded deftly, then turned to his lords and generals. "We are done here. You are all dismissed."

Bravaro's shoulders slumped forward, but he held his tongue. However, one of the other lords stepped forward in protest. "But, Your Majesty, we must make a decision—"

"I have spoken," Nissim said, the air hanging with a finality that made the air leave the room. "You may go, Lord Tzichen." The middle-aged man backed down, bowed, then left the room without even trying to conceal his frustration.

Tamil and Shoram waited at the back of the room, keeping quiet until everyone had filtered out. Only when the door closed did she and Shoram move to his side. "Are you well?" she asked.

Nissim uttered a long sigh. "Not really," he answered. He rubbed the back of his neck and winced as he moved it this way and that. "Lord Tzichen will be upset for a while yet at being dismissed."

"He is Kouraso's father, is he not?" Shoram chimed in. "He comes to the training ring when we are practicing with the older boys sometimes."

"Yes, I do believe his youngest son is living in the barracks now," Nissim said. His tone immediately changed when he saw his son.

"Why is everyone so angry?" Shoram asked.

Tamil held her breath at what Nissim might say. "Well, there are some very difficult decisions that need to be made. But don't you worry. We will do what is best for Luminia, will we not?"

"Yes, Papa," Shoram said.

Tamil drew her husband away from his desk and they exited the study. Shoram walked ahead of them, carrying the lantern. Nissim rested his arm over her shoulder. "What are you two doing out so late? I did not think I would see you until you were well asleep."

"We went for a walk in the gardens," she replied, somewhat distracted. "We ran into Lord Adagio as he was heading out through the secret gate on the north side of the gardens." She still did not feel easy about that meeting, but did not want to burden him with it.

"Oh? He must have been studying in the library. He often does these days."

Nissim did not seem worried that his old friend was skulking around the library at all hours of the night. The hair on her arms stood on end just the same. Shoram was right. Lord Adagio had been acting very strange as of late. Whatever the cause, she could only pray it would work itself out on its own. As they had just seen, her husband had enough to worry about.

CHAPTER 41

ADAGIO

His heart was going to leap out of his throat. Adagio descended the steps from the Musicians Terrace, his footsteps keeping in time with his wildly racing heart. He had to remind himself to slow his pace.

"Act natural," he whispered to his wife and girls as they entered the kitchens. Hot cups of *chatla* were waiting for them, as usual. But Adagio knew he could never keep it down with the knowledge of what he must face in the next few hours.

"No, thank you, Suptil." He said to the young serving girl. "I think we are all a bit tired, and would like to go home to check on Molto before we come back and start our day. Please thank your mistress for us."

"I hope Master Molto feels better soon, my lord." Suptil bowed and took the four clay cups away. Hopefully, she would not suspect anything was amiss with this slight deviation from their routine. Adagio placed his hand on the small of Ritenueta's back, leading her away from the chattering groups of Musicians who were, taking a rest before their busy day began. His heart twisted with grief as he took a moment to glance at all of their precious faces. The children

NICOLE C. BOYD

would be most difficult to leave behind. Their potential was so great, yet he knew it would likely never be fostered within them as it should be. Not if Delgadas succeeded in his plans. What would Delgadas do with the rest of the Musicians? Guilt twisted in his gut, and he thought he might be sick. Should he try to warn them?

No. His son's life was hanging in the balance. He had spotted the spies that Delgadas had slipped into the palace under the guise of serving girls and messenger boys. He even suspected some of the lords were on Delgadas' side as well, like that snake, Lord Tzichen. There was no time to weed them out now, no way to warn the king with Molto's life at stake. He would have to find a way to get word to King Nissim after Molto and the rest of his family was safe.

They hurried through one of the side gates, traveling down a narrow alleyway connecting with the main street in front of their mansion. They slipped into the kitchen, retrieving the small bundles they had packed over the last two days. The serving maids were surprised when they entered through the servant's door, but Ritenueta did her best to calm them.

They were traveling down the back alleyways leading to the bridge that connected the inner city with the outer banks a few minutes later. "Put your hoods on," Adagio instructed, drawing his further over the top of his unmistakable white shock of hair. He did not need anyone to recognize them, trying to waylay them with conversation during their escape.

Adagio's throat grew dry as they neared the end of the bridge leading into the outer city rim. The marketplace was a bustle of activity, no one suspecting their way of life was about to crumble. "How can we leave them?" Ritenueta's small voice whispered beside him. He shook his head deftly, commanding silence.

"We must keep going, love. The other Musicians will rise to the occasion. Our only thought must be for Molto, now." He grasped her hand as they walked out of town and started down the road, the forest quickly taking over the landscape. A cloaked figure appeared at his side only a few minutes into their hike.

"This way." A Tzotoen soldier said from beneath a heavy hood. Adagio nodded at his wife and girls and followed the man.

The guard waved them into the surrounding Redwoods and thick ferns. They traveled on a deer trail for about three hundred yards, coming out in a shaded clearing. Delgadas stood at the opposite edge, with Molto on his knees in the center of the clearing. A pole rested over his shoulders and behind his neck. Leather straps clinched his wrists together behind his head, tethered under his triceps, rendering him incapacitated.

His expression held no fear, only calm, rage-filled silence for his captors. When Molto saw his family entering the clearing, his face fell. "Papa—" came his strangled plea. A soldier stepped up, hitting Molto over the head with the handle of his sword. Molto crumpled to the ground, his face landing hard in the dirt. He did not move, unable to roll to the side with his hands lashed behind his head.

Adagio rushed forward but was held back by two other guards. Adagio thrashed, but the men pushed him backward. He stumbled for a moment, Ritenueta coming to his aide.

Delgadas held up his hand to stay his men's hands. "All in good time." He nodded to one of his guards, who hauled Molto upright and made him kneel once more. His son shook his head, the left side of his face smudged with black earth and blood.

Delgadas regarded Adagio briefly, his eyes flickering to Ritenueta and the girls. "I see you have followed my instructions. My informants tell me that you have kept quiet. Well done."

Adagio's heart skipped with terror for his son's well being. Molto swayed dangerously to one side, shaking his head slightly. His heart went out to his boy. *Hang on, son. Just hang on and do not do anything rash,* he pleaded silently.

Adagio glared at Delgadas, a slight, cool breeze moving the giant fern leaves. The wind whistled through the clearing, making a shiver travel up and down Adagio's spine. "Our bargain?" Adagio asked, his voice sounding more confident than he felt.

"Ahh, yes, of course. You understand that if you show your faces

in Luminia again, I will personally hunt you down and kill you all."
Delgadas's words rang out over the forest with sickening clarity.
"You have brought what I asked?"

Adagio swallowed, nodding that he understood. He took the
satchel from around his shoulder and let it drop to the moist earth.
"They are all there."

"Very good. I must admit, I did not think you would go through
with that part of the bargain." Delgadas motioned to one of his
soldiers, who picked up the satchel and took it to Delgadas. After
looking through its intents, Delgadas smiled that taught, wicked
grin, and nodded. "Give him what he deserves," Delgadas instructed,
and the soldier who had retrieved the satchel moved to free Molto.

But Adagio realized the other soldiers' purpose too late. A scream
erupted from Ritenueta as the guard to her right clasped a handful of
her lengthy, black hair, pulling her backward. Adagio lunged but was
pushed into the clearing and away from his wife by two other
soldiers.

"Ritenueta!" he yelled, a guttural, agonized sound escaping from
deep in his throat. "Delgadas, you lying *kall'ak!*"

Delgadas only smiled as Adagio was restrained by the two
soldiers on either side, reveling in the pained cries of his wife. "Insur-
ance, my dear Adagio. Now, you may leave with your daughters. But
if I hear a whisper of your name again, I will not hesitate to do my
worst." He flicked his wrist toward the forest as if shooing a fly. "Be
gone, now," he said in his annoying, high-pitched tone.

"Ritenueta! Molto!" He cried as the soldiers shoved him back
toward the road. "I will find you! I swear on my life, I will find you!" he
told them, struggling all the while. Two more soldiers had grabbed his
daughters. All of them were pressed toward the opposite end of the
clearing. Adagio was finally able to shake the men off of him. They
pushed him away, unsheathing their swords if he decided to fight back.

Delgadas turned, a low chuckle escaping his wretched throat as
Ritenueta and Molto were hauled into the covering of the jungle. The

soldiers shoved Adagio yet again. He could not keep his balance this time and landed hard on his side, twisting his foot the wrong way. He heard a snap, and a sharp pain raced down his leg, starting at the hip.

"Be gone, old man," one of the soldiers hissed disdainfully. He turned to his compatriot and smiled wickedly, eyes roving over Haarmonae's body. "It is a pity Delgadas insisted on bringing the boy and the old woman. We would have had much more fun with these two," he said in a menacing tone. Adagio tried to stand, but a soldier kicked him hard in the belly. He gasped and coughed, trying to draw breath. Melodia and Haarmonae were at his side in an instant, shielding him. He finally was able to fill his lungs with air, albeit painfully.

"Adagio!" He heard Ritenueta's scream growing fainter as they were dragged away, further out of reach. He tried to rise, but the soldier pressed a blade to his throat.

"Do not," the soldier warned. He sliced the tip of the dagger across Adagio's face, pain searing through his cheek. Adagio cried out and pressed a hand on the wound, turning away before the soldier inflicted more injury. However, the man turned and jogged back the way they had come, disappearing into the foliage.

"Come, Papa. Hurry," Melodia said softly, tears spilling down her cheeks. "We must away while we still have a chance," she whispered. Haarmonae went to his other side and helped haul him to his feet. Adagio's eyes watered, and his vision blurred. His wife, son and their captors had disappeared into the forest.

His daughters tried to get him to leave, but he turned, stumbling back toward the clearing.

"I cannot leave them—" he croaked in agony.

He stood on one leg, unable to put pressure on his injured leg. He allowed the blood to trickle down his cheek, determined to follow Delgadas and rescue his wife and son.

"We must, Papa, for now. We are no match against their spears and bows," Haarmonae said. "We must go back to Lunthá to get help. Bravaro will–"

"No," he said firmly. "We cannot go back. You heard Delgadas. He will kill them!" His heart clenched. Why had he ever listened to that traitorous wretch?

They made their way slowly into the dense foliage, heading North away from Lunthá. They did not stop until they were several hundred yards into the forest. He sank onto a fallen log when he felt they were far enough from the danger.

"I must stop for a moment," Adagio said through clenched teeth. The pain in his leg grew with each pounding beat of his heart, swelling the injury. He tried to move, but the pain was intolerable, and he slowly brought it back to rest on the ground. "It is dislocated," he said. That was the least of his worries. Delgadas had his wife and son. *Ilyo Na'ada* alone knew what that monster would do to them now. He should have listened to Molto and never gone along with the plan.

The pounding of horses' hooves assailed their ears, and the girls panicked. Adagio craned his neck and realized they were quite close to the road leading into the outer city. He breathed a sigh of relief. "It is one of the squadrons returning from the survey of the borderlands, no doubt to make their report to the king."

"We must try to warn him somehow," Haarmonae said, pacing. "I wish I had brought my bow! I could have done something back there."

"They would have taken it from you," he said, motioning for them to help him back to his feet. "Let us make haste." First, he would find them a suitable hiding place for the night and then they would devise a plan to warn the king.

THE KING barely had a chance to enter the threshold of his rooms late that night when the figure appeared from the shadows. He almost

300

raised the alarm, but he showed himself before he could do so. The king sighed with relief. "Adagio, my friend, you startled me. What a time we have had—"

"Delgadas is back," was Adagio's abrupt reply.

The king's mouth hung open. "Surely, not," he breathed.

The light from a single candle illuminated the king's face, giving him a ghostly visage. "What has happened to you? You're hurt."

Adagio hobbled further into the light, his rudimentary crutch making a hallow *ker-thud* on the floor , wincing as he moved the hood off his head. "Delgadas came to my home and kidnapped Molto three days ago. He told us that we must leave Luminia in exchange for him. We went to the rendezvous point this morning after we played for the sunrise. However, when he was about to give Molto back, he betrayed us and captured Ritenueta as well. He's taken them, Your Majesty," he said frantically. "Please. Help us get them back before—" his words trailed off in a choked sob.

"How could this happen?" The king placed a hand on his shoulder.

"Man!" The king called his attendant, who appeared almost immediately in the doorway. "Call Bosenia immediately."

"Yes, Your Majesty."

Adagio stood up. "There is no time. Delgadas has spies all over the palace. I am sorry, Your Majesty, but I am only putting you in more danger by staying here."

Nissim helped him gently to the cushions before the low table where he sometimes took his meals. "Nonsense, my friend. We will protect you. Now, tell me what he is planning."

Adagio shook his head. "I know not. I cannot think of anything but the fact he has my wife and son. Please, Your Majesty. We must save them."

"Of course. I will send out scouts as soon as possible to find the traitor. For now, let Bosenia set your arm." He waved the physician over, and he was soon checking the extent of Adagio's injuries. "Where are the girls?" Nissim asked, motioning for his

301

attendant to pour Adagio a glass of water from the pitcher on a side table.

Adagio winced again as Bosenia felt the bones around his hip. "It is not broken. But I will have to put it back in the socket." Bosenia nodded to Nissim's attendant, instructing him to hold Adagio steady.

The doctor tried several times to get it back in place, to no avail. Adagio sucked in short breaths through his teeth, trying to combat the pain. After several seconds, he stood, leaning heavily on the staff "I must away, Your Majesty. Haarmonae and Melodia are waiting for my return at the house."

"Stay here, my friend. You will be safer."

Adagio's eyes flickered with a look that Nissim could not quite decipher. He then nodded in agreement and started toward the hall. "Very well. I will fetch them and return as soon as I can."

"Well, I will send my aide with you, to ensure your protection and safe return to the palace. Lidotz, send out a contingency of eighty men to go and search out Delgadas' men and bring back Lady Ritenueta and Master Molto."

"Please, do not—" Adagio said. "If he suspects anyone is following them, he will kill them."

"Do not worry, my friend. Delgadas has the disadvantage of being on foreign ground. We have the standing army, and he a rabble of bandits." He nodded curtly to the aide, who promptly held a fist over his heart and went out into the hall to wait for Adagio.

There was no use arguing against an escort. He would simply have to lose him when they were outside the palace. Adagio turned slowly and mumbled a word of thanks. "I will return as soon as I can."

CHAPTER 42

KING NISSIM

Nissim watched Adagio slink down the darkened hallway and disappear around a bend. "Make sure they are accommodated." He nodded to another of his attendants, who immediately went to prepare rooms for Adagio and his daughters. "Post guards outside their rooms when they return. I want round-the-clock protection for him and his girls."

Nissim fell onto his bed when his attendant had gone, exhausted from the long day. He had been working non-stop since returning from the borderlands Thankfully, nothing had been amiss on their new border. The wall had appeared to be doing its job of keeping out the raiders. Or so he had thought. Nothing could have prepared him for what Adagio had told him that night.

He was unsure how long he had slept, but he awoke with a start. One of his attendants stood over his shoulder, the room growing gray with the light of dawn. "Your Majesty, an urgent message from one of your soldiers."

Nissim rubbed his eyes, looking around the room in confusion. "How long have I been asleep?"

"Several hours, Your Majesty."

Nissim stood up. Where was Tamil? He had not even gone to the nursery to see the girls. He would go and see them after sunrise.

The soldier stood in the antechamber, covered from head to toe with dust—and blood. "What has happened?" Nissim asked. His heart started pounding in his chest.

"We were attacked, Your Majesty, on the road leading back to Lunthá. We went out to search for Delgadas' raiding party, to see if we might retrieve the Lady Ritenueta and her son. But we found no trace. On our way back, we were attacked. It happened so fast, we barely had time to—" The man met his gaze, his lips drawn into a thin line. "I am the only survivor, Your Majesty."

"And it was Delgadas' men?"

"Tzotoen bandits, as far as we know. Delgadas did not seem to be among them, but they outnumbered us two to one. They attacked before dawn, a little over an hour ago, surrounded all eighty of us and struck us down in a matter of minutes. I pretended to be dead, and waited for them to leave. They are on their way here, to take Lunthá, as we speak."

The attendant, who had remained quietly by the door as the soldier relayed the news of the lost battle, was met by his aide. "Let me pass," his aid grunted, the attendant trying to keep him out.

"Let him," Nissim ordered. "Are you and Lord Adagio only now returning?" he demanded.

The man shook his head. It was only then that Nissim saw the stream of dried blood marring the side of his brow. "I went with Lord Adagio, as you asked, Sire. But when I arrived and started helping the ladies with the packs, someone struck me. When I awoke, Lord Adagio and his daughters were gone."

CHAPTER 43

DELGADAS

"What day did he come?" Delgadas asked, pacing like a caged animal. His soldiers had reminded him of the boy they had captured and lost on the outskirts of Hotun all those years ago. The boy from the Other World. It had long been foretold that a savior would come and restore music. That One, whoever they might be, was the only thing standing in Delgadas's way. If he could silence him before he was able to rise, there would be nothing to interrupt his plans.

The sage went to the table and opened the scrolls that Adagio had brought to him from the royal library. Delgadas peered over his shoulder at the Luminian signs written on the thick bark parchment. Delgadas hated looking at them, knowing that the words could also be transposed into music, each character standing with an accompanying music note. Even worse, the words of the Chronicles could never be destroyed since the bark of the eternal tree would not burn. He turned away from the scroll, preferring to let the captured sage do the reading.

"It says here that the Outsider came on the twelfth day of *Sibbi'*, in the ninth year of the reign of Nissim." The sage looked up at

Delgadas, awaiting his next instruction. The sniveling dolt. None of these slaves ever took the initiative. Of course, what else could be expected of such backward people? They took orders from an unseen god and sat around playing their instruments. They were content to follow King Nissim. Hopefully, that would not be the case for much longer.

Delgadas shook his head in frustration, "No, no, then this is not the right boy. The prophecy says that the one who will come to deliver Luminia will arrive on the eleventh day of *La'oun*." He began pacing in front of the low table, the skin on the right side of his body itching with tingling pain. It was as if a torch was being held above the surface of his skin. The malady had started just after his escape from Lunthá nearly twelve years ago. Each time he had a flare-up, these cursed scales replaced more of his smooth, olive skin. He wondered how long it would take for his whole body to be covered by the hideous black scales.

"3.3.3," Delgadas said through clenched teeth. "This *savior* will appear on the third day, of the third week, of the third month." Delgadas pounded the desk with each 'third' as if he had explained this a hundred times.

The sage splayed his hands. "Then you have nothing to worry about, my lord. This person, whoever they may be, has either appeared and is still to be revealed, or they have not arrived yet."

"What else do the Chronicles say?" Delgadas twisted his neck to the left, trying to loosen the stiffness in his muscles.

"There is nothing else, my lord. It only says when this person will come and that they will restore music to Luminia." The sage licked his lips nervously, backing away from the table slightly.

"I want this person caught!"

"But how can we begin to prepare to capture this man if we do not know the year, my lord? We may be waiting until the end of the *bu'athe'*, for all we know." Delgadas would indeed have nothing to worry about, if that were the case. The end of the current *bu'athe'* would not come for another hundred years, when the sacred and solar calendars realigned on the same day, and began the next *bu'athe'* cycle all over again.

Delgadas was not appeased. "It could be sooner than that, and I need specifics if I am to plan my strategy in overthrowing the king." Delgadas peered at the man, his right eye twitching. He rubbed at the raw flesh surrounding his eyeball, fearing the inevitable. Soon, the tight skin surrounding it would cover the orb entirely, leaving him blind on one side. Pain tore at his flesh as he scraped the back of his hand against the cursed member. Why was his body intent on fighting against him?

"I will consult the Chronicles with my fellow sages again, my lord. But you must be patient. I—"

The sage ducked, but too late to dodge Delgadas's fist as it collided with the side of his head. The man fell to the floor, scrambling away. He wrapped an arm around his head for protection, tripping over cushions and tables as he went.

"Get out of my sight! And do not ever tell me to be patient again!" Delgadas followed him, growling with each menacing step. If the sages were not so vital to his cause, he would kill the whole lot of them on the spot. "You are a so-called *wiseman*. Figure it out!!" Delgadas screamed.

The sage left the tent hurriedly, and Delgadas picked up the first thing within reach, throwing it at the man's back. He missed his target, just barely. The tent flap moved with the wind, snapping back and forth as Delgadas stood there, seething. He hobbled over to the table and looked at the Luminian markings again. He turned away in disgust, rubbing his thigh as he went to a pile of cushions. His joints were growing stiffer now that he was back in Luminia.

Perhaps it was his punishment for turning traitor. Regardless, he would continue with his mission. Soon, all of Luminia would be within his grasp. And then, he would have all the power he had craved since he was young, dithering in the shadow of Nissim's father. When he had wrested control from Nissim, he would find a way to heal himself, and no one would ever dictate to him again.

CHAPTER 44

PRINCE SHORAM

Eleven-year-old Shoram looked out the window of his bed chamber as his father's soldiers spread out around the royal city by the light of the Three Sisters. For days, the palace had been in an uproar, news of Delgadas's return causing terror to rip through them like a piercingly high musical note shattering glass. To compound things, the Head Musician and his girls had vanished after his wife and son were kidnapped by Delgadas. The day after they were discovered missing, a contingency of at least a thousand Tzotoen soldiers had moved to the shores of the outer city, their war drums echoing incessantly over the lagoon to spell their impending doom.

War was imminent. Of course, his father was not casting this news abroad to the rest of the country. Most everyone had taken refuge in the royal city, or had been scattered around the hill country to fend for themselves. The king had quietly begun mobilizing what few troops they had left in Lunthá, but Shoram knew it was too few to hold off Delgadas' troops, of whom more arrived everyday. And rumors were rampant in the palace, that people were starting to slip away in the dead of night to escape the coming fury, rather than stay and fight. It was said only those foolish enough to stay and die were left.

A shiver of trepidation coursed through Shoram's body. He could not imagine the pressure his father was under. The country was under attack, and unrest would soon reach a boiling point in Lunthá. Some would say his father had waited too long to do anything to ward off the attack.

He could not help but wonder what would become of his father if Delgadas succeeded.

And what of him? As the heir to the throne, he had little chance of surviving if Delgadas' men were able to break through their meager defenses.

Shoram swallowed hard as he tried to keep the fear at bay. He turned away from the window, feeling more lost and lonely than ever. He slipped out of the private room his father had given him upon his tenth birthday. It had been difficult to be away from the comfort of the nursery.

Shoram made his way down the eerily silent halls toward the nursery, the need to ensure his sisters' safety too much for him to ignore.

Thankfully, the rains had stopped. After Lord Adagio and the girls had been discovered missing, the lower classes of Musicians had tried to take over the immense responsibility of playing for the sunrise and sunset. But it was not the same. That first morning they were gone they had woken to gray skies and rain clouds releasing a deluge from the heavens. Usually when there were rains like that, it portended a royal death.

Shoram had rushed to the nursery, praying that his little sisters were unharmed. Thankfully, his sisters were well and safe. Even so, Shoram had not traveled far from the nursery since.

When he opened the door and slipped through, he nearly knocked Dosanyata over. He helped steady her, apologizing for his rudeness. "Are they well?" he asked, looking around the room.

Dosanyata waved him in and closed the door to the nursery. "All is well, Your Highness. At least, the girls are safe and and your baby sister is sleeping." Dosanyata smiled weakly as she looked to the small adjoining room where the girls slept. "No one has come to tell us what is going on."

Five-year-old Petella was the spitting image of his stepmother, with bright green eyes and unruly red curls. She lay sprawled over the cushions that made up the shared bed, taking up the most room. Poor Tamila. At four years old, she could not be more the opposite of her elder sister. She had inherited the same thick, dark curls as Shoram and their father, with wise blue eyes. Tamila was quiet, while Petella was never without something to say. Right now, she lay just barely clinging to the edge of the cushions, her red hair partially covering her face. Dosanyata went to scoot Petella over and ensure Tamila would be able to stay abed.

While she did so, Shoram walked over to the crib where the newest addition to the family slept. Baby Shos-Hinta lay slumbering without a care in the world, her tiny thumb tucked between her lips. He smiled at the soft snoring noises that escaped her parted lips every time she exhaled.

"Are you alright?" Dosanyata asked, joining him at the crib. "It is so late."

"I could not sleep," he admitted, turning from the crib. "Honestly, who can with tidings such as these?" He nodded toward the east-facing window and the army laying just beyond the waters that surrounded the island-city. "What I cannot understand is why they haven't attacked yet."

Suddenly, the door swung open, and they both jumped as the door banged against the wall. Dosanyata instantly got in front of him, shielding him with her body.

The king stood in the doorway, alert and watchful as he scanned the darkness. When he saw them, he made toward them. They both let out a sigh of relief as he strode across the room. "Why were you not in your room?" he demanded.

All relief vanished, and Shoram frowned. "I came to check on the girls—"

His father didn't wait for any more of an explanation. "Dosany-ata, pack the girls' things. Just a few things—a change of clothes, shoes, a cape, and some blankets." He took Shoram's arm and almost dragged him out of the room. "We'll be back in a moment!" he called over his shoulder.

Shoram's mind spun. "What's happened? I do not understand." They soon arrived at his room, and his father barked an order at the soldier to keep watch. His father burst into action, heading to the closet where his plethora of fine garments were hung. Shoram followed his father, rummaging through the cupboard.

"No *titzake lumpay*, son. You will need wool. Cotton. If you do not have anything like that, I can have something procured for you from the servant's quarters." His father took only a moment to look down at his son, no doubt trying to keep the rising panic at bay.

Shoram swallowed hard. He went to the very back of the closet and chose a warm green wool shirt and tan ballooned trousers, something only a commoner might be seen wearing. Until now, Shoram had used them as practice garments during his military training exercises.

His father explained as he continued to rummage through his closet. "It is not safe for you and the girls here. I am sending you to Saardonae to wait this out."

Shoram froze, swallowing back sudden tears. He grabbed a black wool cape and backed out of the wardrobe. His father was holding a knapsack for him, no doubt procured from the kitchens in a hurry. "You are sending me away?"

His father knelt before him, firmly taking him by the shoulders. His tortured eyes searched Shoram's, pleading for him to under-stand. "I do not want to send you from me, but I must. For your own safety and the legacy of Luminia, I must." His father touched his cheek. "I can almost see your mother staring out at me through your eyes." He took a deep breath and rose. "There is no time. We have to act now if you are to get them out in time."

Shoram nodded slowly. His father wrapped his strong arms around him, the smell of sandalwood and incense greeting his nostrils. Shoram tucked his face closer to his father's chest, wanting to cling to every last memory of him. "And you will join us there later?"

His father released him, standing. "When Luminia is safe once more, I will send for you. Now, make haste. We do not have much time."

Shoram retrieved an extra pair of sturdy boots he used when he trained with Bravaro and followed his father out the door. Tamil met them outside the nursery with a knapsack slung over her shoulder. She hurried into the room, gathering Petella and Tamila close, and his father picked up Shos-Hinta from her crib, cradling her in his strong arms. Shoram's heart twisted. What would they do without that quiet strength?

"Please conceal their departure for as long as possible. Have their meals delivered here as usual, but do not let any of the servants see that they have gone. Is that clear?" His father instructed Dosanyata and Kyin.

"Yes, Your Majesty," Dosanyata said, tears streaming down her face. "We shall miss you all terribly."

Shoram tried to be brave but could not hold the tears at bay as he hugged her. Would it be the last time he ever saw her? He leaned up and whispered in her ear so only she could hear. "Thank you, Dosanyata. You have been a mother to me when I had none. I—I love you."

Dosanyata hugged him even tighter against her chest. "I love you, too, my boy." He felt her tears wetting the top of his head as she planted a quick kiss on his hair.

"Are you sure you will not go with them?" his father asked Dosanyata.

She deftly shook her head. "No. We will only slow you down. And seven of us will look suspicious. Better that the five of you get away as quickly as possible." She smiled at the girls whimpering as they clung to their mother's neck. "We will see each other again very soon, I am sure."

Shoram watched his father nod curtly. "We must away."

His father led them down the corridor and then slipped into a shadowy hidden staircase tucked behind a tapestry. Shoram had never known of the secret stairwell. His father closed the door behind them, lighting a small torch to show them the way. The stone walls were slick with moisture, and the flickering torch flame made his insides twist with trepidation. Down, down, down they went until he was sure they were in the heart of the mountain. After what seemed like hours, they came to a small wooden door.

"Stay here for a moment," his father instructed. He then slipped through the door and closed it, leaving them in total darkness.

"I am scared, Mama," came Tamila's mousy voice.

Tamil gave a short laugh. "There is nothing to be afraid of, dearest. Papa is just making sure that no one can see us before we go out."

"Like the game we play with Dosanyata?" Tamila asked.

Tamil shushed her. "Yes, much like that. Now, quiet, dearest."

Shoram gulped. He had to be strong for his little stepsisters and his stepmother. It would be up to him to guide them safely to Saardonae.

His father slipped back through the door, the torch extinguished. "Listen carefully," he whispered. "There is a boat waiting at the shore, which will take us to the opposite side of the lake. Horses are waiting to take you to Saardonae—"

Tamil gripped his father's arm, her voice plaintive and frightened for the first time that night. "Surely you are coming with us, Nissim?"

Shoram heard a rustling as his father gathered his wife into his arms. "I cannot leave yet. But I promise to come and get you as soon as it is safe. Luminia depends on me."

Tamil said nothing, but Shoram could feel the tension in the dark passageway. The girls began to cry. His father shushed them gently, opening the door of the hidden staircase. Clouds covered the light of the moons. He stepped out into a meadow, looking behind him at the island-mountain rising high into the sky. They had indeed traveled under the city via the secret tunnel. Shoram wondered what other secrets the old citadel held.

His father helped Tamil and the girls into the boat, and then Shoram stepped up, bounding into the boat unaided. His father pushed the skiff away from the shore, his feet plunging into the tepid waters for a moment before he jumped into the vessel. Shoram took an oar and helped his father row to the opposite shore. Tamil's face was a stony mask of silence. She had taken to gazing over the gently lapping water. She met his gaze, and he realized how torturous this must be for her. He must try to find a way to comfort her. This would be the second time she had abandoned everything to start a new life in a foreign country. But at least they would be safe in Saardonae, his mother's homeland.

When they reached the opposite shore, gray light was slowly starting to touch the sky. The musicians would soon be waking to play for the sunrise. His father jumped out of the boat and helped them all climb out. Shos-Hinta was strapped securely to Tamil's chest with a long piece of cotton cloth. His father then helped Tamil mount a black steed who stomped the ground in expectation. His father handed Tamila to her, and her mother wrapped one arm around her waist, using the other to grip the reins.

"You next, son." His father helped him mount a chestnut-colored stallion, and Petella was settled before him. Thankfully, his training had included three months with the cavalry, so Shoram was comfortable on a horse. It would be another matter entirely to keep Petella steady, however.

"Travel north first, then turn east. Give Delgadas' army a wide berth. When you reach the mountains, turn south and head for the border." His father ensured his foot was securely in the stirrup. "Travel only at night, and stay clear of the main roads." His father handed him a packet of papers tied with leather straps and a wax seal. "These are for your grandfather's eyes only, do you understand? If he wishes to show them to you later, that is his affair."

He rested a hand on Shoram's knee, squeezing it to ensure he understood his task's gravity. "You may count on me, Papa. I will not disappoint you."

Shoram could see his eyes were filled with tears, the light of the waning moons reflected in them. "You could never disappoint me, my son. I love you." He paused for a moment, digging in his vest pocket. He brought out a necklace with a white stone shining in the moonslight. "Your mother wanted you to have this when you were old enough. I should have given it to you long ago, but I suppose I wanted to keep a piece of her close for as long as possible. She would be proud of the young man you have become. Wear it with pride." Shoram took the necklace from his father, awed by its beauty glowing with an ethereal light.

"Thank you, Papa." Shoram said with an awed hush. His father nodded, too overcome with emotion to say anything else.

He then turned to Petella. "I love you, my *hitun-zitke*." *My songbird.*

Shoram felt his heart clench, reluctant to leave him alone in the royal city. Of course, he had his officials and servants, but what would he do without the comfort of his family around him?

He went over to Tamil and Tamila, whispering his goodbyes to them. He ran a hand over Shos-Hinta's head, still covered in short, downy hair. Tamil leaned down and kissed his father before he stepped away, nodding to Shoram to lead the way. Shoram pushed down all emotion, focusing on the task at hand. It was his job to see they arrived in Saardonae safely. But before they disappeared into the forest, he turned slightly, eyeing his father again. He raised a hand, and his father did the same, his body silhouetted by the moonslight. "*Ilyo Na'ada* go with you, my family!" he called before disappearing into the night.

CHAPTER 45

PRINCE SHORAM

Shoram looked down from the hill at the wall separating them from Saardonae, breathing a sigh of relief. They were almost there. He was exhausted from the constant strain of riding through the night and trying to sleep through the day. It seemed impossible that any of them had managed to sleep, with even the slightest noise waking them from their slumber. To make matters worse, poor Shos-Hinta had contracted a cold on the way to safety, making the journey even more treacherous.

He jerked his head around as a twig snapped, but he saw nothing on the road behind them. Were their enemies lurking in the shadows? Or was the whistling wind simply playing tricks on his sleep-deprived mind?

"There it is," he whispered, pointing to the southeast. "We only need to find a way to cross the border without being seen by Delgadas's soldiers." Thankfully, his father had had the wisdom to ensure they dressed in the plainest clothes they owned. Even if Delgadas did not yet know of their escape, he soon would. He would be none too pleased to discover that the heir to the throne of Luminia had escaped his clutches.

Shoram climbed off the horse's back, Petella whimpering softly. "Do not worry, little sister. I shall return soon."

Tamil shook her head vehemently. "You cannot go alone, Shoram. You are the heir and your father expressly bade me—"

"Mama, what else would you have me do? I will not send you down alone. The girls need you." He splayed his hands. "I will ensure it is safe and then come back for you."

"The *country* needs *you*." She shook her head again, an air of finality in her visage. There would be no arguing with her. "I know some of the tongue from Saardonae, and I can disguise my speech. No one will suspect the queen of Luminia to be traveling alone, without an armed guard. We will go together and pretend to be from Saardonae, fleeing back to our home country."

Shoram thought for a moment. It was not a bad plan, but he was still nervous about allowing her to take the lead at the gates. Any number of things could go wrong, not least running into a band of raiding Tzotoen soldiers. He had nothing but a small dagger to defend them.

His stepmother looked up at the sky. "We should cross now, before the sun sets. If we do meet anyone on our way, they will think it odd if a lone woman and four children are traveling after nightfall."

Shoram nodded. He saw no other way. He mounted his steed, wrapping his arms around Petella to support her. She snuggled into him, so exhausted that she did not even grasp the danger they were about to face. Tamil led the way down the incline toward the newly constructed wall. Now, the construction of the foreboding structure seemed obsolete. Even with the wall and the constant patrolling, Delgadas had still found a way in.

When they neared the gate, his throat was as dry as sun-bleached bone. A desolate strip of land that was now under Tzotoeh's control lay Luminia's newly apportioned borders and Saardonae's ancient borders beyond. All they had to do was cross this strip of deserted forest land and get through Saardonae's gates, and they would be safe.

Gulping, he spurred his horse forward so he was neck and neck with Tamil's mount. "What are you going to say to the guards?" He nodded his head toward the two Luminian sentries standing in the tower.

"You leave that to me."

When they approached the gates, the sentry called for them to halt. He climbed over the ramparts and shimmied down a long, thin ladder that had once been a Redwood sapling. It was stripped of its branches, and spikes had been driven into the sides at alternating heights to act as rungs. Within seconds, the soldier was standing before them, sword drawn. The sentry above pulled back his longbow, ready to loose the arrow at the slightest provocation.

Tamil took the hood off, letting it settle on her shoulders. She looked up at the sentry without a flicker of fear. Her horse sidestepped with nervousness, no doubt sensing Tamil's tension. Placing a protective hand on Shos-Hinta's back, she glared at the sentry. "Would you really shoot a defenseless woman and her children? Search us if you will, but I assure you, you will find no weapons on our person."

Shoram swallowed, hoping the man would not go through with her suggestion. He had not told his stepmother of the secreted knife. Hopefully, he would not need to use it.

The sentry lowered his sword. Shoram was shocked and pleased, for Tamil had impersonated a Saardonaenian accent perfectly.

"Where do you come from?" The Luminian sentry asked, looking a little more at ease.

"We are traveling from Lunthá on our way home to Saardonae. The king has issued a decree that all foreigners should go home to escape the coming war. And here we are." His stepmother spread her cloak wider so the sentry could see the top of Shos-Hinta's head. He lowered his sword the rest of the way.

The sentry looked alarmed, calling one of his fellow soldiers to see. Another man joined the long-bow-man, looking over the side of the wall with concern. "But you have no escort? Do you not realize that Tzotoeh now holds the mile strip of land between Luminia and Saardonae?"

Tamil went on, and Shoram could tell she was growing more agitated. The sun was setting, and it would be the death of them to try and cross the stretch of ground between Luminia and Saardonae in the dark. "We are aware. My husband can no longer protect us, as he passed away some three months ago. But we have faith that *Ilyo Na'ada* will protect us. Will you let us through the gate, kind sir?"

The sentry above thought for a moment. "The boy does not look much like his mother, if I may say so." He leaned over the wall, peering at them closer. Had he recognized them?

Shoram tensed, but Tamil barely missed a beat in answering. "That is impertinent, I must say. If this is the way the king's men treat women, I will have to file a formal complaint. Really, the idea—"

"I meant no offense, my lady." The sentry visibly started sweating, no doubt assuming Tamil was a high-born Saardonaenian noblewoman.

Tamil sighed. They were running out of time. "If it is payment you are after, then take this," she said. She dug into the small pouch around her shoulder and soon brought out a sparkling sapphire necklace. "It is a family heirloom that will fetch a handsome price."

The sentry looked guilty. "No, my lady. We could not take that—"

"Enough of this chatter, then. Will you let us through or not?" Tamil snapped, wrapping Shos-Hinta back up in her cloak. She shifted on the horse, making ready to move as if they had already given their blessing.

The sentry straightened and stepped out of the way. "Of course, my lady. My partner and I will keep a watch over you until you are safely on the other side of the border. I suggest you make haste. We have not seen any hostiles in the area for the last few days. But they are a wily lot. One cannot be too careful."

"I thank you. That is very kind," Tamil said, flashing the young man a charming smile.

Shoram tried to still the wild beating of his heart as the heavy wooden and steel-clad gate was opened. The sentry that had come down scurried up the ladder and pulled it up behind him. The great cogs and wheels creaked as the gate was drawn into the right side of the wall, which seemed to take ages. But soon, there was enough room for the two horses to pass, and Shoram waved gratefully to the two sentries. They started forward, slowly at first, as the soldiers watched their progress. In all likelihood, they need not have worried about the sentries. They seemed loyal to Luminia's cause. Still, his father had warned them not to reveal their identities to anyone lest they be spies for Delgadas.

When they cleared the gate, Shoram heard it being pushed back into place, manned by a dozen soldiers from within the heart of the wall. The gate rattled into place with a sound of finality. There was no going back now.

At a signal from Tamil, he spurred his horse into a gentle lope and then into an all-out gallop.

She looked to the Eastern horizon. "The sunlight will be gone soon. Let us go." She spurred her horse forward, and Shoram followed suit.

"Make haste, my lady! And may *Ilyo Na'ada* be with you!" Shoram heard the sentry atop the wall call down to them. His words seemed to give the horses wings. Shoram did not look to the right or the left as the scenery rushed by them, blurred at the speed at which they traveled. His heartbeat seemed to match the pounding horses' tread, their hooves eating up the ground.

It was worse than Shoram could have imagined. The Tzotoen-controlled strip of land was a waste. The mighty Redwood trees had been cut down and used for building the walls, no doubt. The vegetation had been stripped. Swirling dust was all that was left. Whatever trees still left were gnarled and dry, their evergreen foliage long gone. A cold wind whipped at Shoram's cloak, and he pulled it tighter around him, wrapping an arm around Petalla's waist. Tamil pulled her mount up beside him and did the same for Tamila.

Finally, the Saardonaenian border came into sight, surrounded by its own impressive wall. Shoram sighed in relief. However, Tamil yelped with surprise and despair. He turned just in time to see six Tzotoen bandits riding up behind them, coming out of nowhere from the north. He ducked as an arrow buzzed by his head, covering Petella. His sister screamed. "Hang on!" he commanded, digging his heels into the horses' sides.

He glanced over his shoulder for a split second. The Tzotoen soldiers were closing fast. Shoram looked up at the wall, only a few hundred yards away. "Open the gate!" he yelled desperately. He could see the Saardaenian sentries scrambling atop the wall, shouting orders. Bows were at the ready in seconds, ready to loose on the approaching horsemen.

"Faster, Mama! Faster!" Shoram called to Tamil. He looked again to the sentries, but they still had not given the order to open the gates.

"Open the gate!" he yelled again in Saardaenian, hoping they would hear him this time. The gate began slowly opening a second later, but Shoram knew it would not be fast enough. He chanced another glance over his shoulder. The Tzotoen renegades were now busy deflecting arrows from the sentries, holding up rudimentary wooden shields. They turned to the left and started to fall back, but Shoram and his family were not out of danger yet. He sped ahead of Tamil, willing the men working inside the wall to open the gate faster. Another arrow whizzed past Shoram's shoulder, and he ducked to the side, doing his best to shield Petella from the onslaught.

Shoram raced through the gate, followed in the next second by Tamil. The Tzotoen soldiers halted and fell back with nothing but sporadic oak brush to hide behind. The gate began to close as soon as the soldier saw they were safely through, locking out the threat for good. Seeing their prey had escaped, the Tzotoen soldiers turned and sped away, cursing the travelers as they went.

Shoram turned to his stepmother, both of them out of breath. Of course, the girls wept with fright, but Shos-Hinta miraculously still slept, strapped to Tamil's heaving chest. Soldiers surrounded them in the next instant. One helped Shoram dismount, and Tamil nearly collapsed from her steed, weak with fright and exertion. But they had made it, and they were unharmed.

"That was a mad dash if ever I saw one. What were you thinking, lad?" said one of the soldiers.

Shoram straightened to his full height, which he knew was nothing compared to the soldier. He produced the packet of papers for his grandfather and held up his father's seal. "I am Prince Shoram, heir to the throne of Luminia. King Nissim has sent us here to seek asylum with King Botzena."

A hush fell over those standing around. The man who had spoken to Shoram stepped forward and examined the seal. "It is King Nissim's mark," he confirmed. He looked over Shoram, amazement filling his gaze. "I will take you to the king immediately. The situation in Luminia must be more dire than we were led to believe."

Shoram gave a grim nod, looking back toward his homeland. "It is."

PART THREE
ECLIPSE

"Ilyo Na'ada will uplift the righteous,
the ones who keep his sacred melody.
But the one who is proud and full of greed,
He will repeal the gift to hearken."

-Ancient Luminian Proverb

CHAPTER 46

BRAVARO

Lunthá, Luminia
Three Days Later

Bravaro had never worked so hard in all his life. Sweat dripped from his forehead and into his eyes. He wiped his brow with his forearm, allowing nothing to slow his pace as they did their best to ensure the city was impenetrable. Straightening, he felt the all-too-familiar trickle of sweat run down his spine and the tingle of fear that accompanied being out in the open.

Building the blockade on the far end of the bridge leading to the inner city was one way to combat his rising sense of unease. He had been against the idea of securing the city. Should they not abandon Lunthá and find somewhere easier to defend? Perhaps the strong-hold of Chinelt on the cliffs further inland? However, he was only a lowly foot soldier, and the lords would not listen.

Why the army did not attack was beyond him. There had to be over three-thousand men camped in the forests surrounding the outer city. The ear drums had stopped, adding even more anxiety to the inhabitants of Lunthá. Somehow the quiet was even worse than the maddening ruckus.

Working on these fortifications felt like he was sealing himself in his own tomb and the rest of the inhabitants with him. The outer city was abandoned, with more people trying to cram into the inner city every day. It seemed like the whole of Luminia had congregated in Lunthá. Of course, that is only how it felt. He knew that many of the remaining inhabitants from rural Luminia had fled to Saardonae for sanctuary, which King Botzena had gladly given, along with a promise of thirty thousand troops. But the promised troops had yet to arrive.

Thankfully, the queen, Shoram, and the princesses had safely crossed the border. A messenger had ridden in from the wall, saying they had met them at the gate, thinking they were ordinary folk. But the sentries from Saardonae had soon put them right about that. Bravaro's heart clenched. He missed his young friend. Shoram would be gone for who knew how long. And Valian was still in training, only twelve years old. He shivered at the thought of Valian. If his young friend had been one year older, he would have been used as a messenger for the army, running messages from the general to his commanders on the battlefield. He gulped and bent down to pick up a chunk of limestone the size of his torso, placing it atop the barricade. He had seen what Delgadas and his men were capable of at the burning of Hotun all those years ago. Would a pile of stones and rubble be able to stop them?

As sunset approached, Bravaro's squadron finished preparations on the bridge's far end. Now, they would work in the middle of the bridge through the night. King Nissim had ordered the bridge to be weakened in the center. When the Tzotoen army marched across, the weight of the soldiers would plunge them into the lagoon's waters. Perhaps it would only buy them a little time, but at least it was something.

Bravaro had suggested they destroy the bridge from the start, not even giving Delgadas and his men the option of crossing. But the king had been reluctant to see the old structure go. It had been built centuries before and was a national landmark, something they all looked to with pride. Bravaro had argued that saving the people was better than keeping a bridge intact. Finally, the king had given in to a compromise. They would catch the Tzotoens in a trap, and with any luck, they would abandon their assault on the city.

Bravaro made his way silently to the center of the bridge, where another squadron was already hard at work weakening the supports. "Hello down there!" he called, leaning dangerously over the side to see their torch-lit faces. "How is it coming?"

"Almost done, sir. We have chipped away at all the stone supports, and will disguise any cracks on the surface with dust and the like. Delgadas will not even know what hit him."

The boy who answered could not have been more than sixteen, yet he had volunteered to help defend his country. Several men who peered up at him were young, barely older than himself. He gave a curt nod. "Good work, men. Finish here and then make haste into the city. I would not want to be on this bridge any longer than necessary."

They all forced brave smiles, no doubt imagining Delgadas and his horde falling into the chilly waters. Bravaro doubted Delgadas would be with the first assault. Undoubtedly, he would stand back like a coward and wait for his mercenaries to take the city and make his way to the palace when all the excitement was over.

No. He could not afford to think like that. Surely they would win out in the end, shielded by *Ilyo Na'ada's* mighty hand. With every passing hour that inched by with no help arriving, he struggled to believe *Ilyo Na'ada* would come through for them. Why did he wait? Why did He not come in and save them as Bravaro had heard in the stories of old? If *Ilyo Na'ada* loved them as a father, why had he not saved them from this torment?

Or perhaps He was cruel and cold, like Bravaro's birth father...

Bravaro shook his head and strode to the other end of the bridge, his heart hardening. His father should have been a long-forgotten memory. But especially as of late, he had frequented his dreams, tormenting him with a fury.

He pushed the thoughts away, anxious for a hot meal and rest before his night watch began in a few hours. People still milled about the streets, and Bravaro made his way to the palace with difficulty. The noise was deafening: babies cried, and men shouted at each other as they haggled for a loaf of bread. Women sang softly to their infants to try and get them to sleep. It was an impossible feat with everyone crammed together so closely.

Bravaro stepped over a pair of legs, tripping when their owners shifted slightly. He caught himself before he landed in an older man's lap, looking over his shoulder at the person he had disturbed. A pair of hollow, hungry eyes looked up at him. If he had to guess, the child was no more than eight years old.

"I beg your pardon, my boy. Please forgive me." Bravaro reached for him, but the child shrank away. He halted, looking around at the people milling about. No one had even noticed their exchange, as everyone seemed too engrossed in their own suffering. "I mean you no harm, lad. I am sorry I tripped over your legs. Did I hurt you?"

The boy shook his head but did not say anything. Bravaro looked around but saw no adult figure that looked like they belonged with the boy. "Where are your parents?"

The boy stilled, looking up with eyes too large for his face. "Gone." He said simply. Hanging his head, he studied the frayed hem of his sleeveless shirt.

"I am sorry," Bravaro said softly. "When did they pass?"

The boy looked up at him with a confusion. "They are not dead," he corrected. "They left for Saardonae. Left me and my little sister to fend for ourselves. But she's dead now."

White hot rage seared his chest, and Bravaro looked around at the others in the square. He had not thought Luminians could be so heartless as to abandon their children, especially with war looming. "Come along with me." Bravaro reached out his hand, but the boy did not take it.

"Leave me. Just let me die. We are all going to die in a few days anyway." The boy turned away and lay down on the cold, hard cobblestones. He pressed the side of his face into the stones, and Bravaro's heart shattered. How long had it been since the boy had had a decent meal? How long since someone had taken care of *him*?

"I will not," Bravaro said firmly. He leaned down and picked the boy up, cradling him like an infant. He could not have weighed more than a four-year-old, his rib cage sticking out at sharp angles. The boy did not give a fight as Bravaro carried him the rest of the way to the palace, falling asleep to Bravaro's gentle, rocking strides.

Anger welled up inside him once more. How had they allowed it to get this bad? When he arrived at the palace, he barked orders at the guard to let him pass. The man did so, undoubtedly shocked that Bravaro would bring an urchin into the palace. He went straight up to the royal nursery, pounding on the door. Dosanyata opened, looking frightened, until her eyes alighted on the poor child.

"Oh, my. Bring him in. What happened?" Dosanyata opened the door wide, stepping aside so Bravaro could pass through. He lay him down on one of the large cushions in the sitting area.

"I tripped over the lad in the street." He brushed the hair away from his sunken face. "His parents abandoned him and his little sister so they could save their own lives," he said dully.

Dosanyata sucked in a breath, sinking onto a cushion beside the boy. She placed her fingers on his forehead, checking for fever. "I cannot imagine it. How awful. And his sister?"

Bravaro shook his head. "Dead." He breathed a frustrated sigh, raking a hand through his hair. "The people are starving, Dosanyata! There are too many of us crammed into the city. It's filthy out there, dangerous for men, let alone women and children. We have to do something!"

Dosanyata sat beside the boy and moved the hair away from his forehead. Bravaro's anger dissipated a bit. At least the boy would receive the greatest of care with Dosanyata, just as Bravaro had when he first came to the palace all those years ago. "You'll take care of him for me?"

"Of course, I will." Dosanyata was already moving to the now abandoned bed that had belonged to one of the princesses. She retrieved a blanket and spread it lovingly over the boy. Bravaro and Valian, had been too preoccupied as of late to see what a toll an empty nursery had on the woman who had spent most of her adult life caring for children. The nursery must have seemed utterly depressing in the days since Petella, Tamila, and Shos-Hinta had been forced to leave it.

"He will be most blessed to have you by his side when he awakes," Bravaro said, patting her hand. "We all have been blessed to have you."

Dosanyata looked up at him, tears in her eyes. "I will do all I can for him. I fear he may be too far gone for me to bring him back from the grave."

Bravaro nodded. "But, you will try?" he asked.

She nodded curtly, determination shining in her eyes. "How many more are there, Bravaro? How many more children have been abandoned by their selfish parents?" she asked. Bravaro had never heard her speak so vehemently, and he could not blame her.

Bravaro stood. "I am going to the king with this news. If parents are abandoning their children, they should be punished."

Dosanyata let out a long, sad sigh. "I agree with you, Bravaro," she stood and approached him after tucking the blanket snugly over the child's shoulders. The boy snuggled into the warmth. "But what can the king do right now? He is too busy preparing for an attack from Delgadas. I think parents abandoning their children is the least of his worries, not to sound crass."

"But it is crass! If we abandon our morals—the very fabric of what makes us Luminian—then we deserve the ruin that is upon us!" Bravaro was too angry to measure his words.

Dosanyata drew him away from the boy and into the main room. "Keep your voice down," she scolded. She need not have worried, for the boy did not even stir. "People do terrible things when faced with fear. I am not condoning their actions, son. Believe me, I am as angry as you to hear that people are leaving their children behind to save themselves. But we cannot focus on that right now. All we can do is try to help the children."

Bravaro nodded, scrubbing a hand over his face. He was so exhausted. It would seem he would not get a square meal and a rest before his guard duty began that night after all. Of course, the boy was worth it, but his selfish side rose. How could he lead the men who depended on him if he were not at his best? Dosanyata was right. Would Bravaro have walked past the boy if he had not accidentally tripped over his little legs? He assumed that Dosanyata was correct and that many more children needed nourishment and protection.

Bravaro made his way to the window. His face fell, looking beyond the palace walls to the suffering he knew was running rampant in the streets. "There are so many," he whispered despondently. "How can we help them all?"

Dosanyata said nothing for several seconds. When Bravaro looked down at her again, he saw tears spilling onto her cheeks. He drew her into a protective embrace, her forehead brushing against his jawline. "I am sorry. I should not have troubled you with all of this. I know you and Kyin are under enough pressure with his new position as one of the king's advisors."

"It is not that. I am sad that I cannot do more." She straightened, stepping away from him. "I can care for one boy. But what could I do if I were not here in the palace? You know of our humble origins. Kyin was a lowly brick maker before the king brought me here to be Shoram's nurse. How can I stay encased behind these walls while there are so many more children in need?"

Bravaro nodded, relieved that at least one child was off the street, warm and safe. For now. "Perhaps the king can be persuaded to open the palace to more of the needy children? I am sure he has not been told of the situation, as I have only just found out about it." He turned, kissing her lightly on the top of her head with familial affection. "I will check in on him in the morning. Thank you again, Dosanyata."

He turned and strode from the room, searching for King Nissim and the General. He found them in the courtroom, which had been transformed into a makeshift headquarters for army operations. Two guards stepped in front of the door as he approached, but when the general looked up and saw who it was, he waved Bravaro in.

Once inside, General Zalim gave him a cursory glance before returning his attention to the map before him. "How goes the preparation for the bridge defenses?"

"The blockades at both ends of the bridge have been completed, and the center supports have been weakened. If he brings his army over the bridge, it is sure to crumble with the weight."

"Excellent," the General replied, although he did not sound enthused. How long had he gone without sleep? How long had they all gone without it? Bravaro feared the General would start making grave mistakes if he did not rest soon.

"I would like a word with the king, if I may?" Bravaro requested. General Zalim did look up then. He furrowed his brow, glancing over his shoulder where the king was in conference with his lords.

"He is quite busy at the moment."

"It is important," Bravaro insisted, cutting off the General. His heart pounded in his ears, his anger giving him courage. "It is about the safety of the city, sir. I am afraid not all our problems lie outside the gates."

General Zalim eyed him for a moment and finally consented. "Very well." He sighed and motioned for him to follow, approaching the arguing group of lords as quietly as possible. Bravaro stepped up beside them, unafraid.

King Nissim looked up, bearing the signs of exhaustion, just as they all did. His clothes were rumpled, and great dark circles marred the undercarriage of his eyes. "Bravaro? What is it?"

Bravaro stepped forward, placed a hand over his heart and

bowed at the waist. He cleared his throat, all the lords turning to regard him. "I come with a report of the city, Your Majesty."

"Oh? Very well, continue." King Nissim looked slightly confused at the abrupt interruption but allowed him to speak.

"People are starving, Your Majesty. We are packed in here too closely. I fear that if we do not do something soon, disease will break out. I suggest we send food provisions to the people within the city and try to find better shelter until this is all over."

Lord Lamik huffed, giving a mirthless laugh. "And where do you suggest we get the food from?"

Bravaro licked his lips nervously. "I—"

"And where do you suggest we give them shelter? And medical attention? There is nothing left, boy." Lord Lamik snapped, glaring at him. No doubt they had been trying to solve the same issues Bravaro was bringing forward.

"We need to get as many people off this island as we can." Bravaro squared his shoulders. "We cannot hope to defend the island forever. Tzotoeh is too strong for us, especially in the state we now find ourselves. People are abandoning their children to die, Sire." Bravaro let those last words drop like a stone *slitsike* at an execution. So final. So absolute.

King Nissim's head shot up. "What is this?"

"I came upon a boy this eve as I was returning from the bridge. His parents left him and his sister to fend for themselves so they could make it over the border unencumbered. His sister is dead now, but I brought him to the palace to care for him."

A collective utterance of alarm spread through the lords, angry scowls marring their faces. "You cannot be serious?! I suppose you will say we should take in all the orphans, house them right here in the palace?"

Bravaro frowned at the man. "It is not my palace to give, but if it were, I would do so in a heartbeat. Do you not realize how many hundreds—even thousands—of people might be given shelter if we open the courtyards and gardens?" Bravaro had never openly shown hatred for anyone save for Lord Delgadas. But this pompous, selfish lord was now the only other person in Luminia who had earned his utmost scorn. "How many rooms lay vacant in your palatial villa, my lord? How many cold, hungry children could you provide for?"

Lord Lamik looked ready to scream at him, but King Nissim held up his hand for silence. "Bravaro is right. We must try to do something to ease the people's suffering." He looked up at Bravaro with tortured eyes. "I am sorry, Bravaro. It is too late to get the people off the island. Delgadas and his horde have already surrounded the lake. It would mean certain death or capture for anyone who tried to get away now."

The king stood, sighing heavily. "Open the courtyards, gardens, and hallways—any place that might house the people. Leave only the courtroom, library, and my quarters reserved from the public."

"But Sire, your palace. What of the valuables—?" Lord Lamik tried to argue.

King Nissim looked over at Lord Lamik, then at the rest of the assembled lords. "And you would do well to open your homes as well. The teachings of *Ilyo Na'ada* command us to look after orphans and widows."

"Sire—" Lord Lamik seemed bent on arguing. The king silenced him with a scowl.

"What value do those trinkets have now?" The king roared, surprising all of them. "We are in a fight for our lives, man. It matters not what earthly possessions they take. My guess is they will not care. Food is what they need, not gold." King Nissim strode through the middle of the circle, leaving the courtroom in a huff. Bravaro secretly smiled at the tongue-lashing Lord Lamik had received. He slowly turned and joined General Zalim at the table he used to spread out his maps.

"Well done, boy. I think you made an enemy of every one of those lords." A small smile tugged at the corners of the General's mouth. "It's about time someone riled them out of their stupor."

Several whispers could be heard as the lords dispersed. Some of them strode angrily out of the courtroom. Bravaro glanced over his shoulder. A few were not so angry, nodding to him respectfully as they left.

When they were alone, Bravaro let out a breath, frustrated once more. "They pretend like this is not happening, like they can close themselves behind the palace walls and this will all go away."

"They have been raised soft, Bravaro. They have never had to fight a war or even prepare for one. I think they are all just now realizing that this is not a game we are playing." General Zalim straightened, wincing as he placed a hand on his lower back. The man had never seen all-out war either. But at least he had been involved in a few skirmishes with the Tzotoen bandits. He would at least have some knowledge of how to roust them.

"Would that they had realized it much sooner. Maybe something could have been done for the people before it got this bad." Bravaro threw up his hands. "What if people could be taken out through the harbor? Surely Delgadas has not had time to surround us on every front?" If they could take people out by the sea—perhaps call on Detallma to take in some refugees—or even drop them off in Saardonae, they could ease some of the suffering of Lunthá. At least, if the women and children could be smuggled out, Bravaro would breathe easier.

"I'm afraid he has, Bravaro. The sentries on the seaside cliffs have just brought me reports of over a dozen Tzotoen ships resting outside the harbor." General Zalim sighed and placed a hand on Bravaro's shoulder. "You are a good man. You are at once compassionate and fierce. That is needed in a leader." He hung his head. "I think someday you will have my job, perhaps sooner than either of us is prepared for." The general looked back up at him, his eyes filled with sadness.

Bravaro tried to conceal the shiver of dread that ran up his spine. Before, he would have jumped at the chance for a place of leadership on General Zalim's war council. Now, he saw just how serious it all was. These were no war games. This was real. And he knew he had neither the experience nor wisdom to lead the men as he should.

"I do not want the assignment, Sir," he said. All he wanted was to see Luminia safe from Delgadas. He wanted Adagio, Melodia, and Haarmonae reunited with Ritenueta and Molto. He wanted things to go back to the way they had been.

Bravaro shuddered again. So many families had been torn apart. The Musicians could barely keep the sun rising and setting.

The General nodded, placing a heavy hand on his shoulder. Bravaro was forced to look him in the eye. "And that is precisely why you are one I would trust to take it. If it comes to that, you will face impossible situations like this, having to choose between what is right for the people and your men." General Zalim sighed again. "But you cannot save everyone."

CHAPTER 47

MELODIA

Melodia's lungs ached as she rushed after her father's shadowy form, tripping over tree roots and rocks in the dark. Her breath sounded loud in her own ears, and she did her best to quiet it. Perhaps she should have done more hiking instead of keeping to the palace halls. If she had, she might not feel like her heart was about to burst from the exertion. Still, she was unsure if there was anything she could have done to prepare her for their midnight flight from Lunthá.

"Hurry!" her father whispered for what must have been the hundredth time. For someone who had a dislocated hip, he was moving uncommonly fast. Haarmonae grunted as she tripped, nearly falling to the ground behind her.

Melodia knelt to help steady her, catching hold her sister before she collided with the ground. Their father never once turned around. "Papa has never acted like this before," Haarmonae said, huffing as she stood up. Refusing the hand Melodia offered, she brushed the dirt and mud off her skirts as best she could. Even dressed in their plainest garments, they were both unprepared for their trek through the maze that was the redwood forest. Haarmonae nodded toward

339

their father's disappearing form. "We had better catch up if we don't want him to leave us behind." She gave a harsh laugh. "I do not think he even remembers we are here."

"He is afraid." Melodia said, a lame attempt to defend him.

"We all are. For the love of all that is pure, Melodia! Mama and Molto were just kidnapped by a maniac! All he can think about is running away, saving his own neck. What is the rest of Luminia to do while we cower in the woods?" Haarmonae did not even try to keep the venom from her voice. They had traveled further from Lunthá over the last week than any of them had ever been. It was as if their father was running from his grief. But no matter how far he ran, he could not escape himself.

Melodia grabbed Haarmonae's arm, trying to get her to quiet her angry tone. "What else would you have us do? You heard Delgadas. He will kill them both if we do not disappear." She looked up once more and saw that their father had finally stopped to wait for them. She had never seen her father show fear, but everything had changed since their mother and brother had been kidnapped. It was almost as if her father had given up his fighting spirit, thinking that Delgadas would spare their family if they followed his instructions to the letter. Bile rose in her throat. Melodia did not believe anything would induce Delgadas to spare her brother's life. Perhaps he would let their mother live for a time, but Molto was much too vocal with his opinions. He would become a nuisance and get himself killed. Her heart twisted. In a way, she respected his bravery. But another piece of her hoped he would see sense and keep his mouth shut—at least for Mama's sake.

How had her life crumbled so entirely in a matter of a few days? They had been forced to hide in the forests surrounding Lunthá for a those few days after they had gotten out of the royal city. Delgadas and his army had drawn closer every day, until it was no longer safe for them to remain in the area. They had lived in terror as the marching of the soldiers grew louder, shaking the ground. None of them had slept. Perhaps it explained her fathers crazed mumblings as they made their getaway through the forest.

She glanced back at Haarmonae when they joined their father. He gripped Melodia's hand as he led them further into the maze of foliage. He said nothing, only nodded once and kept on going. Did he even know where he was taking them? Or were they destined to wander aimlessly in the woods until Delgadas could be brought to heel?

After what seemed like hours, their father stopped in front of a great Redwood tree. He planted his hands on his hips, looking up into the shadowed branches far above their heads. "Yes—" he said absently. It was as if she and Haarmonae were no longer there.

Melodia followed him as he walked around the tree, mumbling to himself as to the suitability of the place. "Papa, what are you doing?" The tree was larger than the ones around it, making her wonder if it might be one of the oldest trees in the area. What was he mumbling about?

He turned as if he had suddenly remembered she was there. "Did you not see? Here, come along with me." Melodia followed him to the place he had started. When they came around the trunk, Haarmonae still stood where they had left her, her arms crossed over the leather breastplate she had often worn during her training exercises. Her father barely noticed her twin, motioning toward some climbing vines wrapped around the base of the trunk, curling as they climbed up and around the side of the tree.

Melodia furrowed her brow. Had he completely lost his mind? "Do you mean for us to climb the tree, Papa?" She looked back at her sister, who had plopped down in the dirt when they entered the clearing. She was picking at a frayed piece of her skirt hem, pouting in stony silence.

"No, child," he said with a huff of frustration. Melodia was taken aback by his harsh tone but chose to ignore it. Now that they were safe, maybe the Papa she knew would resurface. "Look!" He approached the trunk and pulled away a section of the vines. Hidden behind them was a door carved right into the tree trunk. Melodia gave a little gasp, looking up at her father in wonder.

"What is this place?"

Her father smiled for the first time in days. "I will show you." He started to carefully move the vines aside, making sure that they were still intact. "My great grandfather built this house when he was in training for the job I now hold. He and my great grandmother lived here for over fifty years, before he was made Head Musician and moved to Lunthá." He gave the door a slight jerk, and Melodia heard something crash on the other side. He winced. "No one has been here for a long time."

Melodia helped him push the door open. The smell of dust and aging wood immediately slapped her in the face. Her father stepped inside the tree house first, the dim light from outside barely illuminating the space. He went in further, looking up into the large, dome-shaped room. The rustic surroundings made him look out of place, so used to seeing him amidst gleaming white marble halls and lavish furnishings. Melodia took a moment before stepping inside, allowing the dust clouds to settle.

She looked up at the hollowed-out space of the main room. It held a small table and four hand-hewn chairs next to a large river rock hearth. On the opposite wall was a compact counter space with a wash basin and cupboard for storing plates, bowls, and cutlery. Directly in front of her was a doorway, once covered by a piece of sackcloth but long since chewed away by the giant forest moths. Melodia stepped over one of the insect's carcasses, its wings spanning the length and breadth of her hand.

Her father gave a heavy sigh. "It needs quite a bit of cleaning up, but it should do nicely."

Melodia joined her father near the table, stepping over a cushion that had long ago lost its stuffing. "We are going to live here, Papa?"

"Yes, of course! We will be perfectly safe here." Her father started putting the chairs upright, stirring up more dust. Melodia coughed, covering her mouth with the crook of her elbow.

Melodia turned, looking around the dank, dimly lit space. "But for how long, Papa?" She picked up her skirts, walking over to the small window carved high in the tree trunk. From the outside, no one would suspect it was a window but rather a home for a woodpecker or some such burrowing, winged creature.

He turned sharply, almost glaring at her. "For as long as it takes." He looked around once more, lost in memories from happier times, by the look on his face. "We will be safe here until I figure out how to rescue your mother and Molto." He looked down at his injured leg. "I will let my leg heal, and then we will devise a plan. When I'm able to rescue them, we will bring them here to wait out the fighting. Until then, we shall have to do with what we have." He raised his hands and let them fall back to his sides with a thud. Dust billowed out from his clothing. It was so opposite of how she had always seen him, brilliant and courageous. It was as if losing her mother and brother had broken his mind and spirit. Tears spilled onto Melodia's cheeks to see what he had been reduced to.

Haarmonae finally ventured through the door, screwing up her nose at the smell of the place. Melodia turned her attention back to her father. "But how will we live? What will we do for food? And water?"

"And light," Haarmonae added, squinting as she tried to take in their new surroundings. Her father motioned for her to close the door, and she did so out of obedience rather than willingness. Melodia shivered when the door was closed all the way. She felt encased in a dark tomb, the only light coming from the small, irregularly shaped windows set high in the walls. Her father could not be serious about wanting to stay here while the rest of their friends fought for *Ilyo Na'ada* and country.

"There is a drip system that my grandfather developed. It collects water from the tops of the trees when it rains and stores it in drums below ground. You can hear it running down the inside of the tree when it rains. It sounds like the instruments we used to play that were made of hollowed tree branches filled with dried grain." He looked up as if they might hear it now, but only silence greeted them. "As for food, I shall hunt, and we can forage. I know where there are edible plants and berries. We shall live like kings out here! Just wait and see."

Melodia was not so sure. Should they not be back in Lunthá, helping King Nissim and the other Musicians fight against Delgadas? Obviously, their fellow Musicians had taken up the call and started playing for the sunrise again. The sun did rise each morning, but it lacked the brilliance of the past. Somehow, she assumed their fear came through in their melodies, no matter how they tried to mask it.

She was a coward. They all were. How could she voice this sentiment to her father? He would likely take her questions as criticism. She bit her tongue. It would be better to go along with his plan. For now, she would let him settle down before voicing her thoughts.

"I can help you, Papa. With hunting, I mean. I have always wanted to learn how," Haarmonae offered. She glanced at Melodia, who gave her an annoyed scowl. But it was true. She had never felt like she really belonged with their family. They all adored their jobs as Musicians, while she felt guilty for wanting something different. Melodia knew she wanted to fight. At least in their present circumstances, she might finally be useful.

Adagio turned, nodding at Haarmonae. "And you shall. You may both come with me, if you like." He looked up at the cavernous space above their heads. "But there is plenty to do here, if you do not wish to come along, Melodia?"

Melodia shook her head. She did not have the stomach for such things. Foraging she could do. Killing, no.

"Melodia cannot shoot as well as I can, Father," Haarmonae said, seeing her discomfort. "Leave the hunting to me." Melodia brushed past them and walked further into the room. She parted the hole-ridden curtain and peered into what must have been a bedroom. It was a fraction of the size of the room she had shared with Haarmonae back home.

344

"I will stay here and keep the house, ensure the fires are burning," Melodia mumbled.

"Very good," her father said with a nod of approval. He walked about the room again, and they all choked on the dust clouds. She wished her father would stand still, but he continued rummaging around, saying a loud "aha!" when he found what he was looking for. He gripped a broom handle and grabbed it as if he had found a treasure trove. "Now, let us get to work."

LATE THAT NIGHT, Melodia lay awake, listening to the rainwater dripping down the storage system. Its clinking made a tune as it went, just as her father had said. Haarmonae slept fitfully by her side, with their sleeping mats stretched before the fire. Melodia had never worked so hard in her life as she had cleaned the tree house. They had cleared a mountain of dust, spreading it evenly outside so it would seep into the ground over time. Her father was paranoid about Delgadas and his spies finding their hideout.

They had cleaned the furniture as best they could and found the bedrolls in one of the two rooms. Cleaning a room for herself and Haarmonae would be a task for the morrow. For now, she lay on her back and stared at the ceiling, counting the tree rings visible in the dancing firelight. The tree had seen over four hundred years come and go. What stories would it have to tell if only it could speak? Tears streamed down the sides of her face and into her ears, but she did nothing to wipe them away.

She missed Mama and Molto. Never in her life had they been separated for more than a few days at a time. If ever Mama and Papa had to travel with the king, they were usually allowed to go with them, especially since Molto had been training to take over as Head Musician someday. She drew in a shaky breath. What was to become of them all? Were Mama and Molto well?

Melodia knew that the Musicians must have discovered they

were missing by now. She glanced at the tiny round window high in the tree trunk wall. Gray light was fighting to come over the horizon. What would happen if Delgadas decided to capture the rest of the Musicians and forbade them to play? What would happen to the royal city and their nation without someone to play for the sunrise? The rain came down all the faster at this thought, and Melodia wondered if the underground drums that stored the water would overflow.

She wiped at her eyes, holding back the gut-wrenching sobs that threatened to come bubbling to the surface. She loved her Papa but felt she did not know him anymore. Where was the strong, steady, confident man she had grown up knowing? Had losing Mama so broken him that he was beyond repair?

Melodia turned over, whimpering softly so as not to wake Haar-monae or Papa. *Ilyo Na'ada, where are you? We need your help to fight against Delgadas. I have grown up hearing about your mighty works. So why do you remain silent now?*

No answer was forthcoming, only the tinkling of the rain running down the midst of the trunk. Feeling lost and alone, she turned on her side and gave way to silent gut-wrenching sobs.

CHAPTER 48

PRINCE SHORAM

Shoram was walking along the corridor abutting the courtroom when he heard voices raised in alarm. It had been a week since their arrival in Raellu, the Saardonaenian capitol, and Shoram was finally feeling more at ease. His grandfather was kind and generous. Although he had only met him once when he was younger, he felt a kinship toward him that surpassed their shared blood.

Peeking into the courtroom, Shoram saw the king and his grandfather looking stunned, reading over a missive that had no doubt just been delivered. The messenger stood before them, breathless, his shoulders heaving with each inhale. Without thinking, Shoram entered the courtroom uninvited.

"What is it, Grandfather?" Shoram asked. Instinct told him that whatever it was, it had to do with Luminia.

The king's features softened, and Shoram's grandfather came off the dais to meet him. "Shoram, what are you doing here? Should you not be with your tutor?" His grandfather tried to steer him out of the room, but Shoram gently brushed his hand away and turned to face the king.

"I was passing by when I heard your voice. What is it? Has something happened back home?" King Botzena looked to Shoram's grandfather before allowing anyone to speak. The messenger backed up slowly, bowing his head.

The king and his grandfather shared a worried glance. "I suppose he is old enough to know?" The king asked, waiting for his brother to give his permission. His grandfather turned to Shoram, studying him for a moment.

"He is next in line to the throne," he replied, his usually rich, comforting voice sounding anything but. Shoram's heart began to hammer inside his chest.

"What is it? Please, tell me, Your Majesty," Shoram pleaded with King Botzena, splaying his hands before him.

His grandfather sighed, taking the scroll that the king offered him. He gave it to Shoram to read. "We have had reports from Luminia. Apparently, Delgadas' forces are closing in on Lunthá. We believe they mean to lay siege to the city."

Shoram scanned the document, but his eyes soon blurred with tears. He returned the message to his grandfather, turning hurriedly to leave the courtroom. "I should be there with Papa right now. I have to go—"

Tamil appeared in the doorway, her face white. She had donned the lavish attire of a Saardaenian diplomat's wife, everything they had escaped with being too worn for the palace courts. However much she might have looked the part of a queen in the dress, she looked more the worry-worn traveler, even after days of rest in their lavish rooms. "No, Shoram. I cannot allow you to do that." She held up her hands, her eyes meeting his. No matter how he pleaded, his stepmother would not allow him to leave, but it would not stop him from trying.

His grandfather stammered an apology. "I am sorry, Your Majesty. I should have asked you first—" he said to his stepmother. Tamil captured Shoram in her arms, discouraging him from moving. She hugged him close as he tried to pull away.

"No. You were right to show him." Tamil's voice cracked with emotion. What must she be feeling at this news? Shoram pushed away gently, reaching for her hand. "Nissim?" she asked.

His grandfather now looked to Shoram for guidance. He did not know Tamil as he did. Shoram squeezed her hand. "There was no news of Papa. We must therefore assume he is yet well."

"For now," she replied.

"I am sorry, Mama," he said softly. She gave him a weak smile, looking up at the king.

"May I see the letter?" She entered the room, gripping Shoram's hand as if she needed his support to stay upright. She scanned the letter slowly, worry lining her face. When she came to the end of it, her head shot up. "We have to do something. Your Majesty, is there any way to get help to them before it is too late?"

The king splayed his hands. "I am doing everything I can to mobilize my troops, but Delgadas is moving so fast. I hate to tell you this, but we may not be ready in time. He is already laying siege to Lunthá."

"Has there been any word from my father? Surely Detallma might come to their aid by sea?" Tamil's eyes darted to and fro, overcome with anxiety. Shoram had not realized how very much Tamil loved his father, until then. He had not always been sure growing up. He had often felt the outcast as the only son of his late mother amongst his sisters born of Tamil. Tamil and his father's love had blossomed slowly from what he had seen. Now, he did not think she could imagine life without his father.

The king sighed heavily, keeping his eyes trained on his step-mother. "We have heard nothing from them as of yet. You know your father better than I do. Will they be able to travel quickly enough to defend Luminia's harbor?"

Tamil bit her lip, tossing Shoram a worried glance. "I do not know. Detallma may be on the other end of our world for all we know." She turned away from the dais.

Shoram's grandfather came to his side, touching his shoulder.

"We will pray that the missive reaches Detallma in time. Who knows —perhaps they are on their way as we speak." Shoram looked up into his grandfather's kind, brown eyes.

"I must leave immediately. I should be there with Papa," Shoram said, brushing his grandfather's hand off his shoulder and striding toward the door again. He could not stand idly by. He may never see his father again, and that was a reality he could not imagine.

Tamil grabbed his arm, halting him in his tracks. "No, Shoram! Your father told me to protect you. I cannot just let you ride back into danger. He would want you to remain here, where it is safe."

"But who is to say Delgadas will stop when Lunthá falls? What if he has his sights on Saardonae? If we do not stand up to him, what is to stop him from taking over the world?"

The king stood, striding down the dais steps over to him. "You are the heir to the throne of Luminia, Prince Shoram. Queen Tamil is right. You need to stay here where it is safe. Do not worry. Saardonae is well-defended."

"I am not worried for my own safety!" he railed. Shoram turned from his grandfather to his stepmother. "Papa is all alone right now. The message said that Adagio and his family have gone missing. The Musicians will soon be too afraid to play for the sunrise. Already, we can feel the effects of their fear." Shoram said, feeling frantic to make them understand. The skies had been murky gray for the last three days, sputtering rain. Had most of the Musicians fled the city in preparation for Delgadas's attack, or did some still hold on and try to fill the gap left by Adagio? "Who will be there to stand by Papa? Who will encourage *him*?"

Tamil's eyes softened. "It should have been me," she replied softly. "But we cannot go back and change what has been. We are here now, and His Majesty is doing everything in his power to prepare his army." She glanced at King Botzena, although Shoram could see she was trying to mask her disappointment and anger at the delay.

"Of course," King Botzena replied. "I will try to send a contingent of soldiers as soon as possible, and the rest can follow when all is prepared. Do not worry, Shoram. We will stop Delgadas, whatever the cost."

Shoram felt a stab of fear run through his heart. The king was trying to make him feel better, but Shoram sensed they were only offering false hope. Perhaps the adults did not want to believe that Luminia could fall to Delgadas—that centuries of peace and prosperity could not be undone in a matter of weeks.

Shoram started toward the door, Tamil walking beside him. The king and Shoram's grandfather returned to work, speaking with the messenger who had brought the news in hushed tones.

"Everything will be well, Shoram. Now, why do you not go back to your lessons? There is nothing to be gained by worrying," Tamil said. However, even her tone was laced with anxiety. Shoram nodded silently, heading back down the hall toward the school room. Even as he sat and listened to his tutor, his mind was far away, worrying about the homeland he loved so much.

CHAPTER 49

HAARMONAE

Days passed, and still, Haarmonae and her sister could not draw their father out of his deep depression. Since arriving at the tree house, he had initially worked as hard as they, making repairs and hunting for food. In all reality, it was more of a tree *fortress* than a house. It was true what their father said —no one would find them. Not even their friends would be able to locate them. The tree had passed from memory with Melodia's grandparents. From the outside, it looked like all the others. From within, they had access to a labyrinth of staircases and underground tunnels that snaked under the forest for who knew how many miles.

Her sister wiped at the sweat beading on her forehead, bent over as she scrubbed a pot. Melodia had been working non-stop the last few days. The thick layer of dust had been removed from the floor and the furnishings. Haarmonae stopped, stretching her lower back after nearly an hour of scrubbing the floor. They had done their best to make the house portion of the tree more livable. Still, their father would not allow them to hang curtains in the windows, nor clear the vines from the front of their new abode—nothing that would give the enemy suspicions of their hiding spot.

Haarmonae glanced at her sister and dropped the newly veined arrow in her quiver. "You have been scrubbing the same pot for the last half hour. Was the stew that burnt?" she asked. Her sister had been quiet—quieter than usual. She supposed Melodia had the right after everything that had happened. But she still worried for her.

"Come on. Leave it for a while," Haarmonae said. "You need a break from washing. And I need a break from watching you wash," she teased. She rose from the floor and took her sister's hand, hauling her to her feet.

"I cannot leave it. I must start the evening meal," Melodia said feebly, but Haarmonae would hear none of it. She kept a firm grip on her sister's hand and, lifting her emerald green skirts, started up one of the winding staircases that led up into the heart of the tree.

Melodia snatched up her light blue skirts, shimmering in what little light crept through the hallowed knots of the tree and shone down on the living space. There was a rare break in the weather that day. She wondered if a Musician somewhere had been able to play a few notes, coaxing the sun out of its gray prison. "Where are you taking me?" Melodia asked. Haarmonae knew she did not mind being dragged up the steps, however annoyed her tone might sound. She needed a rest, at least for a few moments.

"We are going to explore a bit. If this is to be our new home, we ought to know more about it," Haarmonae said as they climbed higher and higher.

The steps had been carved straight into the side of the tree, winding up and around the trunk's hollowed interior. It had taken a masterful hand and careful planning—probably a lifetime. Melodia was fascinated by everything. She looked down momentarily, then decided it was better not to, the higher up they went. There was no railing to keep them from slipping and falling over the side.

"There are nets," Haarmonae said as if reading her thoughts. "You cannot see them from this height, with how dark it is. But if you were to fall, you would not die."

Melodia followed her sister until they were at the very top of the tree. It took a long time for them to climb all the way up, but once there, they came out on a balcony where they could look out on the whole of Luminia.

"This is—" Melodia breathed, unable to catch her breath or come up with the right words to describe it. She had never been up this high before. And she had certainly never been able to see as far as this. Since the towering Redwood forests surrounded the royal city, she had barely seen past their sheltered island home.

"Stunning," Haarmonae finished.

"It makes me feel so small," Melodia said. She walked out to the edge of the half-moon-shaped balcony. Thankfully, this one had a railing around it. She gripped the smooth wood, looking out over the forest. There was green foliage as far as the eye could see. She looked to the south, in the direction that Lunthá lay. She could not see it now, but it was as if her heart drew her there.

"Are you well?" Haarmonae asked after a moment's pause.

"I miss home," Melodia admitted. "Even more than that I am eaten away with guilt for what we have done." She looked back at Haarmonae and motioned her to join her.

Haarmonae frowned. "What do you mean?"

Melodia looked up at the sky. There were still some branches covering their heads, with about fifty feet of tree thinning as it came to a point in the sky. Melodia felt like they were flying, with clouds almost near enough to touch. She closed her eyes and took a deep breath, feeling as if her chest might cave in from the weight of her guilt. "We left them there, Haarmonae. We fled to save our own lives. Even now, our friends might have been captured by Delgadas, or worse, and we never lifted a finger to try to stop him."

"That is the worst part about being trapped here: not knowing. We should be doing something, but father will not budge. If only we could go back and—"

Melodia wished it too, but what could two of them do against the power of Delgadas' army? She grabbed Haarmonae's hand. It was as cold as her own. "And what? Get ourselves killed?" Melodia asked. "That would finish Papa. He is so worried about Mama and Molto." A shiver ran down Haarmonae's spine at her sister's words. "If something were to happen to us, who knows what lengths he would be pushed to."

"We cannot accomplish anything by hiding out here. Surely you see that," Haarmonae pleaded. She had to make her sister understand, to get some kind of blessing for what she had been contemplating. However, the look of horror in Melodia's eyes told her that she could not trust her with her secret. Not yet.

"You are not planning what I think you are planning," Melodia stated. Her eyes flashed with indignation and fear. No, Haarmonae could not tell her.

"What? What could I possibly be planning?" Haarmonae asked, brushing her off. She turned her attention back to the forest. "I just feel so helpless, Melodia. What if Delgadas breeches our defenses. What do you think he is going to do to the Musicians then?" she asked. Her heart clenched with worry. "We abandoned them to their Fate. I cannot forgive Papa for that."

Melodia gasped. She had never heard her sister speak that way about their father. Melodia would certainly never dream of voicing such things. However, there was a part of her that felt the same. She felt like a coward. "I do not know what he will do. I suppose they will be taken captive, as Mama and Molto were." Her stomach tightened with fear. Bile rose in her throat just thinking of the persecution that would come to their fellow Musicians if Delgadas was indeed able to break through Lunthá's defenses.

"All I know is that I cannot sit here and do nothing while they suffer. What if there is a way to get people out? Were not Queen Tamil and the children able to escape?"

Melodia shook her head. "That was before Delgadas and his horde closed in on the city. It would take a miracle for anyone to sneak out of Lunthá now." She studied her sister's face. She looked away, her hazel eyes filled with guilt of another kind. "Or for someone to sneak *in*."

Melodia reached over and grabbed her sister's hand. "Promise me that you will not go back there."

"Melodia—" Haarmonae started, trying to argue. But Melodia cut her off.

"No, you have to promise me," Melodia pleaded. Tears stung her eyes. "I do not know what I would do if we lost you, too." Her voice broke, and a single tear making tracks down her cheek.

Haarmonae sighed in resignation. "Alright. I promise," she agreed slowly. Melodia hugged her tightly, and Haarmonae clung to her as well. They had never been apart for more than a few hours since birth.

And Haarmonae had just told her first lie.

CHAPTER 50

KING NISSIM

Lunthá, Luminia

"Your Majesty, Delgadas is at the gates." The sentry bowed before him, keeping his eyes lowered. He could be no more than fifteen years old, shaking in his oversized armor. Nissim straightened, his mind reeling. He had received a communique from his enemy the day before, asking for a meeting. Nissim saw no other way with the city on the brink of chaos.

"Let us go, then," Nissim ordered. He mounted his steed, nodding to his general. A band of soldiers and dignitaries accompanied him down the steep, winding streets. *Ilyo Na'ada, grant us peace.* He prayed all the way to the gates that protected the outer city. Delgadas had ordered him to open the gates so that he might come to the palace for their rendezvous, but Nissim was not about to let him see how weak they really were.

Treading lightly over the bridge, Nissim gasped when he saw the destruction already wrought by the Tzotoen bandits on the outer city of Lunthá. There were no people to be seen, all of them no doubt huddled in their hovels. Or had they escaped while they still had a chance? How were Adagio and his daughters faring, he wondered? Guilt stabbed at his heart for what must have been the hundredth time. He should have protected his friend better. If he had, perhaps he would have stayed to help him deal with the crisis they were facing.

They walked up to the gates, and he ordered his soldiers to open them. Once on the other side, Nissim could see a huddle of about thirty soldiers sneering and mocking him. Nissim held his head high despite their derisive laughter. He would not give in to their jeers, for he was the king of all Luminia. *At least, for the time being*, he thought. He shook his head slightly. *Do not think like that, Nissim. You must trust that Ilyo Na'ada has this in hand.*

A gasp ran through his soldiers when Delgadas revealed himself. Indeed, Nissim would never have recognized him if not for the arrogant sneer on his face. Murmurs traveled around the company, and Nissim held his hand up for silence. Nissim stepped forward, meeting his old adversary face-to-face for the first time in over a decade. "Delgadas," he said flatly. "I would say that you look good, but I cannot tell a lie."

Nissim's soldiers snickered at his remark, but he maintained his icy stare. The whole right side of Delgadas's face had turned black, with large scales growing where the skin used to be. Nissim had never seen anything like it.

Delgadas only gave a lopsided grin. "Ahh, your words have a bite to them. And here I thought that the teachings of *Ilyo Na'ada* forbade such unkind words. Perhaps your faith is slipping, my old friend?"

Nissim's ire rose, not only that Delgadas had thrown the teachings of *lyo Na'ada* in his face, but that he had called him *old friend*. However, Nissim knew he could not answer with anger. He clenched his fists and continued. "You asked for a meeting, Delgadas. Now, what is it you want?"

Delgadas began to pace slowly back and forth. He eyed Nissim with his good eye, which had turned an unearthly shade of bright green. The other was covered with a patch, but Nissim assumed it was because the scales had grown over his eyelid. Delgadas fixed him with a piercing stare, giving a short laugh. "I come to offer a truce, my friend."

"You? A truce?" Nissim asked in disbelief. He knew Lunthá would not be on the winning side of any truce that Delgadas had to offer. "What are the terms of your so-called truce?"

Delgadas feigned hurt and continued, "All I ask is that you abdicate the throne to me. If you do so, I will spare the city." Obviously, Delgadas could see that Nissim was in no mood to negotiate. He tried to sweeten the deal. "I will even give you a title and a position in my new regime. You will see, my plans for Luminia are much more, let us say—" Delgadas paused, a smirk crossing his lips. "—progressive."

Nissim could not believe what he was hearing. He looked to his general, who was sizing up the situation. They could not be sure how many of Delgadas' soldiers were lurking beyond the city, hidden in the shadowed foliage of the forest. "Progressive? You meant destructive, surely."

"Not so! You have seen the destruction that comes from relying on music. If you even miss playing for one sunrise, the whole world falls apart. What do you think will happen, if music is abolished for good?" Delgadas spat.

Nissim's heart froze. "You mean to abolish music? But that is suicide!"

"No. I have found a way to bring our world to life without this accursed *music*. We will never again be at it's mercy."

Nissim's arms crawled with gooseflesh. "But why? *Ilyo Na'ada* provides all that we need. We do not need another way. All we need to do is follow his ways—" The rest of the words caught in his throat. Delgadas did not want to bend his will to the will of *Ilyo Na'ada*. He wanted only his own way.

Delgadas snarled at him. "You are a fool, Nissim. If you band with me, we would be unstoppable. There would be no one to stand in our way!"

Nissim took a steadying breath, knowing that he would never bend to Delgadas' truce. "And if I refuse?"

Delgadas cocked his head to the side like a vulture, watching greedily as its next meal expired. "Then I will take it by force. And your people will pay the price for your selfishness." His voice came out in a fierce, low whisper that made Nissim's skin crawl.

"I will give you three days to decide, Nissim." Delgadas took the edge of his cloak and turned sharply, making it ripple in the wind. "Three days and no more," he yelled over his shoulder. His men started to close in around him as Delgadas walked away into the forest cover, disappearing like a thief in the night.

Nissim nodded to his general and retreated to the relative safety of the outer city walls. "What are we going to do, Your Majesty?" General Zalim asked, walking at a brisk pace to match Nissim's.

"I know not. But we must pray. We must charge the whole city to fast and pray." It was all he knew to do. He cursed himself for not moving sooner. He and the whole country had been lulled into a false sense of security. All the while, their enemy had been planning his attack, waiting until they were most vulnerable.

"That will not be too difficult, since there is little food to be had," General Zalim mumbled under his breath.

Nissim halted in his tracks, facing the men around him. "Is that what you think? That all is lost? Where is your faith, General Zalim? All of you?" His voice rose over the abandoned city. "If we give up hope now, then we must also admit that *Ilyo Na'ada* has forsaken us! And I would rather die than admit such a thing." His men eyed him hesitantly.

After several seconds, Nissim turned back to the inner city, gazing at its once-sparkling marble structures left to deteriorate and gardens to grow wildly at will. Lunthá looked like a bride who had been jilted at the altar. Her visage was no longer bright and clear but smudged with tears, dirt, and despair. Her gown was no longer purest white but covered in filth, and her head was no longer lifted with hope and promise. Was it *Ilyo Na'ada's* will to humble them? If it were his will, there would be no escape for any of them. But Nissim refused to believe that. They must stand up and fight. He headed toward the bridge, climbing onto his horse. He pondered what he should do as they rode gingerly across the weakened bridge.

"General, take down a decree once we arrive at the palace. I want it distributed throughout the city." Nissim said. The general nodded, waiting. "Tell the people that there is to be a solemn fast. For three days and three nights, we will pray—"

And hope that Ilyo Na'ada hears.

CHAPTER 51
BRAVARO

Bravaro awakened with a start as a white-blue light flashed through his window. Seconds later, thunder crashed, shaking the ground. It had been raining since King Nissim returned from the meeting with Delgadas the previous morning. Since then, the whole city had been pressed to fast and pray. Even the Musicians had held off playing for the sunrise and sunset. The storm had come quickly as the whole country went into a state of mourning. The King was in an impossible situation. How could he choose between giving control of the country over to Delgadas and the safety of his own people?

Bravaro stood up slowly, going to the window to look at the ravaged city. Lighting cracked once more, illuminating the winding streets for a split second. Bravaro's heart froze as movement near the harbor caught his eye. "What in the world?" he whispered. He turned, reaching for his looking glass and held it to his right eye. He kept the instrument trained on the harbor, waiting for the next lightning strike.

When the next one came, he spotted several shadowy figures creeping toward the palace. Alarmed, he lowered the looking glass, peering with his naked eye. However, darkness had once again settled over the city, making it impossible to decipher whether he had imagined things. He shook his head, wondering what anyone would be doing out in a storm like this. There was no reason for the townspeople to be about. With the storm raging, no one was brave enough nor had the strength to venture outside.

Bravaro knew that time was of the essence. He tucked the looking glass under his arm and hurried out of the room, bumping into two guards as he went. They stood on the defensive, pointing their long, obsidian-tipped spears at him. Bravaro held up his hands.

"Stand down," he said, and they lowered their weapons.

"Forgive us, sir. We thought—"

"It is alright. Come with me. We must raise the alarm." Bravaro did not waste another moment to explain but instead looked over his shoulder as he raced down the hall toward the king's chambers. "I've seen something down at the harbor, soldiers coming this way. I do believe Delgadas is going back on his word."

"Delgadas is attacking the city? But he said we had three days!" one of the men exclaimed. Bravaro slowed as they approached the king's chambers.

"Well, he is taking the city now," Bravaro replied. "Or at least, he is going to try. Open the doors," he ordered, and the two soldiers outside the king's chamber glanced at each other.

"The king ordered that no one was to be admitted. He is praying—"

"This is a matter of life and death, man!" Bravaro yelled, frantic to save Lunthá. "Delgadas is attacking," he said and brushed the soldier aside. He could not have been more than a year or two older than Bravaro. He rushed into the room, only to see the king rising from the end of the bed where he had knelt in prayer. He lowered his head. "Forgive me, Your Majesty. I bring grave news."

"What is it, Bravaro?" King Nissim asked, his face drawn and tired.

"I saw something down at the docks. You had better come have a look," Bravaro said.

King Nissim nodded grimly, turning to the soldiers who had followed Bravaro into the room. "Sound the alarms and rally the troops. Find General Zalim and tell him to meet us on the roof."

Bravaro's heart skipped a beat. "Should we not get you to safety, Your Majesty? There is a boat waiting at the edge of the lagoon–"

"I will not abandon my people to save myself," he snapped. He hurried down the hall, and Bravaro sprinted to keep up with him. Ever since he had sent Queen Tamil and the children to safety, it was near impossible for anyone to convince the king to take care of himself or consider his safety. What would they do if King Nissim was captured? Or worse?

Bravaro tried to push the disturbing thoughts away as they bounded up the steps to the rooftop. He would not allow Delgadas to capture their king. He would give his life before he let that happen.

When they arrived on the roof, Bravaro handed over his looking glass, and they walked over to the edge of the flat precipice. The king raised the looking glass to his eye and waited for the next lightning strike. They had only a moment to wait, for the next strike crackled across the dark violet clouds above like tree roots spreading across the sky. Bravaro held his breath, hoping that this was not a false alarm. He began to doubt as the king stood frozen, looking toward the harbor.

"What do you see, Your Majesty?" one of the soldiers asked.

King Nissim lowered the glass slowly, looking at Bravaro. "There was nothing there, son," he said, returning the glass to Bravaro.

Bravaro could not believe his ears. "Your Majesty, I–"

"That does not mean they are not on their way. It would not have taken long for them to sneak through the city to the palace gates, which is exactly their intent, I am sure."

"Delgadas promised you three days. Why would he attack now?" The soldier who had asked the question before was again voicing his disbelief. Bravaro could see he was on the verge of losing all control.

He dropped his spear and backed away from the roof's edge. "We have to get out."

Bravaro stepped over to him, clamping his hands on his shoulders and shaking him. "Keep your head, man. We need everyone if we are to defend the city."

Bravaro looked around, wondering what was keeping General Zalim. At that second, a flash of lightning illuminated the roof, and he saw several men coming up from the staircase. He recognized the soldiers from his platoon. They approached without a sound, just as they had all been trained, fanning out to create a perimeter around the king. They turned outward, training their spears in front of them to fend off would-be attackers. The leader of the group came and stood at attention before King Nissim.

"We went in search of General Zalim, but he is not in his quarters, Your Majesty."

"Not in his quarters? Where would he go?"

However, King Nissim could not finish his thought, for a loud crack echoed through the night. A whistling sound followed, and Bravaro yelled for the king to get down, diving in front of him just as a large boulder hit the roof's edge. The impact sent large chunks of marble and dust spraying over their heads. Bravaro took a piece of rubble to the face, just above his left eye. He scrambled and covered the king with his body, as did several fellow soldiers.

In the next second, Bravaro began barking orders. "Get the king to safety! And get the archers up on this wall. Now!" He pushed the king to his feet, and six of their best fighters surrounded him, taking him to the stairs leading into the heart of the palace. They would take him to the servants' quarters below the palace to keep him safe until the fighting was over.

Bravaro followed the king and his men, but as he motioned for the soldiers to come to the roof's edge, another projectile hit the palace wall just below the first target. The roof and part of the wall began to crumble under his feet. He yelled for the rest of the men to get out of the way, but one of his men started to fall backward over the edge. Bravaro reached out and grabbed his forearm in the nick of time. He lurched forward, and were they both nearly dragged over the side.

Bravaro gripped a bit of wall that was still intact, hanging on for dear life. The other soldier dangled like a worm on a hook hundreds of feet above the cobblestone square. He clung to Bravaro's arm with both hands, allowing his spear to fall to the ground. It landed on a balcony about thirty feet below them, and he heard the obsidian tip shatter.

Lighting laced the sky, and Bravaro saw the boy's eyes wide with fear. "Do not look down," Bravaro instructed, trying to keep his voice calm. Leaning over the side of the roof was crushing his ribs, cutting off his air supply. He had to get him up and over the edge before the next boulder came careening toward them.

As the darkness enveloped them again, Bravaro could hear the soldier huff, trying to hold on. However, his grip was starting to loosen as the rain-slicked their hands. "Let me go," the soldier said. Bravaro held on all the tighter.

"Never. I will not let you go. Here, pull yourself up, if you can. Are you injured?" Bravaro asked.

The boy did not respond to this question. "Let me go, sir. I dropped my spear, and you know that is an offense punishable by death."

Bravaro heaved, trying to pull his soldier up with brute strength. However, he slid back down again, his rib cage pressing painfully against the roof's edge. "This is not a punishable offense, man. We need you," Bravaro ordered. "Get up on this roof and help us defend the king, as is your duty!"

"I am slipping, sir. I cannot get up. My arm—" his words trailed off, and as another bolt of lightning hit, Bravaro could see that the man's left arm was dripping blood. Bravaro closed his eyes, summoning all the strength he had in reserve.

"I am not going to let you die like this. Now, when I count to three, you grip with your good arm, and I shall pull you the rest of the way. One, two, three!" he yelled, letting out a growl as he pulled with all his might. The soldier released a gasp of pain, pulling him over the roof's edge and dragging him a few feet away to safety.

They lay there, breathing heavily in a heap for a moment. The tell-tale whistling met his ears the next instant, and Bravaro burst into action. "Another missile! Get out of the way!"

He hauled the boy up to his feet and placed a hand under his arm. They ran toward the stairs to get away from the next projectile. Several of their comrades ran for the safety of the stairs, and Bravaro handed off the injured man to another of their fellow soldiers. Bravaro stood by the opening to the stairwell, yelling for them to hurry until all were accounted for. Another missile hit, shaking the palace, but this time, it hit further down, closer to where the royal court was situated.

Bravaro dove into the stairwell just as it hit. The force sent him careening down the stairs. He covered his head and neck out of instinct, rolling down the stone steps with nothing to slow his progress until he hit the back of one of the other soldiers. They stopped a few stairs down, grunting and moaning in pain. Bravaro slowly opened his eyes, taking stock. Had he broken his neck?

A soldier's face appeared above him, reaching out his hand to assist him. Bravaro took it, relieved he could still move. "Come on, sir. We have to move," the man said. Bravaro nodded, suddenly aware of all the places on his body where he would be bruised from the fall. Several ribs felt like they had been cracked, making it painful to inhale. He would have to worry about that later. Right now, he had to defend the palace.

"Where are the archers?" he yelled as he limped down the remaining stairs. Once on the main floor where the royal bedchambers were located, he looked around to see that a large, gaping hole stood where a bedroom had once been. Fear coiled in the pit of his stomach. He hurried down the hall, but when he came to another hole, he took a moment to look out. He had a clear view of the courtyard in front of the palace. His heart nearly stopped with the drama unfolding before him. He turned and went out onto the rickety balcony. Half of it had already crumbled away from the force of the projectile.

Delgadas stood before the palace gates, which had been forced open. A fire had been built in a large brass drum, the flames reaching high despite the rain pouring down from the heavens. Behind the fire, Bravaro could see Delgadas' marred face, set in a permanent sneer. And beside him was General Zalim, beaten and bloody. Two Tzotoen soldiers held him, laughing and mocking as they smiled at the destruction they had wrought on the palace.

"Nissim!" Delgadas boomed. "Where is Nissim!"

Without thinking, Bravaro stepped forward, but someone clamped a hand around his arm, holding him back. Bravaro glanced at his face and recognized Valian in the low light. "Do not," he warned. Even though he was still only a boy, Bravaro was surprised by the fierceness shining in his gaze.

Bravaro shook him off, boiling with anger. "The king is no longer within the walls!" Bravaro shouted. It took Delgadas a moment to decipher where Bravaro's voice was coming from. He soon found him and shot a hate-filled glare at Bravaro.

"What a pity. I suppose we ransacked the city for nothing. Oh, well. I had hoped he would be here to see the show, but I suppose you and your ragged band of leaderless soldiers will have to do." Delgadas turned to his soldiers, nodding once. One of them pulled out a long obsidian blade and held it to General Zalim's throat. Bravaro could not help but lurch forward, holding his hand out for them to stop. But there was nothing he could do. In the next instant, General Zalim sank to his knees, holding his hands over the gaping slit in his throat.

"No!" Bravaro cried, even as he hung over the railing, desperate to help the man. Valian took him by the arm and pulled him backward. Bravaro was shocked by the strength Valian demonstrated. He was wiry and lank at twelve, his firm grip pulling him back to reality.

"We have to go. Get the king to safety," Valian insisted breathlessly.

"There is nowhere you can run! I am the Lord of Lunthá, now!" Delgadas said. "I will find the king, and then Luminia will be mine!" His voice echoed around the courtyard with a sickening crescendo. "Gather all the Musicians you can find, and bring them to the roof!" He ordered his men. The Tzotoen bandits spread over the palace grounds, looking like vengeful ants who had had their hill destroyed by a fiery poker.

His heart stopped, but Valian had a firm hold and was dragging him from the balcony. Once back in the hall, they lit out for the servant's quarters. "We have to find the king and get him out of Lunthá!" Valian insisted.

Bravaro nodded, unable to speak, shocked by what he had just seen. "*Ilyo Na'ada,* save us," he whispered, forcing his legs to keep moving forward. They hurried down the steps, weaving around terrorized people running for their lives. Just before they reached the palace's underground ramparts that housed the servants' quarters, they heard a massive crash above them. Dust rained down from the ceiling, and they covered their heads with their arms. Bravaro looked up, listening for a moment, and then glanced at Valian.

"They've broken down the doors," Valian said, fear lacing his tone.

Bravaro nodded grimly. "The king," he said to remind his charge of their mission.

They headed down the dark corridor, stumbling about like blind men until their eyes adjusted to the gloom. They checked every room, Bravaro with his sword at the ready should Delgadas' soldiers overtake them. Valian pulled out a small dagger, but Bravaro was not about to discourage him from using it. It would do little against the trained Tzotoen mercenaries. However, Bravaro again admired the boy's courage. Most boys his age would have tried to hide from the coming onslaught.

Screams sounded from above, floating down to them from the

stairs. Bravaro's heart sank, knowing they would likely not escape with their lives. Worry for their king propelled them forward. When they had checked every room, they leaned against a wall, exhausted. Valian pointed to Bravaro's head. He reached up and touched the spot, and only then did he realize he was bleeding profusely from the wound he had taken when the first catapult had released its fury on the roof. He tore the hem of his shirt and wrapped it around his head. "It will have to do."

He straightened and nodded toward the end of the corridor. "Perhaps they took him to the dungeons. There are many more places to hide down there," Bravaro said. Valian nodded, and they started back the way they had come. However, just as they set off, they heard angry voices accompanied by crashing footsteps. Bravaro shoved Valian into a room, hurrying him into a tiny closet. "Stay down," he said. Bravaro joined him a second later, shielding Valian with his body. They held their breath as someone burst into the room, pilfering through the servant's belongings for signs of life.

"There's no one here. Move on," the man said, his voice gravelly and deep.

"You did not check the closet," another man said, and Bravaro's muscles tensed, ready to fight his way out.

The man grunted, and Bravaro heard their footsteps approaching. His heart raced, the blood pumping in his ears. The tip of a sword parted the curtains hanging over the closet opening, and Bravaro gritted his teeth, ready for a fight. The last thought to pass through his mind before he sprang into action was for the safety of his king. "For King Nissim and for Luminia!" he yelled and charged into the fray.

CHAPTER 52

KING NISSIM

Nissim's heart pounded, his lungs refusing to fill with oxygen, partly from fear and partly from the acrid smoke that filled the halls. What had he done? He should have evacuated the city while he still had the chance. Because of his foolishness, his people would pay the price just as Delgadas had foretold.

"This way, Your Majesty," one of the guards whispered. They made their way through the maze of hallways beneath the palace. It had been years since he had been anywhere near the servant's quarters, and he was easily turned around.

"I should be helping them. Hand me a sword! I will fight!" Nissim whispered harshly. "We cannot leave them."

"Your Majesty, our only hope lies with you. You have to survive," the soldier replied. His young face was twisted with fear and resolve. Nissim squeezed his eyes shut. The boy should never have been put in this position, never should have had to fight. It was Nissim's job to keep them all safe, and he had failed miserably.

"*Ilyo Na'ada,* forgive my pride," he wheezed.

"Come, Sire. There is little time," his soldier replied, thrusting him forward. He kept a hand on his arm, helping to steady him.

Nissim's mouth curved in a sardonic smile. Is this what he had come to, an old man cowering in the dark while others fought his battles for him?

The soldiers in front of them suddenly stopped, and the next second, he heard an evil laugh pierce through the smoke. "You are mine, Nissim," came Delgadas' voice. Nissim's heart quit beating for a moment.

Delgadas moved through the smoke, flanked by six nasty-looking bandits. "I am surprised at you. I thought your capture would be much more difficult."

Nissim straightened, fear turning to anger. He said nothing as the Tzotoen soldiers poked their spears menacingly at his guards' bellies. Nissim held up his hand. "There is no need to harm them. I will come with you willingly."

Delgadas cocked his head to the side. "You have no authority to beg for anyone's life, Nissim. You are no longer king of Luminia," he spat. He nodded once, and his soldiers sprang into action like starving lions pouncing on easy prey. Nissim struggled against the two men who dragged him away into the darkness, shouting as his men were cut down without mercy.

"No! Delgadas, you—!" Nissim could not finish with the foul name he had been about to call Delgadas, for a blade was swiftly held to his throat. He stopped thrashing, but his chest heaved with the heartbreak of losing his soldiers. "You did not have to do that! They were only boys!"

Delgadas frowned slightly but then smiled. "I can do whatever I want, Nissim. Neither you nor anyone else will tell me what to do again. You had your chance to join me, and you refused. You brought this on yourself." He wound up and slapped him hard across the cheek. "I am king! Do you hear me? *I* am king!"

Nissim knew all too well where Delgadas was taking him. His arms were shoved painfully behind his back, and his wrists lashed together with leather thongs. The soldiers then prodded him with razor-sharp stone spears, mocking him as he was led to the dungeons.

A large, iron door was opened, and they descended into the heart of the island mountain. The narrow, uneven stone steps were slick from centuries of rainwater that ran like rivers during storms. Humid, stale air hit him in the face, smelling of standing water, excrement, and death. Oppressive darkness pressed in on all sides, sending his heart into convulsions. He had never liked small spaces but did his best to mask his growing dread.

Delgadas ordered that the torches lining the aisle between cells to be lit when they stepped down onto the main dungeon floor. Nissim was shoved down the aisle, nearly losing his balance. His head began to swim. He had barely eaten during the last week, trying to spread the rations to the people who had suffered so much. He had eaten nothing through the fast he had ordered the day prior. Bravaro had been right to bring as many people as he could into the palace to try and ease that suffering. However, now he was unsure if they would live to remember it. He had unwittingly brought them into the trap Delgadas had laid for him.

Delgadas turned to the right, uttering a low, sinister laugh. "You might recognize this cell, hmm, Nissim?"

Nissim's heart lurched. It was the same cell he had banished Delgadas' to all those years ago. From what he could remember, it had been the deepest, darkest cell they could find in the dungeon. Nissim said nothing, stepping forward voluntarily.

"Why lock me in here, Delgadas? Why not kill me now and have done with it?" Nissim asked. A hand shoved him hard, and he fell into the cell. Nissim grunted in pain as he hit the stone floor knees first. He felt a kneecap slip out of place, pain lacing his entire leg. He nearly blacked out from the pain but shook his head and gritted his teeth. He would not shame himself further by slipping into unconsciousness. At least, not yet.

"All in good time, Nissim. All in good time," Delgadas said in a sing-song voice. He motioned for the door to be shut and quickly turned away, heading back down the aisle between the cells. "Lock up anyone who remains loyal to Nissim. I want these dungeons filled with them!"

The iron door of his cell creaked shut, banging with a finality that made Nissim's heart wrench with pain. The torch was taken away, and he was left with an inky blackness, dissipated only by a faint orange glow from his burning city. He looked up at the tiny window set high in the wall. The stones below it were worn smooth by rainwater and stained with refuse from the street above. He hung his head, moving his leg out in front of him. His right leg looked odd, with his kneecap twisted to the side. He winced and tried to straighten it to get it back into place. However, with his hands still bound behind his back, he could do little to coax it into alignment.

He lay on the floor, not caring that he was sprawled on a pile of rotting straw mixed with human filth. *"Ilyo Na'ada,"* he cried weakly into the darkness. "Why have you forsaken us?"

NISSIM AWOKE WITH A START. He did not remember having fallen asleep. The sounds of battle from the streets above his cell no longer filtered through the window. Crackling flames and the occasional hiss of water drops on the embers alerted him that the city was still at a slow burn. He sat up with difficulty, forced to lay on his side since his wrists were bound. He licked his lips, parched. He could not remember the last time he had had a cool drink of water.

He ran his tongue over the roof of his mouth, trying to find moisture. However, his throat had gone dry from all the running and the faint wisp of smoke filtering through the tiny iron-barred window.

"So, the great Nissim has finally awakened," came a voice to his left.

Nissim turned his head, trying to see in the darkness. A form moved in the opposite cell, and Nissim winced as he turned to get a better look.

"Lord Danib?" Nissim asked, squinting.

"Yes. Lord Danib. Once-powerful ruler of the *Thosmin District*. Now look at us," he said bitterly, giving a derisive laugh. "Reduced to ash and rubble."

"What is going on up there? Have you heard anything?" Nissim pressed closer to the bars, each movement sending pain racing up and down his right leg. "Tell me. Has anyone escaped?"

Lord Danib said nothing for several seconds. "There is no escape," he said dully. "Not for anyone. The Tzotoen hordes are too numerous for us. Our allies have abandoned us." He gave a short laugh. "Not even Detallma was able to come in time. We are lost, Your Majesty." The bleakness that filled his tone made Nissim shrink back.

"Where are all the other lords?" Nissim asked.

"I am here, Your Majesty!" a voice sounded from another cell. "Lord Haztup. And Lord Lletzoun." There was a pause before Lord Haztup spoke again. "I fear he will not make it through the night."

Nissim hung his head. "And the others from the council? Have they been killed?"

Neither of the lords spoke for a long while. Nissim's heart grew frantic. "Well? Tell me!" he ordered.

"The rest of the council has been spared, Your Majesty." Lord Danib answered without inflection.

Nissim breathed a sigh of relief, but their silence alerted him that there was more. "And?" he asked, almost afraid to hear their answer.

He heard Lord Haztup grunt, sighing with frustration. "The rest of the council was spared because they defected to Delgadas, Your Majesty. We are the only three who remained loyal to you."

Nissim felt like the whole dungeon was crashing down on him, the heavy stone pressing on his chest, making breathing impossible. "Defected?"

"I am so sorry, Your Majesty. There were several of the lords who were feeding information to Delgadas. That Snake offered the rest of your council mercy, if they would give him their allegiance," Lord

Danib spat. "He's been spouting some insanity about abolishing music, that he has found another way to make Luminia come to life."

"And what of the servants?" Nissim asked. All the fight had gone out of him. "What of the people?"

"Most of the servants have remained loyal to you, Sire. The people ran as soon as the Tzotoen soldiers raided the palace. I do not think Delgadas was as worried with them as much as with capturing the Musicians. Last I knew, he was rounding up all the Musician families and taking them to the palace roof."

Nissim's heart began to pound again. "Oh, no," he breathed. What would Delgadas do to them? Force their allegiance, or face death? It was unthinkable. If none of the Musicians were left alive, they were doomed, Tzotoen and Luminian alike. "He is mad."

"Yes, Your Majesty," Lord Haztup replied, his voice sounding further away. "He is mad with pride and jealousy. He always has been."

Nissim scooted closer to the iron bars and leaned his shoulders against them. It was more comfortable than laying on his side on the cold stone floor. However, his right leg still caused him great pain. "Thank you, my lords. You have shown great courage standing with me this night. I will remember you in the Beyond. Hopefully, we will meet there again someday."

"It is not over yet, Your Majesty. Perhaps Bravaro and his men will find a way to free us so we can escape," Lord Haztup said, his voice filled with hope. Nissim leaned his head against the bars, shaking his head. He said nothing, trying to grasp onto the hope that Lord Haztup offered. If Bravaro were smart, he would leave this place and never look back.

CHAPTER 53

HAARMONAE

Haarmonae gritted her teeth as she pulled herself up on a rooftop, careful to stay low when she reached the top. Her father would kill her when he discovered she had disobeyed him and traveled back to Lunthá. It had taken her some time to figure out the correct tunnels to take, but after days of wandering and marking her way, she had finally made it, coming out at the lagoon's outer shore.

Swimming across the lagoon in her underclothes had been an experience. She had been able to slip onto the shore in the dead of night and hide out on the abandoned leeward side of the island where no one would think to search. She had climbed an ancient maple tree, careful to keep herself covered behind the branches. Her plan had been to try to get people off the island via the tunnel she had discovered. Shortly after her arrival, Delgadas's army had snuck into the harbor and begun storming the palace, waking her from a fitful slumber.

Instead of retreating back across the lagoon to safety, she had snuck deeper into the bowels of the city. Now, she inched toward the edge of what had been her family's mansion roof. Her family home lay in ruin, gutted by catapulted projectiles. The beams that held the roof up had come down into the common room. Haarmonae carefully avoided the gaping holes in the roof as she made her way to its edge.

The sun had begun to rise but was still hanging low behind the horizon. There was no warmth in its rays with nasty-looking clouds blotting out the sun's surface. They were in for another thunder and lightning storm.

Haarmonae took her longbow off her shoulder, resting it and her quiver of arrows against the low wall surrounding the roof. She craned her neck and saw people milling about the Musician's Terrace, which she could see with surprising clarity from her rooftop perch, only a stone's throw away from the palace. She ducked as Delgadas appeared at the stairwell, screaming orders at his soldiers. Haarmonae gasped. Several of her friends from Musicians' families were bundled under and around the pergola. Indeed, she could make out almost all the faces from their troop, being poked and prodded into a tight circle. A sinking feeling assailed her insides, and she swallowed the urge to vomit. "*Ilyo Na'ada,* no. Please, no," she prayed fervently, unable to tear her eyes away from the scene.

Tzotoen soldiers filed up from the palace stairwell, carrying their precious instruments: woodwinds and harps, violins, drums and guitars. They set them in a pile before the Musicians, who eyed them like long-lost children, yearning to hold them in their arms.

Haarmonae choked back a sob, knowing what was coming. Delgadas hated all that was music, all that was good.

The Monster stood before the Musicians, screeching in his gravelly tone. Haarmonae could not understand what he said, but she knew it was not good from the horrified faces of the Musicians. Delgadas waved his wrist with a snap toward the pile of instruments, and his soldiers began taking up armfuls at a time. They walked to the roof's edge and threw them over, their sick laughter mingling with the moans of her fellow Musicians. Haarmonae lurched forward, unthinking.

As if she could save any of them.

Most of the instruments were carved from the trunks of the eternal tree, handed down for generations. She sobbed silently, watching them remove the pile like so much refuse. But Haarmonae sensed that Delgadas's rampage was far from over.

Delgadas again yelled orders to his men. The Musicians were separated into two groups. Over 300 men, women and children had to be on that roof, and Haarmonae was helpless to save any of them.

He paced before the crowd, venting his poisonous words, instilling fear into the hearts of her loved ones. "*Ilyo Na'ada,* save us! Come like you did in the days of old and smite our enemies!" Haarmonae pleaded. However, there was no fire from heaven. No myriad of spirit warriors appeared in the sky to rain down justice on Delgadas or his followers. Silence reigned from above, and Haarmonae turned back to watch.

Delgadas finished, waving his hand one more time. The soldiers advanced on one of the groups of Musicians, the men, women and children lifting their voices in screams of terror as they were dragged to the edge of the roof. Haarmonae covered her eyes, wanting to close her ears to the carnage. One by one, they were pushed over the side, their screams sounding for a split second and ending with a thud on the cold cobblestone square amidst their instruments.

Haarmonae's head shot up, tears of rage and grief making tracks down her dust-covered face. "No!" she lamented in agony. "Stop it!" She screamed, standing up on the rooftop. But no one heard her, the wind and thunder snatching away her words.

She collapsed on the rooftop, pulling her knees up to her chest and wrapping her arms around them. She rocked back and forth, praying, pleading for *Ilyo Na'ada* to intervene.

Finally, after what seemed like hours, the distant screams stopped, replaced by guttural moans from the remaining Musicians. Haarmonae risked a glance and saw that the killing had stopped. She did not move to wipe her tear-stained cheeks, her heart thudding with a dull beat.

Delgadas nodded to one of his soldiers, and the rest of the Musicians were put in chains and led down the stairs through the heart of the palace.

Haarmonae watched, frozen by grief. All she could do was watch helplessly as the Musicians were prodded down the stairs and out of the palace. Who knew what their fate would be? When all was quiet, she stood, retrieving her bow. Her limbs felt like they were weighted with sandbags, pulling her down into despair.

As she climbed off the roof and landed on one of the balconies of a neighboring house, she heard people yelling and running thought the streets below. She ducked, watching as women and children ran for their lives, hunted by the Tzotoen soldiers. A few men also ran, but they were quickly cut down.

Haarmonae's escape was blocked as the soldiers took to the streets to round up the citizenry that had not already fled. She looked behind her, trying to think of another way. Even more dire than the soldiers on the prowl were several men holding torches, setting the mansions nearest the palace on fire. Haarmonae had to get out, or she would be trapped by flames or soldiers. Glancing behind her, she knew the only way to safety would be to weave through the maze of alleyways to the north and make for the lagoon and the hidden tunnel. It would be a challenging swim, weighed down by her skirts, bow, quiver, and dagger. It was the only way.

She shimmied over the balcony railing, looking down so she would land on another terrace below. She let out a breath and hung suspended at least five feet above safety. She landed with a soft crunch as her boots hit the pebble-strewn marble.

"Alright. One more," she said under her breath. She repeated her movements, hanging over the edge of the last balcony. This time, the drop was more like eight feet. She sent up a silent prayer for protection and let go.

She landed on her feet but felt her left ankle give way as she hit an uneven cobblestone in the road. She yelped as she fell, landing hard on her side. Pinpricks ran up and down her legs from the force of her fall, and her ankle throbbed with pain.

"This way! I think I heard something!"

Haarmonae heard a masculine voice behind her, none too pleasant. She scrambled to her feet and ran as fast as her injured leg could carry her. Limping, she ducked into an alleyway and hid in the shadows, halting to listen for her pursuers. For a moment, all she could hear was the blood thundering in her ears.

She stopped, backing into a recessed doorway encased in shadow, relieved that no one seemed to be coming after her. She turned and went deeper into the dark alleyway and headed north to the lagoon shore. After several minutes of wandering, losing her way, and correcting, she finally saw a break in the houses and a meadow spreading out before her. An orange glow reflected off the water. Its surface was oddly calm after the night of horrors she had witnessed. "Just a little further," she mumbled. Soon, she would be at the lagoon shore and could cross to safety.

Safety.

She no longer knew if there was such a thing in Luminia. Delgadas had just destroyed everything she had ever known.

CHAPTER 54

KYIN

"Are they gone?"

Kyin peeked out from behind the ruined wall of the nursery. He glanced back at his wife, huddled with several of the street urchins that Bravaro had brought to them for protection. "I believe all is quiet," he whispered. They would need to move fast if they were to make it to the hidden tunnel and swim across the lagoon to safety. He looked again at the frightened faces of the children that had been put into his care. Did any of them know how to swim? He doubted it, being from outlying farm districts.

"We have to move quickly," Kyin instructed. Dosanyata was at his side in an instant, carrying one small child on each of her hips.

"Where will we go? Delgadas' men are crawling all over Lunthá," she said. Her voice was firm, trying to ensure her fear was not transferred to the children. "And we must find Valian."

"He will be with his squadron," Kyin said. Fear coiled around his heart. His son might have been a boy in training, but after this night, he would be a boy no longer. Not after the horrors that he had likely already witnessed. "We must trust that Bravaro and the rest of his squadron will watch over him."

A sob escaped her throat, but there was nothing more they could do for their son if they were to get these children out alive. Kyin inched out of hiding, and motioned for Dosanyata and the rest of the children to join him near the doorway. One of the other servant girls, not much older than his son, had been assisting his wife when the catapults had started unleashing their fury. There were seventeen children in all. "You, take the first group to the secret tunnel. You know of its whereabouts, I am sure?"

"Yes, Master Kyin. I have lived in the palace all my life," the girl said, her voice shaking with fear.

"Very well. You take these eight who can walk on their own. Dosanyata and I will follow with the younger ones, and a few of the older children to help us." Kyin counted off some of the younger children, to follow the servant girl. Then he separated some of the older children, those about eight to ten years old to help with the ones who could not walk on their own and would need to be carried.

The girl left as soon as Kyin checked the corridor was clear. He waited for several minutes, listening. There was no sound that reached his ears, save for the distant screams from the streets of Lunthá. He went back into the room, resting his hands on his wife's shoulders. "Are you ready?" he asked.

"Yes," she choked. "But our son. How can we leave him?" she pleaded.

"We must trust that he will be well," Kyin said.

She nodded, but he knew her heart was breaking. His heart was breaking as well. "We have to move before it is too late—" he started, but Dosanyata's eyes suddenly snapped to a distant point behind him. As he turned, he was met with a sickening laugh coming from the shadowy corridor.

"Well, well, well, what have we here?" came a gravelly voice.

Kyin turned on his heel to meet their attacker. "Delgadas," he breathed.

"Tzinetzin," Delgadas greeted. "Son of Lady Shes-Tia and Nobelitzin. Grandson of the infamous Lady Tzizenah herself."

Delgadas laughed, shaking his head. "Lord Lamik and his son, Lord Tzichen, told me you had resurfaced. After all these years, I was doubtful he had recognized correctly. But it seems he was right after all."

"Lord Lamik told you of me?" Kyin asked, his heart jumping into his throat. There was no use denying his connection to the famed seer. She had foretold of these events nearly a hundred years ago. He had never thought he would live to see their fulfillment, even though his family had suffered at the hands of past royals who would silence the warnings that his grandmother had tried to give. His family had been ripped apart by men like Delgadas, who would keep the prophecies from coming true. Thus, his years of hiding. However, his familial connections had found him out. It pained him to know that Kouraso's father and grandfather were traitors. He should have been more careful of the spies he knew were in the palace. He should have gotten his wife and son out long before now. Kyin instinctively stepped in front of his wife. "So, he is a traitor."

"Yes, indeed. There were many traitors in your midst. And yet you still chose to come out of hiding to serve the king," Delgadas said and slowly started to pace around the room. Dosanyata pressed closer to Kyin and he put a protective arm around her shoulder.

"What do you want of me then?" Kyin asked.

"I want to know where your grandmother and mother are," Delgadas demanded.

"You should know, since they were killed at your orders."

Delgadas gave a derisive laugh. "Ahh, no, Tzinetzin. Your father, Nobelitzin, did die trying to cover your mother's escape. She was able to warn your grandmother in time, and they escaped my soldiers. As did you. What I want to know is where they went. Where have they been hiding all this time?"

"I have no idea," Kyin replied. It was strange hearing the name his mother and father had given him at birth, a variation of his grandmother's name and that of his father's. It had been bestowed on him as a sign of honor, but only served as a reminder of his former privileged high rank which had been his birthright, and had been ripped away from him. "What do you want them for? My grand-mother, if she is still alive, would be of no use to you. She was an old woman when she warned the king of what was coming. And you are the fulfillment of her frightening visions."

"This is getting me nowhere," Delgadas growled. "Do you possess the second sight?" he demanded.

Dosanyata pressed even closer, huddling the children close to her. He looked down at their frightened faces. Kyin could lie, to keep himself alive. There was no guarantee that a lie would keep his family or the children in his charge safe. "I do not know. Allow this woman to go free, along with the children. They have no quarrel with you."

"You are in no position to be making demands, Tzinetzin. I know this *woman* is your wife. I will ask you only once more. Do you possess the second sight, as your grandmother did?"

Kyin lowered his head, submitting to whatever fate *Ilyo Na'ada* had in store. "I do not know," he said again. And it was true. He had never been given to visions as his mother and grandmother had. Perhaps it only blessed the females of the family line.

"Then you are of no use to me," Delgadas said. He gave a curt wave of his wrist as he exited the nursery. "Do it! And find their son. He must be cowering here somewhere."

Kyin held his wife close, turning his back on the advancing soldiers. "Forgive me," he whispered into his wife's hair, enveloping the children between them to try to protect them. He touched the hilt of the secreted dagger in the folds of his robe. He knew his efforts were futile, but he would not go down cowering. With his last breaths he thought of Valian, his brave son, and prayed that someday he would find a way to defeat Delgadas and bring peace to their beloved homeland.

CHAPTER 55

BRAVARO

"That should be the last of them." Bravaro grunted, helping Valian drag yet another fallen Tzotoen soldier into the shadows. He and Valian had fought their way out of their hiding spot, only to sneak around the servants quarters and several more guards before they made it out undetected. Now, they made their way to the rear of the palace toward the training facilities, trying to find what was left of their squadron.

However, they were waylaid when a group of bandits came around the corner, their menacing laughs echoing through the halls. Thankfully, they did not notice them. "King Nissim looked like he was ready to wet himself when we captured him. The fool."

Bravaro grabbed Valian and made him hide deeper in the fold of shadows. It was not difficult, for the palace was in chaos, with no lanterns or torches to light their way. Valian pressed his back against the smooth marble walls, slowing his breathing so the soldiers would not hear. It was a difficult feat, especially with the news that King Nissim had been captured.

Valian shifted, and Bravaro clamped a hand to his chest to make him be completely still. The invaders had not discovered they were in the hall, and he wanted to keep it that way.

"Well, the fool will soon be dead, and then we can enjoy the spoils," one of the other soldiers said in a suggestive tone. The others laughed. They rounded a corner and were gone, but Bravaro did not allow Valian to move. He listened, waiting.

He stepped gingerly from the shadows when he was sure they were alone. He looked about before motioning Valian to follow him. "Come on. We must find the king."

They wove their way around rubble and the bodies of the fallen comrades, their silent advance undiscovered by their attackers. Bravaro opened the dungeon door and slipped inside, dragging Valian along. They wound down the uneven steps, stopping to listen every few seconds to be sure they would not meet a guard from Delgadas's hordes. When they reached the dungeons, Bravaro was overcome by the stench.

They slipped through the cells, searching each one for the king before moving on. Suddenly, a hand slipped through the bars of one of the cells and grabbed Bravaro's arm. He instinctively drew his sword and jumped back, ready to fight.

"Calm yourself, boy. It is I, Lord Danib," the man whispered hoarsely. Blood colored his white beard at the corner of his mouth.

Bravaro let out a breath he had not even realized he had been holding. "My lord. Forgive me—"

"The king is in the last cell. Just there," Lord Danib interrupted. Bravaro glanced in the direction that Lord Danib nodded, barely able to discern in the gray light. He and Valian tiptoed over to the cell, his heart pounding.

They made their way silently toward the last cell, light shining in from a single window barely the width of his shoulders. "King Nissim? Your Majesty?" he whispered. He peered in, fearing the worst when the form inside the cell did not move.

"Your Majesty," Bravaro he called again. The king stirred, and turned over to look at him, horror quickly seeping into his features.

"At last, we have found you." He motioned to Valian. "See if there is something we can use to pry the door from the hinges."

"Bravaro, you must get out of here. There is no time—" he choked.

"I am here to break you free," he whispered.

Nissim's heart lifted with hope. "Have you the keys?" he asked.

"No," Bravaro answered, glancing over his shoulder to where Valian was scouring for something to use for prying. There had to be a way to get him out. "But we shall force the doors open. Somehow." He started looking at the hinges, feeling for a way to snap them out of place. Nissim reached through the bars and stayed his hands. The rust alone would keep the bolts in place.

"It is no use. These are solid iron, built to keep the most dangerous of criminals secure." The king smiled sadly, his eyes full of tender feeling. "Thank you for risking your life to try to free me." An orange glow bounced off the king's face, and an explosion followed from above, shaking the stone cell. The king lurched against the bars, leaning down to shield his eyes from the rubble. Bravaro did the same, hanging onto the bars to steady himself. Dust and small rocks rained down on them. When the shaking stopped, he looked up at the ceiling.

"You have to go." He nodded toward the stairs.

"I cannot leave you here, Your Majesty. He's lost his mind, I tell you!" Bravaro's heart was breaking. He would not lose another father figure. Not again. All the pent-up grief of losing his mother, the rejection of his birth father, and the death of Manemna and then of Souni came rushing upon him, threatening to drag him down like a powerful undertow. "I would never forgive myself."

"This is not of your doing, Bravaro. My son, you have served me well. I should have listened to you." His voice broke.

Valian jogged back over to them. "I cannot find anything," he said out of breath. "Perhaps your sword—"

"No, Valian. Bravaro, please listen. Delgadas and his men will be back. You have to go now, and lead the people who are able to escape. I am told General Zalim is dead."

Bravaro hung his head. "He is."

"Well, then. Take Valian and go now before you are captured." The king touched his hand, making him look up at him. "You have to be strong. I am glad I had the privilege of watching you grow into the young man you are today. You have made me proud," he said. "And I hope someday you will be able to forgive my foolishness. I should have listened to you and to the other lords, and gotten everyone out."

Bravaro swallowed, his Adam's apple bobbing up and down.

He shifted, the pain in his leg throbbing uncontrollably. He winced, sucking a breath through his teeth. "Take a message to Saardonae for me," he said, desperation lacing his tone.

"We cannot escape Lunthá, much less get to Saardonae," Valian said.

"You will. Most of Delgadas's soldiers will be busy with the plunder for the next few days. That will give you an opportunity to slip through the lines unnoticed. Steal a Tzotoen uniform, if you can." He turned around, nodding toward his arms. "Untie me."

Bravaro reached through the bars and cut his bonds. The king sighed with relief, stretching his shoulder for a moment. He then took the signet ring off his finger and slipped it through the bars. "Guard this with your life. And when you come to my wife and son in Saardonae, tell him that the reign of Luminia has passed to him."

Valian took the golden ring, cradling it in both hands. "I will," he promised, tears welling in his eyes.

"No matter what happens, I am in *Ilyo Na'ada's* hands. No one can take me from Him, my boy, as it is with all His children. Now, go. Prince Shoram must not leave Saardonae. Tell him to wait for the appointed time, to search the prophecies of Tzizenah the Seer. It was foretold a rescuer would come. I had no idea we would even need one until now." The king took a breath before he went on. "And tell my son—" he faltered, choked by emotion. "Tell my son I love him, and his mother would be proud."

Valian nodded, rising from his feet. He took a leather strand from about his neck, untied the ends, and slipped the signet onto it. Bravaro leaned close then, clasping the king's hand through the bars. "How can I lead these people, Sire? I am not you. I am not General Zalim."

His Majesty took a steadying breath. "You do not have to be. You are Bravaro, and that is more than enough."

Tears came to his eyes, and for the first time that night, he let them fall. He nodded, urging them to go. Bravaro rose and headed for the stairs where Valian waited. He halted at the bottom step, looking back at his sovereign. He gave a bolstering nod. "We will see that your message gets to Prince Shoram."

"I know. Go, now, my boy. And *Ilyo Na'ada* go with you."

CHAPTER 56

BRAVARO

It took several seconds for Bravaro to collect himself. He sensed that he had just said his last goodbye to his beloved king. Guilt ate at him as they skulked up the dungeon steps and came out on the deserted landing. The light of dawn was growing, but was accompanied by dark, heavy clouds. Valian shut the heavy wooden door behind him, and they moved into the shadows.

"This way," Bravaro whispered. He motioned Valian to follow him outside, and they snuck through the gardens. They rounded the corner of the palace and saw the high walls looming over the training center.

All was quiet inside the palace now, save for the sounds of the city burning and the occasional high-pitched scream of a woman. Bravaro gritted his teeth. He did not want to think of what the soldiers were doing to the women they had allowed to live. Delgadas would pay for the destruction he had wrought that night. He was unsure how or when, but justice must win, no matter the cost.

"On your left!" Valian hissed, pushing Bravaro to the right just in time to save his head from being skewered by an arrow. He and

Valian collapsed on the gravel-covered path, tiny stones spraying above them as they slid to safety behind a stone pillar. Bravaro tucked and rolled, landing in a squatting position near the outer wall of the palace. Valian soon joined him, crouching low as they scanned the training facility walls for their assailants.

"There, on the eastern lookout tower. Two men. I cannot see anymore than that," Valian said.

The boy had eyes as sharp as an eagle, and he trusted the boy's judgment. Bravaro nodded, spotting the two men as they moved silently through the greying light. There would be no true dawn this day, not with the destruction that Delgadas had wrought. He motioned to show Valian that he would move forward and that Valian should break off to the right. If they could climb up the tower without being seen, maybe they could get around their attackers and take them by surprise.

Bravaro nodded, and they both sprang into action. He stayed low, moving quickly over the grass toward the training facility. He sheathed his sword as quietly as possible and took out a five-inch dagger. He clamped the blade between his teeth and began to climb the wall, using the window sills as hand and footholds. With the agility of a cat, he scaled the wall and waited for Valian to take his place. A second later, he saw Valian's silhouette racing over the rooftops toward him. Bravaro took the dagger out of his mouth, made ready, and burst into action as Valian jumped off the neighboring rooftop and soared toward the two sentries.

They had no idea what hit them, dead before they hit the ground.

Bravaro grabbed Valian's arm and pumped it up and down several times, congratulating him on the clean kills. "Well done. Now, let's move," Bravaro said. They headed swiftly and silently toward the courtroom, scaling the walls and balconies and slinking through corridors fraught with destruction while searching for Delgadas. If they could kill him, they would cut the head off the snake and might have a chance at taking back their country.

They were almost to the third story when Valian motioned him to stop. They both froze, listening as the sound of shuffling feet came near. They readied their weapons, prepared to defend themselves. Valian nodded, and they pulled themselves over the balcony railing, ready to strike.

However, before Bravaro sunk his blade into the back of one of them, he noticed that they wore the uniform of Luminia. He turned the soldier around and saw terror shining in the man's eyes. "Koura-so!" Bravaro breathed, taking the blade away from his fellow soldier's rib cage. Without thinking, he hugged him, pounding his back with relief. "We thought we would never see any of you again," he whispered.

Kouraso's face was beaded with sweat, no doubt thankful that Bravaro had stayed his blade at the last second. "General Bravaro," he answered, taking a knee and placing a hand over his heart. "We are glad to see you alive and well."

Bravaro blinked. "*General?*"

Three more faces appeared behind Kouraso, all of them bloodied from battle. He glanced at Valian, who nodded with a mixture of pride and sadness gleaming in his eyes.

"Yes, Master Bravaro. You were General Zalim's aide—the best trainee. Delgadas has killed the General and all the other seasoned warriors and commanders below him. You are all we have left to lead us," Kouraso said, motioning to the teenage boys behind him.

Bravaro let out a breath, motioning for them all to hide in the shadows. Now was not the time for them to argue over who would lead. It was a job he had thought to have when he was much older and after he had gained much more experience. Never in his life had he imagined his experience would come so quickly on the streets of Lunthá-turned-battlefield.

"We have to get out of Lunthá and regroup. We will not be able to overpower Delgadas unless we have help." Bravaro thought again of Saardonae and Detallma. Their ally to the east had promised help and protection, but that lifeline had failed. And word had yet to arrive from Detallma. They were on their own—for now.

"Are there any others of our squadron left alive?" Bravaro asked.

"We have searched the palace as best we could, but we are the only ones left," Kouraso said. "If there are others, perhaps they have already escaped."

Bravaro nodded. "We have to move. We will go out through the king's secret stair. I am afraid we will be taking an icy dip this morning, boys," he said. They all nodded, and Kouraso peeked his head into the dimly lit hall. He came back into the shadows of the balcony, whispering furtively.

"The Tzotoen soldiers raided the wine cellars and many of them are passed out now, with only a few sentries parading the halls. We should be able to make it without being spotted."

Valian touched Bravaro's arm, pulling him aside. "My parents. The nursery is on the way. I have to try to get them out," he said, his eyes pleading.

Bravaro nodded. "We need to split up. Valian, Cheltlla, and I will go around through the east wing and retrieve Dosanyata and Kyin. Kouraso, you take Dutza and Adall through the west wing. We will meet up at the king's stairwell and make our escape."

They all nodded, and the group of six split up. They snuck out into the corridor, and Bravaro felt his heartbeat racing again. Sticking to the darkest shadows, they made their way through the palace like phantoms. Disappointment stung his heart. He had hoped to find Delgadas and end his miserable life, but the lives of his men were more critical.

Valian took the lead as they neared the royal nursery. This end of the palace seemed relatively untouched, with only a few pieces of furniture upended. No bodies lay strewn about, as there had been near the front of the palace. That is where the heaviest of the fighting had been.

Clay vases had been shattered, and tapestries dislodged from their hooks, most likely from the force of the projectiles hitting the eastern wall. They stepped over the shards and debris, trying to conceal their footsteps. When they rounded the corner, Valian sprinted for the nursery doors. He opened them silently and slipped inside while Bravaro and Cheltlla kept watch.

However, as the minutes dragged on, Bravaro's nervousness increased. Cheltlla glanced at him, worry lining his face. "What is taking them so long?" he whispered, barely audible.

Bravaro shook his head, frowning. "I will go," he said. "You keep watch." Bravaro opened the door a crack and slipped inside. The room seemed empty at first glance. However, he walked into the room braced for an attack.

"Valian," he called softly, looking this way and that. "Valian?" he asked as his eyes alighted on his friend's still form, kneeling near one of the bedroom archways.

Bravaro drew closer, stopping when he saw the bodies strewn about the room. He inched closer to see Valian cradling his mother in his arms, her eyes wide and staring. Valian looked up at Bravaro with tortured eyes, and Bravaro sank to his knees. Grief tore at his heart for the woman who had been like a mother to him since his arrival at the palace six years before, and he reached to touch her sweet face. He pulled his hand away at the iciness of her skin.

"I am so sorry, my friend," Bravaro choked. He looked over her still form, wondering who would ever want to harm such a sweet soul.

"Papa is over there, near the window," Valian said dully. Bravaro looked around to see several children's bodies lying about, none of them moving. What had happened to the rest of them? Rage billowed inside his chest. He wanted to hunt down the soldiers who had done this. These children were no threat, and yet they had been cut down in cold blood.

Bravaro followed his friend's gaze and saw his tutor crumpled in a heap, moonlight shining off a dagger clasped in his hand. Two Tzotoen bandits lay lifeless near Kyin. "He died fighting, my friend." It was little comfort, and Bravaro immediately regretted his words.

What could he say to ease the pain of his young friend? Nothing. He knew all too well what it was to grieve. Silence was preferable to empty, callous words.

Valian leaned forward to cover his mother's body, holding her close as he wept. Bravaro touched his shoulder, wanting to give him time to mourn but knowing they were not safe. "We have to go, Valian. Our men are counting on us."

Valian sniffed hard, looking up at him. The tears still streamed down his boyish features, wetting his mother's cheeks. "Why did she have to die?"

Bravaro looked down at her face again, illuminated by the light of the Three Sisters and the struggling, rising sun. The rain had stopped, the clouds breaking to allow the moons to emerge. Their light had betrayed them that night. The moons were meant to be their guides when all other light failed. What were they supposed to hold onto now when their last resort had given the upper hand to the enemy?

"I do not know, Valian. She and your father are at peace in the great Beyond. There is nothing we can do for them now." Bravaro's sense of urgency heightened. They would be late in meeting the others at the secret stairway as it was. He had to find a way to get Valian out of there. "Come, my friend," he urged.

Valian clung to his mother's lifeless body for a moment. "I cannot just leave them here," he said.

"You must. Their bodies are simply husks meant to house their eternal spirits. They are safe in the arms of *Ilyo Na'ada*. But you are not. Your parents would want you to live to see the restoration of Luminia. We must hurry. We are Luminia's last hope, my friend." Bravaro touched his shoulder again, giving it a light squeeze. His heart was racing, knowing they were tempting Fate if they stayed much longer.

Valian kissed his mother's cheek and laid her down gently on the marble floor where she had fallen. He placed her hands on her abdomen, arranging the hair to frame her face. "Goodbye, Mother," he whispered and stood. He did not follow Bravaro as he would have hoped. He went to his father and knelt, lifting his head so he could maneuver a chain from around his neck. "He would have wanted me to keep this safe. It was his prized possession," Valian whispered hurriedly. He slipped a long chain around his neck, a bronze key dangling from the end. Valian slipped the key under his breastplate, then stood and joined Bravaro at the door.

Bravaro drew him away toward the door, his heart breaking for him. He, too, knew what it was like to have to leave his family behind. At least Valian knew his parents were safe in the bosom of *Ilyo Na'ada*. He still did not know what had become of Souni and Intza. "What does the key unlock?" Bravaro asked.

"I do not know," Valian said. "My father said he would tell me when I was a man."

Valian might never know what the key opened then, but there was no time to dwell on it now. Bravaro half coaxed, half dragged Valian to the nursery door. He poked his head out, and Cheltlla nodded that the coast was clear. He and Valian slipped through the door and started down the hall again. His heart raced, sensing that danger was near. Or was his exhaustion-riddled mind simply creating more fears to distract him?

The three moved silently through the halls, the moons illuminating their steps. Bravaro would have rather had the cover of darkness, but the sun seemed intent on fighting its way over the mountains. They were out in the open and vulnerable to attack.

When they were almost to the secret stairway, they suddenly heard a loud crash and voices filtering down from somewhere on the roof. Bravaro, Valian, and Cheltlla flattened their backs against the west wall, stepping as far away from the east-facing windows and the traitorous light. He listened for several seconds for another crash. It was not long in coming. Outside the window, they saw things being thrown over the side of the roof. Bravaro pushed himself away from the wall to get a better look. "They are throwing the instruments down," he said in shock. His men followed him, watching in horror as the precious heirlooms were tossed like refuse to the cobblestone courtyard, where they were smashed to pieces.

Bravaro looked up as if he could see through the marble to the Musicians Terrace. No wonder it had been so quiet in the halls. Everyone was up on the roof. Voices floated down to them, first those tinged with sickening glee at the destruction they were causing. Then, other sounds began to assail his ears. Wails and moans of despair mixed with the macabre sounds of revelry from the victors who had laid waste to their once beautiful Lunthá.

Bravaro turned to his men. "Come, we must make haste," he gritted his teeth. They hurried through the hall, throwing caution to the wind. No one waylaid them as they made their way the short distance to the secret stairwell. Bravaro moved a large tapestry and opened a masked door disguised as just another piece of the marble wall. He motioned his men inside and slipped through, replacing the tapestry over the door as best he could before closing it.

Kouraso was on him in an instant. "Where have you been? We were about to leave without you!" he whispered harshly. He glanced behind Bravaro down the corridor, suddenly realizing what must have happened. "Where are Dosanyata and Kyin?"

Valian started down the stairs, not wanting to speak of the horror he had witnessed that night, no doubt. Bravaro motioned the other men forward, hanging back with Kouraso. "They are dead," he replied.

Kouraso hung his head. "I am sorry. I know you were close with them."

"I was. But I fear for Valian. Help me keep an eye on him, will you?" Bravaro asked. Valian would need comfort in the days ahead. They would all have to pull together if they were to survive this loss.

"Of course," Kouraso said, gripping his shoulder. "You can count on me."

"I know I can. Now, let us hurry. We shall need every second they are distracted to make our escape."

Cheltlla turned slightly as they made their way down the

winding staircase. "Something tells me that the sun will not be able to fully rise this morning," he said with an air of finality that made Bravaro's heart jump into his throat. Fear for the Musicians and what Delgadas planned to do with them assailed him. Regardless, Lunthá would be plunged into perpetual mourning, until Delgadas could be brought to heel.

CHAPTER 57

HAARMONAE

Haarmonae hurried over to a rock outcropping, watching in the stillness to ensure she was alone. Nothing moved save for the long grass blown about by the wind. She was about to step out when a calloused hand wrapped around her head and covered her mouth. She screamed, her eyes going wide with fear. Another strong arm encircled her waist and pulled her into the shadows. She cried and thrashed with all her might, kicking at unknown assailants. Her attacker turned her around to face him, pressing her against the rocks. He clamped a hand around her wrists, pinning her arms above her head while he kept his other hand over her mouth.

She was going to die. But she would not be an easy conquest. Haarmonae continued to struggle, not caring if they heard her screams now.

"Haarmonae, it's me," a voice whispered furtively. "It's Bravaro!"

It took a moment for her mind to compute what he was telling her, but she opened her eyes, searching his face. He slowly took his hand away from her mouth, no doubt waiting to see if she would be silent.

"Bravaro?" she questioned, unable to believe her eyes. He slowly let go of her wrists and moved his arm to encircle her waist. She went weak at the knees and collapsed. Her forehead fell against his chest as if it were too heavy for her neck to hold up any longer. "I thought—" she choked, unable to finish.

He stroked her hair as if she were a small child. "It is alright," he whispered in her ear. His warm breath sent shivers up and down her spine. "I am here. You are safe."

Haarmonae leaned into him, burying her face in his chest. She covered her face with her hands, giving rise to silent sobs. His arms encircled her in an even tighter embrace as she shook with grief.

"It is alright, you are safe," he said again. "But we have to move. Can you walk?" he asked. He let her go, keeping his hands on her elbows should she collapse again. She sniffed, looking at him through a blur of tears. He still did not understand.

"They are gone," she said.

Bravaro frowned. "Who is?" he asked. "I heard about your mother and Molto."

Haarmonae gripped his shirt front and shook him. "The Musicians! He killed them, Bravaro! Delgadas killed them. Threw them off the Musicians Terrace as if they were nothing!" she choked. She leaned her forehead against his chest and rocked back and forth. He placed a hand on her back.

He glanced at Valian and Kouraso standing a few paces away. "We have to go," Kouraso said.

Bravaro nodded. He grabbed Haarmonae's shoulders and shook her gently. "I know you are undone but we have to go. Can you walk?" he asked again, more firmly this time.

She nodded, tears streaming down her face. She knew she had to keep it together and save her grief until after they had made their escape. She straightened. "Yes."

Bravaro motioned for the half-dozen soldiers to follow him down to the lagoon. He took her hand, his touch at once firm and gentle. "Stay close, and I will help you," he instructed.

Haarmonae pulled him to a momentary halt, picking up her bow, which she had dropped during their struggle. They hurried to the shore, and she dove into the cold waters. She did as Bravaro instructed, sticking close to his side. The weight of her skirts made the swim across to shore more difficult than she had imagined.

"Here, hand me your bow," he said. She did so without argument and kept going. She then flipped over on her back and kicked with all her might. Gazing at the sky, she again felt tears pricking her eyes. Rain drops spattered her face, dark clouds covering most of the light that the tired sun would have given out.

"It's alright now. We've made it," Bravaro said after half an hour of hard swimming. He touched down on the rocky lake bottom first and slid his arms under her back and legs. He lifted her out of the water as if she was weightless.

Exhausted, she allowed him to carry her until they were under cover of the forest, far from prying eyes. He laid her down in a soft patch of grass and brushed the damp tendrils away from her face. Water dripped down his face, his mouth set in a grim line. He gave her a sad smile, his fingers lingering on her forehead. Once again, her heart fluttered.

"You did well, Haarmonae," he whispered. She should not be feeling anything but grief at a time like this, and yet her heart yearned to be held again, to have this whole night disappear as if it were only a dream.

She turned her face away and stood up. Haarmonae silently shielded herself, crossing her arms over her chest. Water dripped down her dress, pulling her toward the ground. "Look at it," she said, barely above a whisper.

They all turned, watching as the city spit forth billowing smoke, the flames still dancing across the water with their orange glow. The once beautiful city, gleaming white as a beacon of hope for all the world, was reduced to death and destruction.

Haarmonae reached for her bow, and Bravaro gave it to her. She put her arm between the handle and taut band, slinging it over her left shoulder.

"I have to go," she said, turning away from the misery.

Bravaro caught hold of her arm. "Wait. Take us to your father. I have to see him."

Haarmonae thought for a moment. She glanced at the soldiers with him, wondering for the first time if all of them were loyal. The only other person she knew was young Valian. "Very well. But only you and Valian may join me," she whispered.

"These men are all from my squadron. I would trust them with my life," Bravaro argued.

Haarmonae shook her head. "Then you may not come with me." She nodded toward the others behind him. "What of that one? Lord Lamik's grandson, I believe? You know where his grandfather's sympathies lie." And those of his father, Lord Tzichen. She could not be too careful.

Bravaro thought for a moment. Lord Lamik had not been among the lords who had been taken to the dungeon, and the king had said there were many who defected. He glanced over his shoulder. Lord Lamik, also Kouraso's grandfather, had voiced many times that they should sue for peace with Delgadas.

Bravaro nodded deftly when he saw the fire in her eyes. "Kouraso, take these men with you to the Castle Hachep-Tzuay. Gather anyone you meet along the way who has escaped and offer them refuge there. Valian and I will join you in a few days."

Kouraso straightened in salute, keeping one arm glued to his side. "Yes, General!" He motioned for the other three soldiers to follow him and disappeared into the foliage.

Valian approached him, doing his best to keep control of his emotions. "What about the message for Prince Shoram? The king asked us to go deliver the news of his capture."

"Unfortunately, that will have to wait. I would not trust that message beyond either of us." Bravaro nodded to Haarmonae. "Lead the way, my friend."

Haarmonae turned, motioning to the East and the sun still struggling to rise. "This way."

CHAPTER 58

DELGADAS

Delgadas could feel the terror pulsating off the people gathered in the courtyard. He relished the sight of their soot-smudged faces, drawn with exhaustion and defeat. Tzotoen drums sounded, filling the large square with an ominous promise of destruction. Delgadas closed his eyes, feeding off the palpable fear. The pain that had so racked and tormented him the last twelve years suddenly left as he felt a dark presence possess his body. He opened his eyes, lifting his hands into the air.

"People of Luminia! Behold, your *king*!" Mocking words dripped off his tongue. Nissim appeared at the courtyard's edge, his fingers laced behind his head. Leather cords had been tightly wrapped under his triceps, crossed over behind his head, then lashed again to his wrists, making it impossible for him to move or lower his arms. The guards pushed him to the center of the courtyard and forced him to his knees before a stake. One of them stepped forward, ripping the king's shirt from top to bottom off his back. He held it up triumphantly as if it were a prize. The gathered Tzotoen soldiers lifted a sadistic cheer.

Delgadas's heart began to beat in time with drums, their cadence growing faster and louder. "Behold the beginning of a new era, my people!" Delgadas said, stepping up beside Nissim. The king's eyes were filled with tears as he looked out at the horrified masses. However, Delgadas sensed he did not share the same fear of dying that they held. "No longer will you be held by this regime's archaic principles!" He shouted over the sound of the drums. He walked around the courtyard, waving his arms wide.

The lords who had defected to Delgadas' side were brought to the front of the gathering. This display was as much for their benefit as for the people. He hopped to stave off any last vestiges of fighting spirit by this potent example. He turned to glare once more at Nissim, but his captive did not cower. He did not plead for his life. Instead, the pain began to return to Delgadas' joints, thanks to Nissim's fighting spirit. Delgadas hunched over, growling low with frustration. The fear had given him momentary relief from the wracking pain that was his constant companion. Nissim's refusal to give in to the terror brought the pain back with increased force.

He turned to face Nissim, looking down his nose at him. "You are reduced to nothing, Nissim. Luminia is mine."

Nissim said nothing to that, only looked at him with what might have amounted to pity. "I am sorry it has come to this, Delgadas. Once, I might have called you friend." He hung his head. "*Ilyo Na'a-da's* will be done."

Delgadas surged forward, smashing him with his fist across the face. "My will be done! Do you understand? *Ilyo Na'ada* has forsaken this land! All is within my power, *my* might!" Delgadas turned around, raising his arms once more. "*My* will be done!"

NISSIM WATCHED HIM SADLY. Delgadas's body and wasting sickness proved that his will was already being done. His hatred had given rise to this insanity, this sick obsession with grasping power at any cost. The eternal fires of *Atuksach'* would be his reward in the end.

He looked over the heads of the crowd, past the guilt-ridden faces of his lords and a few who sneered at him in contempt. His eyes lifted to the distant eastern mountains, praying under his breath as the drums swelled. For mercy's sake, he hoped his end would be quick.

Delgadas turned back around, glaring daggers at him. "Despair and perish," he spat. "Your son and heir will soon join you."

Nissim's eyes flew open at these words, fear for Shoram overwhelming him. However, he could not utter a sound, for the next instant, the lashing around his wrists were cut, and re-tied behind his back. He was shoved forward and made to lean over a large, flat boulder with a depression carved into the center, just large enough for a human skull to rest. The drums quickened, his heart matching the beat. The people around the edges of the courtyard gasped, some of them closing their eyes, others unable to tear their gazes away. Several began to wail and plead for his life, but he knew it was futile. He looked at several of his people, now held captive by this madman. He had failed them.

He could hear the executioner raise the *slitsike* above his head with a grunt.

"Forgive me," Nissim pleaded of a woman who refused to look away, her eyes rimmed in red as she watched in horror. Then he closed his eyes in preparation for the tapered stone hammer to come down on his head, never to open them again.

CHAPTER 59

RITENUETA

Trumpets sounded from above, alerting Ritenueta that something or someone was approaching. She grimaced as she pushed herself off the cold, damp stone floor. Looking down from their cliff-side prison, she could hear the captives before she saw them break from the trees into the clearing. She would have recognized her fellow Musicians anywhere, dressed in deep purples and blues. However, their clothing was shredded and dirtied from the long trek through the woods, just over the newly conquered Luminian territory where Delgadas had set up his offensive headquarters.

Had they been forced to march all the way from Lunthá? Ritenueta's heart shattered for them. It looked as if they had been led in chains from the royal city, beaten and bloody. She squatted, careful not to lean too far out of the opening to their tiny cell as she looked down upon their fellow Musician's suffering.

Her heart slipped into her belly. These were only a fraction of the Musicians. She looked back at Molto, huddled in the corner of the crammed space. The cell was only about four feet tall, forcing them to lay down or squat at all times. Water dripped from the ceiling, making their clothes perpetually damp.

"Molto," she called hoarsely. She waved him over after he roused and scooted aside so he could see.

He had to squat even more painfully, now that he was even taller than his father. Ritenueta's heart again clenched. How was Adagio faring? Were he and the girls among the captives? If Delgadas had gotten his hands on Adagio, would he even still be alive? She prayed that he had followed Delgadas' instructions and disappeared from the city. If for nothing else, at least Melodia and Haarmonae would be safe.

"What is he planning to do with them?" Molto asked. His voice no longer held the vivacious intonation it had once. His words came out dull and colorless—just like their world. Ritenueta attributed the change partly to the hardships they had faced after coming to this place and partly to the dreariness of their cliffside prison. There was no hope of escape. The fortress of *Hitzena,* or the Stone Fortress, had been carved out of the stone cliffs themselves. Once a beautiful palace belonging to Luminia, the ruins sat on top of the cliff, just over the recently redrawn borders of Tzotoeh.

The labyrinth dungeons had been hewn out of the mountain, the earliest prisoners forced to fashion their own cells-turned-tombs from the unforgiving rock. Some confining spaces did not even have windows to let in what little light remained in their muted land. The darkness was so oppressive she could hear people in adjoining dungeons going mad from the solitary confinement and utter blackness.

The only way up the cliff side was a system of platforms and pulleys. Ritenueta watched for what seemed like hours as the prisoners were unchained several hundred feet below them, loaded onto the platforms and brought up to the cells. They were shoved into their hole-like prisons and left to rot. It was ingenious, really, in a sadistic sort of way. Delgadas would never have to worry about prisoners trying to escape. Either they would stay in their prison cells, or they would throw themselves out and perish after the hundred-foot fall to the bottom of the cliffs.

"Come away, Mama," Molto said.

Ritenueta glanced over her shoulder at her son. She had a difficult time remembering how long it had been since they had been put in this awful place. Days? Weeks? She was no longer sure. Days seemed to blur together with the monotony of prison life. The only thing they had to look forward to was their rations of food and water, as meager as it was. There was a small hole in the roof of their cell where food was dropped down to them. Molto stationed himself below it, lying on his back. They sent down crusts of bread each morning and evening. There was never any fresh fruit or vegetables, none of the delicacies they had been used to before Luminia had fallen.

"What are we going to do?" Ritenueta asked.

Molto gave a mirthless laugh. "You speak as if there is something we can do." He sat up suddenly, wrapping his arms around his knees as he brought them to his chest, careful not to bang his head on the low ceiling. "There is nothing we can do for them, Mama. There is no hope."

Ritenueta hated to see the life draining out of his eyes. He had lost hope, but she had not. "There has to be a way out of here." Delgadas had taken them out to question them a few times. Perhaps there was a way they could escape the next time he did so.

"It will not work, Mama. Whatever you are planning, it will not work. You will only get yourself killed," Molto said.

"I will not sit by idle while that man destroys everything Luminia stands for! Now, get up. I did not teach you to lay down and accept evil. We must fight back, son."

Molto only looked at her. "How, Mama? I tried to fight back in Lunthá, to warn everyone that this was coming. But no one would listen." He lay back down and stared at the ceiling.

Ritenueta did not have an answer for him. It was true that he had devoured the ancient prophecies since he was a boy. He had sensed Delgadas' maneuverings, but he was right, no one had listened.

She sank to the floor and propped her back against the cold stone wall. Night was fast approaching, but she no longer heard the sound of ropes creaking outside their cell, signaling the last of the prisoners had been deposited in their gloomy cubbies.

Ritenueta had to find a way to reignite her son's fight. She fingered her shorn hair absently. After only a few days of being in the cell, they had both been forced to shave their heads with bits of sharp obsidian rock they had chipped from the walls. Lice and other creatures infested the straw used for bedding. She doubted it had ever been changed, rotting under them. It was a torture all its own. There was not even a place for them to rest from their imprisonment, to find solace in happier dreams far from this hell.

She rested her head against the stone wall and dozed. The sound of dripping water from the ceiling soothed her to sleep. She was in the middle of a sweet dream, holding her daughters hands as they danced on the Musicians Terrace. Suddenly, she was jarred awake. The sound of one of the baskets scraping against the cliffs near their opening made her heart lift with hope. A Tzotoen soldier poked his head in. "Both of you, come here. Delgadas wants to see you."

Ritenueta nudged Molto awake as she started crawling on all fours to the mouth of the cell. Rough hands clasped her under the arms and pulled her through the hole. She stood stock still on the far side of the platform, gripping the rickety railing and trying not to let her dizziness overcome her. *Do not look down. Do not look down.* Molto was taken from the cell the same way she had been, but she knew he hated being handled as if he were an infant.

They were hauled up to the top of the cliffs, the two guards leering at her. Ritenueta did her best to ignore their lewd stares. Molto stepped in front of her, shielding her from their gazes. When they reached the top, she and Molto were pushed out of the platform and over to a small half-moon-shaped amphitheater that lay in ruins. A wooden table and chair had been placed in the center of the ancient stage. Delgadas stood hunched beside it.

Ritenueta was glad her son was just behind her as they were led to the palace ruins where Delgadas kept his command headquarters. If she were alone and had not been summoned by Delgadas, she cringed to think what these two men would do to her.

Delgadas moved behind the table, pouring over maps. No doubt, he was planning his next move.

"My Lord, the prisoners you asked for," said one of the soldiers. One pushed her from behind, but she was unprepared for the momentum. She gritted her teeth as she landed hard on her palms and knees on the stone. Pain exploded through her body. When she lifted her hands, they came away dripping with blood. She was afraid to stand and see what her knees looked like.

"Mama!" Molto shouted, fighting against the soldiers. She turned in time to see the soldier unsheathe his short obsidian blade and put it to her son's throat.

"No, please!" she begged. "Delgadas, tell me what you want. I will do anything. *Tell* you anything."

Delgadas nodded once, and the soldier released Molto. She let out a sigh of relief. "I am afraid that is what I fear most. I do not want you to tell me *anything*. I want you to tell me the truth."

Ritenueta grimaced as she stood, her limbs in so much pain she could hardly breathe. "I did not think you had any use for Truth, Delgadas."

Delgadas swiped his hand over the table and sent his maps and papers flying. "Stupid woman! Did any of the other Musicians get off the island?"

Ritenueta blinked. "I do not know. I was *escorted* out of the city before you stormed our defenses." She tried to remain calm, but her terror rose as Delgadas walked around the table and came nearer. Delgadas looked even more hideous than before. His face was covered almost entirely by the grizzly black scales. Between the cracks, raw red skin showed through. It looked painful. On anyone else, she would have felt pity. But it was what he deserved.

"I want to know Nissim's plans. He was able to get his son and wife out of the city before we took it. Is he hiding other Musicians outside our reach as well? Where would they have gone?" Delgadas snarled. He came within inches of her face, and she held her breath so she wouldn't have to smell his foulness.

"I do not know," she answered truthfully.

"Very well, then perhaps you can aid my mages. We need to know how we can get the sun to rise without the use of traditional music."

"You mean by your dark arts?" Ritenueta spat, then gave a derisive laugh. "Never will I aid you. You might as well kill me now."

Delgadas leaned back, studying her face. After what seemed like ages, he finally nodded, waving at the soldiers. "Very well. I have no more need for you, then. Or your boy, for that matter." He headed back up the stage steps and walked over to the table. "My mages are already on the verge of breakthrough. Bow to my will, Ritenueta. Here, we shall strike a bargain. Pledge fealty to me, and I will let your son live."

Ritenueta's heart began to race all the more. She looked at her son, held captive by the burly soldier at his back and the blade at his throat. His eyes were filled with silent pleading, but a split second later, her heart slowed, and she was filled with an inexplicable calm. *I am your shield, sweet one.*

The words echoed in her mind, and she knew it was the voice of *Ilyo Na'ada* Himself speaking to her heart.

Delgadas smirked as he turned around, planting his hands on the tabletop as he faced her. But his smile quickly faded when he saw the look on her face.

"I will not bow to you, Delgadas," she said firmly. She jerked her arm free of the soldier at her side and strode toward Delgadas. Taking a deep breath, she began to sing at the top of her lungs.

Delgadas stumbled back, shrieking and covering his ears as he tried to scramble out of reach of the sound.

"Get her! Get her away!" Delgadas ordered.

However, the soldiers were slow to do his bidding. Ritenueta continued to sing, drawing boldness from *Ilyo Na'ada*. "I will never bow! We will not go quietly!" she sang. "*Ilyo Na'ada* will avenge what you have done this day!"

Delgadas cursed her, but she knew where her strength came from. She had to alert the other Musicians. Their strength did not lie in bending to Delgadas' will. "We will never bow!" she continued to sing.

Before she could utter another sound, a bear-like hand clasped around her mouth and pulled her roughly back. Her neck strained dangerously to the side, and she feared the soldier would break it if he made a fraction of a movement. He wrapped one around her waist and hoisted her toward the cliff's edge. Her eyes went wide with fear, but again she was surrounded by the peaceful Presence.

Your will be done, she prayed in surrender. She bowed her heart to the One who held her life in His hands. If it was her day to die, then so be it. She would not bow to Delgadas.

"Wait!" She heard Delgadas shriek, and the soldier stopped. "Bring her and the boy," he ordered. "But keep your hand over her mouth," he added, sounding like a frightened child.

She and Molto were forced to stand before Delgadas, both of them with hands over their mouths. Delgadas straightened his ratty cloak that had once been the most luxurious *titzake lumpay*. Even his clothes were rotting off his body, infected by his hate.

"Take them to the deepest cells you can find—and be sure they are separated. I don't want anyone to hear them, no matter how loud they scream," Delgadas snarled. "Fit her with the device we spoke about."

Ritenueta's heart broke. To be separated from her boy was a torture she was unsure she could survive. She tried to scream and thrash, but another soldier appeared with two helmets. The face mask was made of metal, with the mouthpiece protruding like a flattened beak.

She shook her head, but the soldier wrenched her head forward as the other fitted it over her face and around her head. She tried to open her mouth to scream, but no sound was allowed to issue from her lips. Panic settled over her, and she thrashed her arms and legs, trying to escape. The man behind her wrapped his arms around hers, pinning them to her sides. She stopped kicking, and the other soldier tightened the straps around the back of her head. A small lock kept everything in place.

They released her, and she stood there, trying to speak. Somehow, the enchanted device stole the sound from her lips before it could pass the mouthpiece.

Delgadas smiled his wicked smile. "There now. That is better," he said. He still looked shaken from when she had sung a moment before. "An ingenious device, is it not? It still allows the prisoner to eat and drink, but no sound may issue from their lips. Your stay in my dungeons will be blessedly quiet, my dear." He laughed. Ritenueta only glared at him through the eye holes in the metal mask. Silent tears streamed down her face, and she gazed at her son. At least they were still alive. And while there was breath in their lungs, there was still hope.

"If and when you decide to cooperate, I will have the device removed. All you have to do is bow to me, Ritenueta. The same will go for your son. Now, I think an extended stay in the dungeons will help you change your mind. Take them below," Delgadas said, waving them away.

Ritenueta reached for her son, and they clasped hands for a moment before they were ripped apart. She tried to scream, to tell him to hold onto what she had taught him. More than anything, she did not want him to give up.

Molto met her gaze, and his eyes softened, nodding as if he understood her silent pleadings. He looked up, and she followed his gaze, catching his meaning. They were not alone. She tried to convey encouragement through her eyes. They would both need the strength that could only come from the One who had created them in the first place.

They were taken to two holes carved straight down into the bowels of the mountain, no more than five feet in diameter. A pulley system was constructed around it, with a large bucket hanging from a rickety-looking rope at its center.

"Get in," the soldier said without inflection.

Ritenueta was shoved into the bucket and swung dangerously from side to side. She gripped the ropes above her, and they quickly began lowering her into the mountain's depths. She could not know what was waiting for her below, but she still clung desperately to hope. If only the rest of Luminia knew what she had discovered. She must stay alive to tell them. Their power did not rest in hiding away but in letting their song rise. Someday, their rescuer would come. She had to believe it.

When that day came, he would put all the wrongs in Luminia right.

CHAPTER 60

MELODIA

Melodia huddled beside the small fire, trying to keep her hands from freezing. The rain had turned to snow that afternoon, an anomaly for so low an altitude in Luminia. Anxiety settled in the pit of her stomach, unwilling to let her be for even a moment. The snow was steadily piling up in heaps all around their hidden tree house. Her father was outside, trying to shore up the holes where cold air continuously poured through, making her efforts to keep the house warm futile. What did this freak storm mean?

Fear for her sister was more problematic than her chilled limbs. Haarmonae had disappeared nearly a week ago with no trace. Her father had been distraught, but with no clue where she had gone, they were at a loss as to how to go after her. Melodia picked up a stick and poked at the fire, wishing she could sink into a deep sleep and forget all that had happened. At least for a little while.

Suddenly, the door opened, and snow began blowing into the main room. She scrambled to her feet and went to the door, thinking her father might need help. However, looking at the man's face, she was stunned to see an old friend staring back at her.

"Bravaro!" she exclaimed, holding a hand over her heart. A moment later, Haarmonae appeared, followed by her father. Melodia's heart flooded with relief, and she rushed to Haarmonae, pulling her into a tight embrace.

"Where did you go? Papa and I were worried sick," she said, slapping her sister on the back as she pulled her even tighter. "Never do that to me again." She had not realized it, but it felt like she had been holding her breath since her twin had disappeared, and only now could she take a deep breath.

"You should never have brought them here!" her father growled at Haarmonae, anger creasing his brow as he stomped into the house. Snow continued to billow around him and started to pile at the door. Melodia stepped forward.

"Close the door and get out of the cold," Melodia ordered. A boy appeared behind her father, slipping in as if trying to take up as little space as possible so no one would notice him. He lifted the hood off his head, and she was again filled with joy and relief at seeing Valian. Melodia let go of Haarmonae and approached the boy, drawing him into a hug. "Thank *Ilyo Na'ada,* you are safe," she whispered against his hair.

"Not all of us," he said bleakly and walked toward the hearth. He raised his hands toward the flames, and Melodia shot Haarmonae and Bravaro a confused glance.

Bravaro stepped to her side and lowered his voice. "Dosanyata and Kyin are no more," he whispered. Melodia took in his face. His stubbled chin was caked with dirt, blood, and soot. How long had they traveled without stopping to rest? They must all be exhausted.

"Come in and sit down. I will make you something to eat," Melodia choked.

Haarmonae went to change while Bravaro joined Valian at the table. He placed a hand on his shoulder, and the boy hung his head ever further. Melodia's heart went out to the boy. "How awful."

Her father did not seem to hear and stepped toward Haarmonae menacingly as she made her way to the small chamber they shared. "You should not have brought them here!" he said again.

Haarmonae's shoulders stiffened, then she turned. She glared at their father, fire dancing in her eyes. "I had to, Papa. Bravaro is our friend. Or have you forgotten even that?" Haarmonae shot back.

Melodia gasped. Neither she nor her siblings had ever spoken to their father in such a disrespectful tone. Haarmonae immediately looked guilty and hobbled over to the low table that rose from the very floor, carved straight from the tree. Sinking down, she buried her face in her hands.

Melodia hurried over to her, kneeling at her side. "What happened?"

Haarmonae winced as she tried to remove her boot. "I twisted my ankle in the fall."

"What fall? Where did you go?" Melodia asked, standing to face off with Bravaro. "You let her fall?"

Bravaro held up his hands. "I had nothing to do with her injury. She is the one who came back to Lunthá."

A charged silence hung in the air. "Against my wishes!" their father exploded.

"That is enough!" Melodia said, bringing herself to her full height and facing off with her father. Her father looked at her as if she had sprouted antlers. She took a steadying breath. "Now, sit down. We cannot undo what has been done. For now, we are safe."

She motioned for him to sit beside Haarmonae, and he did so without further comment. "Sit down, all of you and I shall make you some *chatla*. It will warm you." The tea brewed from the fire flower would help quicken the healing process for Haarmonae's ankle and hopefully calm everyone's tempers. "Would that it could be used as a sleeping potion," she muttered as she walked over to the hearth.

They all remained silent, staring at nothing in particular, until her father spoke up. "What news of Lunthá and the king?" She breathed a sigh when he sounded more like his old self. They all sat down at the table, save for Valian. It was as if he were rooted to his spot near the fire, staring into the flames. She touched his arm and gave him a tight-lipped smile. He nodded, silently thanking her.

Bravaro said nothing for a long while. Melodia turned once she had finished putting a large pot of water on to boil over the fire. She sat beside Haarmonae, touching her shoulder as if she needed to connect with her. She had been so worried.

"Lunthá has fallen. Last we heard, Delgadas had captured King Nissim and was holding him in the dungeons. We barely escaped with our lives." Bravaro said, his voice shaking with emotion.

"Just the three of you?" his father asked.

"There were four more members of our squadron who made it out. I sent them to Castle Hachep-Tzuay." Bravaro scrubbed his hands over his face. He looked like he was ready to collapse.

Her father turned an incredulous look on him. "Hachep-Tzuay? That is little more than a pile of rubble," he said.

Bravaro shrugged. "It is close enough to Lunthá. I hope to send out rescue parties and get any survivors out of Delgadas' clutches before he takes them over the border to Tzotoeh. We can regroup there and then go on to a better hiding place in the mountains."

"I see," her father replied.

"There is more," Bravaro said. Melodia's stomach twisted into a knot as he paused. "Delgadas has killed half of the Musicians and taken the rest into captivity."

Silence reigned. Melodia's heart felt as if it would shatter with grief. "Killed them?" she repeated after a long pause. It was almost too much for her mind to understand. Half of her friends—gone. Just like that? What could Delgadas hope to gain by killing them? They were not warriors. All they had were their songs and instruments. Melodia stood from her spot near Haarmonae and began to pace, chewing on the end of her thumb nail.

Bravaro looked over at her, his eyes tortured orbs. "Yes. He—he threw them off the roof at the Musician's Terrace." Bravaro sat forward, barely giving pause between his following words. "Come with us. The Musicians are scattered. We will need your wisdom and the power of music to help us if we are to win back our country."

Melodia's heart lifted at this. More than anything, she wished to be useful again. "Yes, Papa. We should leave at once—" she moved to start packing, but he held up his hand.

"No. We cannot leave this place," her father said. His eyes darted from Bravaro's grim face to her pleading eyes.

Melodia stilled, as did everyone around the table. "But Father—" Haarmonae was about to argue, but her father slammed his fist onto the table.

"I have spoken!" he said and rose. Adagio looked around the table and raked his hands into his hair, giving a low moan. "You know what Delgadas will do if he ever hears our names again. What do you think will happen if he sees that the sun is rising and setting as it once did? He will *know* it is us and where to find us. And he m will kill your mother and brother."

Melodia approached him carefully, placing a hand on his arm. "Papa. We cannot be sure he has not already made their lives forfeit. We have to fight back."

"No. It is he who has brought this upon our land!" Her father jabbed a bony finger at Bravaro. "You should go back to the Other World and leave us be."

"Papa!" Melodia gasped.

Her father hung his head, and she touched his cheek gently. She knew he was suffering, but hiding was not the answer. "I cannot lose you, too," he muttered, glancing at Haarmonae who was seated a few paces away. "It is too much for me to bear," he pronounced, then turned and walked from the room into one of the adjoining chambers. Melodia's shoulders slumped. She was unsure what to do, walking over to the front door and closing it against the cold to give herself time to think.

"Your father is not himself," Valian said. "I have never seen him like that in all my life."

Melodia lowered her voice. "Nor have we. It is as if the fear has changed his personality. He sits in front of the fire sometimes, just staring into its depths, unmoving for hours. I fear the loss of my mother and brother has broken him."

Bravaro stood and closed the distance between them, taking her hand. "He will come out of it," he offered. "He must."

Melodia gave him a sad smile. "We can only hope." She raked her teeth over her lower lip. "I am sorry for what he said. He does not mean it."

"I know." He gave her a weak smile. Bravaro glanced over his shoulder at Valian and nodded that he should join him at the door. "Well, we must be away before we are snowed in. We have to rejoin Kouraso and the rest of the men."

"No, surely you must stay and rest for a few days. You've been on the move for days as it is," Melodia argued.

"No, we must rejoin what is left of our ranks. But I thank you," Bravaro said. "Are you sure you cannot convince him to come with us?"

Melodia shook her head. "We will try to convince him, but it may take some time."

He nodded and headed toward the door. Haarmonae followed the boys, whispering with Bravaro for a moment. Melodia went to the store cupboard and took down their last loaf of bread. She went over to Valian and offered it to him. "It is not much, but hopefully, it will give you strength for the journey."

Valian took it, nodding. "Thank you."

She touched his shoulder and drew him into an impromptu hug. "Safe journey, my friend," she whispered. He wrapped his free arm around the small of her back, and they clung to each other for a moment. When they separated, there were tears in his eyes. "What is it, Valian?"

He sucked in a breath, hanging his head. "I cannot believe they are gone."

Melodia's heart broke for him. "I am so sorry," she said.

He only nodded, opening the door and heading out into the snow before he could lose control of his emotions, no doubt. Melodia stepped up and hugged Bravaro. "Send word when you arrive, if you can."

"We will," he whispered. "And perhaps you two might keep working on your father? It would be better if we were all together. We could protect you."

Melodia looked over at her sister. They could try, but she was unsure how successful their pleadings to convince their father to leave the tree house would be. Haarmonae only nodded and returned to the table to rest her injured ankle. Melodia gave him a brave smile. "Go with *Ilyo Na'ada*, my friend."

"You as well," he said, and then he was gone. Melodia closed the door, feeling a sense of loss as keen as when she had watched Delgadas rip her mother from her. She could surely use some of Mama's wisdom now.

No sooner had the door closed than her father reappeared, holding his guitar and Haarmonae's violin. Tucked under his arm was Melodia's wooden flute. Fire blazed dangerously in his eyes, and a warning voice told her to step in front of him. She did so, holding up her arms.

"Papa, what are you doing? I did not even know you had brought our instruments with us."

"Of course I did. But it was a mistake," he said, trying to step around her. He gave a low growl when she sidestepped, his eyes flashing with anger.

"Stand aside, Melodia," he said, but she again refused.

"No, Papa. Whatever you are planning, you cannot go through with it." He brushed past her, but Haarmonae was soon standing, barring his way.

Without warning, he dropped everything except his guitar, raising it above his head. Haarmonae scrambled out of the way as he brought it down on the edge of the table. Melodia turned as it shat-

433

tered, shielding her eyes from the pieces that went flying. The strings made a buzzing sound as the tension holding them to the instrument was broken. He then gathered the pieces and tossed them into the fire.

"There shall be no more music. Do you understand? None!" he cried, throwing Haarmonae's violin into the flames. The fire surrounded the instruments but did not consume them, for they had been fashioned out of wood from the eternal tree.

Haarmonae lunged at their father, holding back his arm as he held Melodia's flute suspended over the hearth. "No, Papa! Please!" They struggled for a moment, and after a while, he stilled, letting his hand fall to his side still clutching the flute. Tears streamed down her cheeks, and Melodia found hers were also wet.

Melodia approached her father slowly. She reached slowly for the instrument, as if any sudden movement might send him into a rage once more. "Papa, please. Give it to me," she begged. He looked at her, his eyes rimmed with dark circles.

"I am doing this for your own good," he said, promptly breaking the flute in half over his knee. "I forbid you to touch them, do you understand?" He then threw it into the fire, returning to his room. Melodia lurched for it, but Haarmonae held her back.

"No, do not," she whispered against her ear. "Wait until the fire dies down, and then we will secret them away."

They sat on the floor, crying and holding each other for a long time, watching the flames slowly burn out. When the embers cooled, they retrieved their instruments, wiping off the soot and ash as best they could. Other than being a bit dirty, the wood was unharmed. Melodia's poor flute, however, would need a little more mending. Haarmonae touched her arm, glancing toward their father's bedroom. "It is alright. We shall find a way to fix it."

She held a finger to her lips and scooted a chair over to the hearth. She then stood on it and secreted the instruments in a knothole in the ceiling, pushing them deep in the shadowy recess.

434

Melodia had not even noticed it, but it was the perfect hiding spot for their treasures.

Haarmonae climbed down from the chair. "Now, this is where they shall stay until the time is right."

CHAPTER 61

BRAVARO

Bravaro grunted as he pulled himself up on a large boulder near the river bed. He and Valian had met up with Kouraso and the other three from their squadron. In the days following Luminia's fall, they had been reunited with several stragglers who had slipped out of the city before Delgadas's soldiers had been able to capture them. Others had hidden during the attack and escaped when Delgadas left the city after its collapse.

Now, a ragged band had formed of a hundred people or more. He was unsure how, but people found their way to him, joining his small band of remnants. He looked over the crowd, slowly making their way down the gorge. It was the same river that flowed out from the lagoon surrounding Lunthá. The river grew increasingly treacherous as they traveled further North. Its water had carved out the rock through which it flowed until the gorge's walls rose a hundred feet on either side. The people had to swim in the raging waters or traverse the precarious sides of the river's rocky ledge.

"This way!" he called, motioning to Kouraso, who had taken up the rear. Kouraso waved and turned to encourage the older people and the children who tended to lag. Indeed, their band comprised

437

only a handful of soldiers and young women. The rest were either infirm, too young, or too old for Delgadas to have bothered with. Bravaro looked out over the group of ragged survivors that were now his responsibility to protect. How was he to raise an army with pickings such as these?

Bravaro jumped from the boulder and hurried through the icy waters to retake the lead. The sound of rushing water grew louder as he approached a bend in the river. Bravaro's heart quickened. He hurried forward, leaving Valian in charge for a moment. The sound of crashing water grew more deafening with each step, and when he came around the next bend, he saw a waterfall flowing over the face of a half-moon-shaped cliff. He smiled, waving the band forward. "Hurry! We are almost there!"

Bravaro dove into the waters, the shock of cold water making his heart seize momentarily. He pushed his arms through the water, which grew deeper the closer he got to the waterfall. He came to the shore near the waterfall's edge and walked up on the bank, his clothes dripping. He then got as close to the cliff as possible and made his way behind the waterfall. Sure enough, a cave opening lay there in the darkness, forgotten by time. The cave wall above the opening was covered in ancient Luminian carvings, and he ran his fingertips over the prayer with a mixture of reverence and deep sadness.

"Shield us with your mighty hand, *Ilyo Na'ada,* King of luminance and melody," he recited as he read the characters curving over the archway. Legend had it that this is where Enrikae and Elee-ash had made their entrance into this world. There would be time to look deeper into these legends later, though. For now, his people needed shelter and rest.

He walked back behind the waterfall and out into the open, waving everyone over. A narrow ledge ran around the pool's edge at the bottom of the falls. He directed Valian to lead the people uncomfortable with swimming around that way. Some of the younger people and children decided to swim for it.

Bravaro directed them into the cave, having one of his soldiers find dry tinder and set to making torches. "We will be safe here," he said to a pair of children, both drenched and shivering from their swim.

However, his respite was short-lived. When about half of the people had made it into the safety of the large cavern, he spotted three people approaching. They had not been with them before. One led a donkey by a frayed rope, and the other two steadied a blanket-wrapped bundle flung over the donkey's back. Bravaro waved to Valian, pointing out the travelers. Only then did he realize that the large bundle was wrapped in a red mourning cover. His heart stilled.

"Stay here," he said to Valian, diving into the waters to swim to the opposite shore. He hurried to meet the travelers, holding up his hand for them to halt. He could not be sure whether they were friends or foes.

"What brings you here?" he asked, fingering the dagger in his belt.

Bravaro looked over the children. The boy, who could not be more than ten years of age, stood stock still holding the donkey's lead. The girl, probably fifteen, hung back, looking out at him from under her cloak's hood with only her eyes visible.

An older woman stepped forward, her eyes red-rimmed. "We are refugees from Lunthá. My children and I have come to seek safety with the new general."

"I am Bravaro," he said, glancing at the bundle on the donkey's back. The girl's head snapped up, and she frowned at him. He tore his gaze away, turning his attention to the mother. "What have you there?"

The woman hung her head, looking like she was on the brink of tears. "It is the body of King Nissim," she said softly.

Bravaro's head reeled. Sinking to his knees, he let the water flow around him, stunned and disbelieving. He barely noticed the icy chill crawling up his thighs. King Nissim had known, but Bravaro's heart wrenched at the thought that Delgadas had done the unthinkable.

"Show me," he said, still in shock. He had to see for himself before he would believe it.

The young boy turned the donkey aside and moved the red cloth from the corpse's face. Bravaro gasped as if someone had punched him in the gut. The king was nearly unrecognizable, the side of his head bashed in. Bravaro let go of the corner of the blanket, closed his eyes, and took a moment to swallow the bile rising in his throat. The king had not only been his monarch and a man he had sworn to protect, but a man who had taken the place of a father. Bravaro had failed to protect him as he had vowed.

"We have brought him to give him a proper burial, Sir," the woman said. Bravaro rose on one knee and pushed himself to stand.

He nodded, glad when the woman put the cloth back over the king's head. "You did well. Thank you for risking your lives to bring him here," he choked. He glanced over his shoulder at his men, standing watch outside the waterfalls' edge. Valian stepped forward, watching and waiting. How would he tell the boy their beloved king was dead, a man who had also been like a father to him?

The woman's eyes welled with tears. "It was the least we could do, Sir."

Bravaro touched her shoulder, seeing how exhausted they were. "My men will take care of his body from here. Go to the cave and get some rest."

The woman and boy moved off, but her daughter stayed behind. Bravaro stilled, confused as to why the girl would not want to seek refuge inside the cave. "Is there something wrong?" he asked.

The girl moved the hood off her head. Her long, flowing brunette hair fell over her shoulders. Her green eyes welled with tears. "Bravaro?" she said slowly.

It took a moment for recognition to dawn. "Intza—" He stumbled back as if seeing a ghost.

"Yes, it is me, Bravaro!" she said. A short laugh escaped her lips the moment before she sailed into his arms. He picked her up, her laughter ringing out through the gorge. He still could not believe it but hugged her close, weeping into her hair.

"Sister? Is it really you?" he asked. She leaned away so she could see his face. He touched her cheek as if fearing she would disappear if he did not keep hold of her. "I cannot believe it."

"I'm here, Bravaro," she cried, hugging him tightly. "I thought you were dead."

He released her, setting her back on her feet. "I thought you were dead as well. I looked all over the forest for you after the attack. What happened?"

Intza beamed up at him, her cheeks red from tears. "I hid as Mama told me to. She said you would come and find me, but I got lost. I walked and walked and finally came to one of the other villages." She nodded toward the woman and boy she had come with. "Yusenti and her husband took me in."

He cupped her face, wiping her tears with his thumbs. "Thank *Ilyo Na'ada* you are safe." She hugged him again, and he turned her toward the cave. "We will be safe here, until we can rally and find a way to take back Luminia."

Intza gave him a wry smile. "Yes, I heard. I had no idea it was you they spoke of when they said there was a new general rallying the remnants."

His voice filled with sadness. "Yes. Not by choice," he said. He had nearly lost hope since watching Lunthá burn and Delgadas massacre the Musicians. He kept his arm wrapped around his sister's shoulders. "Your return has given me hope, sister."

They halted before they reached the pool, where the water deepened. People were swimming across or trailing around the stone ledge. She sighed. "I am sorry you have been alone all this time. I wish I could have been with you."

Bravaro felt as if a weight was being lifted off his shoulders, years of guilt at having failed his mother and sister starting to ebb away. "You are here now. That is all that matters." The months ahead would be difficult, to be sure. With Intza safe, he felt as if he could face anything.

"Yes, I am here now." She moved away from him, looking up into his face. "Mama would have been proud."

LATE THAT NIGHT, they laid King Nissim's body to rest at a solemn ceremony held in the cave's confines. After filling in the shallow grave, each person picked stones of varying sizes and put them in a heap over his grave, paying their respects to their fallen leader. Bravaro watched as the people filed by. Some wept and others passed in silent remembrance and mourning.

When it came his turn, the pile of rocks had grown as tall as a man and spread out over a ten-foot radius. Bravaro touched the rise, laying down his stone last. His king should have had a hero's burial, laid to rest beside his beloved wife, Lutep-Tzia, in the temple. For now, this was the best they could do.

He turned to those assembled and held up his hand. "To Nissim, king of Luminia! May his soul find its way to the bosom of *Ilyo Na'ada* in the Great Beyond."

They repeated his words in unison, their words echoing through the cave. Their words settled into silence, and all were quiet for a long while.

"Long live, Bravaro! May you rule us in righteousness and justice," a man's voice rang out. Bravaro's head shot up, looking for who had said the words. However, he could not distinguish who had said it as several more people took up the chant. Soon, the cave was thundering with calls for Bravaro to take up leadership.

At once humbled and frightened, Bravaro called for silence. He stepped up on a rock not far from the king's burial heap, holding his hands up for quiet. "Good people of Luminia, I am not king. I am honored and humbled that you would bestow this responsibility on me, but I am not a leader."

"You are the only leader we have!" an older man croaked from the shadows. "If not you, then who?"

Bravaro glanced at Intza and then around at his men. He knew they would stand by him. Valian nodded encouragement, and Bravaro gulped. "Again, I say that I am not king. I will lead our warriors, but nothing more. Prince Shoram is king, whenever he may be able to return and take his rightful place. Until then, we will fight to free Luminia from Delgadas's clutches."

The cave erupted in cheers and applause, but all Bravaro could do was bound down from the boulder and join Valian. He shook his head, feeling the weight of leadership pressing down upon him. "I do not know if I can do this, Valian."

Valian nodded firmly. "You can, Sir. You can, because you must."

EPILOGUE

S everal nights after King Nissim's burial, Bravaro sat in a private alcove he had claimed for himself and Intza. He sat beside a small fire, where Valian and Kouraso slept between watches. Smoke stung his eyes since there was nowhere for the smoke to go. It hung like a noxious mist above his head, swirling among the stalactites. Bravaro knew they could not stay in this cave forever. True, it was large and could be a good hiding place in times of dire need. But they needed a more permanent shelter and ways to grow and forage for food. Their numbers had swelled to two hundred over the last few days. Bravaro sent out scouts daily to find lost and wandering Luminians. They were reeling in the wake of Delgadas's overthrow of the government. How was he to care for them all? He took a stick from the wood pile at his left, broke it in half and threw it into the fire.

His one comfort was Intza. She had grown into a beautiful young woman, strong and wise. They had stayed up late the last several nights, catching up on what the other had missed. He vowed he would never let her out of his sight again.

Bravaro searched the dimly lit cave and spotted Intza visiting with a group of older women. She carried a pot of stew, dishing it out to anyone in need. Her smile had a bolstering effect, chasing away the gloom from their faces, even if it was just for a little while.

Suddenly, an older woman appeared from the shadows, carrying something under her arm. "Forgive the interruption, General Bravaro. May I have a word?" she asked, her voice quaking with age. He stood, offering her the small boulder he had been sitting on.

"Of course. May I offer you something to eat?" Bravaro asked, wondering what complaint she had to bring to him. He had seen several people over the last few days and had had to settle disputes between them. Being confined in such close quarters and forced to wander about tripping over each other in the dark had made everyone testy.

"No, thank you, I have not come to make a request. I have come to talk with you about a matter of great importance," she replied. She took a piece of rolled bark out from under her arm and handed it to him. He squatted on the opposite end of the fire, looking at it with awe.

"What is this?" he asked.

"It is a partial copy of the ancient prophecies. Someday, the savior of music will come to us, and set right all that is wrong."

The hair on his arms stood on end as she spoke. "Are you a seer?" he asked, an awed hush coming over him. He knelt beside her, paying homage.

"No," she laughed softly. "I am a humble scribe, set with the task of copying all the important manuscripts in the royal library. For the last seven years, I have been in the king's library, saving the Chronicles of Kings and many other important works for posterity. Just in case something as we have just been through should happen."

Bravaro held the bark scroll with reverence. "You mean that we have not lost these manuscripts to the flames after all?" So much culture, history, and religious teaching would have been lost, stored in the king's library. Hope sparked inside him, like a tiny flame that he thought had all but been snuffed out.

"That is what I mean. King Nissim knew it was important for these works to be saved, should Delgadas try to destroy or change our histories. I have put them away for safekeeping in a location known only to myself, now that our dear king is gone." She handed him the piece of slightly curved bark, and he squinted to see the Luminian signs delicately carved into the surface.

Bravaro looked up at her, gratitude swelling in his heart. "I cannot express how thankful I am, uhh–?"

"Shes-Tia," the woman introduced herself. She studied him for a long moment, her gray-blue eyes filling with tears. "I sense the pain you bear, young Bravaro. You are not alone," she said softly. He nodded, handing the bark manuscript back to her. However, she shook her head, pushing it back toward him with gnarled fingers. She flashed him a smile. "You keep it. It is a copy of Tzizenah's Prophecy. It has given me comfort over the years, watching as the darkness has crept in on our beloved Luminia. I pray it will give you the same comfort in the months and years to come."

"Thank you," he whispered, hanging his head. Hopefully, it would only take months for them to regain their strength and raise an army to go after Delgadas. If Melodia and Haarmonae successfully convinced their father to join them, they could gain the upper hand, bringing music back on their own.

"The Savior of Music will not only bring peace to Luminia, but also to you, General."

Bravaro's head shot up. "To me? What do you mean?" All he wanted was for Luminia to be restored and the rightful heir placed on the throne. If he were able to accomplish that, he would be at peace.

Shes-Tia bowed her head for a moment, listening. "Your mother still searches for you. But do not fear. *Ilyo Na'ada* promises that your eyes will not see death until you see her face again."

Bravaro raised a brow. "My mother? Souni?" he asked. His heart started beating wildly with excitement. Intza would be pleased to hear she was alive.

The old woman shook her head. "No, I do not speak of your adoptive mother. I speak of your birth mother, Dee-ahnna," she stated matter-of-factly. Bravaro nearly fell over. He had not spoken her name in years. How did this woman know of her if she was not a seer? Perhaps *Ilyo Na'ada* had endowed her with a temporary sight.

"I think you *do* have a bit of the seer about you, Shes-Tia," he said, drawing a laugh from her thin lips. He had so many questions.

"Perhaps. Rest assured, your mother is well, and you will see her before she passes into the Beyond. And your father, as well."

Bravaro's stomach lurched. The last person he wanted to be reunited with was his birth father. He had worked hard over the years to put his father's abuse and rejection behind him.

"It is best my father remains in the past. That is where he belongs."

Shes-Tia stood on shaking legs. Bravaro helped her the rest of the way with a supportive hand under her elbow. She smiled, walking away into the shadows. He watched her go, his head spinning.

He looked again at the rolled bark, reached over to his satchel and placed it gingerly inside. He moved over and sat down on the boulder Shes-Tia had vacated, gazing into the fire. Until recently, the Savior of Music had been little more than a myth. Indeed, there had been no need for a rescuer. Now, Bravaro was curious to know all he could of him. It had been foretold that someone would arise and save Luminia when they needed him most. The question now was, when?

"What did she want?" Intza asked, joining him at the fire. She set the empty pot down and sank to her haunches. She put her hands out, warming them in the soft orange glow.

"She told me that I would see my mother again. My *birth* mother."

Intza screwed up her nose. "What do you mean?"

Bravaro let out a breath. "You do not remember how I came to be here in Luminia, do you? You were so young."

"No, I remember," Intza corrected him. "We talked of it many times when we were young. But how can you see her again? I thought the cave had vanished."

"It did." Bravaro leaned back, studying his sister's face in the firelight. "I do not know how it will happen," he said. "I did not ever think I would see you again, but here you are."

Intza smiled sadly, taking his hand. They both stared at the fire. If it was *Ilyo Na'ada's* will that he saw his mother again, rest assured that not even the fires of hell could keep His promise from coming to pass.

The End

A Note from the Author

Hey there! Thank you so much for reading Bravaro's story. This is the first of three novels, and I cannot wait to share the next part of Luminia's story with you. First, if you enjoyed this book, would you consider posting a review for Amazon? As a new author, this helps me so much, and I would love to hear what you thought of this first book in the Dawn Land Series.

This series has been a long time in the making. Originally, the book was just a high school creative writing assignment, but I quickly fell in love with the characters and knew it had to become a book someday. Over the last seventeen years, God has been speaking and moving, even when it felt like this dream was long dead. I believe that storytelling is such a powerful tool, and hope that you have walked away with some things to ponder. What I hope is that you see you do not have to stay stuck in past mistakes or trauma. There is One who wants to bring healing–to love and cherish you like the treasure you are.

In this series, He goes by the name of *Ilyo Na'ada*. In ours, He goes by Yahweh, Adonai, Father God. In Bravaro's journey, he has walked through trauma inflicted by his earthly father and is struggling to find his identity, as so many of us do. This idea of finding our identity is not a new one, and a task that seems even more difficult in our current culture. However, I pray that you are encouraged from what you have read of Bravaro's story so far, and know that you are loved by God Almighty, the One True and Living God who knit you together in your mother's womb. You are not here by accident. And He loves you more than you can imagine.

Thank you once again for taking this journey with me, and I hope you'll join me for the next installment of the Dawn Land Series, *Songs of Freedom.*

With love,
Nicole C. Boyd

Turn the page and read the sample to
get ready for the next book in the Dawn Land Series!

Also, don't miss *The Anthem's Return,*
coming soon!

SONGS OF FREEDOM
LADY TZIZENAH

Lunthá, Luminia
The Year of the Trumpet, 897

Rain beat down in torrents on the cobblestones as Lady Tzizenah climbed the palace steps, chilled to her bones with the message she knew she must speak. Her breaths came in quick succession, not from cold, for the rain was warm and refreshing after so many years of drought. The chill that radiated her body was of another kind.

"Mama, perhaps now is not the time," her son said as they neared the palace courtroom where sounds of revelry could be heard. Her son had tried to deter her from venturing out in the downpour, but the urging of *Ilyo Na'ada* had been unmistakable. Tzizenah might very well find herself thrust from the palace on this night of celebration, for the words of *Ilyo Na'ada* would be difficult for the young king to hear. She could only hope that his pride would not overtake his will to listen to wisdom.

"Wait for me here," Tzizenah said to her son, Nobletzin. He had allowed her to lean heavily on his arm for support.

455

"No, *sheska-tziksoe*," he started to argue.

However, Tzizenah held up her hand for silence. "I must do this, my son. *Ilyo-Na'ada* does not hold me responsible for the reaction to his messages, only that I am obedient."

Nobletzin, now entering into his thirties, was a grown man with children of his own. But he still obeyed her, and for that she was grateful. "I will not be long," she said as she began to climb the steep stone steps leading up to the courtroom where her king and his officials celebrated a reprieve from dry skies.

Tzizenah paused at the top of the steps, catching her breath and looking out over the royal city. The rain was a blessed relief, for the country had been in a drought for eight long years, despite the Musicians' faithful playing each morning and evening. Finally, *Ilyo Na'ada* had heard as the country had turned wholeheartedly to him once more, repenting of their pride. For some, it had been too late, as had been the case for her beloved Enrikae. The previous king, His Majesty King Reisen, had died five years into the drought. Enrikae had suffered at his hands, and then vanished.

The young king had obeyed the old ways for a time, bringing in this new season of blessing. He now stood in danger of falling prey to the same pride that had afflicted his late father in leading Luminia astray. She hoped he would hear her words, and humble himself.

Light from the open doorway greeted her, as well as the sounds of chatter and laughter amidst the music of their skilled instrumentalists. The royal family and their attendants celebrated in the great hall, thanking *Ilyo Na'ada* for his blessing of rain for their drought-weary land. Little did they know that she was about to disturb their gaiety.

She entered the hall, dripping from head to toe. As she caught her breath, a puddle formed at her feet, running down the water repelling fur robes of finely woven *titzake-lumpay*. The cloak was heavy, just like the words weighing down her heart. She did not lift her hood, not until the king acknowledged her. It took several seconds for the clamor to diminish. The music suddenly stopped as someone whispered her name and all turned to look at the famed seer.

Tzizenah descended the steps into the sunken area inside the pyramidal structure, walking across the marble floor toward the dais, leaving a trail of water behind her. When she arrived at the foot of the dais, she lifted the hood, rain splashing to the cool marble at her bare feet. She moved her long white hair, hanging in wet tendrils around her face. Although she was only in her early fifties, her white hair made her feel much older. She had earned every one of her white strands of hair.

The king wore a look of profound shock as Tzizenah waited for him to invite her to speak. He stepped down the first stair of the raised dais, reaching toward her. "Lady Tzizenah, please come next to the fire. You must be chilled to the bone," King Nizalom stood and walked down the dais, ready to lead her to a chair near the brazier.

"No, thank you, Your Majesty," she replied, "I am sorry to interrupt your festivities. *Ilyo Na'ada* has shown me a vision far into the future." She handed him a small scroll, sealed with her family's royal blue crest. The seal's indent was that of a dove in flight, clutching a scroll in its beak. It was the seal of the Seers who carried messages from *Ilyo Na'ada* himself. With her missive delivered, she prepared to exit the hall, but the king called for her to stop.

"Please, Lady Tzizenah, come into the courtyard so we can talk," he pleaded. She turned, nodding silently as he motioned for her to follow him out of the great hall and into a courtyard. Three of his advisors followed at his bidding.

Tzizenah tried to calm the wild beating of her heart, knowing that the message she had to deliver was not one that the king would likely reject. While he was a good leader, he had a tendency to turn a blind eye to warnings. Their country had seen many strange things as of late—first with the Spanyaards from the Other World, then the drought. She could not blame the king for wanting a bit of relaxation and time to reflect. But there was more trouble on the horizon.

They seated themselves in the covered courtyard, rain coming down like curtains from the eaves. She was the only one who remained standing. She took a deep breath as the king and his three advisors waited. Thankfully, they did not try to rush her. She nodded to the unopened scroll that the king still clutched in his hand.

"I have seen a great war that will divide the country. A man will arise to challenge all that is honest, and pure, and good. Many will be killed and captured, forced to bend to this one man. But a remnant will remain to fight against him. In that day, a great shaking of the earth will occur, and a deliverer will come to free the people from their misery. That one will bring peace to the land."

King Nizalom shifted uncomfortably in his seat. "When will this happen?"

"I do not know the exact times and seasons, but it has been revealed to me that on the third day of the third month of La'oun, the deliverer will come. One of your descendants will be on the throne. He will fight against the evil one, and lose for a time, but his son shall take his place and restore peace to the realm." Tzizenah bowed her head, her vision finished. She then slowly turned and prepared to leave the palace.

King Nizalom jumped up, following close at her heels as she hurried down the hall. They appeared at the side entrance to the great hall, and she stilled when her vision suddenly blurred. She closed her eyes, shaking her head slightly to try and rid herself of the images flashing through her mind. As she peered into the courtroom, she saw it transformed before her eyes. The room was filled with smoke and screams echoed in her ears. People ran for their lives against a ruthless enemy, tripping as they were cut down. Her heart clenched, seeing a small girl hunched in the corner of the room, trying desperately to hide from the attackers behind a large potted fern.

Almost as soon as the vision had come, her sight cleared, and all was as it had been when she had first entered. People stared at her in awe and concern. They began to whisper to each other, bringing

Tzizenah to the present. Tzizenah started when King Nizalom touched her arm.

"But this will not happen in my lifetime, will it Lady Tzizenah?"

Tzizenah turned, glaring at him in dismay. What she had just seen had shaken her to the very core, and all he could worry about was if he would be directly affected. "Because of your selfishness, Your Majesty, you will not long sit on the throne of Luminia. Instead, your position will be given to another more worthy."

The king's eyes grew wide with shock, then narrowed in fury. Tzizenah went on. "You cannot stop this, King Nizalom, however much you wish to try. All you can do is prepare. Keep the vision in the royal library. Pass it down. Perhaps, if you will humble yourself, *Ilyo Na'ada* will see fit to forgive you and the suffering of your descendants will not be so heavy."

She jerked her arm free of his grasp and started down the steps toward the entrance. Placing her hood back over her head, she rushed across the now-silent hall. Her voice carried a strange echo as she gave her last instructions, turning at the opposite end of the great hall before everyone's dazed stares. She was not long for this world, if her late husband's fate was any indication of what awaited her. Indeed, she doubted if she would ever deliver another prophecy.

Tzizenah turned, still graceful despite how shaken she was. "Hand down the prophecy, father to son. In time, all will be revealed." And with that, she returned to the stormy night.

Outside the Village of Hotun

PRONUNCIATION KEY

What's in a Name?

Below are the names of characters in the book, their Luminian pronunciation, and their meanings:

Nations, cities, villages, landmarks:

- Luminia (Loo-Mih-nee-uh) - "Dawn Land, Land of First Light"
- Saardonae (Ss-air-Doe-Nay) - "Sea Breeze, Land of Refreshing"
- Tzotoeh (Tsoh-Toh-eh) - "Nomad Land, Restless Wanderers"
- Lunthá (Loon-Thah) (royal city of Luminia) - "Torch"

CHARACTER NAMES:

- Joshua - (Shohss-Hoo-ah) - "Savior, Deliverer"
- Bravaro (Brah-Var-oh) - "Mighty warrior, Leader to victory"
- Nissim (Niss-ihm) - "Miracles, wonders, His justice is everlasting"
- Lutep-Tzia (Loo-tehp Tsee-ah) - "A light shines"
- Shoram (Shor-ahm) - "God is exalted, compassion, unconditional love"
- Melodia (Meh-Loh-dee-ah) - "Leader of songs, sweet melody"
- Haarmonae - (Hare-moh-Nay) - "spirited, free, unafraid, Pillar of Support"
- Adagio (Ah-dah-j'io - french 'je') - "steady pace, strong, wise"
- Ritenueta (Rit-eh-neeoo-tah) - "dazzling beauty, mysteries of God"
- Molto (Mole - toe) - "Heartbeat of God, strength of a generation"
- Delgadas (dehl-Gah-dass) - "Stealthy, deceiver, Keeper of the Night"
- Souni - (Soo-Nee) "Her song arises"
- Manemna (Mah-Nehm-Nuh) - "Prosper in the land, steadfast"
- Intza (Een-Tsuh) - "Happy, bubbling spring, life-giver"
- Dosanyata (Doe-sahn-yah-tah) - "Flower of the dawn, soft, protector"
- Kyin (Kee-yin) - "Father of peace"
- Valian (Va-lee-ahn) - "Shield of Bravery, Brother, unbroken loyalty"
- Untah (Oon-tah) - "Spring of Hope"
- Sesen (Seh-ssen) - "Music Calls"
- Nargo (Nar-goh) - "Greed, Revolter, Merciless"

- Ilyo-Na'ada - (Eel-yoh Nah-adah) - Ilyo - "Unfathomable, beyond comprehension" Na'ada - "Closer than a breath, Creator of Life"

Objects:

- Atzanta (Ah-tsahn-tah) - Highest form of currency, eight sided gold coin with a round hole in the middle. Two atzanta's = a full year's wages.

Hello, my name is Adagio. Are you ready for your Luminian lesson? Very good.

The Luminian language can be broken down into several sub-dialects. The most commonly spoken in Luminia is called *Luminsilkis*. Each letter in the Luminian alphabet coincides with a note on the musical scale and covers five scales. The Luminian characters do not necessarily stand for one "letter" as in many of your languages, like English, but represent sounds or a pair of sounds. Characters are written from top to bottom, left to right.

Essentially, when a word is written, that word can also be turned into a song by arranging the notes on a musical scale. For example, the name "Mary" can also be sung in order to call the person. Now imagine putting whole sentences together in song form? If one had an inkling, one could send whole coded messages in song form...

Luminian Musical Scale

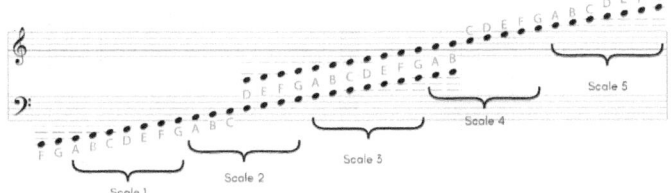

LUMINIAN CHARACTERS

MUSICAL NOTES	Scale 1		Scale 2		Scale 3	
A		ay		tz		ae
B		cha		ee		uh
C		na		ah		ta
D		ba		za		re
E		mn		th		zhe
F		ha		oo		fa
G		pe		gñ		ya

LUMINIAN CHARACTERS

MUSICAL NOTES	Scale 4		Scale 5		Punctuation	
A		aa		sa		quotation
B		ih		oh		period
C		i (eye)		ka		question mark
D		ky		ma		comma
E		sh		da		guttural stop
F		va		ga (rare)		excalmation point
G		la		oa		hyphen

BRAVARO

Here is an example of a "name song". By arranging the Luminian characters with their corresponding musical notes on the sheet music, one can compose a a "name song". Try yours below:

NAME:

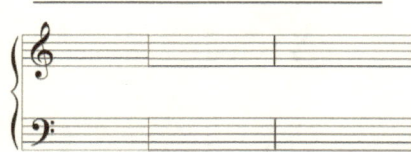

RESOURCES

1. *Konapee wreck.* (n.d.). https://www.oregonencyclopedia. org/articles/konapee-wreck/
2. Barry, J. Neilson. "SPANIARDS IN EARLY OREGON." *The Washington Historical Quarterly*, vol. 23, no. 1, 1932, pp. 25–34. *JSTOR*, http://www.jstor.org/stable/23908770. Accessed 22 Mar. 2025.